THIRST
NO. 1

THIRST

NO. 1

INCLUDES
THE LAST VAMPIRE
BLACK BLOOD
RED DICE

Christopher Pike

Simon Pulse
NEW YORK   LONDON   TORONTO   SYDNEY

This book is a work of fiction. Any references to historical events, real people, or real locales are used fictitiously. Other names, characters, places, and incidents are the product of the author's imagination, and any resemblance to actual events or locales or persons, living or dead, is entirely coincidental.

SIMON PULSE

An imprint of Simon & Schuster Children's Publishing Division
1230 Avenue of the Americas, New York, NY 10020
The Last Vampire copyright © 1994 by Christopher Pike
Black Blood copyright © 1994 by Christopher Pike
Red Dice copyright © 1995 by Christopher Pike
All rights reserved, including the right of reproduction in whole or in part in any form.
SIMON PULSE and colophon are registered trademarks of Simon & Schuster, Inc.
Designed by Mike Rosamilia
The text of this book was set in Adobe Garamond.
Manufactured in the United States of America
This Simon Pulse paperback edition August 2009
10 9 8
Library of Congress Control Number 2008938619
ISBN: 978-1-4169-8308-8

These titles were previously published individually.

CONTENTS

THE LAST VAMPIRE

For Dr. Pat

ONE

I am a vampire, and that is the truth. But the modern meaning of the word *vampire,* the stories that have been told about creatures such as I, are not precisely true. I do not turn to ash in the sun, nor do I cringe when I see a crucifix. I wear a tiny gold cross now around my neck, but only because I like it. I cannot command a pack of wolves to attack or fly through the air. Nor can I make another of my kind simply by having him drink my blood. Wolves do like me, though, as do most predators, and I can jump so high that one might imagine I can fly. As to blood—ah, blood, the whole subject fascinates me. I do like that as well, warm and dripping, when I am thirsty. And I am often thirsty.

My name, at present, is Alisa Perne—just two words, something to last for a couple of decades. I am no more attached to them than to the sound of the wind. My hair is blond and silklike, my eyes like sapphires that have stared long at a volcanic fissure. My stature is slight by modern standards, five two in sandals, but my arms and legs are muscled, although not unattractively so. Before I speak I appear to be only eighteen years of age, but something in my voice—the coolness of my expressions, the echo of endless experience—makes people think I am much older. But even I seldom think about when I was born, long before the pyramids were erected beneath the pale moon. I was there, in that desert in those days, even though I am not originally from that part of the world.

Do I need blood to survive? Am I immortal? After all this time, I still don't know. I drink blood because I crave it. But I can eat normal food as well, and digest it. I need food as much as any other man or woman. I am a living, breathing creature. My heart beats—I can hear it now, like thunder in my ears. My hearing is very sensitive, as is my sight. I can hear a dry leaf break off a branch a mile away, and I can clearly see the craters on the moon without a telescope. Both senses have grown more acute as I get older.

My immune system is impregnable, my regenerative system miraculous, if you believe in miracles—which I don't. I can be stabbed in the arm with a knife and heal within minutes without scarring. But if I were to be stabbed in the heart, say with the currently fashionable wooden stake, then maybe I would die. It is difficult for even a vampire's flesh to heal around an implanted blade. But it is not something I have experimented with.

But who would stab me? Who would get the chance? I have the strength of five men, the reflexes of the mother of all cats. There is not a system of physical attack and defense of which I am not a master. A dozen black belts could corner me in a dark alley, and I could make a dress fit for a vampire out of the sashes that hold their fighting jackets closed. And I do love to fight, it is true, almost as much as I love to kill. Yet I kill less and less as the years go by because the need is not there, and the ramifications of murder in modern society are complex and a waste of my precious but endless time. Some loves have to be given up, others have to be forgotten. Strange as it may sound, if you think of me as a monster, but I can love most passionately. I do not think of myself as evil.

Why am I talking about all this? Who am I talking to? I send out these words, these thoughts, simply because it is time. Time for what, I do not know, and it does not matter because it is what I want and that is always reason enough for me. My wants—how few they are, and yet how deep they burn. I will not tell you, at present, who I am talking to.

The moment is pregnant with mystery, even for me. I stand outside the door of Detective Michael Riley's office. The hour is late; he is in his private office in the back, the light down low—I know this without seeing. The good Mr. Riley called me three hours ago to tell me I had to come to his office to have a little talk about some things I might find of interest. There was a note of threat in his voice, and more. I can sense emotions, although I cannot read minds. I am curious as I stand in this cramped and stale hallway. I am also annoyed, and that doesn't bode well for Mr. Riley. I knock lightly on the door to his outer office and open it before he can respond.

"Hello," I say. I do not sound dangerous—I am, after all, supposed to be a teenager. I stand beside the secretary's unhappy desk, imagining that her last few paychecks have been promised to her as "practically in the mail." Mr. Riley is at his desk, inside his office, and stands as he notices me. He has on a rumpled brown sport coat, and in a glance I see the weighty bulge of a revolver beneath his left breast. Mr. Riley thinks I am dangerous, I note, and my curiosity goes up a notch. But I'm not afraid he knows what I really am, or he would not have chosen to meet with me at all, even in broad daylight.

"Alisa Perne?" he says. His tone is uneasy.

"Yes."

He gestures from twenty feet away. "Please come in and have a seat."

I enter his office but do not take the offered chair in front of his desk, but rather, one against the right wall. I want a straight line to him if he tries to pull a gun on me. If he does try, he will die, and maybe painfully.

He looks at me, trying to size me up, and it is difficult for him because I just sit here. He, however, is a montage of many impressions. His coat is not only wrinkled but stained—greasy burgers eaten hastily. I note it all. His eyes are red rimmed, from a drug as much as fatigue. I hypothesize his poison to be speed—medicine to nourish long hours beating the pavement. After me? Surely. There is also a glint of satisfaction in his eyes, a prey finally caught. I smile privately at the thought, yet a thread of uneasiness enters me as well. The office is stuffy, slightly chilly. I have never liked the cold, although I could survive an Arctic winter night naked to the bone.

"I guess you wonder why I wanted to talk to you so urgently," he says.

I nod. My legs are uncrossed, my white slacks hanging loose. One hand rests in my lap, the other plays with my hair. Left-handed, right-handed—I am neither, and both.

"May I call you Alisa?" he asks.

"You may call me what you wish, Mr. Riley."

My voice startles him, just a little, and it is the effect I want. I could have pitched it like any modern teenager, but I have allowed my past to enter, the power of it. I want to keep Mr. Riley nervous, for nervous people say much that they later regret.

"Call me Mike," he says. "Did you have trouble finding the place?"

"No."

"Can I get you anything? Coffee? A soda?"

"No."

He glances at a folder on his desk, flips it open. He clears his throat, and again I hear his tiredness, as well as his fear. But is he afraid of me? I am not sure. Besides the gun under his coat, he has another beneath some papers at the other side of his desk. I smell the gunpowder in the bullets, the cold steel. A lot of firepower to meet a teenage girl. I hear a faint scratch of moving metal and plastic. He is taping the conversation.

"First off I should tell you who I am," he says. "As I said on the phone, I am a private detective. My business is my own—I work entirely freelance. People come to me to find loved ones, to research risky investments, to provide protection, when necessary, and to get hard-to-find background information on certain individuals."

I smile. "And to spy."

He blinks. "I do not spy, Miss Perne."

"Really." My smile broadens. I lean forward, the tops of my breasts visible at the open neck of my black silk blouse. "It is late, Mr. Riley. Tell me what you want."

He shakes his head. "You have a lot of confidence for a kid."

"And you have a lot of nerve for a down-on-his-luck private dick."

He doesn't like that. He taps the open folder on his desk. "I have been researching you for the last few months, Miss Perne, ever since you moved to Mayfair. You have an intriguing past, as well as many investments. But I'm sure you know that."

"Really."

"Before I begin, may I ask how old you are?"

"You may ask."

"How old are you?"

"It's none of your business."

He smiles. He thinks he has scored a point. He does not realize that I am already considering how he should die, although I still hope to avoid such an extreme measure. Never ask a vampire her age. We don't like that question. It's very impolite. Mr. Riley clears his throat again, and I think that maybe I will strangle him.

"Prior to moving to Mayfair," he says, "you lived in Los Angeles—in Beverly Hills in fact—at Two-Five-Six Grove Street. Your home was a four-thousand-square-foot mansion, with two swimming pools, a tennis court, a sauna, and a small observatory. The property is valued at six-point-five million. To this day you are listed as the sole owner, Miss Perne."

"It's not a crime to be rich."

"You are not just rich. You are very rich. My research indicates that you own five separate estates scattered across this country. Further research tells me that you probably own as much if not more property in Europe and the Far East. Your stock and bond assets are vast—in the hundreds of millions. But what none of my research has uncovered is how you came across this incredible wealth. There is no record of a family anywhere, and believe me, Miss Perne, I have looked far and wide."

"I believe you. Tell me, whom did you contact to gather this information?"

He enjoys that he has my interest. "My sources are of course confidential."

"Of course." I stare at him; my stare is very powerful. Sometimes, if I am not careful, and I stare too long at a flower, it shrivels and dies. Mr. Riley loses his smile and shifts uneasily. "Why are you researching me?"

"You admit that my facts are accurate?" he asks.

"Do you need my assurances?" I pause, my eyes still on him. Sweat glistens on his forehead. "Why the research?"

He blinks and turns away with effort. He dabs at the perspiration on his head. "Because you fascinate me," he says. "I think to myself, here is one of the wealthiest women in the world, and no one knows who she is. Plus she can't be more than twenty-five years old, and she has no family. It makes me wonder."

"What do you wonder, Mr. Riley?"

He ventures a swift glance at me; he really does not like to look at me, even though I am very beautiful. "Why you go to such extremes to remain invisible," he says.

"It also makes you wonder if I would pay to stay invisible," I say.

He acts surprised. "I didn't say that."

"How much do you want?"

My question stuns him, yet pleases him. He does not have to be the first to dirty his hands. What he does not realize is that blood stains deeper than dirt, and that the stains last much longer. Yes, I think again, he may not have that long to live.

"How much are you offering?" he ventures.

I shrug. "It depends."

"On what?"

"On whether you tell me who pointed you in my direction."

He is indignant. "I assure you that I needed no one to point me in your direction. I discovered your interesting qualities all by myself."

He is lying, of that I am positive. I can always tell when a person lies, almost always. Only remarkable people can fool me, and then they have to be lucky. But I do not like to be fooled—so one has to wonder at even their luck.

"Then my offer is nothing," I say.

He straightens. He believes he is ready to pounce. "Then my counteroffer, Miss Perne, is to make what I have discovered public knowledge." He pauses. "What do you think of that?"

"It will never happen."

He smiles. "You don't think so?"

I smile. "You would die before that happened."

He laughs. "You would take a contract out on my life?"

"Something to that effect."

He stops laughing, now deadly serious, now that we are talking about death. Yet I keep my smile since death amuses me. He points a finger at me.

"You can be sure that if anything happened to me the police would be at your door the same day," he says.

"You have arranged to send my records to someone else," I say. "Just in case something should happen to you?"

"Something to that effect." He is trying to be witty. He is also lying. I slide back farther into my chair. He thinks I am relaxing, but I position myself so that my legs are straight out. If I am to strike, I have decided, it will be with my right foot.

"Mr. Riley," I say. "We should not argue. You want something from me, and I want something from you. I am prepared to pay you a million dollars, to be deposited in whatever account you wish, in whatever part of the world you desire, if you will tell me who made you aware of me."

He looks me straight in the eye, tries to, and surely he feels the heat building up inside me because he flinches before he speaks. His voice comes out uneven and confused. He does not understand why I am suddenly so intimidating.

"No one is interested in you except me," he says.

I sigh. "You are armed, Mr. Riley."

"I am?"

I harden my voice. "You have a gun under your coat. You have a gun on your desk under those papers. You are taping this conversation. Now, one might think these are all standard blackmail precautions, but I don't think so. I am a young woman. I don't look dangerous. But someone has told you that I am more dangerous than I look and that I am to be treated with extreme caution. And you know that that someone is right." I pause. "Who is that someone, Mr. Riley?"

He shakes his head. He is looking at me in a new light, and he doesn't like what he sees. My eyes continue to bore into him. A splinter of fear has entered his mind.

"H-how do you know all these things?" he asks.

"You admit my facts are accurate?" I mimic him.

He shakes his head again.

Now I allow my voice to change, to deepen, to resonate with the fullness of my incredibly long life. The effect on him is pronounced; he shakes visibly, as if he is suddenly aware that he is sitting next to a monster. But I am not just any monster. I am a vampire, and in many ways, for his sake, that may be the worst monster of all.

"Someone has hired you to research me," I say. "I know that for a fact. Please don't deny it again, or you will make me angry. I really am uncontrollable when I am angry. I do things I later regret, and I would regret killing you, Mr. Riley—but not for long." I pause. "Now, for the last time, tell me who sent you after me, and I will give you a million dollars and let you walk out of here alive."

He stares at me incredulously. His eyes see one thing and his ears hear another, I know. He sees a pretty blond girl with startlingly blue eyes, and he hears the velvety voice of a succubus from hell. It is too much for him. He begins to stammer.

"Miss Perne," he begins. "You misunderstand me. I mean

you no harm. I just want to complete a simple business deal with you. No one has to . . . get hurt."

I take in a long, slow breath. I need air, but I can hold my breath for over an hour if I must. Yet now I let out the breath before speaking again, and the room cools even more. And Mr. Riley shivers.

"Answer my question," I say simply.

He coughs. "There is no one else."

"You'd better reach for your gun."

"Pardon?"

"You are going to die now. I assume you prefer to die fighting."

"Miss Perne—"

"I am five thousand years old."

He blinks. "What?"

I give him my full, uncloaked gaze, which I have used in the past—alone—to kill. "I am a vampire," I say softly. "And you have pissed me off."

He believes me. Suddenly he believes every horror story he has been told since he was a little boy. That they were all true: the dead things hungering for the warm living flesh; the bony hand coming out of the closet in the black of night; the monsters from another page of reality, the unturned page—who could look so human, so cute.

He reaches for his gun. Too slowly, much too.

I shove myself out of my chair with such force that I am

momentarily airborne. My senses switch into a hyper-accelerated mode. Over the last few thousand years, whenever I am threatened, I have developed the ability to view events in extreme slow motion. But this does not mean that I slow down; quite the opposite. Mr. Riley sees nothing but a blur flying toward him. He does not see that as I'm moving, I have cocked my leg to deliver a devastating blow.

My right foot lashes out. My heel catches him in the center of the breastbone. I hear the bones crack as he topples backward onto the floor, his weapon still holstered inside his coat. Although I moved toward him in a horizontal position, I land smoothly on my feet. He sprawls on the floor at my feet beside his overturned chair. Gasping for breath, blood pouring out of his mouth. I have crushed the walls of his heart as well as the bones of his chest, and he is going to die. But not just yet. I kneel beside him and gently put my hand on his head. Love often flows through me for my victims.

"Mike," I say gently. "You would not listen to me."

He is having trouble breathing. He drowns in his own blood—I hear it gurgling deep in his lungs—and I am tempted to put my lips to his and suck it away for him. Such a temptation, to sate my thirst. Yet I leave him alone.

"Who?" he gasps at me.

I continue to stroke his head. "I told you the truth. I am a vampire. You never stood a chance against me. It's not fair, but it is the way it is." I lean close to his mouth, whisper in his ear.

"Now tell me the truth and I will stop your pain. Who sent you after me?"

He stares at me with wide eyes. "Slim," he whispers.

"Who is Slim? A man?"

"Yes."

"Very good, Mike. How do you contact him?"

"No."

"Yes." I caress his cheek. "Where is this Slim?"

He begins to cry. The tears, the blood—they make a pitiful combination. His whole body trembles. "I don't want to die," he moans. "My boy."

"Tell me about Slim and I will take care of your boy," I say. My nature is kind, deep inside. I could have said if you don't tell me about Slim, I will find your dear boy and slowly peel off his skin. But Riley is in too much pain to hear me, and I immediately regret striking so swiftly, not slowly torturing the truth out of him. I did tell him that I was impulsive when I'm angry, and it is true.

"Help me," he pleads, choking.

"I'm sorry. I can only kill, I cannot heal, and you are too badly hurt." I sit back on my heels and glance around the office. I see on the desktop a picture of Mr. Riley posed beside a handsome boy of approximately eighteen. Removing my right hand from Mr. Riley, I reach for the picture and show it to him. "Is this your son?" I ask innocently.

Terror consumes his features. "No!" he cries.

I lean close once more. "I am not going to hurt him. I only want this Slim. Where is he?"

A spasm of pain grips Riley, a convulsion—his legs shake off the floor like two wooden sticks moved by a poltergeist. I grab him, trying to settle him down, but I am too late. His grimacing teeth tear into his lower lip, and more blood messes his face. He draws in a breath that is more a shovel of mud on his coffin. He makes a series of sick wet sounds. Then his eyes roll back in his head, and he goes limp in my arms. Studying the picture of the boy, I reach over and close Mr. Michael Riley's eyes.

The boy has a nice smile, I note.

Must have taken after his mother.

Now my situation is more complicated than when I arrived at the detective's office. I know someone is after me, and I have destroyed my main lead to him or her. Quickly I go through Riley's desk and fail to find anything that promises to be a lead, other than Riley's home address. The reason is sitting behind the desk as I search. Riley has a computer and there is little doubt in my mind that he stored his most important records on the machine. My suspicion is further confirmed when I switch on the computer and it immediately asks for an access code. Even though I know a great deal about computers, more than most experts in the field, I doubt I can get into his data banks without outside help. I pick up the picture of father and son again. They are posed beside a computer. Riley Junior, I suspect, must know the access code. I decide to have a talk with him.

After I dispose of his father's body. My exercise in cleanup is simplified by the fact that Riley has no carpet on his office floor. A brief search of the office building leads me to a closet filled with janitorial supplies. Mop and pail and bucket in hand, I return to Mr. Riley's office and do the job his secretary probably resented doing. I have with me—from the closet— two big green plastic bags, and I slip Riley into them. Before I leave with my sagging burden, I wipe away every fingerprint I have created. There isn't a spot I have touched that I don't remember.

The late hour is such a friend; it has been for so many years. There is not a soul around as I carry Riley downstairs and dump him in my trunk. It is good, for I am not in the mood to kill again, and murder, for me, is very much tied to my mood, like making love. Even when it is necessary.

Mayfair is a town on the Oregon coast, chilly this late in autumn, enclosed by pine trees on one side and salt water on the other. Driving away from Riley's office, I feel no desire to go to the beach, to wade out beyond the surf to sink the detective in deep water. I head for the hills instead. The burial is a first for me in this area. I have killed no one since moving to Mayfair a few months earlier. I park at the end of a narrow dirt road and carry Riley over my shoulder deep into the woods. My ears are alert, but if there are mortals in the vicinity, they are all asleep. I carry no shovel with me. I don't need one. My fingers can impale even the hardest soil more surely than the sharpest knife can poke through a man's flesh. Two miles into the woods I drop Riley onto the ground and go down on my hands and knees and begin to dig. Naturally, my clothes get a bit dirty but I have a washing machine and detergent at home. I do not worry. Not about the body ever being found.

But about other things, I am concerned.

Who is Slim?

How did he find me?

How did he know to warn Riley to treat me with caution?

I lay Riley to rest six feet under and cover him over in a matter of minutes without even a whisper of a prayer. Who would I pray to anyway? Krishna? I could not very well tell *him* that I was sorry, although I did tell him that once, after holding the jewel of his life in my bloodthirsty hands while he casually brought to ruin our wild party. No, I think, Krishna would not listen to my prayer, even if it was for the soul of one of my victims. Krishna would just laugh and return to his flute. To the song of life as he called it. But where was the music for those his followers said were already worse than dead? Where was the joy? No, I would not pray to God for Riley.

Not even for Riley's son.

In my home, in my new mansion by the sea, late at night, I stare at the boy's photo and wonder why he is so familiar

to me. His brown eyes are enchanting, so wide and innocent, yet as alert as those of a baby owl seen in the light of
the full moon. I wonder if in the days to come I will be burying him beside his father. The thought saddens me. I don't
know why.

TWO

I do not need much sleep, two hours at most, which I usually take when the sun is at its brightest. Sunlight does affect me, although it is not the mortal enemy Bram Stoker imagined in his tale of Count Dracula. I read the novel *Dracula* when it first came out, in ten minutes. I have a photographic memory with a hundred percent comprehension. I found the book delicious. Unknown to Mr. Stoker, he got to meet a real vampire when I paid him a visit one dreary English evening in the year 1899. I was very sweet to him. I asked him to autograph my book and gave him a big kiss before I left. I almost drank some of his blood, I was tempted, but I thought it would have ruined any chance he would have had at writing a sequel, which I encouraged him to do. Humans are seldom able to dwell for any length on things that truly terrify them, even though the horror writers of the present think otherwise. But Stoker was a perceptive man; he knew there was something unusual about me. I believe he had a bit of a crush on me.

But the sun, the eternal flame in the sky, it diminishes my powers. During the day, particularly when the sun is straight up, I often feel drowsy, not so tired that I am forced to rest but weary enough that I lose my enthusiasm for things. Also, I am not nearly so quick or strong during the day, although I am still more than a match for any mortal. I do not enjoy the day as much as the night. I love the blurred edges of darker landscapes. Sometimes I dream of visiting Pluto.

Yet the next day I am busy at dawn. First I call the three businessmen responsible for handling my accounts—each located on a different continent—and tell them I am displeased to learn that my finances have been examined. I listen to each protestation of innocence and detect no falsehood in their voices. My admiration for Mr. Riley's detecting abilities climbs a notch. He must have used subtle means to delve into my affairs.

Or else he'd had help.

Of course I know he had help, but I also believe he turned against the man who sent him to find me. When he realized how rich I was, he must have thought that he could score more handsomely by going after me directly. That leads me to suspect that whoever hired Riley does not know the exact details of my life, where I live and such. But I also realize he will notice Riley's disappearance and come looking for whoever killed him. I have time, I believe, but not much. By nature, I prefer to be the hunter, not the hunted. Yes, indeed, I vow, I will kill those who hired Riley as surely as I wiped him from the face of the earth.

I make arrangements, through my American businessman, to be enrolled at Mayfair High that very day. The wheels are set in motion and suddenly I have a new identity. I am Lara Adams, and my guardian, Mrs. Adams, will visit the school with my transcripts and enroll me in as many of Ray Riley's classes as possible. It has not taken me long to learn the son's name. The arm of my influence is as long as the river of blood I have left across history. I will never meet this fake Mrs. Adams, and she will never meet me, unless she should talk about her efforts on Lara's behalf. Then, if that happens, she will never talk again. My associates respect my desire for silence. I pay them for that respect.

That night I am restless, thirsty. How often do I need to drink blood? I begin to crave it after a week's time. If a month goes by I can think of nothing other than my next dripping throat. I also lose some strength if I go too long. But I do not die without it, at least not readily. I have gone for as long as six months without drinking human blood. I only drink animal blood if I am desperate. It is only when I feed from a human that I feel truly satisfied, and I believe it is the life force in the blood that makes me hunger for it more than the physical fluid itself. I do not know how to define the life force except to say that it exists: the feel of the beating heart when I have a person's vein in my mouth; the heat of their desires. The life force in an animal is of a much cruder density. When I suck on a human, it is as if I absorb a portion of the person's essence, their will. It takes a lot of willpower to live for fifty centuries.

Humans do not turn into vampires after I bite them. Nor do they change into one if they drink my blood. Blood that is drunk goes through the digestive tract and is broken down into many parts. I do not know how the legends started that oral exchange could bring about the transformation. I can only make another vampire by exchanging blood with the person, and not just a little blood. My blood has to overwhelm the other person's system before he or she becomes immortal.

Of course, I do not make vampires these days.

I drive south along the coast. I am in Northern California before I stop; it is late. There is a bar off the side of the road, fairly large. I make a smooth entrance. The men look me over, exchange glances with their buddies. The bartender does not ask me for my ID, not after I give him a hard glance. There are many more men than women around. I am searching for a particular type, someone passing through, and I spot a candidate sitting alone in the corner. He is big and burly, unshaven; his warm jacket is not dirty, but there are oil stains that did not come out from the last cleaning. His face is pleasant enough, sitting behind his frosty beer, but a tad lonely. He is a long-distance truck driver, I know the type. I have often drunk from their veins.

I sit down in front of him, and he looks up in surprise. I smile; the expression can disarm as well as alarm, but he is happy to see me. He orders me a beer and we talk. I do not ask if he is married—though it is obvious he is—and he does not bring it up. After a while we leave and he takes me to a motel, although I would have been satisfied with the back of his truck. I tell him as much, but he pats my leg and shakes his head. He is a gentleman. I won't kill him.

It is while he is undressing me that I bite into his neck. The act makes him sigh with pleasure and lean his head back; he is not really sure what I am doing. He stays in that position the whole time I drink, hypnotized with the sensation, which to him feels as if he is being caressed from the inside out—with the tip of my nails. Which to me feels like it always does, sweet and natural, as natural as making love. But I do not have sex with him. Instead, I bite the tip of my own tongue and let a drop of my blood fall onto his wounds. They heal instantly, leaving no scar, and I lay him down to rest. I have drunk a couple pints. He will sleep deep, maybe wake up with a slight headache.

"Forget," I whisper in his ear.

He won't remember me. They seldom do.

The next morning I sit in Mr. Castro's history class. My cream-colored dress is fashionable, on the rich side; the embroidered hem swings four inches above my knees. I have very nice legs and do not mind showing them off. My long wavy blond hair hangs loose on my shoulders. I wear no makeup or jewelry. Ray Riley sits off to my right, and I study him with interest. Class will begin in three minutes.

His face has a depth his father's never imagined. He is cut in the mode of many handsome modern youths, with curly brown hair and a chiseled profile. Yet his inner character pushes through his natural beauty and almost makes a mockery of it. The boy is already more man than boy. It shows in his brown eyes, soft but quick, in his silent pauses, as he takes in what his classmates say. He reflects on it, and either accepts or rejects it, not caring what the others think. He is his own person, Ray Riley, and I like that about him.

He talks to a girl on his right. Her name is Pat, and she is clearly his girlfriend. She is a scrawny thing, but with a smile that lights up whenever she looks at Ray. Her manner is assertive but not pushy, simply full of life. Her hands are always busy, often touching him. I like her as well and wonder if she is going to be an obstacle. For her sake, I hope not. I honestly prefer not to kill young people.

Pat's clothes are simple, a blouse and jeans. I suspect her family has little money. But Ray is dressed sharp. It makes me think of the million I offered his father.

Ray does not appear upset. Probably his father often disappears for days at a time.

I clear my throat and he looks over at me.

"Hello," he says. "Are you new?"

"Hi," I say. "Yes. I just checked in this morning." I offer my dainty hand. "My name's Lara Adams."

"Ray Riley." He shakes my hand. His touch is warm, his blood healthy. I can smell blood through people's skin and tell if they have any serious ailments—even years before the disease manifests. Ray continues to stare at me, and I bat my long lashes. Behind him Pat has stopped talking to another classmate and looks over. "Where are you from?" he asks.

"Colorado."

"Really? You have a slight accent."

His comment startles me because I am a master at accents. "What accent do you hear?" I ask, genuinely curious.

"I don't know. English, French—it sounds like a combination."

I have lived in both England and France for extended periods of time. "I have traveled a lot," I say. "Maybe that's what you hear."

"Must be." He gestures to his side. "Lara, this is my girlfriend, Pat McQueen. Pat, meet Lara Adams."

Pat nods. "Hi, Lara." Her manner is not the least defensive. She trusts in Ray's love, and in her own. That is going to change. I think of Riley's computer, which I have left in his office. It will not be terribly long before the police come to look around, and maybe take the computer away. But I have not taken the machine because I would have no way of explaining to Ray what I was doing with it, much less be able to convince him to open its data files.

"Hello, Pat," I say. "Nice to meet you."

"Same here," she says. "That's a beautiful dress."

"Thank you." I would have preferred to have met Ray without Pat around. Then it would have been easier for him to start a relationship with me without her between us. Yet I am confident I can gather Ray's interest. What man could resist what I have to offer? My eyes go back to him. "What are we studying in this class?" I ask.

"European history," he says. "The class just gives a broad overview. Right now we're talking about the French Revolution. Know anything about it?"

"I knew Marie Antoinette personally," I lie. I knew *of* Antoinette, but I was never close to the French nobility, for they were boring. But I was there, in the crowd, the day Marie Antoinette was beheaded. I actually sighed when the blade sliced across her neck. The guillotine was one of the few methods of execution that disturbed me. I have been hanged a couple of times and crucified on four separate occasions, but I got over it. But had I lost my head, I know that would have been the end. I was there at the start of the French Revolution, but I was in America before it ended.

"Did she really say, 'Let them eat cake'?" Ray asks, going along with what he thought was a joke.

"I believe it was her aunt who said that." The teacher, Mr. Castro, enters the room, a sad-looking example of a modern educator if ever there was one. He only smiles at the pretty girls as he strides to the front of the room. He is attractive in an aftershave-commercial sort of way. I nod to him. "What's he like?"

Ray shrugs. "Not bad."

"But not good?"

Ray sizes me up. "I think he'll like you."

"Understood."

The class starts. Mr. Castro introduces me to the rest of the students and asks me to stand and talk about myself. I remain seated and say ten words. Mr. Castro appears put out but lets it go. The lesson begins.

Ah, history, what an illusion humanity has of the past. And yet scholars argue the reality of their texts until they are blue in the face, even though something as recent as the Second World War is remembered in a manner that has no feeling for the times. For *feeling*, not events, is to me the essence of history. The majority of people recollect World War II as a great adventure against impossible odds, while it was nothing but an unceasing parade of suffering. How quickly mortals forget. But I forget nothing. Even I, a bloodthirsty harlot if ever there was one, have never witnessed a glorious war.

Mr. Castro has no feeling for the past. He doesn't even have his facts straight. He lectures for thirty minutes, and I grow increasingly bored. The bright sun has me a bit sleepy. He catches me peeking out the window.

"Miss Adams," he says, interrupting my reverie. "Could you give us your thoughts on the French nobility?"

"I think they were very noble," I say.

Mr. Castro frowns. "You approve of their excesses at the expense of the poor?"

I glance at Ray before answering. I do not think he wants the typical teenage girl, not deep inside, and I have no intention of acting like one. He is watching me, the darling boy.

"I don't approve or disapprove," I say. "I accept it. People in power always take advantage of those without power."

"That sounds like a generalization if I ever heard one," Mr. Castro replies. "What school did you go to before moving to Mayfair?"

"What school I went to doesn't matter."

"It sounds as if you have a problem with authority," Mr. Castro says.

"Not always. It depends."

"On what?"

"Whether the authority is foolish or not," I say with a smile that leaves no doubt I am talking about him. Mr. Castro, wisely, passes me over and goes on to another topic.

But the teacher asks me to stay behind when the bell rings. This bothers me; I wish to use this time to speak to Ray. I watch as he leaves the room with Pat. He glances over his shoulder at me just before he goes out of sight. Mr. Castro taps his desk, wanting my attention.

"Is there something wrong?" I ask him.

"I hope not," Mr. Castro says. "I am concerned, however, that we get off to a good start. That each of us understands where the other is coming from."

I stare at him, not strongly enough to cause him to wilt, but enough to make him squirm. "I believe I understand exactly where you're coming from," I say.

He is annoyed. "Oh, and where is that?"

I can smell alcohol on his breath, from the previous night, and alcohol from the night before that, and the night before that. He is only thirty, but the circles under his eyes indicate his liver is close to seventy. His tough stance is only an image; his hands shake as he waits for me to respond. His eyes are all over my body. I decide to ignore his question.

"You think I have a bad attitude," I say. "Honestly, I am not what you think. If you knew me you would appreciate my understanding of history and . . ." I let my voice trail off. "Other things."

"What grade are you hoping to get in this class?"

His question makes me laugh, it is so ridiculous. I lean over and give his cheek a pinch, a hard one that makes him jump. He's lucky I don't do the same to his crotch. "Why, Mr. Castro, I'm sure you're going to give little old Lara just about any grade she wants, don't you think?"

He tries to brush my hand away, but of course it is already gone. "Hey! You better watch it, miss."

I giggle. "I'll be watching you, Mr. Castro. Just to make sure you don't die of drink before the semester's over. I've got to get that good grade, you know."

"I don't drink," he protests feebly as I walk away.

"And I don't give a damn about my grade," I say over my shoulder.

I fail to catch Ray before my next class starts, which I do not share with him. Seems my pseudo guardian was unable to match my schedule exactly to Ray's. I sit through fifty minutes of trigonometry, which naturally I know almost as well as history. I manage to refrain from alienating the teacher.

The next period I don't have with Ray either, although I know fourth period we will be together in biology. Third is P.E. and I have brought blue shorts and a white T-shirt to wear. The *girlfriend,* Pat McQueen, has the locker beside mine and speaks to me as we undress.

"Why did Castro ask you to stay behind?" she asks.

"He wanted to ask me out."

"He likes the girls, that guy. What did you think of Ray?"

Pat is not excessively paranoid, but she is trying to ascertain where I am coming from. "I think he needs lots of love," I say.

Pat is not sure what to think of that, so she laughs. "I give him more than he can handle." She pauses, admiring my momentarily naked body. "You know, you really are incredibly beautiful. You must have guys hitting on you all the time."

I pull on my shorts. "I don't mind. I just hit them back. Hard."

Pat smiles, a bit nervously.

Phys ed is currently educating the boys and girls of Mayfair in the rudiments of archery. I am intrigued. The class is coed and the bow and arrow in my hands bring back old memories. Perhaps, though, the ancient memory of Arjuna, Krishna's best friend and the greatest archer of all time, is not one I should stir. For Arjuna killed more vampires than any other mortal.

All with one bow.

All in one night.

All because Krishna wished it so.

Pat follows me out onto the field, but tactfully separates herself from me as we select our equipment. I have already spooked her, and I don't think that is bad. I wear strong sunglasses, gray tinted. As I gather my bow and arrows, an anemic-looking young man with thick glasses and headphones speaks to me.

"You're new, aren't you?" he asks.

"Yes. My name is Lara Adams. Who are you?"

"Seymour Dorsten." He offers his hand. "Pleased to meet you."

My flesh encloses his, and I know instantly that this young man will be dead in less than a year. His blood is sick—how can the rest of his body not be? I hold on to his hand a moment too long, and he stares at me quizzically.

"You are strong," he says.

I smile and let go of him. "For a girl?"

He rubs his hand on his side. His illness has startled me. I have bruised him. "I suppose," he says.

"What kind of name is Seymour? It makes you sound like a nerd."

He likes my forthright manner. "I've always hated it. My mother gave it to me."

"Change it when you get out of high school. Change it to Marlboro or Slade or Bubba or something like that. And lose those glasses. You should be wearing contacts. I bet your mother even buys your clothes."

I am a revelation to Seymour. He laughs. "She does. But since I *am* a nerd, shouldn't I look the part?"

"You think you're a nerd because you think you're so smart. I'm a lot smarter than you and I look great." I gesture to our bows and arrows. "Where should we shoot these things?"

"I think it would be best if we shot them at the targets," he says wisely.

So that's what we do. A few minutes later we are at one end of the football field sending our arrows flying toward the targets that have been arranged in a neat row on the fifty-yard line. I impress Seymour when I hit the bull's-eye three times in a row. He is further impressed when we go to remove the arrows from the target and they are stuck in so deep he has to use all his strength to pull them out. He does not know that I could have split the shaft of my first arrow with the next two if I had wished. I am showing off, I know, and it is probably not the wisest thing to do, but I don't care. My mood this day is frivolous. My first day of high school. First happy thoughts about Ray and Pat and now I have taken an immediate liking to Seymour. I help him pull the arrows from the target.

"You have shot before," he says.

"Yes. I was trained by a master marksman."

He pulls out the last arrow and almost falls to the ground as it comes loose. "You should be in the Olympics."

I shrug as we walk back toward the goal posts, "I have no interest," I say.

Seymour nods. "I feel the same way about mathematics. I'm great at it, but it bores me to death."

"What does interest you?"

"Writing."

"What do you like to write?"

"I don't know yet. The strange and unusual fascinates me." He pauses. "I read a lot of horror books. Do you like horror?"

"Yes." I start to make a joke of his question, something about how close it is to my heart, but a feeling of déjà vu sweeps over me. The feeling startles me, for I haven't had it in centuries. The sensation is intense; I put a hand to my head to steady myself, while searching for the source of it. Seymour reaches out to help, and once more I feel the sickness flowing beneath his skin. I am not sure of the nature of his disease, but I have a good idea what it is.

"Are you all right?" he asks me.

"Yes." A cool film of sweat has gathered on my forehead, and I wipe it away. My sweat is clear, not tinted pink, as it becomes when I drink large quantities of human blood. The sun burns bright in the sky and I lower my head. Seymour continues to watch me. Suddenly I feel as if he has come so close to me his body is actually overlapping mine. Like the déjà vu, I do not like the sensation. I wonder if I have developed a greater sensitivity to the sun. I have not been out like this, at midday, in many years.

"I feel as if I've met you before," he says softly, puzzled.

"I feel the same way," I say honestly, the truth of the matter finally striking me. Already I have said how I can sense emotions, and that is true. The ability came to me slowly as the centuries of my life passed. At first I assumed it was because of my intense observatory faculties, and I still feel that is part of it. Yet I can sense a person's feelings even without studying them closely, and the ability baffles me to this day because it suggests a sense that is nonphysical, which I am not yet ready to accept.

I am not alone with this ability. Over time I have met the occasional human who was as sensitive as I. Indeed, I have killed several of them because they alone could sense what I was, or rather, what I was not. Not human. Something else, they would tell their friends, something dangerous. I killed them, but I did not want to because they alone could understand me.

I sense now that Seymour is one of these humans. The feeling is further confirmed when once more I pick up my bow and arrow and aim at the target. For my vision is distracted. Mr. Castro stands in the distance behind the school gymnasium, talking to a perky blond. Talking and touching—obviously making a move on the young thing. The teacher is perhaps three hundred yards distant, but for me, with a bow in my strong arms, he is within range. As I toy with my next arrow, I think that I can shoot him in the chest and no one will know—or believe—that it was really me who killed him. I can make it so that even Seymour doesn't see where the arrow flies. Killing Mr. Riley two nights earlier has awakened in me the desire to kill again. Truly, violence does beget violence, at least for a vampire—nothing quite satisfies as does the sight of blood, except for the taste of it.

I slip the arrow into the bow.

My eyes narrow.

Castro strokes the girl's hair.

Yet out of the corner of my eye I notice Seymour watching me.

Seeing what? Sensing what? The blood fever in me?

Perhaps. His next word is revealing.

"Don't," he says.

My aim wavers. I am amazed. Seymour knows I am thinking about killing Castro! Who is this Seymour, I ask myself? I lower my bow and look over at him. I have to ask.

"Don't *what*?" I say.

His eyes, magnified behind their glasses, stare at me. "You don't want to shoot anybody."

I laugh out loud, although his remark chills me. "What makes you think I want to shoot somebody?"

He smiles and relaxes a notch. My innocent tone has done its work on him. Perhaps. I wonder if Seymour is one of those rare mortals who can fool even me.

"I just had the feeling you were going to," he says. "I'm sorry."

"Do I look so dangerous?"

He shakes his head. "You are different from anyone I have ever met."

First Ray notices that I have an accent, and now Seymour reads my mind. An interesting day, to say the least. I decide I should keep a lower profile, for the time being.

Yet I do not really believe he has read my mind. If I did, like him or not, I would kill him before the sun set.

"You're just so dazzled by my beauty," I say.

He laughs and nods. "It isn't often a beauty such as you is caught talking to a nerd like me."

I lightly poke him in the belly with the tip of my arrow.

"Tell me more about the kind of stories you like." I nock the arrow onto my bowstring. Mr. Castro will live another day, I think, but maybe not many more. I add, "Especially your favorite horror stories."

So for the rest of the period Seymour tells me about an assortment of authors and books he has read. I am delighted to learn that *Dracula* is his all-time favorite story. I miss the bull's-eye a few times on purpose, but I don't know if I fool Seymour. He never takes his eyes off me.

The next period I am off to biology. Ray sits in the back at a lab table. I waste no time. I walk straight back and sit beside him. He raises an eyebrow as if to say that someone else has that seat, but then seems to change his mind.

"How did you enjoy archery?" he asks.

"You talked to Pat?" I ask.

"Yes."

There she is again, the girlfriend, between us. Once more I think of the data files at Mr. Riley's office. If the police do examine them, and do decide Mr. Riley has met with foul play, they will be paying me a visit. If I cannot access the files soon, I will have to destroy them. I decide to hasten things, knowing that I run the risk of destroying my whole seduction. I want to look at those files tonight. I reach over and touch Ray's arm.

"Can you do me a big favor?" I ask.

He glances at my fingertips on his bare arm. My touch is warm. Wait till he feels it hot. "Sure," he says.

"My parents are gone for a few days, and I need some help moving some things into my house. They're in the garage." I add, "I could pay you for your help."

"You don't have to pay me. I'd be glad to help this weekend."

"Actually, one of these *things* is my bed. I had to sleep on the floor last night."

"What a drag." Ray takes a breath and thinks. My hand continues to rest on his arm, and surely the soft texture of my skin must be a part of his thought processes. "I have to work after school today."

"Till what time?"

"Nine. But then I'm supposed to go over and see Pat."

"She's a lovely girl." My eyes rest on his eyes. It is as if they say, yes, lovely, but there are other things in life besides love. At least that is my intention. Yet as I stare into Ray's eyes, I can't help but feel that he is one of those rare mortals I could love. This is another startling revelation for me, and already, even before noon, it seems the day is to be filled with them. I have not loved a man—or a woman for that matter—in centuries. And none have I ever loved as much as my husband, Rama, before I was made into a vampire.

Yet Rama comes to mind as I stare at Ray, and at last I know why Ray looks familiar. He has Rama's eyes.

Ray blinks. "We've been going out for a year."

I sigh unintentionally. Even after fifty centuries I still miss Rama. "A year can pass quickly," I say softly.

But not five thousand—the long years stand behind me like so many ghosts, weary, but also wary. Time sharpens caution, destroys playfulness. I think how nice it would be to go for a walk in the park with Ray, in the dark. I could kiss him, I could bite him—gently. I sigh because this poor boy doesn't know he is sitting beside his father's murderer.

"Maybe I can help you," Ray says clearly. My eyes do not daunt him as much as I would expect, and I do not know if that is because of his own internal strength or because my glance is softened by my affection for him. "But I'll have to check with Pat."

I finally take my hand back. "If you check with Pat, she'll say it is fine to help me as long as she gets to come along." I shrug. "Any girl would."

"Can she come over, too?"

"No."

My answer startles him. But he is too shrewd to ask me why. He simply nods. "I'll talk to her. Maybe I can come a little later. What time do you go to bed?"

"Late."

The lecture in biology is about photosynthesis. How the sun's energy is changed into chemical energy through the presence of green chlorophyll, and how this green pigment in turn supports the entire food chain. The teacher makes a comment I find interesting—chlorophyll and red blood cells are practically identical. Except in chlorophyll the iron atom is replaced by a magnesium atom. I look over at Ray and think that in the evolutionary chain, only one atom separates us.

Of course, I know that evolution would never have created a vampire. We were an accident, a horrible mistake. It occurs to me that if Ray does help me examine his father's files, I should probably kill him afterward. He smiles at me as I look at him. I can tell he likes me already. But I don't smile back. My thoughts are too dark.

The class ends. I give Ray my address, but not my phone number. He will not call and cancel on me. It is the address of a new house that was rented for me that morning. Mr. Riley will have my other address in his files, and I don't want Ray to draw the connection when and if we go into his computer. Ray promises to come over as soon as he is able. He does not have sex on his mind, but something else I cannot fathom. Still, I will give him sex if he wants it. I will give him more than he bargains for.

I go to my new home, a plain suburban affair. It is furnished. Quickly, not breaking a sweat, I move most of the furniture into the garage. Then I retire to the master bedroom, draw all the shades, and lie down on the hard wooden floor and close my eyes. The sun has drained my strength, I tell myself. But as I doze off I know it is also the people I have met this day that have cut deep into me, where my iron blood flows like a black river over the cold dust of forgotten ages, dripping onto this green world, onto the present, like the curse of the Lord himself. I hope to dream of Krishna as I fall asleep, but I do not. The devil is there instead.

Yaksha, the first of the vampires.

As I am the last.

THREE

We were the original Aryans—blond and blue eyed. We invaded India, before there were calendars, like a swarm of hornets in search of warmer climates. We brought sharp swords and spilled much blood. But in 3000 B.C., when I was born, we were still there, no longer enemies, but part of a culture that was capable of absorbing every invader and making him a brother. I came into the world named Sita, in a small village in Rajastan, where the desert had already begun to blow in sand from the dead lands to the west. I was there at the beginning, and had as a friend the mother of all vampires. *Amba*, which meant mother in my language. She was a good woman.

Amba was seven years older than my seven years when the disease came to our village. Although separated by seven years, we were good friends. I was tall for my age, she was short, and we both loved to sing, bajans mainly, holy songs from the sacred Vedas, which we chanted by the river after dark. My skin was brown from the harsh sun; Amba's dark from a grandfather who was of original Indian stock. We did not look alike, but when we sang our voices were one and I was happy. Life was simple in Rajastan.

Until the disease came. It did not strike everyone, only half. I do not know why I was spared, since I drank from the polluted river as much as Amba and the rest. Amba was one of the first to fall ill. She vomited blood the last two days of her life, and all I could do was sit by her side and watch her die. My sorrow was particularly great because Amba was eight months pregnant at the time. Even though I was her best friend, she never did tell me who the father was. She never told anyone.

When she died, it should have ended there. Her body should have been taken to the cremation ground and offered to Vishnu, her ashes thrown in the river. But recently an Aghoran priest had entered our village. He had other ideas for her body. Aghora was the left-handed path, the dark path, and no one would have listened to what the priest had to say if the panic over the plague hadn't been in the air. The priest brought his blasphemous ideas, but many listened to him because of their fears for the plague. He said the plague was the result of an evil *rakshasa* or demon that had taken offense at our worship of the great God Vishnu. He said the only way to free our village of the rakshasa was to call forth an even greater being, a *yakshini*, and implore the yakshini to eat the rakshasa.

Some thought this idea was reasonable, but many others, myself included, felt that if God couldn't protect us, how could a yakshini? Also, many of us worried what the yakshini would do once it had devoured the rakshasa. From our Vedic texts we knew that yakshinis had no love for human beings. But the Aghoran priest said that he could handle the yakshini, and so he was allowed to go ahead with his plans.

Aghorans usually do not invoke a deity into a statue or an altar but into the corpse of someone recently dead. It is this practice in particular that has them shunned by most religious people in India. But desperate people often forget their religion when they need it most. There were so many dead at the time, the priest had his choice of corpses. But he chose Amba's body, and I think the fact of her late pregnancy attracted him. I was only a child at the time, but I could see something in the eyes of the priest that frightened me. Something cold and uncaring.

Being so young, I was not permitted to attend the ceremony. None of the women were allowed. Because I was worried what they were going to do with my friend's body, however, I stole into the woods in the middle of the night they were to perform the invocation. I watched from behind a boulder, at the edge of a clearing, as the Aghoran priest with the help of six men—one of them my father—prepared Amba's naked body. They anointed her with clarified butter and camphor and wine. Then, beside a roaring fire, seated close to Amba's upturned head, the priest began a long repetitious chant. I did not like it; it sounded nothing like the bajans we chanted to Vishnu. The mantras were hard on the ear, and each time the priest completed a verse, he would strike Amba's belly with a long sharp stick. It was as if he were imploring her to wake up, or else trying to wake something up inside her.

This went on for a long time, and soon Amba's belly began to bleed, which frightened the men. Because she bled as a living person, as if there were a heart beating inside her. But I knew this could not be. I had been with Amba when she died and sat beside her body for a long time afterward, and not once, even faintly, had she drawn in a breath. I was not tempted to run to her. Not for a moment did I believe the priest had brought her back to life. Indeed, I was tempted to flee back to my mother, who surely must have been wondering where I was. Especially when a dark cloud went over the moon and a heavy breeze began to stir, a wind that stank of decay and waste. The smell was atrocious. It was as if a huge demon had suddenly appeared and breathed down upon the ceremony.

Something had come. As the smell worsened, and the men began to mutter aloud that they should stop, the fire abruptly shrank to red coals. Smoke filled the air, curling around the bloody glow of the embers like so many snakes over a rotting prey. Some of the men cried out in fear. But the priest laughed and chanted louder. Yet even his voice failed when Amba suddenly sat up.

She was hideous to behold. Her face dripped blood. Her eyes bulged from her head as if pushed out from the inside. Her grin widened over her teeth as if pulled by wires. Worst of all was her tongue; it stretched much longer than any human tongue could, almost a foot, curling and licking at the air like the smoking snakes that danced beside what was left of the fire. I watched it in horror knowing that I was seeing a yakshini come to life. In the haunting red glow it turned to face the priest, who had fallen silent. No longer did he appear confident.

The yakshini cackled like a hyena and reached out and grabbed the priest.

The priest screamed. No one came to his aid.

The yakshini pulled the priest close, until they were face to face. Then that awful tongue licked the priest's face, and the poor man's screams gagged in his throat. Because wherever he was touched by the tongue, his skin was pulled away. When the priest was a faceless mass of gore, the yakshini threw its head back and laughed. Then its hands flew up behind the priest's neck and took hold of his skull. With one powerful yank it twisted the priest's head around until it was facing the other way, his bones cracking. The priest fell over dead as the yakshini released him. Then the monster, still seated, glanced around the campfire at the terrified men. A sly glance it was.

It smiled as its eyes came to rest on me. Yes, I believe it could see me even as I cowered behind the huge stone that separated me from the clearing. Its eyes felt like cold knives pressing into my heart.

Then finally, thankfully, the monster closed its eyes, and Amba's body lay back down.

For a long moment none of the men moved. Then my father—a brave man, although not the wisest—moved and knelt beside Amba's corpse. He poked it with a stick and it did not move. He poked the priest as well, but it was clear the man wasn't going to be performing any more ceremonies in this life. The other men came up beside my father. There was talk of cremating both of the bodies then and there. Hiding behind my boulder, I nodded vigorously. The stench had blown away on the wind, and I did not want it to return. Unfortunately, before more wood could be gathered, my father noticed movement inside Amba's belly. He cried out to the others. Amba was not dead. Or if she was, he said, her child was not. He reached for a knife to cut the infant out of Amba's womb.

It was then I jumped from behind the boulder and ran into the clearing.

"Father!" I cried, reaching for his hand holding the knife. "Do not let that child come into this world. Amba is dead, see with your own eyes. Her child must likewise be dead. Please, Father, listen to me."

Naturally, all the men were surprised to see me, never mind hear what I had to say. My father was angry at me, but he knelt and spoke to me patiently.

"Sita," he said. "Your friend does appear dead, and we were wrong to let this priest use her body in this way. But he has paid for his evil karma with his own life. But we would be creating evil karma of our own if we do not try to save the life of this child. You remember when Sashi was born, how her mother died before she came into the world? It sometimes happens that a living child is born to a dead woman."

"No," I protested. "That was different. Sashi was born just as his mother died. Amba has been dead since early dawn. Nothing living can come out of her."

My father gestured with his knife to the squirming life inside Amba's bloody abdomen. "Then how do you explain the life here?"

"That is the yakshini moving inside her," I said. "You saw how the demon smiled at us before it departed. It intends to trick us. It is not gone. It has entered into the child."

My father pondered my words with a grave expression. He knew I was intelligent for my age and occasionally asked for my advice. He looked to the other men for guidance, but they were evenly divided. Some wanted to use the knife to stab the life moving inside Amba. Others were afraid, like my father, of committing a sin. Finally my father turned back to me and handed me the knife.

"You knew Amba better than any of us," he said. "You would best know if this life that moves inside her is evil or good. If you know for sure in your heart that it is evil, then strike it dead. None of the men here will blame you for the act."

I was appalled. I was still a child and my father was asking me to commit an atrocious act. But my father was wiser than I had taken him for. He shook his head as I stared at him in amazement, and took back the knife.

"You see," he said. "You are not sure if what you say is true. In a matter of life and death, we must be careful. And if we are to make an error, it must be on the side of life. If this child turns out to be evil, then we will know as it grows up. Then we will have more time to decide what should be done with it." He turned back to Amba's body. "For now I must try to save it."

"We may not have as much time as you think," I said as my father began to cut into Amba's flesh. Soon he held a bloody male infant in his hand. He gave it a gentle spank, and it sucked in a dry rasping breath and began to cry. Most of the men smiled and applauded, although I noticed the fear in their eyes. My father turned to me and asked me to hold it. I refused. However, I did consent to name the child.

"It should be called Yaksha," I said. "For it has the heart of a yakshini."

And the child's name was as I said. Most considered it an evil omen, yet none of them, in their darkest dreams, would realize how appropriate the name would be. But from that time on, the plague vanished and never returned.

My father gave Yaksha to my aunt to raise, for she had no children of her own and greatly desired one. A simple but loving woman, she treated the child as if it were her own—certainly as if it were a human deserving of her love. Whether she felt any love in return from the child, I don't know. He was a beautiful baby with dark hair and pale blue eyes.

Time went by, and it always does, and yet for Yaksha and for me the years took on a peculiar quality. For Yaksha grew faster than any child in the history of our village, and when I was fifteen years of age, he was already, in stature and education, my age, although he had been born only eight years earlier. His accelerated development brought to surface once again the rumors surrounding his birth. But they were rumors at best because the men who had been there the night Yaksha had come into the world never spoke about what had happened when the priest had tried to invoke the yakshini into Amba's corpse. They must have sworn one another to secrecy because my father occasionally took me aside and reminded me that I should not talk about that night. I did not, of course, because I did not think anyone outside of the six men would have believed me. Besides, I loved my father and always tried to obey him, even when I thought he was making a mistake.

It was at about this time, when I was fifteen, that Yaksha started to go out of the way to talk to me. Until then I had avoided him, and even when he pursued me I tried to keep my distance. At least at first, but there was something about him that made him hard to resist. There was his great beauty, of course, his long shiny mane of black hair, his brilliant eyes, cool blue gems, set deep in his powerful face. His smile was also beguiling. How often it flashed in my direction, his two rows of perfect white teeth like polished pearls. Sometimes I would stop to talk to him, and he would always have a little gift to offer—a spoonful of sandlepaste, a stick of incense, a string of beads. I accepted these gifts reluctantly because I felt as if one day Yaksha would want something in return, some-thing I would not want to give. But he never asked.

But my attraction to him went deeper than his beauty. Even at eight years of age he was clearly the smartest person in the village, and often the adults consulted him on important matters: how to improve the harvest; how best to build our new temple; how to barter with the wandering merchants who came to buy our crops. If people had doubts about Yaksha's origin, they had nothing but praise for his behavior.

I was attracted to him, but I never ceased to fear him. Occasionally I would catch a disturbing glimmer in his eyes, and be reminded of the sly smile the yakshini had given me before it had supposedly vacated Amba's body.

It was when I was sixteen that the first of the six men who had witnessed his birth disappeared. The man just vanished. Later that same year another of the six disappeared also. I asked my father about it, but he said that we could not hold Yaksha to blame. The boy was growing up well. But the next year, when another two of the men vanished, even my father began to have doubts. It was not long after that my father and I were the only ones left in the village who had been there that horrible night. But the fifth man did not just vanish. His body was found gored to death, as if by a wild animal. There was not a drop of blood left in his corpse. Who could doubt that the others had not ended up the same way?

I begged my father to speak up about what was happening, and Yaksha's part in it. By then Yaksha was ten and looked twenty, and if he was not the leader of the village, few people doubted that he would be in charge soon. But my father was soft-hearted. He had watched Yaksha grow up with pride, no doubt feeling personally responsible for the birth of this wonderful young man. And his sister was still Yaksha's stepmother. He told me not to say anything to the others, that he would ask Yaksha to leave the village quietly and not come back.

But it was my father who was not to come back, although Yaksha vanished as well. My father's body was never found, except for a lock of his hair, down by the river, stained with blood. At the ceremony honoring his death I broke down and cried out the many things that had happened the night Yaksha had been born. But the majority of people believed I was consumed with grief and didn't listen. Still, a few heard me, the families of the other men who had vanished.

My grief over my lost father faded slowly. Yet two years after his death and the disappearance of Yaksha, near my twentieth birthday, I met Rama, the son of a wandering merchant. My love for Rama was instantaneous. I saw him and knew I was supposed to be with him, and by the blessings of Lord Vishnu, he felt the same way. We were married under the full moon beside the river. The first night I slept with my husband I dreamed of Amba. She was as she had been when we had sung late at night together. Yet her words to me were dark. She told me to beware the blood of the dead, never to touch it. I woke up weeping and was only able to sleep by holding my husband tightly.

Soon I was with child, and before the first year of my marriage was over, we had a daughter—Lalita, she who plays. Then my joy was complete and my grief over my father faded. Yet I was to have that joy for only a year.

One moonless night I was awakened late by a sound. Beside me slept my husband, and on my other side our daughter. I do not know why the sound woke me; it was not loud. But it was peculiar, the sound of nails scraping over a blade. I got up and went outside my house and stood in the dark and looked around.

He came from behind me, as he often used to when we were friends. But I knew he was there before he spoke. I sensed his proximity—his inhuman being.

"Yaksha," I whispered.

"Sita." His voice was very soft.

I whirled around and started to shout, but he was on me before I could make a sound. For the first time I felt Yaksha's real strength, a thing he had kept hidden while he lived in our village. His hands, with their long nails, were like the paws of a tiger around my neck. A long sword banged against his knee. He choked off my air and leaned over and whispered in my ear. He had grown taller since I last saw him.

"You betrayed me, my love," he said. "If I let you speak, will you scream? If you scream you will die. Understood?"

I nodded and he loosened his grip, although he continued to keep me pinned. I had to cough before I could speak. "You betrayed me," I said bitterly. "You killed my father and those other men."

"You do not know that," he said.

"If you didn't kill them, then where are they?"

"They are with me, a few of them, in a special way."

"What are you talking about? You lie—they are dead, my father's dead."

"Your father is dead, that is true, but only because he did not want to join me." He shook me roughly. "Do you wish to join me?"

It was so dark, I could see nothing of his face except in outline. But I did believe he was smiling at me. "No," I said.

"You do not know what I am offering you."

"You are evil."

He slapped me, hard. The blow almost took off my head. I tasted my own blood. "You do not know what I am," he said, angry, but proud as well.

"But I do. I was there that night. Didn't the others tell you before you killed them? I saw it all. It was I who named you—Yaksha—cursed son of a yakshini!"

"Keep your voice down."

"I will do nothing you say!"

He gripped me tight again, and it was hard to breathe. "Then you will die, lovely Sita. After first watching your husband and child die. Yes, I know they are asleep in this house. I have watched you from afar for a while now."

"What do you want?" I gasped, bitter.

He let me go. His tone was light and jovial, which was cruel. "I have come to offer you two choices. You can come with me, be my wife, become *like me*. Or you and your family can die tonight. It is that simple."

There was something strange in his voice besides his cruelty. It was as if he were excited over an unexpected discovery. "What do you mean, become *like you*? I can never be like you. You are different from anybody else."

"My difference is my greatness. I am the first of my kind, but I can make others like me. I can make you like me if you will consent to our blood mixing."

I didn't know what he was offering, but it frightened me,

that his blood, even a little, should get inside mine. "What would your blood do to me?" I asked.

He stood tall. "You see how strong I am. I cannot be easily killed. I see things you cannot see, I hear what you cannot hear." He leaned close, his breath cold on my cheek. "Most of all I dream things you never imagined. You can be part of that dream, Sita. Or you can begin to rot tonight, in the ground, beside your husband and child."

I did not doubt his words. His uniqueness had been obvious to me from the start. That he could transfer his qualities into another did not surprise me.

"If your blood entered into me, would I also become cruel like you?" I asked.

My question amused him. "I believe in time you would become worse than I." He leaned closer still, and I felt his teeth touch my earlobe. He took a tiny bite and sucked at the blood that flowed, and the act revolted me because of its effect on me. I liked it. I loved it even more than I loved the passion my husband gave to me in the middle of the night. I felt the true essence of Yaksha's power then, the depth of it, the space beyond the black space in the sky where the yakshinis came from. Just with that tiny bite I felt as if every drop of my blood turned from red to black. I felt invincible.

Still, I hated him, more than ever.

I took a step away.

"I watched you grow up," I said. "You watched me. You

know I always speak my mind. How can I be your wife if I hate you so? Why would you want a wife like me?"

He spoke seriously. "I have wanted you for years now."

I turned my back on him. "If you want me so, it must mean you care about me. And if you care about me, then leave this place. Go away and don't come back. I am happy with my life."

I felt his cold hand on my shoulder. "I will not leave you."

"Then kill me. But leave my husband and child alone."

His grip on my shoulder tightened. Truly, I realized, he was as strong as ten men, if not more. If I cried out, Rama would be dead in a moment. Pain radiated from my shoulder into the rest of my body, and I was forced to stoop.

"No," he said. "You must come with me. It was destiny that you were there that night. It is your destiny to follow me now, to the edge of night."

"The edge of night?"

He pulled me up and kissed me hard on the lips. Once more I tasted his blood, mixed with mine. "We will live for eternity," he swore. "Just say yes. You must say yes." He paused and glanced at my house. He did not have to say it again; I understood his meaning. I was beaten.

"Yes."

He hugged me. "Do you love me?"

"Yes."

"You lie, but it doesn't matter. You will love me. You will love me forever."

He picked me up and carried me away. Into the dark forest, to a place of calm, of silence, where he opened his veins and mine with his nails, and pressed our arms together, and held them such, for what seemed forever. In that night all time was lost, and all love was tainted. He spoke to me as he changed me, but it was with words I did not understand, the sounds yakshinis must make when they mate in their black hells. He kissed me and stroked my hair.

Eventually, the power of his transfusion overwhelmed my body. My breathing, my heartbeat—they raced faster and faster, until soon they chased each other, until I began to scream, like one dropped into a boiling pot of oil. Yet, this I did not understand, and still do not. The worst of the agony was that I could not get enough of it. That it thrilled me more than the love any mortal could give to me. In that moment Yaksha became my lord, and I cried for him instead of for Vishnu. Even as the race of my breathing and heartbeat collided and stopped. Yes, as I died I forgot my God. I chose the path my father had rejected. Yes, it is the truth, I cursed my own soul by my own choice as I screamed in wicked pleasure and embraced the son of the devil.

FOUR

*T*he expression "the impatience of youth" is silly. The longer I live, the more impatient I become. True, if nothing much is happening, I can sit perfectly still and be content. Once I stayed in a cave for six months and had only the blood of a family of bats to dine on. But as the centuries have gone by, I want what I want immediately. I enter into relationships swiftly. Therefore, in my mind, I already consider Ray and Seymour friends, although we have just met.

Of course, I often end friendships as quickly.

It is Ray's knocking at my door that brings me out of my rest. How does a vampire sleep? The answer is simple. Like something dead. True, I often dream when I sleep, but they are usually dreams of blood and pain. Yet the dream I just had, of Amba and Rama and Yaksha, of the beginning, is the one I find the most painful. The pain never lessens as the time goes by. It is with a heavy step that I walk from the bedroom to answer the front door.

Ray has changed out of his school clothes into jeans and a gray sweatshirt. It is ten o'clock. A glance at Ray tells me that he is wondering what he is doing at my house after dark. This girl he has just met. This girl that has such hypnotic eyes. If he wasn't thinking about sex before, he might be thinking about it soon.

"Am I too late?" he asks.

I smile. "I'm a vampire. I stay up all night." I step aside and gesture. "Please come in, and please forgive the bare rooms. As I said, a lot of the furniture is still in the garage. The moving people couldn't get into the house when they came."

Ray glances around and nods his approval. "You said your parents are away?"

"I did say that, yes."

"Where are they?"

"Colorado."

"Where did you live in Colorado?"

"In the mountains," I say. "Would you like something to drink?"

"Sure. What do you have?"

"Water."

He laughs. "Sounds perfect. As long as you'll join me.

"Gladly. I might have a bottle of wine as well. Do you drink?"

"I have a beer every now and then."

We head for the kitchen. "Wine is much better, red wine. Do you eat meat?"

"I'm not a vegetarian, if that's what you mean. Why do you ask?"

"Just wondering," I say. He is so darling, it is hard to resist nibbling on him.

We have a glass of wine together, standing in the kitchen. We drink to world peace. Ray is anxious to get to work, he says. He is just anxious. Alone with a mortal, my aura of difference is greater. Ray knows he is with a unique female, and he is intrigued, and confused. I ask how Pat is. May as well confront his confusion.

"Fine," he says.

"Did you tell her you were coming to visit me?"

He lowers his head. He feels a twinge of guilt, but no more. "I told her I was tired and wanted to go to bed."

"You can sleep here if you want. Once you bring in the beds."

My boldness startles him. "My father would wonder where I was."

"I have a phone. You can call him." I add, "What does your father do?"

"He's a private detective."

"Sounds glamorous. Do you want to call him?"

Ray catches my eye. I catch his in return. He doesn't flinch as his father did under my scrutiny. Ray is strong inside.

"Let's see how it goes and how late it gets," Ray says carefully.

He sets to work. Soon he is huffing and puffing. I help him, but only a little. Nevertheless, he comments on my strength. I tell him how I befriended Seymour and he is interested. Apparently Seymour is a friend of his as well.

"He's probably the smartest guy in the school," Rays says, lugging in a couple of dining room chairs. "He's only sixteen years old and he'll be graduating in June."

"He told me he likes to write," I say.

"He's an incredible writer. He let Pat read a couple of his short stories, and she gave them to me. They were real dark, but beautiful. One was about what goes on in the space between moments of time. It was called 'The Second Hand.' He had this character who suddenly begins to live between the moments, and finds that there is more going on there than in normal time."

"Sounds interesting. What made the story dark?"

"The guy was in the last hour of his life. But it took him a year to live it."

"Did the guy know it was his last hour?"

Ray hesitates. He must know Seymour is not well. "I don't know, Lara."

He has not used my name before. "Call me Sita," I say, surprising myself.

He raises an eyebrow, "A nickname?"

"Sort of. My father used to call me that."

Ray is alert to my change of tone, for I have allowed sadness to enter my voice. Or maybe it is the sound of longing, which is different from sorrow. No one I have cared about has used my real name in thousands of years. I think how nice it will be to have Ray say it.

"How long will your family be in Colorado?" Ray asks.

"I lied. My father's not there. He's dead."

"I'm sorry."

"I was thinking about him before you came." I sigh. "He died a long time ago."

"How did he die?"

"He was murdered."

Ray makes a face. "That must have been terrible for you. I know if anything ever happened to my father, I would be devastated. My mother left us when I was five."

I swallow thickly. By the strength of my reaction, I realize how involved I have allowed myself to become with the boy. All because he has Rama's eyes? There is more to it than that. He also has Rama's voice. No, not his accent surely—the average person would have said, had they heard them together, that they sounded nothing alike. But to me, with my vampire ears, the subtle aspects of their voices are almost identical. The silence between their syllables. It was Rama's deep silence that initially attracted me to him.

"You must be very close" is all I can say. But I know I will have to bring up the father again soon. I want in that office tonight. I just hope I mopped up every drop of blood. I have no wish to be with Ray when he learns the truth.

If he ever does.

I let him finish bringing in the furniture, which takes him a couple of hours, although it took me less than twenty minutes to put it in the garage. It is after midnight. I offer him another glass of wine—a large glass—and he drinks it down quick. He is thirsty, as I am thirsty. I want his blood, I want his body. Blood drinking and sex are not that separate in my mind. Yet I am no black widow. I do not mate and kill. But the urges, the lusts—they sometimes come together. But I don't want to hurt this young man, I don't want any harm to befall him. Yet just by being with me his chances of dying are much greater. I have only to think of my history, and of the person who stalks me now. I watch as Ray sets down his empty glass.

"I should get home," he says.

"You can't drive."

"Why not?"

"You're drunk."

"I'm not drunk."

I smile. "I gave you enough alcohol to make you drunk. Face it, boy, you're trapped here for a while. But if you want to sober up quick, then take a hot tub with me. You can sweat the alcohol out of your system."

"I didn't bring my suit."

"I don't own a suit," I say.

He is interested—very—but doubtful. "I don't know."

I step over and rest my palms on his sweaty chest. His muscles are well developed. It would be fun to wrestle with him, I think, especially since I know who would win. I look up into his eyes; he is almost a head taller than I. He looks down at me, and he feels as if he is falling into my eyes, into bottomless wells of blue, twin skies behind which the eternal black of space hides. The realm of the yakshinis. He senses my darkness in this moment. I sense other things about him and feel a chill. So much like Rama, this boy. He haunts me. Could it be true? Those words of Krishna's that Radha had told me about love?

"Time cannot destroy it. I am that love—time cannot touch me. Time but changes the form. Somewhere in some time it will return. When you least expect it, the face of a loved one reappears. Look beyond the face and—"

Odd, but I cannot remember the last part of it. I of the perfect memory.

"I will not tell Pat," I say. "She will never know."

He draws in a breath. "I don't like lying to her."

"People always lie to one another. It's the way of the world. Accept it. It doesn't mean you have to hurt with your lies." I take his hands; they tremble slightly, but his eyes remained fastened on mine. I kiss his fingers and rub them on my cheek. "What happens with me will not hurt her."

He smiles faintly. "Is that a lie to save me hurt?"

"Maybe."

"Who are you?"

"Sita."

"Who is Sita?"

"I told you already, but you weren't listening. It doesn't matter. Come, we'll sit in the water together and I'll rub your tired muscles. You'll love it. I have strong hands."

Not long after, we are naked in the Jacuzzi together. I have had many lovers, of course, both male and female—thousands actually—but the allure of the flesh has yet to fade in me. I am excited as Ray sits with his bare back to me, my knees lightly hugging his rib cage, my hands kneading deep into the tissue along his spine. It has been a long time since I have massaged anybody and I enjoy it. The water is very hot. Steam swirls around us and Ray's skin reddens. But he says he likes it this way, so hot he feels he's being boiled alive. I, of course, don't mind boiling water. I lean over and bite him gently on the shoulder.

"Careful," he says. He does not want me to leave any marks for Pat to find.

"It will be gone in the morning." I suck a few drops of blood from his wound. Such a pleasant way to spend a night. The blood flows like an elixir down my throat, making me want more. But I resist the urge. I pinch the tip of my tongue with my teeth and a drop of blood oozes onto the small bite. It vanishes instantly. I return to my massage. "Ray?" I say.

He moans with pleasure. "Yes."

"You can make love to me if you want."

He moans some more. "You are an amazing girl, Sita."

I turn him around, slowly, easily, pleasurably. He tries not to look at my body and fails. I lean over and kiss him hard on the lips. I feel what he feels. His initial surprise—kissing a vampire is not like kissing a mortal. Many men and women have swooned just from the brush of my lips. Such is the pleasure I can give. Yet there is the painful side—my kiss often sucks the breath from a person, even when I don't intend it to. Inside, I feel Ray's heart begin to pound. I release him before there is any danger. The later it gets, the more I vow not to harm him, and the more inevitable it seems. He hugs me, all slippery and wet, and tries to catch his breath while resting his chin on my shoulder.

"Are you choking on something?" I ask.

"Yes." He coughs. "I think it's you."

I chuckle as I continue to stroke his back. "You could do worse."

"You are not like any girl I've ever met."

"You don't want just any girl, Ray."

He sits back, my naked legs still around him. He is not afraid to look me in the eyes. "I don't want to cheat on Pat."

"Tell me what you do want."

"I want to spend the night with you."

"A paradox. Which one of us is going to win?" I pause, add, "I am a master at keeping secrets. We can both win."

"What do you want from me?"

His question startles me, it is so perceptive. "Nothing," I lie.

"I think you want something."

I smile. "There is your body."

He has to smile, I sound so cute, I know. But he is not dissuaded. "What else do you want?"

"I'm lonely."

"You don't look lonely."

"I'm not when I'm looking at you."

"You hardly know me."

"You hardly know me. Why do you want to spend the night with me?"

"There is your body." But he loses his smile and lowers his head. "There is something else, too. When you look at me I feel—I feel you are seeing something nobody else sees. You have such amazing eyes."

I pull him back toward me. I kiss him. "That's true." I kiss him again. "I see right through you." Again, another kiss. "I see what makes you tick." A fourth time, a hard kiss. He gasps as I release him.

"What is that?" he asks, sucking in a breath.

"You love Pat, but you crave mystery. Mystery can be as strong as love, don't you think? You find me mysterious and you're afraid if you let me slip away you'll regret it later."

He is impressed. "That is how I feel. How did you know?"

I laugh. "That is part of the mystery."

He laughs with me. "I like you, Sita," he says.

I stop laughing. His remark—so simple, so innocent—pierces me like a dagger. No one in many years has said something as charming as "I like you" to me. The sentiment is childish, I know, but it is there nevertheless. I reach to kiss him again, knowing this time I am going to squeeze him so tight he will not be able to resist making love to me. But something makes me stop.

"Look beyond the face and you will see me."

Krishna's words to Radha that she has given to me. There is something in Ray's eyes, a light behind them, that makes me reluctant to soil them with my touch. I feel it then, that I am a creature of evil. Inside I swear at Krishna. Only the memory of him can make me feel this way. Otherwise, if we had never met, I would not care.

"I care about you, Ray." I turn away. "Come on, let's get out and get dressed. I want to talk to you about some things."

Ray is shocked at my sudden withdrawal, disappointed.

But I sense his relief as well.

Later we sit on the floor in the living room by the fire and finish the bottle of wine. Alcohol has little effect on me; I can drink a dozen truck drivers under the table. We talk of many things and I learn more details of Ray's life. He plans to go to Stanford the next fall and study physics and art—an odd double major he is quick to admit. The tuition at Stanford worries him; he doesn't know if his father can afford it. He should be worried, I think. He is a fan of modern quantum mechanics and abstract art. He works after school at a supermarket. He does not talk about Pat, and I don't bring her up. But I do steer the conversation back to his father.

"It is getting late," I say. "Are you sure you don't want to call your father and tell him that you've been sitting naked in a Jacuzzi with a beautiful blond?"

"To tell you the truth, I don't think my dad's home."

"He has a girlfriend of his own?"

"No, he's been out of town the last few days, working on a case."

"What kind of case?"

"I don't know what it is, he hasn't told me. Except that it's big and he hopes to make a lot of money on it. He's been working on it for a while now." Ray adds, "But I'm getting worried about him. He often leaves for days at a time, but he's never gone so long without calling."

"Do you have an answering machine at home?"

"Yes."

"And he hasn't even left you a message?"

"No."

"How long has he been out of touch?"

"Three days. I know that doesn't sound long, but I swear, he calls me every day."

I nod sympathetically. "I would be worried if I were you. Does he have an office in town?"

"Yes. On Tudor, not far from the ocean."

"Have you been by his office?"

"I've called his secretary, but she hasn't heard from him, either."

"That is ridiculous, Ray. You should call the police and report him missing."

Ray waves his hand. "You don't know my dad. I could never do that. He would be furious. No, I'm sure he just got wrapped up in his work, and he'll call me when he gets a chance." He pauses. "I hope."

"I have an idea," I say as if it just occurred to me. "Why don't you go down to his office and check his files to see what this big case is. You'd probably be able to find out where he is."

"He wouldn't like me looking through his files."

I shrug. "It's up to you. But if it were my father, I would want to know where he was."

"His files are all on computer. I'd have to go into his whole system, and there would be a notation left that I had done so. He has it set up that way."

"Can you get into his files? I mean, do you know the password?"

He hesitates. "How did you know he has it set up that a password is required?"

There is a note of suspicion in his question, and once more I marvel at Ray's perceptive abilities. But I do not marvel long because I have waited for this very moment since I killed his father two days ago, and I have no intention of upsetting my plan.

"I didn't," I say. "But it is a common way to protect files."

He appears satisfied. "Yeah, I can get into his files. The password is a nickname he had for me when I was a kid."

I do not need to ask him what it is, which may only increase his suspicion. Instead I jump to my feet. "Come on, let's go to his office right now. You'll sleep better knowing what he's up to."

He is startled. "Right now?"

"Well, you don't want to go looking at his files when his secretary's there. Now is the perfect time. I'll come with you."

"But it's late." He yawns. "I'm tired. I was thinking I should go home. Maybe he'll be there."

"That's an idea. Check to see if he's at home first. But if he's not, and he hasn't left you a message, then you should go to the office."

"Why are you so worried about my father?"

I stop suddenly, as if his question wounds me. "Do you have to ask?" I am referring to the comment I made about my own poor dead father and feel no shame using him that way. Ray looks suitably embarrassed. He sets down his glass of wine and gets up from the floor.

"Sorry. You may be right," he says, "I'll sleep better knowing what's going on. But if you come with me, then I'll have to bring you back here."

"Maybe." I give him a quick kiss. "Or maybe I'll just fly home."

FIVE

t Ray's house I wait in the car while he goes in to see if his father has returned, or if there is a message from him. Naturally, I am not surprised when Ray returns a couple of minutes later downcast. The cold has sobered him up, and he is worried. He climbs into the car beside me and turns the key in the ignition.

"No luck?" I ask.

"No. But I got the key to his building. We won't have to break in."

"That's a relief." While I had Ray look away, I intended just to break the lock.

We drive to the building I visited only forty-eight hours earlier. It is another cold night. Throughout the years I have gravitated toward the warmer climates, such as my native India. Why I have chosen to come to Oregon, I am not sure.

I glance over at Ray and wonder if it has something to do with him. But of course I don't believe that because I don't believe in destiny, much less in miracles. I do not believe Krishna was God, or if he was God—*maybe* he was God, I simply do not know for sure—then I do not believe he knew what he was doing when he created the universe. I have such contempt for the lotus-eyed one.

Yet, after all these years, I have never been able to stop thinking about him.

Krishna. Krishna. Krishna.

Even his name haunts me.

Ray lets us into the building. Soon we are standing outside Mr. Michael Riley's office door. Ray searches for another key, finds it. We step inside. The lights are off; he could leave them off and I would still be able to find my way around. But he turns them on and heads straight into his father's office. He sits at the computer while I stand off to one side. I survey the floor. Minute drops of blood have seeped into and dried in the cracks between the tiles. They are not noticeable to mortal eyes, but the police will find them if they search. I decide, no matter what happens, that I must return and do a more thorough cleaning. Ray boots the computer and hastily enters the secret password, thinking that I do not catch it. But I do—*RAYGUN*.

"Can you check what his latest entries were?" I ask.

"That's exactly what I'm doing." He looks over at me. "You know about computers, don't you?"

"Yes." I move closer so I can see the monitor. A menu flashes on the screen. The computer is equipped with a mouse. Ray chooses something called *Pathlist*. A list of files appears on the screen. They are dated. The number of bytes they occupy on the hard disk is also listed. A rectangular outline flashes around the file at the top.

ALISA PERNE.

Ray points to the screen. "He must be working with this person. Or else investigating her." He reaches for the Enter button. "Let's see who this woman is."

"Wait." I put my hand on his shoulder. "Did you hear that?"

"Hear what?"

"That sound."

"I don't hear anything."

"I have sensitive hearing. I heard someone outside the building."

Ray pauses and listens. "It could have been an animal."

"There it is again. Didn't you hear it?"

"No."

I appear mildly anxious. "Ray. Could you please see if anyone's there?"

He thinks a moment. "Sure. No problem. Stay here. Lock the door. I'll call to you when I return." He goes to get up.

But he exits the files before he leaves, although he leaves the computer running.

Interesting, I think. He was willing to sleep with me, but he doesn't trust me alone with his father's files. Smart boy.

The moment he's out the door, I lock it and hurry to the computer. I enter the password and call up the files. I can speed read like no mortal and have a photographic memory, yet I cannot read nearly as fast as a modern computer can copy. From the other night I know Mr. Riley has a few spare zip drives in his desk. I remove two from the drawer and plug one into the computer. I am familiar with the word processor. I set it to copying the file. Mr. Riley had accumulated a lot of information on me. The Alisa Perne file is large. I estimate, given the equipment I am using, that it will take me five minutes to copy the file onto both zip drives. Ray will return before then. While the file copies, I return to the office entrance and study the lock. I can hear Ray walking down the stairs. He hums as he walks. He doesn't think there is anyone outside.

I decide to jam the lock. Taking two paper clips from Riley's desk, and bending them into usable shapes, I slip them into the tumblers. The first drive finally fills as Ray returns from his quick outside inspection. I plug in the second drive.

"Sita," Ray calls. "It's me. There was no one there."

I speak from the back office. "You want me to open the door for you? I locked it like you said."

"Never mind, I have the key." He inserts the key into the lock. But the door does not open. "Sita, it won't open. Have you thrown the latch?"

I approach the door slowly so that my voice will sound closer, but I have turned the monitor around so that I can keep an eye on it. The bytes accumulate quickly, but so, I suppose, do Ray's suspicions.

"There is no latch," I say. "Try the key again."

He tries a few times. "Open the door for me."

I give the appearance of trying real hard to open it. "It's stuck."

"It opened a few minutes ago."

"Ray, I'm telling you it's stuck."

"Is the lock latch turned up?"

"Yes."

"Turn it sideways."

"I can't get it to turn. Am I going to be stuck in here all night?"

"No. There's got to be a simple solution to this," He thinks a moment. "Look in my father's desk. See if you can find a pair of pliers."

I am happy to return to the desk. In a minute I have to remove my second drive and exit the files. I open and close the drawers while I wait for the copying to finish. When it is complete, I jump into the file, scan the first page, then highlight the remainder of the file—which is several hundred pages long—and delete it. Now the Alisa Perne file contains only the first page, which holds nothing of vital importance. I return to the screen that requests the password. I put both drives in my back pocket. Striding back to the door, I pull out the paper clips and slip them in my back pocket as well. I open the door for Ray.

"What happened?" he asks.

"It just came unstuck."

"That's weird."

"Are you sure there's no one outside?"

"I didn't see anyone."

I yawn. "I'm getting tired."

"You were full of energy a few minutes ago. You want me to take you home now? I can come back later and study the file."

"You may as well look at it while you're here."

Ray returns to the computer. I lounge around the reception area. Ray lets out a sound of surprise. I peek in the door at him.

"What is it?" I ask.

"There isn't much in this file."

"Does it say who Alisa Perne is?"

"Not really. It just gives some background information on who contacted my dad to investigate her."

"That should be helpful."

"It's not, because even that information is cut off in midsentence." Ray frowns. "This is an odd file for my dad to create. I wonder if it's been tampered with. I could have sworn . . ." He looks at me.

"What?" I ask.

He glances back at the screen. "Nothing."

"No, Ray, tell me. You could have sworn what?" I worry he may have registered how big the file was when he first started on the computer. Certainly it is much smaller now. Ray shakes his head.

"I don't know," he says. "I'm tired too. I'm going to look at this stuff tomorrow." He exits the files and turns off the computer. "Let's get out of here."

"Okay."

Half an hour later I am at home, my real home, the mansion on the hill overlooking the ocean. I have come with the zip drives because I need my computer. My good night kiss to Ray was brief. His emotions were difficult for me to read. He is clearly suspicious of me, but that is not his dominant feeling. There is something in him that feels like a mixture of fear and attachment and gladness—very strange. But he is worried about his father, more than he was before we went to the office.

I have a variety of word processors and have no trouble loading the Alisa Perne file and bringing it up on the screen. A glance at the information shows me that Mr. Riley investigated me for approximately three months before calling me into his office. The data he dug up on me is interspersed with personal notes and comments on his correspondence with someone named "Mr. Slim." There is an e-mail address for Slim, but no phone number. The number indicates an office in Switzerland. I memorize it and then proceed through the file more carefully. Riley's initial contact note is interesting. Nowhere in the file are copies of Mr. Slim's faxes, just comments on them.

Aug. 8th

This morning I received an e-mail from a gentleman named Mr. Slim. He introduces himself as an attorney for a variety of wealthy European clients. He wants me to investigate a young woman named Alisa Perne, who lives here in Mayfair. He has little information on the woman—I have the impression that she is but one of many people he or his group is investigating. He also mentioned a couple of other women that he might have me look into in this part of the country, but he did not give me their names. He is particularly interested in Miss Perne's financial situation, her family situation, and also—and this is surprising— whether anyone she has been associated with has died violently recently. When I wrote back and asked if this woman was dangerous, he indicated that she was far more dangerous than she appeared, and that I was not to contact her directly under any circumstances. He said she appears to be only eighteen to twenty years of age.

I am intrigued, especially since Mr. Slim has agreed to deposit ten thousand dollars in my account to start me on my investigation. I have already e-mailed back that I will take the case. I have the young woman's address and Social

Security number. I do not have a picture but
intend to take one for my records, even though
I have been warned to keep my distance. How
dangerous can she be, at that age?

There followed an account of Riley's preliminary investigation into me. Apparently he had a contact at TRW that gave him access to information not usually available to a common investigator. I suspect Mr. Slim knew of this contact and hired Riley for that reason. Almost immediately Riley discovered that I was rich, and that apparently I had no family. The more he found out, the more eager he was to pursue the investigation, and the less information he wrote back to Mr. Slim. At one point Riley made what to him was a major decision, to use a contact on the New York Stock Exchange. By going to the man he was using up a valuable favor. But I suppose he thought I was worth it.

Sept. 21st

Miss Perne has gone to extremes to hide
her financial holdings, and not just from the
IRS. She has numerous accounts at various
brokerage houses set up under different
corporations, some off shore. Yet they appear
to be coordinated by a single law firm in New
York City—Benson and Sons. I tried to contact
the firm directly, speaking as a rich investor,
but they rebuffed my inquiries, making me
suspect they handle Perne's account and no
other. If that is true it is another example of this
woman's wealth, for Benson and Sons has
investments in the range of half a billion dollars.

Yet I have seen her—this girl—and she is as young as Mr. Slim says and very attractive. But her age confuses me, and I wonder if she has a mother somewhere who has the same name. Because many of her business dealings go back two decades, and they can all be traced to the name Alisa Perne. I am tempted to talk to her directly, despite Mr. Slim's warning.

Mr. Slim is not happy with me, and the feeling is mutual. He has the impression I have been withholding information from him and he's correct. But he has done the same with me. He still refuses to tell me the reason for his interest in this young lady, although I can imagine several scenarios. But his initial comment about her dangerous nature keeps coming back to me. Who is Alisa Perne? One of the richest people in the world obviously. But where did she get her wealth? By violent means? From her nonexistent family? I must, before I give up this case, ask her these questions myself.

I have been thinking that Mr. Slim has been paying me well, but that Alisa Perne may want to pay me more. I see already, though, that it would be unwise to let Mr. Slim know I have gone behind his back. There is a certain ruthless tone to his faxes. I don't think I ever want to meet the man. Yet I find myself looking forward to talking to Alisa.

Late September and he is on a first-name basis with me. But he did not contact me till November. What did he do during that time? I read farther and learned that he investigated my international dealings. He discovered I have property in Europe and Asia, and passports from France and India. This last fact was a revelation for him, as well it should have been. Because it appeared, accurately, that I had held the passports for more than thirty years. No wonder, I think, he asked me my age so quickly.

Finally, though, he found a violent act connected to my past. Five years earlier, in Los Angeles. The brutal slaying of a Mr. Samuel Barber. The man had been my gardener. I killed him, of course, because he had a bad habit of peering into my windows. He had seen things I didn't want talked about.

Oct. 25th

According to the police report, this man worked for her for three years. Then one morning he was found floating facedown in the ocean not far from the Santa Monica pier. His throat had been ripped out. The coroner—I spoke to him myself—was never able to determine the type of weapon. The last person to see him alive was Miss Perne.

I don't think she killed him. I like to think she didn't—the more I have studied her, the more I have come to admire her cunning and stealth. But perhaps this man learned things about her she didn't want known, and she had him killed. Certainly, she has the resources to hire whomever she pleases. When I meet with her

I must ask her about her gardener. It will be
another thing I can use as a bargaining chip.

And I have decided I will see her soon. I have
broken off all contact with Mr. Slim. In my last
e-mail I told him that I was not able to verify any
of my earlier claims about Miss Perne's personal
wealth. I have since changed my e-mail address,
so I do not know if Mr. Slim has tried to contact
me again. I imagine he is not happy with me, but
I am not going to lose any sleep over it.

How much should I ask from Miss Perne? A
million sounds like a nice round number. I have
no doubt she'll pay it to keep me quiet. What
I could do with that much money. But in truth,
I don't think I'll touch it. I'll just give it to Ray
when he's old enough.

I will arm myself when I meet with her, just in
case. But I am not worried.

That was his last entry. I am happy I have deleted the file in
the computer. If the police had such information on me, they
wouldn't leave me alone. It might not be a bad idea to burn
down the entire office building, I muse. It wouldn't be hard
to arrange. Yet such an act might draw Mr. Slim's attention to
peaceful Mayfair. To young and pretty Alisa Perne.

Yet Mr. Riley was a fool to think Mr. Slim stopped watching him just because he changed his e-mail address. I am quite
sure Slim observed him all the closer, and now that the detective has disappeared, Slim and company might even be in the

neighborhood. Slim clearly has a lot of money at his disposal, and therefore a lot of power.

Yet I am confident in my own power, and I resent this unseen person shadowing me. I hold the Swiss e-mail address in my memory, and I contemplate what I would say to this fellow should I meet him face to face. I know that my message would be short because I do not think I would let him live long.

But I do not forget that Slim knows how dangerous I am.

That does not necessarily mean he knows I am a vampire, but it is worrisome.

I turn to my computer and press the On button.

Dear Mr. Slim,

This is Alisa Perne. I understand you have hired a certain Mr. Michael Riley to investigate me. I know you haven't heard from him in a while— I don't know what could have happened to him— so I thought I would contact you directly. I am prepared to meet with you, Mr. Slim, in person, and discuss whatever is on your mind.

Yours Truly,

Alisa

I send the message. Then I wait.

I do not have to wait long. Ten minutes later a brief, and to the point, e-mail appears in my inbox.

Dear Alisa,

Where would you like to meet and when? I am
available tonight.

Sincerely,

Mr. Slim

Yes, I think, as I read the message, Slim and company are
probably close by, the Swiss address notwithstanding. I figure
the message went to Europe and was then sent back here—
nearby. I type in my return message.

Dear Mr. Slim,

Meet me at the end of Water Cove Pier in one
hour. Come alone. Agreed?

Again, ten minutes later.

Dear Alisa,

Agreed.

SIX

The pier is a half hour from my house, in the town of Water Cove, twenty miles south of Mayfair. I arm myself before I leave the house: a snub-nosed forty-five in the pocket of my black leather coat; another smaller pistol in my right boot; a razor-sharp knife strapped inside my left boot. I am handy with a knife; I can hit a moving target a hundred yards away with a flick of my wrist. I do not believe Slim will come alone, knowing how dangerous I am. Yet he will have to bring a small army to contend with me.

I leave immediately. I want to arrive before Slim does. And I do. The pier is deserted as I cruise by in my black Ferrari. I park two blocks down from the pier and climb out. My hearing is alert. I can hear the bolt of a rifle being pulled back from over a mile away. Slim would have to come at least that close to try to assassinate me outright, and that is a possibility

I consider. But all is calm, all is quiet. I walk briskly toward the end of the pier. I have chosen the meeting place for two reasons. Slim will only be able to approach me from one direction. Also, if he does arrive with overwhelming odds, then I should be able to escape by diving into the water. I can swim out a mile along the bottom of the ocean before having to surface. My confidence is high. And why shouldn't it be? In five thousand years I have never met my match.

Almost to the hour of our agreement to meet, a long white limousine pulls up to the entrance to the pier. A man and a woman climb out of the back. The man wears a black leather coat, a dark tie, a white shirt, smart black trousers. He is approximately forty-five and has the look of a hardened Navy SEAL or CIA agent: the short crew cut, the bulging muscles, the quick shifting eyes. I see that his eyes are green even from two hundred yards away. His face is tan, deeply lined from the sun. There is at least one gun in his coat, possibly two.

The woman is ten years younger, an attractive brunette. She is dressed entirely in black. Her coat is bulky, as are her hidden guns. She has at least one fully automatic weapon on her. Her skin is creamy white, the line of her mouth set and hard. Her legs are long, her muscles toned. She may be an expert in karate or some such discipline. Her mind is easy to read. She has a nasty job to do and she is going to do it right. Her promised reward is great.

Yet it is clear the man is the leader. His smile is straight

and thin lipped, more chilling than the girl's frown. This is
Slim, I know.

Four blocks down the street I can hear another limousine
parked, its engine idling. I cannot see the second car—it is
hidden behind a building—but I am able to match the sound
of the engines. The cars could hold maybe ten people each, I
estimate. In all the odds might be twenty to one against me.

The man and the woman walk toward me without speaking. I consider escaping over the side of the pier. But I hesitate
because I am a predator first and foremost; I hate to run. Also,
my curiosity is high. Who are these characters and what do
they want with me? Yet if they reach for their weapons, I will
jump. I will be gone in the flick of an eye. It is clear to me that
neither of these approaching creatures is anything but mortal.

The woman stops walking thirty yards from me. The man
approaches to within ten yards but comes no closer. They do
not reach for their weapons but they keep their hands ready.
Down the street I hear three people get out of the second
limousine. They spread out in three different directions. They
carry weapons: I hear the metal brush their clothes. They take
up positions—I am finally able to see them out of the corner
of my eye—one behind a car; another next to a tree; the last
crouched behind a sign. Simultaneously three people inside
the limousine at the pier level high-powered rifles at me.

My hesitation has cost me already.

I stand in the sights of six sets of cross hairs.

My fear is still manageable. I figure I can take a bullet or two and still escape over the side. As long as they don't get me directly in the head or heart. Still, I do not want to run. I want to talk to Slim. He is the first to speak.

"You must be Alisa."

I nod. "Slim?"

"In the flesh."

"You agreed to come alone."

"I wanted to come alone. But my associates didn't think it would be wise."

"Your associates are all about. Why so many soldiers for one girl?"

"Your reputation precedes you, Alisa."

"What reputation is that?"

He shrugs. "That you are a resourceful young woman."

Interesting, I think. He is almost embarrassed by the precautions that have been taken to abduct me. He has been told to take them—ordered. He doesn't know that I am a vampire, and if he doesn't know, then probably no one with him knows since he is clearly in command of the operation. That gives me a huge advantage. But the person above him knows. I must meet this person, I decide.

"What do you want?" I ask.

"Just that you come with us for a little ride."

"To where?"

"To a place not far from here," he says.

That is a lie. We will drive a long distance if I get in his limousine. "Who sent you?"

"You will meet him if you come with me."

Him. "What is his name?"

"I'm afraid I'm not at liberty to discuss that at this time."

"What if I don't want to come?" I ask.

Slim sighs. "That would not be good. In fact, it would be very bad."

They will shoot me if I resist, without question. It is good to know.

"Did you know Detective Michael Riley?" I ask.

"Yes. I worked with him. I assume you met him?"

"Yes."

"How is he?"

I smile, my eyes cold. "I don't know."

"I'm sure you don't." He gestures with his hand. "Please come with us. A police car might be along at any moment. I'm sure neither of us wants to complicate matters."

"If I do come with you, do I have your word I will not be harmed?" I ask.

He keeps his face straight. "You have my word, Alisa."

Another lie. This man is a killer. I can smell the blood on him. I shift slightly on my feet. The rifles aimed at me all have telescopic sights. They move as I move. I estimate at least one of the shooters will hit me before I can get over the pier rail. I don't like being shot, although I have a few times.

I have no choice but to go along, I decide, for the moment.

"Very well, Mr. Slim," I say. "I will come with you."

We walk toward the limousine, Slim on my right, the woman on my left. As we are almost at the entrance to the pier, the limousine down the street suddenly appears. Without picking up the men it deposited, it drives until it is parked behind the first limousine. Four men jump out. Their clothes are all similar—black sweatsuits. They point automatic weapons at me. My fear escalates. Their precautions are extraordinary. If they decide to open fire now, I will die. I think of Krishna, I don't know why. But he did tell me I would have his grace if I listened to him. And in my own way I have not disobeyed him. Slim turns in my direction.

"Alisa," he says. "I would like it if you would slowly reach in your coat and remove your gun and toss it on the ground."

I do as he asks.

"Thank you," Slim says. "Do you have any other weapons on you?"

"You will have to search me to find out."

"I prefer not to search you. I'm asking you if you have any other weapons, and that you surrender them now."

These are dangerous people, highly trained. I have to go on the offensive, I think, quickly. I stare at Slim, my eyes boring into him. He tries to glance away but is unable to. I speak softly, knowing he hears my words as if they were whispered between his ears.

"You do not have to be afraid of me, Mr. Slim," I say. "It does not matter what you have been told. Your fear is unnecessary. I am nothing more than I appear."

I am planting a suggestion deep in his psyche, pushing buttons he already feels. But the woman takes a sudden step forward. She speaks. "Don't listen to her. Remember."

Slim shakes his head as if trying to clear it. He gestures to the woman. "Search her," he orders.

I stand perfectly still while the woman works her way down into my boots and discovers my remaining pistol and knife. I consider grabbing her and holding her as a hostage. But a study of the eyes of the men assembled tells me that they will kill her to get to me, and lose no sleep over the act. The woman disarms me and jumps back from me as if afraid she will catch something from me. All of them, without exception, are confused about why I have to be treated with such caution. Yet all of them are determined to follow orders. Slim removes two pairs of handcuffs from inside his coat. They are gold colored, and don't smell like steel—probably some special alloy. They are three times thicker than normal cuffs. Slim tosses them toward me and they land at my feet.

"Alisa," he says patiently. "I would like you to put one pair of these around your wrists, the other pair around your ankles."

"Why?" Now I want to stall for time. Maybe a police officer will come by. Of course, these people would just kill the officer.

"We have a long drive ahead of us, and we want you safely tucked away before we allow you in our car," Slim says.

"You said we didn't have far to go?"

"Put on the cuffs."

"All right." I put them on, marveling once more at their preparation.

"Press them together so that they lock," Slim suggests.

I do so. They click. "Happy?" I ask. "Can we go?"

Slim removes a black eye mask from his pocket, similar to the kind people wear to bed. He steps toward me. "I want you to put this on," he says.

I hold out my cuffed hands. "You'll have to put it on me.

He takes another step toward me. "Your hands are free enough to put it on."

I catch his eye again; it may be my last chance. "You do not have to be so afraid of me, Slim. Your fear is ridiculous."

He hurries toward me and covers my eyes. I hear his voice.

"You're right, Alisa," he says.

He grabs my arm and pulls me toward the limousine.

We drive south on the Coast Highway. All is dark, but I still have my sense of direction. All my senses with the exception of my eyes are very alert. Slim sits on my right, the woman on my left. Four burly men sit across from us; two up front. I count the breaths. The second limousine follows a hundred yards behind. They picked up their three marksmen before we hit the road.

There are no incidental smells in the limousine. The car is new. There is no food in the limousine, but there is drink in the bar: sodas, juice, water. There is a faint smell of gunpowder in the air. One or more of the guns in the vehicle has recently been fired. Everybody has his gun out, in his hands or resting in his lap. Only the woman keeps hers aimed at me. She is the most afraid of me.

Several miles go by. The breathing of the people around me begins to slow, to lengthen and deepen. They are relaxing, except for the woman. They think the difficult part is over. Careful, I test the strength of the cuffs. The metal is incredibly hard. I will not be able to break it. But that doesn't mean I can't get around. I can hop, even bound, far more quickly than any mortal can run. I might be able to grab one of the automatic weapons from the lap of one of the men across from me and shoot and kill most of the people in the limousine before they can shoot me back. Then again, the woman might put a bullet in my brain first. Also, I know the car behind us is operating under strict instructions. The pattern in the abduction is clear. If they see me attacking, they will open fire without hesitation. Everyone in the first limousine will die, and I will be one of them. This is why there are two cars, not one.

I must try another way.

I let another thirty minutes go by. Then I speak.

"Slim. I have to go to the bathroom."

"I'm sorry, that's not possible," he says.

"I have to go bad. I drank an entire bottle of Coke before meeting you."

"I don't care. We are not stopping."

"I'll pee all over the seat. You'll have to sit in it."

"Pee if you must."

"I will do it."

He doesn't respond. More miles go by. Since Slim carried the cuffs, I decide he must be the one who has the key to open them. The arm of the woman beside me begins to tire. She lowers her weapon hand: I hear the rustling of her clothing. I estimate our speed to be sixty miles an hour. We are maybe fifty miles south of Water Cove. Seaside is approaching; I can hear the town up ahead; the two all night gas stations; the twenty-four-hour doughnut shop.

"Slim," I say.

"What?"

"I have a problem besides having to pee."

"What is it?"

"I'm having my period. I have to get to a rest room. I need only two minutes. You and your lady friend can come with me into the rest room. You can point your guns at me the whole time if you want, I don't care. If you do not stop, we will have a mess here and we will have it soon."

"We are not stopping."

I raise my voice. "This is ridiculous! I am bound hand and foot. You are armed left and right. I just have to go to the bathroom for two minutes. For God's sake, what kind of sick person are you? Do you like piss and blood?"

Slim considers. I hear him lean forward and glance at the woman. "What do you think?" he asks.

"We are not supposed to stop for any reason," she says.

"Yeah, but what the hell." He adds a line, and as he does so, I hear my implanted suggestion. "What harm can she do?"

"She must be guarded at all times," the woman insists.

"I already said you two can follow me into the rest room," I say.

"So we have your permission?" the woman asks sarcastically. The sound of her voice is aggravating. She is from Germany— the east side. I hope she follows me into the bathroom. I have a surprise for her. "I have no sanitary napkins," she says.

"I will use whatever is available," I say softly.

"It is up to you," the woman says to Slim.

He considers, studying me, I know. Then he decides. "Hell, call the others. Tell them we're stopping at the first gas station. We'll pull around back."

"They won't like that," the man up front says.

"Tell them they can talk to me if they are worried," Slim says. He turns toward me. "Happy?"

"Thank you," I say in my velvety voice. "I won't cause any problems. You really can accompany me if you want."

"You can be sure I will, sister," Slim says—as if it were his own idea. I want those keys.

The call is made. We slow as we enter Seaside. The driver spots a gas station. I hear the all-night attendant making change. We drive around the side, the second limousine close behind us. The car stops. Slim opens his door.

"Stay here," he says.

We wait for Slim to return. The woman has her gun pointed at my head again. She just doesn't like my looks, I suppose. But the men are relaxed. They are thinking, all this security for what? Slim comes back. I hear him unholster his weapon.

"There will be two of us on you," he says. "Don't get smart."

"You have to take this thing off my eyes," I say. "I'll make a mess if I can't see."

Of course I can reach up and remove it myself, when I make my move. But to have it removed now will save me the extra step. Also, I want my vision to plan when to attack. Finally, by asking them to take it off, I emphasize my helplessness.

"Any other requests?" Slim asks.

"No."

He reaches over and pulls off the mask. "Happy?"

I smile at him, grateful. "I will be when I get in the bathroom."

He stares at me, doubt and confusion touching his face. "Who the hell are you?"

"A girl with a bad attitude," I say.

The woman pokes her pistol at my temple. "Get out. You have two minutes. No more."

I climb out of the car. The guys in the other limousine are all out, their weapons hidden but handy. They form a wall between me and the front of the gas station. I hope none of them accompanies me into the rest room. But Slim and the woman are determined to stay with me. I give the watching gang a timid smile as I shuffle past. They chew gum. They stare at my body. They, too, wonder what all the fuss is about. The woman goes into the bathroom first. I follow, Slim on my tail. No one else comes in. The door closes behind us.

I strike immediately. I have it all planned.

In a move too fast for a mortal eye to follow, I whirl and knock Slim's pistol away. Raising my cuffed hands over my head, I bring them down on top of his skull. I use only a fraction of my strength; I want to stun him, no more. He topples to the floor as the woman turns, bringing up her gun. I kick it from her hand by lashing out with both my feet. She blinks as I land upright. She opens her mouth to say something when I grab her face with both my hands. My grip is ferocious; there is blood even before I kill her, around her eyes. My nails destroy her vision permanently.

There is lots more blood when I smash the back of her head on the tiled wall. The plaster cracks under the blow sending up a miniature cloud of white dust shot through with streaks of red. Likewise her skull cracks, in many places. She sags in my arms, the blood from her mortal wounds soaking the front of my leather jacket. She is dead; I let her drop.

The door is closed but not locked. Quickly I press it tight and lock it. At my feet Slim lets out a moan. I reach down and grab him and press him against the wall beside the stain of the dead woman's brains. My hands go around his throat. Perhaps five seconds have elapsed since we entered the bathroom. Slim winces and opens his eyes. They focus quickly when they see me.

"Slim," I say softly. "Look around you. Look at your dead partner. Her brains are leaking out of her head. She's a mess—it's terrible. I'm a terrible person. I'm also a very strong person. You can feel how strong I am, can't you? That's why your boss wanted you to be so careful with me. You can't screw with me and get away with it. Please don't even consider it. Now, let me tell you what I want. Reach in your pocket and pull out the key to these cuffs. Unlock them. Don't shout out to the others. If you do these things, then maybe I will let you go. If you don't, your brains will be all over the floor like your partner's. Think about it for a moment, if you want, but don't think too long. You can see what an impatient person I am."

He stammers. "I don't have the keys."

I smile. "Bad answer, Slim. Now I will have to go through your pockets and find them. But I'll have to make sure you're lying perfectly still while I do so. I'm going to have to kill you."

He's scared. He can hardly talk. He accidentally steps in the mess dripping out of the woman's head. "No. Wait. Please. I have the keys. I will give you the keys."

"That's good. Good for you." I release my grip slightly. "Undo the locks. Remember, if you shout out, you die."

His hands shake badly. All his training has not prepared him for me. His eyes keep straying to what I have done to the woman's head. A crumpled accordion of bloody assault. Finally, though, Slim gets my cuffs off. My relief at being free is great. Once more, I feel my usual invincibility. I am a wolf among sheep. The slaughter will be a pleasure. I toss the cuffs in the wastebasket. Just then someone knocks at the door. I press my fingers deep into the sides of Slim's throat.

"Ask what it is," I say. I let go just enough to allow him to speak.

He coughs. "What is it?"

"Everything okay in there?" a man asks. They have heard noise.

"Yeah," I whisper.

"Yeah," Slim says.

The man outside tries the doorknob. Of course it is locked. "What's happening?" the man asks. He is the suspicious type, to be sure.

"Everything is cool," I whisper.

"Everything is cool," Slim manages. It is no wonder the guy outside doesn't believe Slim; he sounds like he's about to weep. The guy outside tries the door again.

"Open the door," he demands.

"If we go out that way," I ask Slim, "will they shoot us both?"

He croaks. "Yes."

I study the bathroom. The wall against which I hold Slim is completely tiled; it appears to be the thickest wall in the rest room. But the wall behind the lone toilet looks flimsy. I suspect on the other side of it might be the late-night attendant's office space. Keeping Slim pinned with my left hand, I reach down and pick up the dead woman's automatic weapon.

"We are going to go through that wall there," I say. "I will kick it in, then we will move. I don't want you wrestling with me. If you do, I will rip out your throat. Now tell me, what is behind this gas station? A field? Another building? A road?"

"Trees."

"Trees like in the forest?"

"Yes."

"Excellent." I drag him into the stall. "Prepare yourself for a fun ride."

Still holding on to Slim, I leap into the air several feet and plant three swift kicks on the wall above the toilet. It splinters and I break through what is left of it with a slash of my right arm. We enter the all-night attendant's office. Before he can turn to identify us, I strike him on the back of the head. He goes down, probably still alive. I kick open the door to the outside. The fresh air is sweet after the staleness of the rest room. Behind me I hear the bathroom door being broken down.

There are shocked gasps when they see what I have done to poor Miss Germany.

Dragging Slim, I come around the two parked limos from behind. There are men inside the rest room, more hovering at the door, still more getting out of the first limo. I raise the automatic weapon, an Uzi, and let loose a spray of bullets. Screams rent the air. Several of the men go down. Others reach for their guns. I empty the clip in their direction and drop the Uzi to the ground. I don't need it, I am a vampire. I need only my natural power.

In a blur, still holding on to Slim, I cross the parking lot and enter the trees. A trail of bullets chases us. One of them catching me in the butt, the right cheek. The wound burns, but I don't mind. The woods are mainly pine, some spruce. A hill rises above us, a quarter of a mile to the top. I pull Slim to the pinnacle, and then back down the other side. A stream crosses our path and we splash through it. The old belief is not true; running water does not bind my steps.

By now I have badly wrenched Slim's neck. Behind us I hear men entering the forest, six of them, spreading out, searching for us. I can hear others at the gas station, moaning in pain, the sputtering breath of still others dying. I literally pick Slim off his feet and carry him a half mile upstream, running faster than a deer in her prime, even with the bullet in me. Then I throw Slim down behind a cluster of bushes. I straddle his chest. He looks up at me with eyes wide with fear. I must be little more than a shadow in his vision. Yet I can see him perfectly. I reach around to my back side, digging my fingers into the torn tissue. I pull out the bullet and toss it aside. The wound begins to heal immediately.

"Now we can talk," I say.

"W-who?" he stutters. I lean over, my face in his.

"That is the magic question," I say. "Who sent you after me?"

He is struggling for breath, although I am no longer holding him by the throat. "You are so strong. How is it possible?"

"I am a vampire."

He coughs. "I don't understand."

"I am five thousand years old. I was born before recorded history began. I am the last of my kind . . . I believe I am the last. But the person who sent you after me knew of my great strength. You were carefully prepared. That person must know that I am a vampire. I want that person." I breathe on his face and know he feels the chill of the Grim Reaper. "Tell me who he is, where I can find him."

He is in shock. "Is this possible?"

"You have seen a demonstration of my power. Do you really want me to give you another one?"

He trembles. "If I tell you, will you let me live?"

"Perhaps."

He swallows thickly, perspiring heavily. "We work out of Switzerland. I have only met my boss a few times. His name is

Graham—Rick Graham. He is very wealthy. I do odd jobs for him, my people and I. Two years ago he set us searching for someone who fit your description."

"How did he describe me?"

"The way you look. Other things as well. He said you would be rich, private, have no family. He said there would be mysterious deaths connected with your name."

"Did he know my name?"

"No."

"Has he had you look for anyone else?"

"No. Only someone who fit your description." He grimaces in pain. "Could you get off me? I think you broke several of my ribs when you pulled me through the trees."

"You were not concerned about my comfort in the car."

"I stopped to let you go to the bathroom."

"That was your mistake." My voice is cold.

He is very afraid. "What are you going to do to me?"

"What is Graham's address? Is he in Switzerland?"

"He is never in one place. He travels constantly."

"Why?"

"I don't know why. Maybe he looks for you."

"But is he on the West Coast now? In Oregon?"

"I don't know."

He is telling the truth. "But you were taking me to him tonight, weren't you?"

"I don't know. We were to drive you to San Francisco. I was

to call from a certain phone booth. I can give you the number. It is in Switzerland."

"Say it." He gives me the number. I consider. "I faxed you in Switzerland earlier tonight. Yet you were here. It is possible Graham is here as well?"

"It is possible. We have relays."

"Do you have a business card, Slim?"

"What?"

"A card. Give me your card."

"My wallet is in my front right pocket."

I rip away his pocket. "So it is." I stuff the wallet in my back pocket. My pants are soaked with blood, some of my own, some of the woman's. In the distance I hear two of the men coming my way. Farther off I hear a police siren, heading south on Coast Highway. The men hear it as well. I can practically read their thoughts, they are so obvious. This woman is a monster. If she has Slim, Slim is dead. She will probably kill us if we do catch up with her. The police are coming. We'd better get the hell out of here and chalk it up to a bad night.

The men reverse their direction, back toward the gas station. I lovingly stroke the sides of Slim's face. Of course there is no possibility I will let him live.

"Why do you work for Graham?" I ask.

"The money."

"I see. Tell me what Graham looks like?"

"He is tall, six three maybe. His hair is dark. He wears it long."

Now I am the one who trembles. "What color are his eyes?"

"Blue."

"Pale blue?"

"Yes. They are frightening."

My voice whispers. "Like mine?"

"Yes. God, please don't kill me. I can help you, miss. I really can."

Yaksha.

It is not possible, I think, after all this time. The stories, why did I listen to them? Just because they said he was dead? He probably invented them. But why does he come for me now? Or is that the most foolish question of all? These people had orders to shoot if I so much as burped. He must want me dead.

He must be afraid of what Krishna told him.

"You have helped me enough," I tell Slim.

He pants. "What are you going to do? Don't do it!"

My fingers reach down to his throat, my long nails caressing the big veins beneath his flesh. "I told you what I am. And I'm hungry. Why shouldn't I suck you dry? You are no saint. You kill without conscience. At least when someone dies in my arms, I think kind thoughts about him."

He cries, "Please! I don't want to die."

I lean over. My hair smothers him.

"Then you should never have been born," I say.

I open him up. I open my mouth.

I take my pleasure slowly.

SEVEN

The body I bury beneath the stream. It is a favorite place of mine. Police seldom look under running water. I hear them in the distance, the law, at the gas station, maybe two black and whites. They have a shoot-out with the boys in the limos. The boys win. I hear them tear away at high speed. They are clever. I believe they will get away.

Yet if I want them, I will have them later.

More police can be heard approaching. I decide to exit the forest the back way. I jog through the trees, setting cross-country records. Six miles later finds me at a closed gas station on a deserted road. There is a phone booth. I think of calling Seymour Dorsten, my archery buddy. It is a mad thought. I would do better to keep running till I find a busier road, a few parked cars. I can hot-wire any car in less than a minute.

I am soaked through with blood. It would be madness to involve Seymour in this night's dirty business. He might tell his mother. Yet I want him involved. I trust the little guy. I don't know why.

Information gives me his number. I call. He answers on the second ring and sounds alert. "Seymour," I say. "This is your new friend."

"Lara." He is pleased. "What are you doing? It's four in the morning."

"I have a little problem I need your help with." I check the street sign. "I am at a gas station on Pinecone Ave. I am six miles inland from Seaside, maybe seven, due east of the city. I need you to come get me. I need you to bring a change of clothing for me: pants and a sweatshirt. You must come immediately and tell no one what you're doing. Are your parents awake?"

"No."

"What are you doing awake?"

"How did you know I was awake?"

"I'm psychic," I say.

"I was having a dream about you. I just woke up from it minutes ago."

"You can tell me about it later. Will you come?"

"Yes. I know where you're talking about. Is it a Shell station? It's the only one on that road."

"Yes. Good boy. Hurry. Don't let your parents hear you leave."

"Why do you need the change of clothes?"

"You'll understand when you see me."

Seymour arrives a little over an hour later. He is shocked at my appearance, as well he should be. My hair is the color of a volcano at sunset. He stops the car and jumps out.

"What happened to you?" he asks.

"A few people tried to rough me up, but I got away. I don't want to say any more than that. Where are the clothes?"

"Wow." He doesn't take his eyes off me as he reaches back into the front seat. He has brought me blue jeans and a white T-shirt and two different sweaters: one green, the other black. I will wear the black one. I begin to strip right in front of him. The boy has driven far and deserves a thrill. "Lara," he says, simply amazed.

"I am not shy." I unbutton my pants and wiggle them down. "Do you have a towel or some kind of old cloth in the car?"

"Yes. You want to wipe off some of the blood?"

"Yes. Get it for me please."

He gives me a stained dish towel. Now I am completely naked, the sweat on my skin sending off faint whiffs of steam in the cold night air. I clean my hair as best I can and wipe the blood from my breasts. Finally I reach for the clothes he has brought.

"Are you sure you don't want to call the police?" he asks.

"I am sure." I pull the T-shirt on first.

Seymour chuckles. "You must have had a bow and a few arrows with you when they caught up with you."

"I was armed." I finish dressing, putting my boots back on, and bundle my clothes together. "Wait here a second. I have to get rid of these."

I bury the clothes in the trees, but before I do so I remove my car keys and Slim's wallet from my pants pocket. I am back with Seymour in ten minutes. He is behind the wheel with the engine on, the heater up high. In his frail condition he must get cold easily. I climb in beside him.

"My car is in Seaside, not far from the pier," I say. "Can you take me there?"

"Sure." He puts the car in gear. We head north. "What made you call me?"

"Your sexy mind."

He laughs. "You knew I was the only one in town who wouldn't immediately report you to the authorities."

"I am serious about you keeping this private."

"Oh, I will."

I smile and pat his leg. "I know you will. Besides your sexy mind, I called you because I know you don't object to a little stroll on the wild side from time to time."

He eyes me through his thick glasses. "You may be a little wild even for my tastes. You can't even tell me a little something about what happened?"

"You would have trouble believing the truth."

He shakes his head. "Not after this dream I had about you. It was amazing."

"Tell me about it."

"I dreamed you were on a battlefield and a whole army of demons was approaching you from every direction. They had all kinds of weapons: axes and swords and hammers. Their faces were hideous. They were jeering loudly, anxious to rip you to shreds. Where you were standing was a bit above the rest of the field, on a grassy knoll. But the rest of the field was a reddish dust color, as if it were a plain on Mars. The sky was filled with smoke. There was only you against thousands. It looked hopeless. But you were not afraid. You were dressed like an exotic goddess. Your chest was covered with silver mail. You had a jeweled sword in your right hand, emerald earrings set in gold that chimed as you slowly surveyed the army around you. A peacock feather stood in your braided hair, and you wore tall boots made of fresh hide. They dripped with blood. You smiled as the front rank of the demons went to strike you. You raised your sword. Then you stuck out your tongue."

"My tongue?"

"Yeah. This was the scary part. Your tongue was real long. It was purple, bloody—it looked as if you had taken a bite or two out of it. When you stuck it out, all the demons froze and acted afraid. Then you made this sound at the back of your throat. It's hard to describe. It was a loud sound, nasal. It echoed across the whole battlefield, and as it reached the ear of each demon, he toppled over dead."

"Wow," I say. The part about the tongue naturally reminds me of the yakshini. There is now no question in my mind. Seymour is supernaturally sensitive to emotional states. More than that he seems to have linked up with me somehow, formed an intuitive bond with me. Certainly, I have with him. I am mystified. I cannot logically understand my great affection for him. It is not the same as my love for Ray, my passion for the son of Riley. For me, Seymour is like a younger brother, a son even. In five thousand years I have never had a child except for Lalita. I would like to play with this young man. "Is there more?" I ask.

"Yes," he says. "But you might not want to hear this part. It's pretty gross."

"I do not gross out easily."

"After seeing you tonight, I imagine you don't. When all the demons were dead, you began to stride about the battlefield. Sometimes you would step on a demon's head and it would be crushed and the brains inside would ooze out. Sometimes you would stop and cut off the head of a demon. You accumulated a number of heads. You were making a necklace out of them. Other times you would find a demon that wasn't entirely dead. These you would grab by the throat and raise up to your mouth." He pauses for effect. "You would open their necks with your nails and drink their blood."

"Doesn't sound so bad." He continues to amaze me. His dream is like a metaphor for the entire night. "Anything else?"

"One last thing. When you were through walking about, and stood still, the flesh of the demons began to decay. In seconds they were nothing but dust and crumbling bones. Then the sky began to darken more. There was something in the sky, some kind of huge bird, circling above you. It disturbed you. You raised your sword to it and let out that weird sound again. But the bird kept circling, getting lower and lower. You were afraid of it. It did not seem you could stop it."

"That hasn't happened yet," I whisper.

"Pardon?"

"Nothing. What kind of bird was it?"

"I can't be sure."

"Was it a vulture?"

"Maybe." He frowns. "Yeah, I think it was." He gives me an uneasy look. "You don't like vultures?"

"They are symbolic of a forsaken ending."

"I didn't know that. Who told you that?"

"Experience." I sit silent with my eyes closed for a few minutes. Seymour knows not to disturb me. The boy saw the present, I think, why couldn't he see the future? Yaksha is circling me, closer and closer. My old tricks will stop him. My strength, my speed, were never a match for his. The night is almost over. The day will soon be. But for us the day is the night, the time to rest, to hide, to despair. I know in my heart that Yaksha is not far.

Yet Krishna said I would have his grace if I obeyed him.

And I have. But what did he promise Yaksha? The same?

I do not believe so.

The scriptures say the Lord is mischievous.

I think Krishna told him the opposite.

I open my eyes. I stare at the road in front. "Are you afraid of dying, Seymour?"

He speaks carefully. "Why do you ask?"

"You have AIDS. You know it."

He sucks in a breath. "How did you know?"

I shrug. "I know things. You know things as well. How did you catch it?"

He nods. "I am HIV positive. I suppose I have full-blown AIDS. I have the symptoms: fatigue; skin cancer; bouts of parasitic pneumonia. But I've been feeling good the last few weeks. Do I look that bad?"

"You look awesome. But sick."

He shakes his head. "I was in a car crash five years ago. Ruptured my spleen. I was with an uncle. He died, but I got to the hospital in time. They operated on me and gave me two pints of blood. It was after the test for HIV was routine with all donated blood, but I guess this batch slipped through the cracks." He shrugs. "So I'm another statistic. Is that why you asked about fear of dying?"

"It was one reason."

"I am afraid. I think anybody would be lying if he said he wasn't afraid of death. But I try not to think about it. I'm alive now. There are things I want to do . . ."

"Stories you want to write," I interrupt.

"Yes."

I reach over and touch his arm. "Would you write a story about me someday?"

"What should I write?"

"Whatever comes to mind. Don't think about it too much. Just whatever is there, write it down."

He smiles. "Will you read it if I write it?"

I take my hand back and relax into the seat. My eyes close again; I feel suddenly weary. I am not mortal, at least I didn't think I was until tonight. Yet now I feel vulnerable. I am as afraid of death as everyone else.

"If I get the chance," I say.

EIGHT

Seymour takes me to my car and tries to follow me back to Mayfair. But I speed away at a hundred miles an hour. He is not insulted, I'm sure. I warned him I'm in a hurry.

I go to my mansion by the sea. I have not described it before because to me a house is a house. I do not fall in love with them as do some mortals. The house is on twenty acres of property, at the top of a wooded yard that reaches from my front porch all the way down to the rocky shore. The driveway is narrow and winding, mostly hidden. The house itself is mainly brick, Tudor style, unusual for this part of the country. There are three stories; the top one has a wide view of the sea and coast. There are many rooms, fireplaces and such, but I do most of my living in the living room, even though it has wide skylights that I have yet to board up. I do not need a lot of space to be happy, although I have lived in mansions or castles since the Middle Ages. I could be quite happy living in a box. I say that as a joke.

My tastes in furniture are varied. At present I surround myself with lots of wood: the chairs, the tables, the cabinets. I sleep on a bed, not in a coffin, a grand mahogany affair with a black lace canopy. I have gathered art over the centuries and have a vast and expensive collection of paintings and sculptures in Europe, but none of it in America. I have gone through phases where art is important to me, but I am not in one now. Still, I have a piano wherever I go. I play almost every day, and with my speed and agility, I am the most accomplished pianist in the world. But I seldom write music, not because I am not creative, but because my melodies and songs are invariably sad. I do not know why—I do not think of myself as a sad vampire.

Tonight, though, I am an anxious vampire, and it has been centuries since I felt the emotion. I do not like it. I hurry into my home and change and then rush back out to my car. My concern is for Ray. If it is Yaksha after me, and I have little doubt now, then he may try to get to me through Ray. It seems a logical course to me based on the fact that Yaksha probably first became aware of me through Ray's father. I now suspect Yaksha has been observing me since I first visited Mr. Riley's office. But why he didn't attack immediately, I don't know. Maybe he wanted to study the enemy he hadn't seen for so long, to probe for weaknesses. Yet Yaksha, more than any living or nonliving being, already knows where I am vulnerable.

I am still in shock that he is alive.

I drive to Ray's house and leap to the front door. I half expect to find him gone, abducted. For a moment I consider not ringing the doorbell, but to just barge in. I have to remind myself that Ray is not Seymour, capable of accepting anything that comes along. I knock on the door.

Pat surprises me when she answers.

The girlfriend is not happy to see me.

"What are you doing here?" Pat demands.

"I have come to see Ray." Pat must have called Ray's house while he was at my place, probably several times. She must have called not long after he came home. He probably invited her over to pacify her concerns. But she does not look that pacified.

"He's asleep," Pat says. She starts to slam the door in my face. I stick out my arm. She tries to force it shut. Naturally, she is not successful. "Get out of here. Can't you tell when you're not wanted?"

"Pat," I say patiently. "Things are not as they appear. They are much more complicated. I need to see Ray because I believe he is in danger."

"What are you talking about?"

"I cannot tell you, not easily. I have to talk to Ray and I have to talk to him now." I put my eye on her. "Please do not try to stop me. It would not be a good idea."

She cowers under my stare. I move to press her farther, but it becomes unnecessary. Upstairs, I hear Ray climb out of bed. I wait a few seconds, then call out his name.

"Ray!" I say. I hear his steps quicken. We both do.

"He's mine," Pat mutters as we wait for Ray to arrive. She is sad, seemingly defeated already. Instinctively she knows I have a power she does not, beyond my beauty. Her love for him is genuine, I can see that, a rare thing in a girl her age.

"Have hope," I say sincerely.

Ray appears. He has on sweatpants, no top. "What's going on?" he asks.

"Lots of things. I need to talk to you, alone." I glance at Pat. "If that would be all right?"

Her eyes are damp. She lowers her head. "I can just go," she mumbles.

Ray puts a hand on her shoulder. "No." He gives me a sharp glance. I have to be careful. "Tell me what it is?"

"It has to do with your father," I say.

He is concerned. "What is it?"

I am stubborn. "I must tell you alone." I add, "I'm sorry, Pat."

Ray rubs her back. "Go upstairs to bed. I'll be up in a few minutes."

Pat shakes her head, giving me a look as she leaves. "I don't think so."

When we are alone, Ray wants me to explain myself. "You told me you wouldn't hurt Pat," he says.

"My coming here could not be helped. I have not been entirely honest with you, Ray. I think you suspect that."

"Yes. You tampered with the file on my father's computer."

"How did you know?"

"When I turned on the computer, I noted the size of the file. It was large. When I returned, most of it had been deleted."

I nod. "That file was about me. Your father was investigating me. He was hired by some people to do so, one man in particular. This man is dangerous. Tonight he sent some people to abduct me. I managed to get away. I believe he may come after you next."

"Why me?"

"Because he knows you are my friend. I believe he has been watching me today and tonight. Also, even though this man hired your father, your father did not part company with him on the best of terms."

"How do you know that?"

"The people who came for me tonight told me."

"What do you mean, they came for you? Were they armed?"

"Yes."

"Then how did you get away from them?"

"They made a mistake, and I am resourceful. I do not want to get into all of that now. What is important is that you come with me now."

"I'm not going anywhere until you tell me where my father is."

"I can't."

"You don't know?"

I hesitate. It is not easy for me to lie to those I love. "No."

Ray is suspicious. His sense of the truth, and therefore of lies, is remarkable. "Do you think my father is in danger?" he asks.

"Yes."

He hears the truth in that word. "We should call the police."

"No!" I grab his arm. "The police cannot help us. You have to come with me. Trust me, Ray. I can tell you more once we are at my house."

"What will we do at your house that we can't do here?"

"You will see," I say.

Ray consents to accompany me. He goes upstairs to say goodbye to Pat. I hear her crying, and wonder if she will not shed a stream of tears in the days to come. I could be wrong. I could be bringing Ray into danger, not away from it. I scan up and down the street but see nothing. Yet I feel eyes on me, powerful eyes such as my own. I wonder if I am not reaching for Ray because I am afraid.

Maybe afraid to die alone.

Ray reappears in a few minutes, dressed. We go to my car. He has not seen it before and marvels that I have a Ferrari. We drive toward my mansion and he wonders why we are not going the same way as before. I tell him I have two houses.

"I am very rich," I say.

"Is that one of the reasons my father was investigating you?" he asks.

"Yes. Indirectly."

"Have you spoken to my father?"

"Yes."

"When?"

"Two and a half days ago."

"Where?"

"At his office."

Ray is annoyed. "You didn't tell me. Why did you speak to him?"

"He called me into his office."

"Why?"

I have to be more careful than ever. "He wanted to tell me that I was being investigated."

"He wanted to warn you?"

"I believe so. But—"

"What?"

"He didn't fully understand who had hired him, the nature of the man."

"But you know this man?"

"Yes. From a long time ago."

"What's his name?"

"He changes his name often."

"Like you?" Ray asks.

The boy is full of surprises. I reach over and touch his leg. "You are worried about your father. I understand. Please try not to judge me too harshly."

"You are not being completely honest with me."

"I'm telling you what I can."

"When you say my father is in danger, what exactly do you mean? Would this man kill my father?"

"He has killed in the past."

The space inside the car is suddenly cramped. Ray hears beyond my words. "Is my father dead already?" he asks quietly.

I have to lie, I have no choice. "I don't know."

We arrive at my house. No one has come while I was away, I can tell. I activate the security system. It is the most elaborate available on the market. Every wire of every section of fence around my house is now heavily electrified. There are motion sensors and laser beams and radar tracking the perimeter. I know it will not stop Yaksha for a second if he wishes to come for me. At a minimum he has twice my strength and speed. In reality I think he is much more powerful than that.

Ray wanders around my house, taking in the sights. He pauses and looks out over the ocean. A waning moon, half full, hangs over the dark shadow of the water. We face west, but behind us, in the east, I detect a hint of dawn.

"What next?" he asks.

"What do you want to do next?"

He faces me. "You are waiting for this man to come here."

"Perhaps. He could come."

"You said something about arming yourself. Do you have guns here?"

"Yes. But I'm not going to give you one. It would not help."

"Are you some kind of expert with guns?"

"Yes."

He is exasperated. "Who the hell are you, Sita? If that is even your real name."

"It is my real name. Few people know it. It is the name my father gave me. The man I am talking about—he is the one who murdered my father."

"Why don't we call the police?"

"This man is very powerful. He has almost unlimited resources. The police would not be able to stop him if he wants to hurt us."

"Then how are you going to stop him?"

"I don't know if I can."

"Then why are we here? Why don't we just get in the car and drive away?"

His question is an interesting one; it has a certain logic to it. I have considered the option since disposing of Slim. Yet I do not believe that I can run successfully from Yaksha, not once he has got me in his sights, which he obviously does. I do not like to postpone the inevitable.

"You can drive away if you want," I say. "You can take my car and go home. Or you can take my car and drive to Los Angeles. That might be the best thing for you to do. I can tell you for a fact that while you are here you are in extreme danger."

"Then why did you bring me here?"

I turn away. "I do not know why. But I think—I don't know."

"What?"

"This man—his real name is Yaksha—he knows you are my friend. You are part of the equation that deals with me—in his mind."

"What do you mean?"

I turn back to Ray. "He has been watching me since I saw your father, I'm sure of it. But he has not come for me personally. Oh, he sent his people after me, but that is not the same thing, not to him and not to me."

"You think that I afford you some protection?"

"Not exactly. More, I think he is curious about my relationship with you."

"Why?"

"I do not make friends easily. He knows that much."

Ray sighs. "I don't even know if I am your friend."

His words sting, more than the bullet I was hit with earlier in the night. I reach out and touch his face. Such a beautiful face, so like Rama's, even though they do not look that much alike. Their essence is similar. Maybe Krishna was right. Maybe their souls are the same, if there are such things. I doubt I have one.

"I care more for you than I have cared for anyone in a long time," I say. "I am much older than I look. I have been more lonely than I have been willing to admit to myself. But when I met you, that loneliness eased. I am your friend, Ray, even if you do not want to be mine."

He stares at me, as if he, too, knows me, then lowers his lips to kiss my hand that touches him. His next words come to me as if from far away.

"Sometimes I look at you and you do not look human."

"Yes."

"You're like something carved from glass."

"Yes."

"Old but always new."

"Yes."

"You said you are a vampire."

"Yes."

But he does not ask me if I am a vampire. He knows better. He knows I will tell him the truth, and he does not want to hear it. He kisses my hand again, and I lean forward to kiss his lips. Long and deep—he does not smother this time and I am glad. He wants to make love, I can tell, and I am very glad.

I start a roaring blaze in the living room fireplace, many logs piled high. There is a rug from ancient Persia on top of the wall-to-wall carpeting in front of the fire; it is where I some-times sleep, when the sun is high. I bring in blankets and pil-lows. We undress slowly; I let Ray take off my clothes. He touches my body, and I kiss his from head to foot. Then we lie down together and the sex is a wonder to him, as well as to me. I am careful not to hurt him.

Later, when he is asleep, I go for an automatic weapon in the attic. I load the clip carefully, making sure all the parts are well oiled, ready for use. Then I return to Ray's side and put the weapon under my pillow. Ray is exhausted; I stroke his head and whisper words that will cause him to sleep away the entire day. I suspect Yaksha will not come until the following night—a fresh night for a fresh slaughter. It would be his way. I know my gun will not stop him. I have only Krishna's promise to protect me. But what is the promise of a God I don't even know if I believe in?

Yet one thing is certain. If Krishna was not God, he was the most extraordinary human who ever lived. Even more powerful than all the vampires combined. I think of him as I lie beside Ray, and I wonder about my feelings of love for the boy. If they are just my longing for the face of Krishna hidden inside him. I do remember Krishna's face well. It was a face that would be impossible to forget even after five thousand years.

NINE

Once more, I go back. We left the area, Yaksha and I. We were quickly joined by two of the men from the village who had disappeared. They were vampires. I was a vampire. But that word did not exist then. I didn't know what I was, except somehow I was like Yaksha.

The horror and the wonder of it all.

My craving for blood did not come over me in the first days, and Yaksha must have told the others not to speak to me about it, because they did not. But I did notice that bright light bothered me. The rays of the midday sun were almost intolerable. This I understood. Because when we were growing up, I had noticed that Yaksha had a tendency to disappear in the middle of the day. It saddened me that I would never again enjoy a wonderful daytime sky.

Yet the nights, they became a thing of great beauty. For

I could see in the dark better than I had been able to see in the day. I would look up at the moon and see that it was not the smooth orb we had all believed, but a pitted and scarred world with no air. Distant objects would appear before me as if only an arm's length away. I could see detail I had never imagined before: the pores of my skin; the multifaceted eyes of tiny insects. Sound, even on a supposedly silent plain, became a constant. I quickly became sensitive to the breathing patterns of different people. What each rhythm meant, how it corresponded to different emotions. My sense of smell took on an incredible vitality. With just a slight shift of the breeze the world was constantly bathed in new perfumes.

My newfound strength I loved most of all. I could leap to the top of the tallest tree, crumble huge boulders with a clap of my hands. I loved to chase the animals, especially the lions and tigers. They ran from me. They knew there was something inhuman about me.

But my blood hunger came over me quickly. On the fourth day I went to Yaksha and told him my chest was on fire and my heart was pounding in my ears. Honestly, I thought I was dying—I kept thinking about bleeding things. Yet I did not think of drinking blood, it was too impossible an idea. Even when Yaksha told me it was the only way to stop the pain, I pushed it out of my mind. Because even though I was no longer human, I wanted to pretend I was. When Yaksha had held me that long night, I felt myself die. Yet I imagined that I was alive as others were alive. But the life in me was not from this world. I could live off that life, but I could never give in to it. Yaksha told me I was sterile at the same time he told me about the blood. It made me cry for Lalita and Rama and wonder how they were doing without their Sita.

But I would not go to see them.

I would not let them see the monster I had become.

I feared I would make them vampires, too.

I resisted drinking another's blood, until pain was all I knew. I grew weak; I couldn't stop moaning. It was as if because I would not drink another's blood, then the thing Yaksha had put inside me would eat me alive. A month after my transformation, Yaksha brought me a half-conscious boy, with his neck veins already partially open, and ordered me to drink. How I hated him then for putting such temptation in front of me. How it rekindled in me my hatred for how he had taken me from Rama and Lalita. Yet my hate did not give me strength because it was not a pure thing. I needed Yaksha after he changed me, and need is a close kin of love. But I would not say I ever loved Yaksha; rather, I looked up to him because he was greater than I was. For a long time he was the only one to look up to—until Krishna.

Yet I drank the boy's blood. I fell upon him even as I swooned. And even though I resolved not to kill him, I couldn't stop drinking once I started. Then the boy was dead. I cried in horror as he took his last breath in my arms. But

Yaksha just laughed. He said that once you killed, it was easy to kill again.

Yes, I hated him then because I knew he was right.

After that, I killed many, and I grew to love it.

The years went by. We headed southeast. We never stopped moving. It never took that long for people in a village to realize we were dangerous. We came, we made friends—eventually we slew, and the rumors went before us. We also made more of our kind. The first vampire I created was a girl my age, with large dark eyes and hair like a waterfall made from the light of the midnight sky. I imagined she could become a friend, even though I took her against her will. By then Yaksha had told me what was necessary: the lifting out of my vein coming from my heart; the merger of her vein going back to the heart; the transfusion; the terror; the ecstasy. Her name was Mataji, and she never thanked me for what I did to her, but she stayed close in the years to come.

Making Mataji drained my strength, and it was several days and many victims later before I regained my full powers. It was the same for all of us except Yaksha. When he created another, he just grew stronger. I knew it was because it was his soul that fed us all. The yakshini embodied. The demon from the deep.

Yet there was kindness in him, but I couldn't understand its source. He was protective of all he created, and he was unusually nice to me. He never again told me that he loved me, however, but he did. His eyes were often on me. What was I supposed to do? The damned could not marry. God would not witness the union as we had been taught from the Vedas.

It was then, maybe after fifty years of being a vampire, that we began to hear stories about a man many said was the Veda incarnate. A man who was more than a man, perhaps Lord Vishnu himself. Each new village we plundered brought us another detail. His principal name was Krishna and he lived in the forests of Vrindavana near the Yumana River, with the cowherders and their milkmaids—the *gopis*, they were called. It was said this man, this Vasudeva—he had many names—was capable of slaying demons and granting bliss. His best friends were the five Pandava brothers, who had the reputation of being the incarnation of more minor deities. Arjuna, one of the brothers, had almost the fame of Krishna. He was said to be the son of the great god Indra, the lord of paradise. We did not doubt, from what we heard, that Arjuna was indeed a magnificent warrior.

Yaksha was intrigued. The rest of us vampires were as well, but few of us wanted to meet Krishna. Because even though our numbers by then were close to a thousand, we felt Krishna would not greet us with open arms, and if half the stories told about him and his friends were true, he might destroy us all. But Yaksha could not bear the thought that there was a man in the land more powerful than he. Because his reputation had grown great as well, although it was the notoriety of terror.

We set out for Vrindavana, all of us, and we marched openly, making no secret of our destination. The many mortals whom we passed seemed happy, for they believed our wandering herd of blood drinkers was doomed. I saw the gratitude in their faces and felt the fear in my heart. None of these people had personally met Krishna. Yet they believed in him. They simply trusted in the sound of his name. Even as we slew many of them, they called out to Krishna.

Of course Krishna knew we were coming; it required no omniscience on his part. Yaksha had a shrewd intellect, yet it was clouded by the arrogance his powers had given him. As we entered the forests of Vrindavana, all seemed calm. Indeed, the woods appeared deserted, even to us with acute hearing. But Krishna was only saving his attack until we were deep into his land. All of a sudden arrows began to fly toward us. Not a rain of them, but one at a time. Yet in quick succession and fired with perfect accuracy. Truly, not one of those arrows missed its target. They went through the hearts and heads of our kind. They never failed to kill that which Yaksha had told us could not be killed. And the most amazing thing is we could not catch the man who shot the arrows. We could not even see him, his *kavach*, his mystical armor, was that great.

Mataji was one of the first to fall, an arrow between her eyes.

Still, we were many, and it was going to take time even for the finest archer of all time to kill us. Yaksha drove us forward, as fast as we could go. Then the arrows began to strike only the rear of our contingent, and then they ceased altogether. It appeared that we had been able to outrun even Arjuna. But we had left many behind. Rebellion stirred against Yaksha. Most wanted to leave Vrindavana, if they knew which way to flee. For the first time Yaksha was losing command. But it was then, in those enchanted woods, that we came across what at first seemed to Yaksha a great boon. We ran into Radha, the chief of the gopis, Krishna's consort.

We had heard about Radha as well, whose name meant "longing." She was called this because she longed for Krishna even more than she desired to breathe. She was picking jasmines by the clear waters of the Yamuna when we came across her. We did not frighten her; she actually smiled when she saw us. Her beauty was extraordinary; I had never seen and never would see in five thousand years such an exquisite female. Her skin was remarkably fair; her face shone with the subtle radiance of moonlight. Her form was shapely. She moved as if in a joyful theater; each turn of her arm or bending of knees seemed to bring bliss. It was because each step she took, she took with the thought of Krishna. She was singing a song about him when we came upon her. In fact, the first words out of her mouth were to ask us if we wanted to learn it.

Yaksha immediately took her captive. She did not try to

hide her identity. We bound her wrists and ankles. I was put in charge of her while Yaksha sent several of our kind calling through the woods that we had Radha and that we were going to kill her unless Krishna agreed to meet Yaksha in single combat. It did not take Krishna long to respond. He sent Yudhishthira, Arjuna's brother, with a message. He would meet us at the edge of Vrindavana where we had entered the woods. If we did not know how to find it, Yudhishthira would show us the way. He had only two conditions. That we not harm Radha, and that he get to choose the form of combat. Yaksha sent Yudhishthira back saying that he accepted the challenge. It may have been that we should have first asked Yudhishthira which way to go. The woods were like a maze, and Radha was not talking. Yet she did not seem afraid. Occasionally she would glance my way and smile with such calm assurance that it was I who knew fear.

Yaksha was ecstatic. He did not believe any mortal could beat him at any form of combat. By such a pronouncement he appeared to discount the stories concerning Krishna's divine origin. Yet when I asked him about that, he did not answer me. He had a light in his eyes, though. He said that he had been born for this moment. Personally, I was fearful of a trick. Krishna had a reputation for being mischievous. Yaksha brushed aside my concerns. He would destroy Krishna, he said, then he would make Radha a vampire. She would be *his* consort. I did not feel jealous. I did not think it would happen.

Eventually we found our way back to the place where we had entered the forest. We remembered the spot because there was a huge pit in the ground. Apparently Krishna intended to use this pit when he challenged Yaksha. His people were gathered about it when we came out of the woods. Yet they made no attempt to attack us, although our numbers were roughly equal. I saw Arjuna, standing near his brothers, his mighty bow in his hands. When he looked my way and saw me holding on to Radha, he frowned and took an arrow into his hands and rubbed it to his chest. But he did nothing more. He was waiting for his master. We were all waiting. In that moment, even though I was not yet seventy years old, I felt as if I had waited since the dawn of creation to see this person. I who held captive his great jewel.

Krishna came out of the forest.

He was not a blue person as he was later to be depicted in paintings. Artists were to show him that way only because blue was symbolic of the sky, which to them seemed to stretch to infinity, and which was what Krishna was supposed to be in essence, the eternal infinite Brahman, above and beyond which there was nothing greater. He was a man such as all men I had seen, with two arms and two legs, one head above his shoulders, his skin the color of tea with milk in it, not as dark as most in India but not as light as my own. Yet there was no one like him. Even a glance showed me that he was special in a way I knew I would never fully comprehend. He walked out of the trees and all eyes followed him.

He was tall, almost as tall as Yaksha, which was unusual for those days when people seldom grew to over six feet. His black hair was long—one of his many names was *Keshava,* master of the senses, or long-haired. In his right hand he held a lotus flower, in his left his fabled flute. He was powerfully built; his legs long, his every movement bewitching. He seemed not to look at anyone directly, but only to give sidelong glances. Yet these were enough to send a thrill through the crowd, on both sides. He was impossible not to stare at, though I tried hard to turn away. For I felt as if he were placing a spell over me that I would never recover from. Yet I did manage to turn aside for an instant. It was when I felt the touch of a hand on my brow. It was Radha, my supposed enemy, comforting me with her touch.

"Krishna means love," she said. "But Radha means longing. Longing is older than love. I am older than he. Did you know that, Sita?"

I looked at her. "How did you know my name?"

"He told me."

"When?"

"Once."

"What else did he tell you about me?"

Her face darkened. "You do not want to know."

Krishna walked to the edge of the pit and gestured for his people to withdraw to the edge of the trees. Only Arjuna remained with him. He nodded to Yaksha, who likewise motioned for our people to back up. But Yaksha wanted me near the pit with my hands not far from Radha's neck. The arrangement did not seem to bother Krishna. He met Yaksha not far from where I stood. Krishna did not look directly at Radha or me. Yet he was close enough so that I could hear him speak. His voice was mesmerizing. It was not so much the sound of his words, but the place from which they sprang. Their authority and power. And, yes, love, I could hear love even as he spoke to his enemy. There was such peace in his tone. With all that was happening, he was not disturbed. I had the feeling that for him it was merely a play. That we were all just actors in a drama he was directing. But I was not enjoying the part I had been selected for. I did not see how Yaksha could beat Krishna. I felt sure that this day would be our last.

Yet it was not day, but night, although the dawn was not far off.

"I have heard that Yaksha is the master of serpents," Krishna said. "That the sound of his flute intoxicates them. As you may have heard, I also play the flute. It is in my mind to challenge you to a combat of instruments. We will fill this pit with cobras, and you will sit at one end, and I will sit at the other, and we will each play for the control of the serpents. We will play for the life of Radha. You may play what you wish, and if the serpents strike me dead, so be it. You may keep Radha for your own pleasure. But if the serpents should bite you so many times that you die, or decide to surrender, then you must swear to me now that you will take a vow that I will ask you to take. Is this a reasonable challenge?"

"Yes," Yaksha said. His confidence leaped even higher, and I knew how strong Yaksha was with snakes. For I had watched many times while he had hypnotized snakes with the sound of his flute. It never surprised me because sometimes yakshinis were depicted as serpents, and I thought Yaksha was a snake at heart. In reality vampires have more in common with snakes than bats. A snake prefers to eat its victim alive.

I knew Yaksha could be bitten many times by a cobra and not die.

Krishna left it to our people to gather the cobras, which took time because there were none in the forests of Vrindavana itself. But vampires can work fast if they must, and travel far, and by the following evening the pit was filled with deadly snakes. Now the feeling in our group favored Yaksha. Few believed a mortal could survive for any length of time in the pit. It was then I saw that even though Krishna had impressed the vampires, they still thought of him as a man, an extraordinary man, true, but not as a divine being. They were anxious for the contest to begin.

I stayed with Radha throughout the day. I talked to her about Rama and Lalita. She told me that they had both passed out of this world, but that Rama's life had been noble and my daughter's had been happy. I did not ask how she knew these things, I simply believed her. I cried at her words. Radha tried to comfort me. All that are born die, she said. All who die are reborn. It is inevitable, Krishna had told her. She told me many things Krishna had said.

Finally, close to dark, Yaksha and Krishna climbed into the pit. Each carried a flute, nothing more. The people on both sides watched, but from a distance as Krishna had wanted. Only Radha and I stood close to the pit. There had to be a hundred snakes in that huge hole. They bit each other and more than a few were already being eaten.

Yaksha and Krishna sat at opposite ends of the pit, each with his back to the wall of earth. They began to play immediately. They had to; the snakes moved for each of them right away. But with the sound of the music, both melodies, the snakes backed off and appeared uncertain.

Now, Yaksha could play wonderfully, although his songs were always laced with sorrow and pain. His music was hypnotic; he could draw victims to feed on simply with his flute. But I realized instantly that his playing, for all its power, was a mere shadow next to Krishna's music. For Krishna played the song of life itself. Each note on his flute was like a different center in the human body. His breath through the notes on the flute was like the universal breath through the bodies of all people. He would play the third note on his flute and the third center in my body, at the navel, would vibrate with different emotions. The navel is the seat of jealousy and attachment, and

of joy and generosity. I felt these as he played. When Krishna
would blow through this hole with a heavy breath, I would feel
as if everything that I had ever called mine had been stripped
from me. But when he would change his breath, let the notes
go long and light, then I would smile and want to give something to those around me. Such was his mastery.

His playing had the snakes completely bewildered. None
would attack him. Yet Yaksha was able to keep the snakes at
bay with his music as well, although he was not able to send
them after his foe. So the contest went on for a long time without either side hurting the other. Yet it was clear to me Krishna
was in command, as he was in control of my emotions. He
moved to the fifth note on the flute, which stirred the fifth
center in my body, at the throat. In that spot there are two
emotions: sorrow and gratitude. Both emotions bring tears,
one bitter, the other sweet. When Krishna lowered his breath,
I felt like weeping. When he sang higher I also felt choked, but
with thanks. Yet I did not know what I was thankful for. Not
the outcome of the contest, surely. I knew then that Yaksha
would certainly lose, and that the result could be nothing other
than our extinction.

Even as the recognition of our impending doom crossed
my mind, Krishna began to play the fourth note. This affected
my heart; it affected the hearts of all gathered. In the heart
are three emotions—I felt them then: love, fear, and hatred. I
could see that an individual could only have one of the three

at a time. When you were in love you knew no fear or hatred. When you were fearful, there was no possibility of love or hate. And when there was hate, there was only hate.

Krishna played the fourth note softly initially, so that a feeling of warmth swept both sides. This he did for a long time, and it seemed as if vampires and mortals alike stared across the clearing at one another and wondered why they were enemies. Such was the power of that one note, perfectly pitched.

Yet Krishna now pushed his play toward its climax. He lowered his breath, and the love in the gathering turned to hate. A restlessness went through the crowd, and individuals on both sides shifted this way and that as if preparing to attack. Then Krishna played the fourth note in a different way, and the hate changed to fear. And finally this emotion pierced Yaksha, who had so far remained unmoved by Krishna's flute. I saw him tremble—the worst thing he could do before a swarm of snakes. Because a serpent only strikes where there is fear.

The group of snakes began to crawl toward Yaksha.

He could have surrendered then, but he was a brave creature even if he was ruthless. He continued to play, now a frantic tune to drive away the snakes. At first it did slow them down, but Krishna did not tire. He continued on the fourth note, his breath quivering up and down through the hole, and at last a large snake slithered up to Yaksha. It bit him on the shin and held on fast with its teeth. Yaksha could not afford to set down his flute to throw it off. Then another snake came forward, and still another, until soon Yaksha was being bitten on every part of his body. He was the king of vampires, the son of a yakshini, yet even his system could absorb only so much venom. At last the flute fell from his hands and he swayed where he sat. I believe he tried to call out; I think he might have said my name. Then he toppled forward and the snakes began to eat him. I could not bear to watch.

But Krishna stood then and set his flute aside. He clapped his hands, and the snakes hurried off Yaksha's body. He climbed out of the pit and motioned to Arjuna. His best friend entered the deep hole and carried out Yaksha's body and dumped it on the ground not far from me. He was breathing, I could see that, but barely, soaked head to foot with black venom; it oozed out of the many wounds on his body.

I let Radha go. She hugged me before leaving. But she did not run to Krishna, but to the other women. Behind me I could hear the main body of the vampires shifting toward the woods, as if they planned to flee. Yet they waited still; they felt compelled to, I think, to see what Krishna would do next. Krishna ignored them. He gestured to me and came and knelt beside Yaksha. My feeling then was so peculiar. As I knelt beside Krishna, this being that would in all probability wipe me from the face of the earth, I felt as if I was under the umbrella of his protection. I watched as he put one of his beautiful hands on Yaksha's head.

"Will he live?" I asked.

Krishna surprised me with his question. "Do you want him to?"

My eyes strayed over the ruin of my old enemy and friend. "I want what you want," I whispered.

Krishna smiled, so serene. "The age is to change when I leave this world. Kali Yuga will begin. It will be a time of strife and short years for humanity. Your kind is for the most part tamasic—negative. Kali Yuga will be challenge enough for people without you on earth. Do you agree?"

"Yes. We cause only suffering."

"Then why do you go on, Sita?"

At his saying my name I felt so touched. "I just want to live, Lord."

He nodded. "I will let you live if you obey my command. If you never make another of your kind, you will have my grace, my protection."

I lowered my head. "Thank you, my Lord."

He gestured toward the other vampires. "Go stand with them. I must talk to your leader. His days are not over. They will not be over for a long time." I moved to leave, but Krishna stopped me. "Sita?"

I turned to look into his face one last time. It was as if I could see the whole universe in his eyes. Maybe he was God, maybe he was simply enlightened. I didn't care right then, in that blessed moment, I just loved him. Later, though, the love was to turn to hate, to fear. They seemed so opposite, the feelings, yet they were all one note on his flute. Truly he had stolen my heart.

"Yes, Lord?" I said.

He bid me lean close to his lips. "Where there is love, there is my grace," he whispered. "Remember that."

"I will try, my Lord."

I went and stood with the others. Krishna revived Yaksha and spoke softly in his ear. When Krishna was done, Yaksha nodded. Krishna bade him climb to his feet, and we saw that Yaksha's wounds were gone. Yaksha walked toward us.

"Krishna says we can go," he said.

"What did he tell you?" I asked.

"I cannot say. What did he tell you?"

"I cannot say."

Yet it was not long before I learned part of what Krishna had told Yaksha. Yaksha secretly began to execute each of the vampires. His acts did not stay secret long. I fled, we all did. But he hunted down the others, over the long years, even after Krishna was gone and Kali Yuga reigned. Yaksha chased them to the ends of the earth over the many centuries until there were none left that I knew of, except me. Yet he never came for me, and in the Middle Ages, as the Black Plague swept Europe, I heard that he was accused of being a witch, and also hunted down, by an entire army, and burned to ash in an old castle. I cried when the news came to me because even though he had stolen what I loved, he had in a sense created what I was. He was my lord as Krishna was my lord. I served both masters, light and darkness, both of which I had seen in Krishna's eyes. Even the devil does God's will.

I never made another vampire, but I never stopped killing.

TEN

Ray stirs as the sun descends toward the western horizon. I sit by my computer on the small table at the end of my living room sofa, with the e-mail addresses Riley and Slim have provided for me. But I do not send Yaksha a message. It is not necessary. He is coming, I can feel him coming.

"Ray," I say. "It's time to get up and enjoy the night."

Ray sits up and yawns. He wipes the sleep from his eyes like a little boy. He checks the time and is amazed. "I slept away the entire day?" he asks.

"Yes," I say. "And now you have to go. I have decided. It is not safe for you here. Go to Pat. She loves you."

He throws aside the blankets and pulls on his pants. He comes and sits beside me and touches my arm. "I am not going to leave you."

"You cannot protect me. You can only get yourself killed."

"If I get killed, then I get killed. At least I will have tried."

"Brave words, foolish words. I can make you leave. I can tell you things about myself that will make you run out of here cursing my name."

He smiles. "I do not believe that."

I harden my tone, though it breaks my heart to treat him cruelly. But I have decided that my reasons for bringing him to my home are selfish. I must have him go, whatever it costs.

"Then listen to me," I say. "I lied to you last night even when I supposedly opened my heart to you. The first thing you must know is that your father is dead and that it was I, not Yaksha, who killed him."

Ray sits back, stunned. "You're not serious."

"I can show you where his body is buried."

"But you couldn't have killed him. Why? How?"

"I will answer your questions. I killed him because he called me into his office and tried to blackmail me with information he had dug up on me. He threatened to make it public. I killed him by crushing the bones of his chest."

"You couldn't do that."

"But you know that I can. You know what I am." I reach over and pick up a small miniature of the Pyramid of Giza that stands on my living room table. "This piece was made for me out of solid marble by an artist in Egypt two hundred years ago. It is very heavy. You can feel it if you don't believe me."

Ray's eyes are dark. "I believe you."

"You should." I hold the piece in my right hand. I squeeze tight and it shatters to dust. Ray jumps back. "You should believe everything I tell you."

He takes a moment to collect himself. "You are a vampire."

"Yes."

"I knew there was something about you."

"Yes."

There is pain in his voice. "But you couldn't have killed my father."

"But I did. I killed him without mercy. I have killed thousands over the last five thousand years. I am a monster."

His eyes are moist. "But you would not do anything to hurt me. You want me to leave now because you do not want me to get hurt. You love me, I love you. Tell me you didn't kill him."

I take his hands in mine. "Ray, this is a beautiful world and it is a horrible world. Most people never see the horror that there is. For most that is fine. But you must look at it now. You must look deep into my eyes and see that I am not human, that I do inhuman things. Yes, I killed your father. He died in my arms. He will not be coming home. And if you do not leave here, you will not return home, either. Then your father's dying wish will have been in vain."

Ray weeps. "He made a wish?"

"Not with words, but, yes. I picked up your picture and he

cried. By then he knew what I was, though it was too late for him. He did not want me to touch you." I caress Ray's arms. "But it is not too late for you. Please go."

"But if you are so horrible why did you touch me, love me?"

"You remind me of someone."

"Who?"

"My husband, Rama. The night I was made a vampire, I was forced to leave him. I never saw him again."

"Five thousand years ago?"

"Yes."

"Are you really that old?"

"Yes. I knew Krishna."

"Hare Krishna?"

The moment is so serious, but I have to laugh. "He was not the way you think from what you see these days. Krishna was—there are no words for him. He was everything. It is he who has protected me all these years."

"You believe that?"

I hesitate, but it is true. Why can't I accept the truth? "Yes."

"Why?"

"Because he told me he would if I listened to him. And because it has been so. Many times, even with my great power, I should have perished. But I never did. God blessed me." I add, "And he cursed me."

"How did he curse you?"

Now there are tears in my eyes. "By putting me in this

situation again. I cannot lose you again, my love, but I cannot keep you with me, either. Go now before Yaksha arrives. Forgive me for what I did to your father. He was not a bad man. He only wanted the money so that he could give it to you. I know he loved you very much."

"But—"

"Wait!" I interrupt. Suddenly I hear something, the note of a flute, flowing with the noise of the waves, a single note, calling me to it, telling me that it is already too late. "He is here," I whisper.

"What? Where?"

I stand and walk to the wide windows that overlook the sea. Ray stands beside me. Down by the ocean, where the waves crash against the rocks, stands a solitary figure dressed in black. His back is to us, but I see the flute in his hand. His song is sad, as always. I don't know if he plays for me or himself, but maybe it is for both of us.

"Is that him?" Rays asks.

"Yes."

"He's alone. We should be able to take him. Do you have a gun?"

"I have one under my pillow over there. But a gun will not stop him. Not unless he was riddled with bullets."

"Why are you giving up without a fight?"

"I am not giving up. I am going to talk to him."

"I'm coming with you."

I turn to Ray and rub the hair on his head. He feels so delicate to me. "No. You cannot come. He is less human than I am. He will not be interested in what a human has to say." I put my finger to his lips as he starts to protest. "Do not argue with me. I do not argue."

"I am not going to leave," he says.

I sigh. "It may be too late for that already. Stay then. Watch. Pray."

"To Krishna?"

"God is God. His name doesn't matter. But I think only he can help us now."

A few minutes later I stand ten feet behind Yaksha. The wind is strong, bitter. It seems to blow straight out of the cold sun which hangs like a bloated drop of blood over the hazy western horizon. The spray from the waves clings to Yaksha's long black hair like so many drops of dew. For a moment I imagine him a statue that has stood outside my home for centuries. Always, he has been in my life, even when he was not there. He has stopped playing his flute.

"Hello," I say to this person I haven't spoken to since the dawn of history.

"Did you enjoy my song?" he asks, his back still to me.

"It was sad."

"It is a sad day."

"The day is ending," I say.

He nods as he turns. "I want it to end, Sita."

The years have not changed his appearance. Why does that surprise me when they haven't changed mine? I don't know. Yet I scrutinize him more closely. A man has to learn something in so many years, I think. He cannot be the beast that he was. He smiles at my thought.

"The form changes, the essence remains the same," he says. "That is something Krishna told me about nature. But for us the form does not change."

"It is because we are unnatural."

"Yes. Nature abhors the invader. We are not welcome in this world."

"But you look well."

"I am not. I am tired. I wish to die."

"I don't," I say.

"I know."

"You tested me with Slim and his people. To see how hard I would fight."

"Yes."

"But I passed the test. I don't want to die. Leave here. Go do what you must. I want nothing to do with it."

Yaksha shakes his head sadly, and that is one change in him—his sorrow. It softens him somehow, making his eyes less cold. Yet the sorrow scares me more than his wicked glee used to. Yaksha was always so full of life for a being that would later be labeled the undead.

"I would let you go if I could," he says. "But I cannot."

"Because of the vow you took with Krishna?"

"Yes."

"What were his words?"

"He told me that I would have his grace if I destroyed the evil I had created."

"I suspected as much. Why didn't you destroy me?"

"There was time, at least in my mind. He did not put a time limit on me."

"You destroyed the others centuries ago."

He watches me. "You are very beautiful."

"Thank you."

"It warmed my heart to know your beauty still existed somewhere in the world." He pauses. "Why do you ask these questions? You know I didn't kill you because I love you."

"Do you still love me?"

"Of course."

"Then let me go."

"I cannot. I am sorry, Sita, truly."

"Is it so important to you that you die in his grace?"

Yaksha is grave. "It is why I came into this world. The Aghoran priest did not call me, I came of my own will. I knew Krishna was here. I came to get away from where I was. I came so that when I died I would be in that grace."

"But you tried to destroy Krishna?"

Yaksha shrugs as if that is not important. "The foolishness of youth."

"Was he God? Are you sure? Can we be sure?"

Yaksha shakes his head. "Even that does not matter. What is God? It is a word. Whatever Krishna was we both know he was not someone we can disobey. It is that simple."

I gesture to the waves. "Then the line has been drawn. The sea meets the shore. The infinite tells the finite what is supposed to be. I accept that. But you are faced with a problem. You do not know what Krishna said to me."

"I do. I have watched you long. The truth is obvious. He told you not to make another of your kind, and he would protect you."

"Yes. It is a paradox. If you try to destroy me, you will go against his word. If you do not try, then you are damned."

Yaksha is not moved by my words. He is a step ahead of me; he always was. He points to the house with his flute. Ray continues to stand beside the window, watching us.

"I have watched you particularly close the last three days," he says. "You love this boy. You would not want to see him die."

My fear is a great and terrible thing in this moment. But I speak harshly. "If you use that as a threat to force me to destroy myself, then you will still lose Krishna's grace. It will be as if you struck me down with your own hands."

Yaksha does not respond with anger. Indeed, he does seem weary. "You misunderstand me. I will do nothing to you while you are protected by his grace. I will force you to do nothing."

He gestures to the setting sun. "It takes a night to make a vampire. I am sure you remember. When the sun rises again, I will come back for you, for both of you. By then you should be done. Then you will be mine."

There is scorn in my voice. "You are a fool, Yaksha. The temptation to make another of our kind has come to me many times in the long years, and always I have resisted it. I will not forsake my protection. Face it, you are beaten. Die and return to the black hell from where you came."

Yaksha raises an eyebrow. "You know I am no fool, Sita. Listen."

He glances toward the house, at Ray, then raises the flute to his lips. He plays a single note, piercingly high. I shake with pain as the sound vibrates through my body. Behind us I hear glass break. No, not just glass. The window against which Ray is leaning. I turn in time to see him topple through the broken glass and plunge headfirst onto the concrete driveway sixty feet below. Yaksha grabs my arm as I move to run to him.

"I wish it did not have to be this way," he says.

I shake off his hand. "I have never loved you. You may yet have grace before you die, but you will never have that."

He closes his eyes briefly. "So be it," he says.

I find Ray in a pool of blood and a pile of glass. His skull is crushed, his spine is broken. Incredibly, he is still conscious, although he does not have long to live. I roll him over on his back, and he speaks to me with blood pouring from his mouth.

"I fell," he says.

My tears are as cold as the ocean drops on my cheeks. I put my hand over his heart. "This is the last thing I wanted for you."

"Is he going to let you go?"

"I don't know, Ray. I don't know." I lean over and hug him and hear the blood in his lungs as his breath struggles to scrape past it. Just as the breath of his father struggled before it failed. I remember I told the man that I could not heal, that I could only kill. But that was only a half truth, I realize, even as I grasp the full extent of Yaksha's plan to destroy me. Once he used my fear to make me a vampire. Now he uses my love to force me to make another vampire. He is right, he is no fool. I cannot bear to watch Ray die knowing the power in my blood can heal even his fatal injuries.

"I wanted to save you," he whispers. He tries to raise a hand to touch me, but it falls back to the ground. I sit up and stare into his mortal eyes, trying to put love into them, where for so many years with so many other mortals I have only tried to put fear.

"I want to save you," I say. "Do you want me to save you?"

"Can you?"

"Yes. I can put my blood in your blood."

He tries to smile. "Become a vampire like you?"

I nod and smile through my tears. "Yes, you could become like me."

"Would I have to hurt people?"

"No. Not all vampires hurt people." I touch his ruined cheek. I haven't forgotten Yaksha's words about coming for both of us at dawn. "Some vampires love a great deal."

"I love . . ." His eyes slowly close. He cannot finish.

I lean over and kiss his lips. I taste his blood.

I will have to do more than taste it to help him.

"You are love," I say as I open both our veins.

ELEVEN

Ray's sleep is deep and profound, as I expect. I have brought him back to the house, and laid him in front of a fire I built, and wiped away his blood. Not long after his transfusion, while still lying crumpled on the driveway, his breath had accelerated rapidly, and then ceased altogether. But it had not scared me, because the same had happened to me, and to Mataji, and many others. When it had started again, it was strong and steady.

His wounds vanished as if by magic.

I am weak from sharing my blood, very tired.

I anticipate that Ray will sleep away most of the night, and that Yaksha will keep his word and not return until dawn. I leave the house and drive in my Ferrari to Seymour's place. It is not that late—ten o'clock. I do not want to meet his parents. They might suspect I have come to corrupt their beloved son.

I go around the back and see Seymour through his bedroom window, writing on his computer. I scratch on his window with my hard nails and give him a scare. He comes over to investigate, however. He is delighted to see me. He opens the window and I climb inside. Contrary to popular opinion, I could have climbed in without being invited.

"It is so cool you are here," he says. "I have been writing about you all day."

I sit on his bed; he stays at his desk. His room is filled with science things—telescopes and such—but the walls are coated with the posters of classic horror films. It is a room I am comfortable in. I often go to the movies, the late shows.

"A story about me?" I ask. I glance at his computer screen, but he has returned to the word processor menu.

"Yes. Well, no, not really. But you inspired the story. It comes to me in waves. It's about this girl our age who's a vampire."

"I am a vampire."

He fixes his bulky glasses on his nose. "What?"

"I said, I am a vampire."

He glances at the mirror above his chest of drawers. "I can see your reflection."

"So what? I am what I say I am. Do you want me to drink your blood to prove it?"

"That's all right, you don't have to." He takes a deep breath. "Wow, I knew you were an interesting girl, but I never guessed . . ." He stops himself. "But I suppose that's not true, is it? I have been writing about you all along, haven't I?"

"Yes."

"But how is that possible? Can you explain that to me?"

"No. It's one of those mysteries. You run into them every now and then, if you live long enough."

"How old are you?"

"Five thousand years."

Seymour holds up his hand. "Wait, wait. Let's slow down here. I don't want to be a pest about this, and I sure don't want you to drink my blood, but before we proceed any further, I wouldn't mind if you showed me some of your powers. It would help with my research, you understand."

I smile. "You really don't believe me, do you? That's okay. I don't know if I want you to, not now. But I do want your advice." I lose my smile. "I am getting near the end of things now. An old enemy has come for me, and for the first time in my long life I am vulnerable to attack. You are the smart boy with the prophetic dreams. Tell me what to do."

"I have prophetic dreams?"

"Yes. Trust me or I wouldn't be here."

"What does this old enemy want? To kill you?"

"To kill both of us. But he doesn't want to die until I am gone."

"Why does he want to die?"

"He is tired of living."

"Been around for a while, I guess." Seymour thinks a moment. "Would he mind dying at the same time as you?"

"I'm sure that would be satisfactory. It might even appeal to him."

"Then that's the answer to your problem. Place him in a situation where he is convinced you're both goners. But arrange it ahead of time so that when you do push the button—or whatever you do—that only he is destroyed and not you."

"That's an interesting idea."

"Thank you. I was thinking of using it in my story."

"But there are problems with it. This enemy is extremely shrewd. It will not be easy to convince him that I am going to die with him unless it is pretty certain that I am going to die. And I don't want to die."

"There must be a way. There is always a way."

"What are you going to do in your story?"

"I haven't worked out that little detail yet."

"That detail is not little to me at the moment."

"I'm sorry."

"That's all right." I listen to his parents watching TV in the other room. They talk about their boy, his health. The mother is grief-stricken. Seymour watches me through his thick lenses.

"It's hardest on my mother," he says.

"The AIDS virus is not new. A form of it existed in the past, not exactly the same as what is going around now, but close enough. I saw it in action. Ancient Rome, in its decline, was stricken with it. Many people died. Whole villages. That's how it was stopped. The mortality rate in certain areas was so high that there was no one left alive to pass it on."

"That's interesting. There is no mention of that in history books."

"Do not trust in your books too much. History is something that can only be lived, it cannot be read about. Look at me, I am history." I sigh. "The stories I could tell you."

"Tell me."

I yawn, something I never do. Ray has drained me more than I realized. "I don't have time."

"Tell me how you managed to survive the AIDS epidemic of the past."

"My blood is potent. My immune system is impenetrable. I have not just come here to seek your help, although you have helped me. I have come here to help you. I want to give you my blood. Not enough to make you a vampire, but enough to destroy the virus in your system."

He is intrigued. "Will that work?"

"I don't know. I have never done it before."

"Could it be dangerous?"

"Sure. It might kill you."

He hesitates only a moment. "What do I have to do?"

"Come sit beside me on the bed." He does so. "Give me your arm and close your eyes. I am going to open up one of your veins. Don't worry, I have had a lot of practice with this."

"I can imagine." He lets his arm rest in my lap, but he does not close his eyes.

"What's the matter?" I ask. "Are you afraid I will try to take advantage of you?"

"I wish you would. It's not every day the school nerd has the most beautiful girl in the school sitting on his bed." He clears his throat. "I know that you're in a hurry, but I wanted to tell you something before we begin."

"What's that?"

"I wanted to thank you for being my friend and letting me play a part in your story."

I think of Krishna, always of him, how he stood near me and I saw the whole universe as his play. "Thank you, Seymour, for writing about me." I lean over and kiss his lips. "If I die tonight, at least others will know I once lived." I stretch out my nails. "Close your eyes. You do not want to watch this."

I place a measured amount of blood inside him. His breath quickens, it burns, but not so fast or hot as Ray's had. Yet, like Ray, Seymour quickly falls into a deep slumber. I turn off his computer and put out the light. There is a blanket on the bed that looks as if it was knitted by his mother, and I cover him with it. Before I leave, I put my palm on his forehead and listen and feel as deep as my senses will allow.

The virus, I am almost sure of this, is gone.

I kiss him once more before I leave.

"Give me credit if you get your story published," I whisper in his ear. "Or else there will be no sequels."

I return to my car.

Giving out so much blood, taking none back in return.

I feel weaker than I have in centuries.

"There will be no sequels," I repeat to myself.

I start the car. I drive into the night.

I have work to do.

TWELVE

Seymour has given me an idea. But even with his inspiration, and mine, even if everything goes exactly as planned, the chances of it working are fifty-fifty at best. In all probability much less than that. But at least the plan gives me hope. For myself and Ray. He is like my child now, as well as my lover. I cannot stand the thought that he is to be snuffed out so young. He was wrong to say I would give up without a fight. I fight until the end.

There is a concept NASA is entertaining to launch huge payloads into space. It is called Orion; the idea is revolutionary. Many experts, in fact, say it won't work in practice. Yet there are large numbers of respected physicists and engineers who believe it is the wave of the future in space transport. Essentially it involves constructing a huge heavily plated platform with cannons on the bottom that can fire miniature nuclear bombs. It is believed that the shock waves from the blasts of the bombs detonating—if their timing and power is perfectly balanced—can lift the platform steadily into the sky, until eventually escape velocity is achieved. The advantage of this idea over traditional rockets is that tremendous tonnage could be shot into space. The primary problem is obvious: who wants to strap themselves atop a platform that is going to have nuclear bombs going off beneath it? Of course, I would enjoy such a ride. Extreme radiation bothers me no more than a sunny day.

Even with my great resources, I do not have a nuclear bomb at my disposal. But the idea of the Orion project inspires a plan in me. Seymour hit the nail on the head when he said Yaksha must be placed in a situation where he thinks all three of us will perish. That will satisfy Yaksha. He will then go to Krishna believing all vampires are destroyed. I theorize that I can build my own Orion with dynamite and a heavy steel platform, and use it to allow Ray and me to escape while a secondary blast kills Yaksha.

This is how I see the details. I let Yaksha into my house. I tell him that I will not fight him, that we can all go out together in one big blast. I know the possibility will entice Yaksha. We can sit in the living room around a crate of dynamite. I can even let Yaksha light the fuse. He will see that the bomb is big enough to kill us all.

But what he will not see is the six inches of steel sheeting under the carpet beneath my chair and Ray's. Our *two* chairs will be bolted to the steel sheet—through the carpet. The chairs will be part of the metal plate—one unit. Yaksha will not see a smaller bomb beneath the floor of the plate. This bomb I will detonate, before Yaksha's fuse burns down. This bomb will blast my amateur Orion toward the wide skylights in my ceiling. The shock wave from it will also trigger the larger bomb.

Simple. Yes? There are problems, I know.

The blast from the hidden bomb will trigger the larger bomb before we can fly clear. I estimate that the two bombs should go off almost simultaneously. But Ray and I need rise up only fifteen feet on our Orion. Then the blast from the larger bomb should propel us through the skylights. If the two bombs are more than fifteen feet apart—ideally twice that distance—then the shock wave from the hidden bomb should not get to the larger bomb before we have achieved our fifteen feet elevation.

Our heads will heal quickly after we smash through the skylights as long as we are in one piece.

The physics are simple in theory, but in practice they are filled with the possibility for limitless error. For that reason I figure Ray and I will be dead before sunrise. But any odds are good odds for the damned, and I will play them out as best I can.

I stop at a phone booth and call my primary troubleshooter in North America. I tell him I need dynamite and thick sheets of steel in two hours. Where can I get them? He is used to my unusual requests. He says he'll call back in twenty minutes.

Fifteen minutes later he is back on the line. He sounds relieved because he knows it's not good to bring me disappointing information. He says there is a contractor in Portland who carries both dynamite and thick steel plating. Franklin and Sons—they build skyscrapers. He gives me the address of their main warehouse and I hang up. Portland is eighty miles away. The time is ten-fifty.

I sit in my car outside the warehouse at a quarter to midnight, listening to the people inside. The place is closed, but there are three security men on duty. One is in the front in a small office watching TV. The other two are in back smoking a joint. Since I have spent a good part of the night thinking about Krishna, hoping he will help me, I am not predisposed to kill these three. I climb out of my car.

The locked doors cause me no problem. I am upon the stoned men in the back before they can blink. I put them to sleep with moderate blows to the temples. They'll wake up, but with bad headaches. Unfortunately, the guy watching TV has the bad luck to check on his partners as I knock them out. He draws his gun when he sees me, and I react instinctively. I kill him much the same way I killed Ray's father, crushing the bones in his chest with a violent kick. I drink a belly full of his blood before he draws his last breath. I am still weak.

The dynamite is not hard for me to find with my sensitive

nose. It is locked in a safe near the front of the building, several crates of thick red sticks. There are detonator caps and fuses. Already I have decided I will not be taking my car back to Mayfair tonight. I will need a truck from the warehouse to haul the steel sheets. The metal is not as thick as I wish; I will have to weld several layers together. I find a welding set to take with me.

There are actually several suitable trucks parked inside the warehouse, the keys conveniently left in the ignitions. I load up and back out of the warehouse. I park my Ferrari several blocks away. Then I am on the road back home.

It is after two when I reenter Mayfair. Ray is sitting by the fire as I come through my front door. He has changed. He is a vampire. His teeth are not longer, or anything silly like that. But the signs are there—gold specks deep in his once uniformly brown eyes; a faint transparency to his tan skin; a grace to his movements no mortal could emulate. He stands when he sees me.

"Am I alive?" he asks innocently.

I do not laugh at the question. I am not sure if the answer is something as simple as yes or no. I step toward him.

"You are with me," I say. "You are the same as me. When you met me, did you think I was alive?"

"Yes."

"Then you are alive. How do you feel?"

"Powerful. Overwhelmed. My eyes, my ears—are yours this way?"

"Mine are more sensitive. They become more and more sensitive with time. Are you scared?"

"Yes. Is he coming back?"

"Yes."

"When?"

"At dawn."

"Will he kill us?"

"He wants to."

"Why?"

"Because he feels we are evil. He feels an obligation to destroy us before he leaves the planet."

Ray frowns, testing his new body, its vibrancy. "Are we evil?"

I take his hands and sit him down. "We don't have to be. Soon you will begin to crave blood, and the blood will give you strength. But to get blood you don't need to kill. I will show you how."

"You said he wants to leave this planet. He wants to die?"

"Yes. He is tired of life. It happens—our lives have been so long. But life does not tire me." I am so emotional around Ray, it amazes me. "I have you to inspire me."

He smiles, but it is a sad smile. "It was a sacrifice for you to save me."

He takes my breath away. "How did you know?"

"When I was dying, I could see you were afraid to give me your blood. What happens when you do? Does it make you weak?"

I hug him, glad that I can squeeze his body with all my strength and not break his bones. "Don't worry about me. I saved you because I wanted to save you."

"Is my father really dead?"

I let go of him, look into his eyes. "Yes."

He has trouble looking at me. Even though he is a vampire now, a predator. Even though his thought processes have begun to alter. He didn't protest when I told him about the blood-drinking. But his love for his father goes deeper than blood.

"Was it necessary?" he asked.

"Yes."

"Did he suffer?"

"No, less than a minute." I squeeze his hand and add, "I am sorry."

He finally raises his eyes. "You gave me your blood out of guilt as well."

I nod. "I had to give something back after what I had taken."

He puts a hand to his head. He doesn't completely forgive me but he understands, and for that I am grateful. He still misses his father. "We won't talk about it," he says.

"That is fine." I stand. "We have much to do. Yaksha is returning at dawn. We cannot destroy him with brute force, even with our combined strengths. But we might be able to trick him. We will talk as we work."

He stands. "You have a plan?"

"I have more than a plan. I have a rocket ship."

Welding the sheets of metal together so that we have six inches of protection does not take long. I work outside with the arc gun so that Yaksha will not notice the smell when he enters the house. He will have to come into the house since I won't go out to him. Cutting a huge rectangle in the floor to accommodate the metal plate, however, takes a lot of time. I fret as the hours slip by. Ray is not much help because he has not acquired my expertise in everything yet. Finally I tell him to sit and watch. He doesn't mind. His eyes are everywhere, staring at common objects, seeing in them things he never imagined before. A vampire on acid, I call him. He laughs. It is good to hear laughter.

As I work, I do not *feel* Yaksha in the area.

It is fortunate.

My speed picks up when I bolt the two chairs to the plate and recover the plate with carpet. Here I do not have to work so carefully; the skirts of the chairs cover much. When I am done, the living room appears normal. I plan to use an end table to hide the detonator to the bomb I will strap beneath the steel plate. I bore a long hole through the table and slip in a metal rod that goes through to the metal plate. I hide the tip of the rod under a lamp base. I place a blasting cap at the bottom end of it. When the time comes, I will hit the top of the small table, the rod will crush the blasting cap, and the first bomb will go off, sending us flying.

The other bomb should go off as well, almost immediately. I keep coming back to that point in my mind because it is the central weakness in my plan. I hope we will be high enough to take the shock from the second bomb from below so the plate will protect us.

Attaching the bomb beneath the plate takes only minutes. I use twenty sticks of dynamite, tightly bound. I place fifty sticks, a whole crate, beside the fireplace in the living room, next to the most comfortable chair in the house. That seat I will offer Yaksha. We will live or die depending on how accurate my calculations are, and how well we play our parts in front of Yaksha. That is the other serious weakness in my plan; that Yaksha will sense something amiss. For that reason I have instructed Ray to say little, or nothing at all. But I am confident I can lie to Yaksha. I lie as effortlessly as I tell the truth, perhaps more easily.

Ray and I sit in our special flight chairs and talk. The bomb in the crate sits thirty feet away, directly in front of us. Above us I have opened the skylights. The cold night air feels good for once. Even with them open, we will still strike glass as we rocket by. I warn Ray, but he is not worried.

"I have already died once today," he says.

"You must have had your nose pressed against the glass to fall with it."

"I didn't until just before he raised his flute."

I nod. "He glanced at the house then. He must have pulled you forward with the power of his eyes. He can do that. He can do many things."

"He has more power than you?"

"Yes."

"Why is that?"

"He's the original vampire." I glance at the time—an hour to dawn. "Would you like to hear the story of his birth?"

"I would like to hear all your stories."

I smile. "You sound like Seymour. I visited him tonight while you slept. I gave him a present. I will tell you about it another time."

I pause and take a breath. I need it for strength. The simple work of a terrorist has exhausted me. Where to begin the tale? Where will I end it? It doesn't seem right that it could all be over in an hour. *Right*—what a word choice for a vampire to make. I who have violated every injunction of the Vedas and the Bible and every other holy book on earth. Death never comes at the *right* time, despite what mortals believe. Death always comes like a thief.

I tell Ray of the birth of Yaksha, and how he in turn made me a vampire. I talk to him about meeting Krishna, but here my words fail me. I do not weep, I do not rave. I simply cannot talk about him. Ray understands; he encourages me to tell him about my life in another era.

"Were you in Ancient Greece?" he asks. "I was always fascinated by that culture."

I nod. "I was there for a long time. I knew Socrates and Plato and Aristotle. Socrates recognized me as something inhuman, but I didn't scare him. He was fearless, that man. He laughed as he drank the poison he was sentenced to drink." I shake my head at the memory. "The Greeks were inquisitive. There was one young man—Cleo. History does not remember him, but he was as brilliant as the others." My voice falters again. "He was dear to me. I lived with him for many years."

"Did he know you were a vampire?"

I laugh. "He thought I was a witch. But he liked witches."

"Tell me about him," Ray says.

"I met Cleo during the time of Socrates. I had just returned to Greece after being away for many years. That's my pattern. I stay in one place only as long as my youth, my constant youth, doesn't become suspicious. When I returned to Athens, no one remembered me. Cleo was one of the first people I encountered. I was walking in the woods when I found him helping to deliver a baby. In those days that was unheard of. Only women were present at births. Even though he was covered with blood and obviously busy, he took an immediate liking to me. He asked me to help him, which I did, and when the child was born, he handed it to the mother and we went for a walk. He explained that he had worked out a better way to deliver babies and had wanted to test his theories. He also admitted that he was the father of the infant, but that was not important to him.

"Cleo was a great doctor, but he was never recognized by his peers. He was ahead of his time. He refined the technique of the Caesarean delivery. He experimented with magnets and how they could restore ailing organs: the positive pole of the magnet to stimulate an organ, the negative pole to pacify it. He had an understanding of how the aromas of certain flowers could affect health. He was also the first chiropractor. He was always adjusting people's bodies, cracking their necks and backs. He tried to adjust me once and sprained his wrists. You can see why I liked him."

I went on to explain how I knew Cleo for many years, and spoke of his one fatal flaw: his obsession with seducing the wives of Athens' powerful men. How he was eventually caught in bed with the wife of an important general, and beheaded with a smile on his face, while many of the women of Athens wept. Wonderful Cleo.

I talk of a life I had as an English duchess in the Middle Ages. What it was like to live in a castle. My words bring back the memories. The constant drafts. The stone walls. The roaring fires—at night, how black those nights could be. My name was Melissa and in the summer months I would ride a white horse through the green countryside and laugh at the advances made to me by the knights in shining armor. I even accepted a couple of offers to jostle, offers the men later regretted making.

I speak of a life in the South during the American Civil War. The burning and pillaging of the Yankees as they stormed across Mississippi. A note of bitterness enters my voice, but I do not tell Ray everything. Not how I was abducted by a battalion of twenty soldiers and tied at the neck with a rope and forced to grovel through a swamp, while the men joked about what pleasure I would give them come sunset. I do not want to scare Ray, so I do not explain how each of those men died, how they screamed, especially the last ones, as they tried to flee from the swamp in the dark, from the swift white hands that tore off their limbs and crushed their skulls.

Finally I tell him of how I was in Cape Canaveral when Apollo 11 was launched toward the moon. How proud I was of humanity then, that they had finally reclaimed the adventurous spirit they had known so well in their youth. Ray takes joy in my pleasure of the memory. It makes him forget the horror that awaits us, which is part of the reason I share the story.

"Did you ever want to go to the moon?" he asks.

"Pluto. Much farther from the sun, you know. More comfortable for a vampire."

"Did you grieve when Cleo died?"

I smile, although there is suddenly a tear in my eye. "No. He lived the life he wanted. Had he lived too long, he would have begun to bore himself."

"I understand."

"Good," I say.

But Ray doesn't really understand. He misconstrues the sentiment I show. My tear is not for Cleo. It is for my long life, the totality of it, all the people and places that are a part of it. Such a rich book of history to slam shut and store away in a forgotten corner. I grieve for all the stories I will never have a chance to tell Seymour and Ray. I grieve for the vow I have broken. I grieve for Yaksha and the love I could never give him. Most of all I grieve for my soul because even though I do, finally, believe that there is a God, and that I have met him, I do not know if he has given me an *immortal* soul, but only one that was to last me as long as my body lasted. I do not know if when the last page of my book is closed, that will be the end of me.

Darkness approaches from outside.

I feel no light inside me strong enough to resist it.

"He is coming," I say.

THIRTEEN

There is a knock at the door. I call out to come in. He enters; he is alone, dressed in black, a cape, a hat—he makes a stunning figure. He nods and I gesture for him to take the chair across from us. He has not brought his flute. He sits in the chair near the crate of dynamite and smiles at both of us. But there is no joy in the smile, and I think he truly does regret what is about to happen. Outside, behind us through the broken windows, a hint of light enters the black sky. Ray sits silently staring at our visitor. It is up to me to make conversation.

"Are you happy?" I ask.

"I have known happiness at times," Yaksha says. "But it has been a long time."

"But you have what you want," I insist. "I have broken my vow. I have made another evil creature, another thing for you to destroy."

"I feel no compulsions these days, Sita, except to rest."

"I want to rest as well."

He raises an eyebrow. "You said you wanted to live?"

"It is my hope there will be life for me after this life is over. I assume that is your hope as well. I assume that is why you are going to all this trouble to wreck my night."

"You always had a way with words."

"Thank you."

Yaksha hesitates. "Do you have any last words?"

"A few. May I decide how we die?"

"You want us to die together?"

"Of course," I say.

Yaksha nods. "I prefer it that way." He glances at the crate of dynamite beside him. "You have made us a bomb, I see. I like bombs."

"I know. You can be the one to light it. You see the fuse there, the lighter beside it? Go ahead, old friend, strike the flame. We can burn together." I lean forward. "Maybe we should have burned a long time ago.

Yaksha picks up the lighter. He considers Ray. "How do you feel, young man?"

"Strange," Ray says.

"I would set you free if I could," Yaksha says. "I would leave you both alone. But it has to end, one way or the other."

This is a Yaksha I have never heard before. He never explained himself to anyone.

"Sita has told me your reasons," Ray says.

"Your father is dead," Yaksha says.

"I know."

Yaksha pulls his thumb across the lighter and stares at it. "I never knew my father."

"I saw him once," I say. "Ugly bastard. Are you going to do it or do you want me to do it?"

"Are you so anxious to die?" Yaksha asks.

"I never could wait for the excitement to begin," I say sarcastically.

He nods and moves the flame to the end of the fuse. It begins to fizzle, it begins to shorten—quickly. There are three minutes of time coiled in that combustible string. Yaksha sits back in his chair.

"I had a dream as I walked by the ocean tonight," he says. "Listening to the sound of the waves, it seemed I entered a dimension where the water was singing a song that no one had ever heard before. A song that explained everything in the creation. But the magic of the song was that it could never be recognized for what it was, not by any living soul. If it was, if the truth was brought out into the open and discussed, then the magic would die and the waters would evaporate. And that is what happened in my dream as this realization came to me. I came into the world. I killed all the creatures the waters had given life to, and then one day I woke up and realized I had been listening to a song. Just a sad song."

"Played on a flute?" I ask.

The fuse burns.

There is no reason for me to delay. Yet I do.

His dream moves me.

"Perhaps," Yaksha says softly. "In the dream the ocean vanished from my side. I walked along an endless barren plain of red dust. The ground was a dark red, as if a huge being had bled over it for centuries and then left the sun to parch dry what the being had lost."

"Or what it had stolen from others," I say.

"Perhaps," Yaksha says again.

"What does this dream mean?" I ask.

"I was hoping you could tell me, Sita."

"What can I tell you? I don't know your mind."

"But you do. It is the same as yours."

"No."

"Yes. How else could I know your mind?"

I tremble. His voice has changed. He is alert, he always was, to everything that was happening around him. I was a fool to think I could trick him. Yet I do not reach for the metal rod that will detonate the bomb. I try to play the fool a little longer. I speak.

"Maybe your dream means that if we stay on earth, and once more multiply, then we will make a wasteland of this world."

"How would we multiply this late in the game?" he asks.

"I told you you can have no children. Krishna told you something similar." It is his turn to lean forward. "What else did he tell you, Sita?"

"Nothing."

"You are lying."

"No."

"Yes." With his left hand he reaches for the burning fuse, his fingers hovering over the sparks as if he intends to crush them. Yet he lets the countdown continue. "You cannot trick me."

"And how do I trick you, Yaksha?"

"You are not waiting to die. I see it in your eyes."

"Really?"

"They are not like my eyes."

"You are a vampire," I say. Casually, as if I am stretching, I move my hand toward the lamp stand. "You can't look in a mirror. There would be nothing there. What do you know about your own eyes?" I joke, of course. I am one bundle of laughs.

He smiles. "I am happy to see time has not destroyed your wit. I hope it has not destroyed your reason. You are quick. I am quicker. You can do nothing that I cannot stop." He pauses. "I suggest you stop."

My hand freezes in midair. *Damn,* I think. He knows, of course he knows.

"I cannot remember what he said," I say.

"Your memory is perfect, as is mine."

"Then you tell me what he said."

"I cannot. He whispered in your ear. He did that so that I would not hear. He knew I was listening, even though I was lying there with the venom in my veins. Yes, I heard your original vow to him. But he did not want me to hear the last part. He would have had his reasons, I'm sure, but the time for those reasons must be past. We are both going to die in a few seconds. Did he make you take a second vow?"

The fuse burns.

"No."

Yaksha sits up. "Did he say anything about me?"

Shorter and shorter it burns.

"No!"

"Why won't you answer my question?"

The truth bursts out of me. I have wanted to say it for so long. "Because I hate you!"

"Why?"

"Because you stole away my love, my Rama and Lalita. You steal my love away now, when I have finally found it again. I will hate you for eternity, and if that is not enough to stop you from being in his grace, then I will hate him as well." I point to Ray. "Let him go. Let him live."

Yaksha is surprised. I have stunned the devil. "You love him. You love him more than your own life."

There is only pain in my chest. The fourth center, the fourth note. It is as if it is off key. "Yes."

Yaksha's tone softens. "Did he tell you something about love?"

I nod, weeping, I feel so helpless. "Yes."

"What did he tell you?"

"He said, where there is love, there is my grace." The sound of his flute is too far away. There is no time to be grateful for what I have been given in my long life. I feel as if I will choke on my grief. I can only see Ray, my lover, my child, all the years he will be denied. He looks at me with such trusting eyes, as if somehow I will still manage to save him. "He told me to remember that."

"He told me the same thing." Yaksha pauses to wonder. "It must be true." He adds casually, "You and your friend can go."

I look up. "What?"

"You broke your vow because you love this young man. It is the only reason you broke it. You must still have Krishna's grace. You only became a vampire to protect Rama and your child. You must have had his grace from the beginning. That is why he showed you such kindness. I did not see that till now. I cannot harm you. He would not wish me to." Yaksha glances at the burning fuse. "You had better hurry."

The sparks of the short fuse are like the final sands of an hourglass.

I grab Ray's hand and leap up and pull him toward the front door. I do not open the door with my hand. I kick it open; the wrong way. The hinges rupture, the wood splinters. The night air is open before us. I shove Ray out ahead of me.

"Run!" I shout.

"But—"

"Run!"

He hears me, finally, and dashes for the trees. I turn, I don't know why. The chase is over and the race is won. There is no reason to tempt fate. What I do now, it is the most foolish act of my life. I stride back into the living room. Yaksha stares out at the dark sea. I stand behind him.

"You have ten seconds," he says.

"Hate and fear and love are all in the heart. I felt that when he played his flute." I touch his shoulder. "I don't just hate you. I didn't just fear you."

He turns and looks at me. He smiles; he always had a devilish grin.

"I know that, Sita," he says. "Goodbye."

"Goodbye."

I leap for the front door. I am outside, thirty feet off the front porch, when the bombs go off. The power of the shock wave is extraordinary even for me to absorb. It lifts me up, and for a few moments it is as if I can fly. But it does not set me down softly. At one point in my trajectory fate makes me a marksman's prized bird. An object hot and sharp pierces me from behind.

It goes through my heart. A stake.

I land in a ball of agony. The night burns behind me. My blood sears as it pours from the wound in my chest. Ray is beside me, asking me what he should do. I writhe in the dirt, my fingers clawing into the earth. But I do not want to go into the ground, no, not after walking on it for so long. I try to get the words out—it is not easy. I see I have been impaled by the splintered leg of my piano bench.

"Pull it out," I gasp.

"The stick?" It is the first stupid thing I have heard Ray say.

I turn my front to him. "Yes."

Ray grabs the end of the leg. The wood is literally flaming, although it has passed through my body. He yanks hard. The stick breaks; he has got half of it. The other half is still in my body. Too bad for me. I close my eyes for an instant and see a million red stars. I blink and they explode as if the universe has ended. There remains only red light everywhere. The color of sunset, the color of blood. I find myself settling onto my back. My head rolls to one side. Cool mud touches my cheek. It warms as my blood pours from my mouth and puddles around my head. A red stain, almost black in the fiery night, spreads down my beautiful blond hair. Ray weeps. I look at him with such love I honestly feel I see Krishna's face.

It is not the worst way to die.

"Love you," I whisper.

He hugs me. "I love you, Sita."

So much love, I think as I close my eyes and the pain recedes. There must be so much grace, so much protection for me if Krishna meant what he said. Of course I believe he meant it. I do believe in miracles.

I wonder if I will die, after all.

BLACK BLOOD

For Teli

ONE

I walk the dark and dangerous streets of L.A. gang-land. A seemingly helpless young woman with silky blond hair and magnetic blue eyes. Moving down filth-strewn alleys and streets where power is measured in drops of blood spilled by bullets sprayed from adolescent males who haven't learned to drive yet. I am near the housing projects, those archaic hotels of hostility where the checkout fee is always higher than the price of admission. Because of my supernormal senses, I know I am surrounded by people who would slit my throat as soon as ask the time of day or night. But I am not helpless or afraid, especially in the dark at night, for I am not human. I, Alisa Perne of the twentieth century, Sita of the ancient past. I am five thousand years old, one of the last of two vampires.

But are there only two of us left? I ask myself.

Something is terribly wrong in gangland L.A., and it makes me wonder. In the last month the *Los Angeles Times* has reported a string of brutal murders that leads me to believe Ray and I are not the only ones with the special blood that makes us impervious to aging and most other human ailments. The victims of these murders have been ripped open, decapitated, and, in some cases, the articles say, drained of blood. It is this last fact that has brought me to Los Angeles. I myself like blood, but I am not eager to find more vampires. I know what our kind can do, and I know how fast we can multiply once the secret of procreation is known. Any vampire I may find this evening will not live to see the light of dawn, or perhaps I should say the setting of the moon. I am not crazy about the sun, although I can bear it if I must.

A full moon rides high above me as I step onto Exposition Avenue and head north, not far from where the last murder occurred—a sixteen-year-old girl found yesterday in the bushes with both her arms torn off. It is late, after midnight, and even though it is mid-December, the temperature is in the midsixties. Winter in Los Angeles is like a moon made of green cheese, a joke. I wear black leather pants, a short-sleeved black top that shows my sleek midsection. My black boots barely sound as I prowl the uneven sidewalks. I wear my hair pinned up beneath a black cap. I love the color black as much as the color red. I know I look gorgeous. Cool stainless steel touches my right calf where I have hidden a six-inch blade, but otherwise I am unarmed. There are many police cars out this fine winter night. One passes me on the left as I lower my head and try to look like I belong. Because I fear being stopped and searched, I do not carry a gun. But it is only for the lives of the police that I fear, and not for my own. A whole S.W.A.T. team couldn't stop me. Certainly, I decide, a young vampire will be no match for me. And he or she must be young to be killing so recklessly.

But who is this youngster? And who made him or her?

Disturbing questions.

Three young males wait for me a hundred yards down the street. I cross to the other side, but they move to intercept me. One is tall and slim, the other squat as an old stump. The third has the face of a dark angel brought up on the wrong side of the pearly gates. He is clearly the leader. He smiles as he sees me trying to get away from him and his buddies, flexing his powerful biceps as if they were laws unto themselves. I see he carries a gun under his dirty green coat. The others are unarmed. The three jog toward me as I pause to consider what to do. Of course, I could turn and flee. Even if they were in training for the Olympics, they couldn't catch me. But I don't like to run from a fight, and I am suddenly thirsty. The smile of the leader will fade, I know, as he feels the blood drain from his body into my mouth. I decide to wait for them. I don't have long to wait.

"Hey, babe," the leader says as they surround me in a fidgety semicircle. "What you doin' here by your lonesome? Lost?"

I appear at ease. "No. I'm just out for a walk. What are you guys up to?"

They exchange smirks. They are up to no good. "What's your name?" the leader asks.

"Alisa. What's yours?"

He grins like the young god he thinks he is. "Paul. Hey, you's one beautiful woman, Alisa, you know that? And I appreciate beauty when I see it."

"I bet you do, Paul. Do you appreciate danger when you see it, too?"

They cackle. I am funny, they think. Paul slaps his leg as he laughs. "Are you saying you're dangerous, Alisa?" he asks. "You look like a party babe to me. Me and my stooges, we're going to a party right now. You want to come? It's goin' to be hot."

I consider. "Are you three the only ones going to this party?"

Paul likes it that I'm sharp. "Maybe. But maybe that's all you need." He takes a step closer. There is alcohol on his breath—a Coors beer—Marlboro cigarettes in his coat pocket close to his gun. A brave boy, he puts his right hand on my left shoulder, and his grin is now more of a leer. He adds, "Or maybe all you need is me, babe. What do you say? Want to party?"

I look him in the eye. "No."

He blinks suddenly. My gaze has been known to burn mortal pupils when I give it free rein. But I have held something in check for Paul, and so he is intrigued, not scared. He continues to hold on to my shoulder.

"You don't want to go sayin' no to me, honey. I don't like that word."

"Really."

He glances back at his friends and then nods gravely in my direction. "You don't look like you's from around here. But around here, there's two ways to party. You either do it with a smile on your face or you do it screaming. You know what I mean, Alisa?"

I smile, finally. "Are you going to rape me, Paul?"

He shrugs. "It's up to you, honeysuckle." He draws his piece from his coat, a Smith & Wesson .45 revolver that he probably got for his last birthday. He presses the muzzle beneath my chin. "And it's up to Colleen."

"You call your gun Colleen?"

He nods seriously. "She's a lady. Never lets me down."

My smile grows. "Paul, you are such a simpleton. You can't rape me. Put it out of your mind if you want to be alive come Christmas Day. It's just not going to happen."

My boldness surprises him, angers him. But he quickly grins because his friends are watching and he has to be cool and in control. He presses the gun deeper into my neck, trying to force my head back. But, of course, I don't move an inch, and this confuses him as much as my casual tone.

"You tell me why I can't just have you right now?" he

asks. "You tell me, Alisa. Huh? Before I blow your goddamn head off."

"Because I'm armed as well, Paul."

He blinks—my gaze is beginning to fry his brain. "What you got?"

"A knife. A very sharp knife. Do you want to see it?"

He takes a step back, letting go of me, and levels the gun at my belly. "Show it to me," he orders.

I raise my right leg in front of him. My balance is as solid as that of a marble statue. "It's under my pant leg. Take it out and maybe we can have a little duel."

Acting like a stud, throwing his pals a lecherous glance, Paul cautiously reaches up inside my pant leg. Throughout the act, he doesn't realize how close he is to having his head removed by my right foot. But I have compassion, and I don't like to drink from a gusher—it might stain my clothes. Paul's eyes widen as he feels the knife and quickly pulls it free from the leather strap. He handles it lovingly, showing his friends. I wait, acting impatient.

"I want it back," I say finally. "We cannot duel if you hold both weapons."

Paul can't believe me. He is tired of my insolent manner. I begin to tire of him as well. "You's a smart-mouthed bitch. Why should I give you this knife? You might stick it in me while I'm lovin' you."

I nod. "Oh, I'm going to stick it in you, be sure of that. I don't mind that you and your buddies prowl these streets like hungry panthers. This is a jungle and only the strong survive. I understand that, better than you can imagine. But even the jungle has rules. Don't take what you don't need, and if you do, be a sportsman about it. But you're not a sportsman, Paul. You have taken my knife and I want it back. Give it to me right now or you will suffer unpleasantly." I stick out my hand and add in a voice as dark as my long life, "Very unpleasantly."

His anger shows; his cheeks darken with blood. He is not a true animal of the jungle, or he would recognize a poisonous snake when he saw it. He is a coward. Rather than hand over my knife, he tries to slash my open palm with it. Of course he misses because my hand is no longer where it was an instant before. I have withdrawn it to my side, at the same time launching my left foot at his gun. I hit only the revolver, not his hand, and see what the other three don't—the weapon landing on the roof of a three-story apartment complex off to one side. Paul's buddies back up, but he continues looking for his gun. His mouth works, but words are slow to form.

"Huh?" he finally says.

I reach out and grab him by the hair, pulling him close, my left hand closing on his hand that holds my knife. Now he feels my gaze as beamed through a magnifying glass set in the hot sun. He trembles in my grip, and for the first time he must realize how many different kinds of animals are in the jungle. I lean close to his ear and speak softly.

"I see that you have killed before, Paul. That's okay—I have killed, too, many times. I am much older than I look, and as you now know, I am also much stronger. I am going to kill you, but before I do I want to know if you have any final requests. Tell me quick, I'm in a hurry."

He turns his head away, but his eyes cannot escape mine. He tries to pull away and finds we are momentarily welded together. Sweat drips from his face like the river of tears the families of his victims have shed. His partners back farther away. Paul's lower lip trembles.

"Who are you?" he gasps.

I smile. "I'm a party girl, like you said." I lose my smile. "No final requests? Too bad. Say goodbye to mortality. Say hello to the devil for me. Tell him I'll be there soon, to join you."

My words, a poor joke to torment a victim I care nothing for. Yet there is a grain of truth in them. I feel a wave of pain in my chest as I pull Paul closer. It is from the wound when a stake impaled me the night Yaksha perished, a wound that never really healed. Since that night, six weeks earlier, I have never been totally free of pain. And I have begun to suspect I never will be. The full extent of the anguish comes upon me at unexpected moments, fiery waves that roll up like lava. I gag and have to bend over and close my eyes. I have suffered a hundred serious injuries in my fifty centuries, I tell myself. Why does this one not leave me in peace? Truly, a life in constant pain is the life of the damned.

Yet I did not disobey Krishna when I made Ray—not really, I try to convince myself.

Even Yaksha believed I still had the Lord's grace.

"Oh, God," I whisper and clench Paul's blood-filled body to me as if it were a bandage that could seal my invisible scar. I feel myself begin to faint, but just when I feel I can take no more of the surging pain, I hear footsteps in the distance. Quick-sounding footsteps, moving with the speed and power of an immortal. The shock of this realization is like cold water on my burning agony. There is another vampire nearby! I jerk upright, open my eyes. Paul's buddies are fifty feet away and still backing up. Paul looks at me as if he is staring into his own coffin.

"I didn't mean to hurt you, Alisa," he mumbles.

I suck in a deep breath, my heartbeat roaring in my ears. "Yes, you did," I reply and slam the knife down into his right thigh, just above the knee. The blade goes in cleanly, and the tip comes out red and dripping on the other side. An expression of pure horror grips his face, but I have no more time for his excuses. I have bigger game to bag. As I let go of him, he falls to the ground like a trash can that has been kicked over. Turning, I run in the direction of the immortal's footsteps. I leave my knife behind for Paul to enjoy.

The person is a quarter mile away, on the rooftops, leaping from building to building. I cut the distance in half before leaping onto the roofs myself, getting above the three stories in two long steps. Dashing between shattered chimneys and rusty fans, I catch a glimpse of my quarry—a twenty-year-old African-American male youth with muscles bulky enough to squash TVs. Yet a vampire's strength has little to do with this muscle power. Power is related to the purity of the blood, the intensity of the soul, the length of the life. I, who was created at the dawn of civilization by Yaksha, the first of the vampires, am exceptionally strong. Leaping through the air, I know I can catch the other vampire in a matter of seconds. Yet I hold back on purpose, I wish to see where he leads me.

That my prey is indeed a vampire I don't doubt for a second. His every movement matches those of a newborn blood sucker. Also, vampires emit a very subtle fragrance, the faint odor of snake venom, and the soul who runs before me smells like a huge black serpent. The smell is not unpleasant, rather intoxicating to most mortals. I have often used it in the past, on lovers and foes alike. Yet I doubt this young man is even aware of it.

But he is aware of me, oh, yes. He doesn't stop to attack, but continues to run away—he is afraid. I ponder this. How does he know my power? Who told him? My questions are all the same. Who made him? It is my hope that he runs to his maker for help. The pain in my chest has subsided, but I am still thirsty, still anxious for the hunt. To a vampire, another vampire's blood can be a special treat, salt and pepper sprinkled on a rare steak. I move forward without fear. If the guy has partners, so be it. I will destroy them all and then fly back to Oregon in my private jet before the sun comes up, my veins and belly full. Briefly I wonder how Ray is doing without me. His adjustment to being a vampire has been long and painful. I know, without me there, he will not feed.

I hear an ice-cream truck nearby.

In the middle of the night. Odd.

My prey comes to the end of the row of apartment buildings and leaps to the ground with one long flying stride. He stumbles as he contacts the earth. I could take this opportunity to land on his back and break every bone in his spine, but I let him continue on his way. I now know where he is headed— Exposition Park, the home of L.A.'s museums, Memorial Sports Arena, and Memorial Coliseum. It is the Coliseum, where the 1984 Olympics were held, that I guess, is his ultimate destination. He speeds across the vacant parking lot like the Roadrunner in the cartoon. It is lucky there are no mortals standing around to watch me chase him because I am the Coyote, and this is not Saturday morning TV. I am going to catch him, and there will be little of him left when I am done.

The tall fence surrounding the Coliseum is already broken open, and this fact slows me slightly. Briefly I reconsider my boldness. I can easily handle five or six vampires such as the guy I am chasing, but not a dozen, certainly not a hundred. And how many there are, I really don't know. For me the Coliseum may turn out to be like the one in ancient Rome. Yet I am a gladiator at heart, and although I enter the Coliseum cautiously, I do not stop.

I am inside the structure only two minutes when I smell blood. A moment later I find the mangled body of a security guard. Flies buzz above his ripped-out throat; he has been dead several hours. My prey has slipped from my view, but I follow his movements with my ears. I am on the lower level, in the shadows beneath the stands. He is inside the Coliseum proper, running up the bleachers. My hearing stretches out, an expanding wave of invisible radar, as I stand rock still. There are three other souls in the Coliseum, and none of them is human. I track the steps. They meet together at the north end of the building, speak softly, then fan out to the far corners. I doubt that they know my exact whereabouts, but their plan is clear. They wish to surround me, come at me from every direction. I don't wish to disappoint them.

Leaving my shelter, I stride openly down a concrete tunnel and out onto the field, where the moon shimmers on the grass like radioactivity on an atomic blast site. I see the four vampires at the same time they see me. They pause as I hurry to the fifty-yard line. Let them come to me, I think. I want time to observe them, see if they have weapons. A bullet in the brain, a knife in the heart, might kill me, although the wooden stake through my chest did not, six weeks ago. The pain awakens with the memory, but I will it away. These four are my problem now.

The moon is almost straight overhead. Three vampires continue to move to their corners; the one at the north end is in place and stands motionless, watching me. He is the only Caucasian, tall, thin, his bony hands like a fossilized skeleton. Even in the silver light, in the distance, I note the startling green of his eyes, the bloodshot veins that surround his glowing pupils like the strings of a red-stained spiderweb. He is the leader, and the cocky smile on his acne-scarred face reveals his confidence. He is thirty, maybe, but he will get no older, because I believe he is about to die. He is the one I wish to question, to drink from. I think of the security guard, the girl in the morning's paper. I will kill him slowly and enjoy it.

None of them appears to carry any weapons, but I look around for one for myself, regretting the loss of my knife, which I can fling over a quarter of a mile with deadly accuracy. It is mid-December, as I have said, but I see a collection of track and field equipment at the side of the field. The person in charge of equipment must have forgotten to put it away. I note the presence of a javelin. As the leader studies me, I move casually in the direction of the equipment. But he is sharp, this cold, ugly man, and he knows what I am going for. With a hand movement he signals to his partners to start toward me.

The three dark figures move quickly down the steps. In seconds they have cleared the bleachers and leaped onto the track that surrounds the field. But in those seconds I have reached the equipment and lifted the javelin in my right hand.

It is a pity there is only one spear. I raise my empty left hand in the direction of the leader, still far away at the top of the bleachers.

"I would like to talk," I call. "But I am fully capable of defending myself."

The smile on the leader's face, over two hundred yards away, broadens. His goons also grin, although not with the same confidence. They know I am a vampire. They eye the javelin and wonder what I will do with it, such silly young immortals. I keep an eye on all three of them, although I continue to face in the direction of the leader.

"It is always a mistake to decide to die hastily," I call.

The leader reaches behind and removes a knife from his back pocket. There is fresh blood on the tip, I see. I am not worried that he can hit me from such a distance since my ability with my knife has only come after centuries of practice. Yet he handles the weapon skillfully, balancing it in his open palm. The young man whom I chased into the Coliseum is in front of me, between me and the leader. Four against one, I think. I will improve the odds. In a move too swift for mortal eyes to follow, I launch my javelin toward the young man. Too late he realizes my strength and agility. He tries to jump aside but the tip catches him square in the chest, going through his rib cage and spine. I hear the blood explode in his ruptured heart. A death grunt escapes his lip as he topples, the long sharp object sticking through his body.

I hear the whistle of a flying blade.

Too late I realize the skill of the leader.

I dodge to the left, fast enough to save my own heart but not fast enough to avoid having the knife planted in my right shoulder near my arm socket—up to the hilt. The pain is immense, and a wave of weakness shakes my limbs. Without wanting to, I fall to my knees, reaching up to pull out the blade. The other two run toward me at high speed, and I know it will be a matter of seconds before they are on me. Taking his time, the leader begins to descend the steps of the bleachers. I realize that the knife I have in me is my *own*. Obviously the leader observed my little episode with Paul, and yet had time to relieve him of my knife and be here to meet me at the Coliseum. How powerful is he? Can I, wounded as I already am, handle him?

I suspect Paul is no longer suffering any pain from his leg wound.

The other two vampires, not the leader, are my immediate problem. I manage to pull the knife free just as the first one lowers his head to ram me. In a slashing motion I let fly my blade and watch as it goes deep into the top of the man's cranium. Yet I am too weak to dodge aside, and although already dead, he strikes me and knocks me over. I hit the ground hard, two hundred pounds of human meat on top of me. Blood pours over my side from a severed artery deep in my shoulder and for a moment I fear I will pass out. But I do not lie down easily, not while an enemy still stands. I shake off the dead vampire as the third one raises a foot to stomp my face. This one lacks speed, however, and I am able to avoid the blow. Still on the ground, rolling in my own blood, I lash out with my left foot and catch his right shin below the knee, breaking the bone. He lets out a cry and falls, and I am on him in an instant, pinning his massive black arms to the grass carpet with my knees. In the distance I see the leader continue to approach slowly, still confident I will be there, easy prey. For the first time I wonder if I should stay around. I have no time to question the vampire below me at length, as I would like to. I grab his hair, pulling at the roots.

"Who is your leader?" I demand. "What's his name?"

He cannot be more than twenty-five and have been a vampire for longer than a month. A babe in the woods. He doesn't realize the full extent of his peril, even after having seen what I did to his friends. He sneers at me and I believe he will have a short experience at immortality.

"Go to hell, bitch," he says.

"Later," I reply. Had the situation been different I would have reasoned with him, tortured him. Instead I wrap my hands around his neck, and before he can cry out, I twist his head all the way around, breaking every bone in his neck. He goes lifeless beneath me. The next moment I am up and removing my knife from the skull of victim number two. The leader sees me grasp the weapon, but neither accelerates nor slows his approach. His expression is an odd mixture of detachment and eagerness. Indeed, only fifty yards from me now, he looks like a neon nutcase. Well, I think, he will be a dead nut in a moment. Placing the knife in my left palm, I cock my arm and let the blade fly, aiming directly for his heart, as he aimed for mine. I know that I will not miss.

And I don't, in a sense. But I do.

He *catches* the knife in midair, inches from his chest.

He catches it by the handle, something even I could not do.

"Oh, no," I whisper. The guy has the power of Yaksha.

I don't suppose he wants to talk out our difficulties.

Turning, I bolt for the tunnel through which I entered the field. My shoulder throbs, my heart pounds. Each step I take I feel will be my last. The knife will come hurtling again, cut me between the shoulder blades, plunge deep into my heart, which has already been so badly injured. Maybe it will be for the best. Maybe then the pain will finally stop. But, in my heart, I don't want it to stop. Because the pain at least makes me know that I am alive, and I cherish my life above all things, even if I do sometimes take life casually from others. And if I do die, before *he* dies, what will become of life on earth? No question. I know this guy is bad news.

Yet he does not cut me down. He does not, however, let me go, either. I hear him accelerate behind me, and I understand he wants to talk to me—under his own terms—before he drinks my blood. He wants to suck away all my power and feel me die in his arms. But that, I swear, is a privilege he will not have.

Running down the long concrete tunnel, my boots pound like machine gun bullets, his steps like burning tracers behind me, closing, yard by yard. I simply do not have the strength to outrun him. Yet it is not my intention to try. After killing the security guard, these brothers of the night did not bother to remove the man's revolver. Entering the Coliseum, over-confident in my invincibility, I didn't either. But now that gun is my last hope. If I can get to it before my assailant gets to me, I can teach him what it is like to bleed from terrible wounds. I am not large, only ninety-eight pounds naked, and I have already lost at least two pints of blood. Desperately I need to stop, to catch my breath and heal. The security guard's gun can give me that opportunity.

I reach the corpse with the monster only a hundred feet behind me. In a flash he realizes my plan. As I pull the revolver free of its holster, out the corner of my eye I see the powerful vampire wind up with the knife. He will use it now, and not care if he spills what is left of my blood. He must know how difficult bullets are to catch, to dodge, especially when fired by another vampire. Yet I still hope to dodge this knife throw. Gripping the gun firmly, I leap up as I pivot, flying high into the air. Unfortu-nately, my maneuver does not catch him by surprise. As I open fire, his knife, *my* knife, for the second time, plunges into my body, into my abdomen, near my belly button. It hurts. God,

I cannot believe how unlucky I am. Yet there is a chance I can survive, and his good fortune is surely over. While coming down from my leap, I open fire, hitting him as best I can even though he jerks to avoid a fatal wound. I put a bullet in his stomach, one in his neck, his left shoulder, two in his chest. As I hit the ground, I expect him to hit the ground.

But he doesn't. Although staggering, he remains on his feet.

"Oh, Christ," I whisper as I fall to my knees. Will this bastard not die? Across the black shadows of the underbelly of the bleachers, we stare at each other, both bleeding profusely. For a moment our eyes lock, and more than ever I sense the disturbance in him, a vision of reality that no human or vampire should want to share. I am out of bullets. He seems to smile—I don't know what he finds so amusing. Then he turns and shuffles away, and I cannot see him or hear him. Pulling the knife from my naked belly, I swoon on the ground, trying to breathe through a haze of red agony. I honestly cannot remember the last time I had such a bad night.

Still, I am Sita from the dawn of humanity, a vampire of incomparable resiliency—unless, of course, I am to be compared to him, this fiend whose name I still do not know. He is not dead, I am sure of it. And after maybe twenty minutes of writhing on the concrete, I know I will survive. Finally my wounds begin to close and I am able to sit up and draw in a deep breath. Before taking the stake through the heart, my wounds would have closed in two minutes.

"I must be getting old," I mutter.

I cannot hear any vampires in the vicinity. But police are closing in on the Coliseum. After putting my knife back in its proper place under my pant leg, I stumble back up the concrete tunnel and onto the field. I find a hose and wash off as much blood as possible. My shoulder, my belly—they are not scarred. Yet I have lost much blood and am terribly weak, and now I have to worry about the police. Their cruisers park outside the arena. Somebody must have called about the gunshots. With so many bodies lying around, it would be a mistake to be caught inside the Coliseum. I would be taken downtown for questioning, where my messy clothes would be difficult to explain. I wonder if I should hide inside until things cool off, but, no, that might take hours, if not days, and I am anxious to return home and speak to Ray to figure out what to do next.

But before I leave the arena, I check on the three vampires to make sure they are indeed dead. It is always possible, despite the severity of their wounds, that they could heal and rise again. To be doubly sure, I crack each of their skulls with the heel of my right boot. The grotesque acts cause me no qualms of conscience. I am, after all, just protecting the officers who might find them.

I hurry in the direction of the least amount of noise and am outside, over the fence, and in the parking lot when a bright searchlight suddenly focuses on me. It is from a cruiser, damn. It pulls up alongside me, and a cop who looks as if he has been eating doughnuts for the last twenty years sticks his head out the passenger side.

"What are you doing here at this time of night, young lady?" he asks.

I appear anxious. "I'm trying to find my car. It broke down about an hour ago and I went looking for help and these boys started chasing me. They threw water balloons at me and threatened me." I shiver, catching his eye, pressing his belief buttons. "But I managed to get away."

The cop looks me over from head to foot, but I doubt he notices the bloodstains on my clothes. In the dark they would be hard to see on black clothes. Plus my gaze has shriveled his will. He is swayed by my great beauty, my obvious youth, my long blond hair, which I have let down. He throws his partner behind the wheel a look, then turns back to me and smiles.

"You're lucky all they threw was water balloons," he says. "This is no area to be walking alone at night. Hop in the back and we'll take you back to your car."

It will appear odd to decline the offer. "Thank you," I say, reaching for the door. I climb in the rear seat of the patrol car. His partner, a younger man, glances back at me.

"Were you inside the Coliseum just now?" he asks.

I catch his eye as well. "No," I say clearly. "How could I possibly be in the Coliseum? The fence is fifteen feet high."

He nods like a puppet. "We've just had some trouble in the area is all."

"I understand," I say.

A man calls on their radio. The fat officer explains how they ran into me. The man on the other end is not impressed with my story. He orders them to hold me until he arrives. There is strength in the man's voice, even over the staticky line. I wonder if I will be able to control him as easily as the other two. We sit and wait for the boss to arrive; the officers apologize for the delay. I consider drinking both officers' blood and leaving them dazed and incoherent, but I've always had a thing for cops. The fat one offers me a doughnut, which does little to satisfy my deeper hunger.

The man who arrives is not LAPD but FBI. He pulls up alone in an unmarked car, and I am told to get in up front. I do not resist. He introduces himself as Special Agent Joel Drake, and he has an aura of authority about him. A young man, he has blond hair almost as light as my own, and blue eyes as well, although these are darker than mine. He wears a sea blue sport coat, expensive white slacks. He is strikingly handsome. I feel, as I climb in beside him, like an actor in a series. *Agent Vampire*—there should be such a show. His face is tan, his features sharp and intelligent. He studies me in the dome light before shutting his door. He notices that I am soaking wet, although, once again, the bloodstains on my black outfit are all but invisible. The other officers drive off.

"What's your name?" he asks.

"Alisa Perne."

"Where's your car?"

"I don't know exactly. I've been walking for an hour, lost."

"You say you got hit with water balloons thrown at you by a bunch of guys? You expect me to believe that?"

"Yes," I say, and I catch his eye, such beautiful eyes really. I hesitate to blunt his will too forcibly, afraid it might damage him. Yet he is strong; he will not be moved without great power. Nevertheless, I cannot let him take me in for questioning. Lowering my voice, I pitch my tone in such a manner that he will feel as if I am speaking between his ears, as if he were in fact thinking what I am saying.

"I have done nothing wrong," I say gently. "Everything I tell you is true. I am a young woman, helpless, a stranger here. The best thing you can do is take me to my car."

He considers what I say for several seconds. I know my voice runs like an echo inside him. Then he shakes himself, seemingly throwing off my implant. I can sense his emotions, although I cannot read his thoughts. His doubt remains strong. He reaches out and shuts his door; the engine is already running.

"Have you been inside the Coliseum tonight?" he asks.

"No. What's inside the Coliseum?"

"Never mind. The police say they found you here, in the parking lot. What were you doing here?"

"Fleeing from the guys who harassed me."

"How many were there?"

"I'm not sure. Three or four."

"We have a report from two young men in the area. They say their buddy was attacked by someone who fits your description. Minutes ago we found their buddy's body, lying in a gutter. What do you have to say about that?"

I grimace. "I know nothing about it. How did he die?"

Joel frowns. "Violently."

I shake my head, looking anxious. "I was just trying to get back to my car. Can't you take me there? It's been a long night for me."

"Where are you from?"

"Oregon. I don't know L.A. I took a wrong exit and then my car stalled. But with your help, I might be able to find it." I reach over and touch his arm, holding his eyes once more, but softly, without fire. "Please?" I say.

He nods finally and puts the car in gear. "Which exit did you get off?"

"I forget the name. It's up here. I can show you, and maybe we can retrace my steps." I point as we pull out of the parking lot and head north in the direction of the freeway. "Honestly, I've never hurt anyone in my life."

He chuckles bitterly. "I don't imagine you had anything to do with what happened tonight."

"I've heard L.A.'s a violent town."

He nods grimly. "Especially lately. I suppose you've read the papers?"

"Yes. Are you in charge of the murder investigation?"

"Several of us are overseeing it."

"Have you any leads?"

"No. But that's off the record."

I smile. "I'm not a reporter, Agent Drake."

He smiles faintly. "You shouldn't get within twenty miles of this area at night. How long are you going to be in L.A.?"

"Why?"

"We might need to ask you more questions later."

"I'll be around. I can give you a number once we find my car."

"That's fine. Did you get off the Harbor Freeway or the Santa Monica?"

"I was on the Santa Monica Freeway. Let's continue north a few blocks. I think I'll recognize the right street."

"How old are you, Alisa?"

"Twenty-two."

"What's your business in L.A.?"

"I'm visiting friends. I'm thinking of going to school here next year."

"Oh. Where?"

"USC."

"The Coliseum is right next to USC."

"That's the reason I was driving around here. One of my friends lives on campus." I shiver again. "But with all this violence I'm seriously reconsidering my choice of universities."

"That's understandable." He glances over, checking out my body this time. He does not wear a wedding ring. "So you're a student. What are you majoring in?"

"History," I say.

We drive without talking for a few minutes, me merely pointing where I think we should turn next. Actually, I do not want to take him to my car because even though he is responding to my suggestions, he still has a will of his own. And he is obviously highly trained. He would memorize my license plate number if I brought him to my rental. A block from where I have parked, passing a red Honda, I signal for him to stop.

"This is it," I say, opening the car door. "Thank you so much."

"Do you think it will start now?" he asks.

"Why don't you pull in front of me and wait to see if I can get it started." I add, a sexy note in my voice, "Could you do that for me?"

"No problem. Alisa, do you have any ID on you?"

I grin foolishly. "I knew you were going to ask that. I'm afraid I'm driving without my license. But I can give you a number where I'll be tomorrow. It's 310-555-4141. This is a genuine L.A. number that will ring through to my house in Oregon. You can call me there any time for the next three days. Do you want me to write the number down for you?"

He hesitates, but I know he is thinking that with my license plate number he can always trace me. "That's not necessary, it's an easy number to remember." He pauses again, studying the damp marks on my shirt. There is no way he can tell they're bloodstains just by looking at them, but I have to wonder if he can smell the odor, even after my heavy washing. Despite my subtle influence, he would never let me go if he definitely saw blood. And I am not free yet. "Can you give me an address as well?" he asks.

"Joel," I say in my special way. "You don't really think I killed anyone, do you?"

He backs away slightly. "No."

"Then why do you want all these things from me?"

He hesitates, shrugs. "If you have an address, I will take it. Otherwise your phone number is enough for me for now." He adds, "We'll probably talk tomorrow."

"Good enough. It was nice meeting you." I step out of his car. "Now I just hope the damn thing starts."

Joel pulls in front of me and waits, as I suggested. It was not a suggestion I made willingly, but felt I needed to allay his suspicions. The Honda door is locked, but I open it with a hard yank and slip behind the wheel. With two fingers I break the ignition switch, noting how Joel studies my license plate number in his rearview mirror. He writes it down as I press the contact wires together and the engine turns over. I wave as I quickly pull away from the curb. I don't want the people in the adjacent house to hear me leaving with their car.

After driving around the block, I get into my own car, and in less than an hour I am in the air, flying in my personal Learjet toward Oregon. Yet I know I will return to Los Angeles soon to finish the war with the powerful vampire.

For good or evil.

Ray is not home when I get there. Our residence is new, obviously, since my original house blew up with Yaksha inside. Our modern mansion in the woods is not far from the old house. It has many electronic conveniences, a view of the ocean, and heavy drapes to block out the midday sun. More than any other vampire I have known, Ray is the most excruciatingly sensitive to the sun. He is made like a Bram Stoker model vampire out of old legends. Many things about his new existence trouble him. He misses his school friends, his old girlfriend, and especially his father. But I can give him none of these things—certainly not his father, since it was I who killed the man. I can only give him my love, which I dreamed would be enough. I am only in the house two minutes before I am back in my car looking for him. Dawn is an hour away.

I find him sitting on his ex-lover's porch, but Pat McQueen is unaware of his nearness. Along with her parents, she is sleeping inside. I know she thinks Ray perished in the blast that supposedly took my life, too. He sits with his head buried in his knees and doesn't even bother to look up as I approach. I let out a sigh.

"What if I was a cop?" I ask.

He looks up, his melancholy consuming his beauty. Yet my heart aches to see him again; it has ached ever since he entered my life, both the physical heart and the emotional one. Radha, Krishna's friend, once told me that longing is older than love, and that one cannot exist without the other. Her name, in fact, meant longing, and Krishna's meant love. But I never saw how their relationship tortured them the way my passion for Ray does me. I have given him the kingdom of eternal night, and all he wants to do is take a walk under the sun. I note his weakness, his hunger. Six weeks and I am still forcing him to feed, even though we don't harm or kill our meals. He doesn't look happy to see me, and that saddens me more.

"If you were a cop," he says, "I could easily disarm you."

"And create a scene doing it."

He nods to the blood on my top. "It looks as if you have created a scene or two tonight." When I don't respond, he adds, "How was Los Angeles?"

"I'll tell you back at the house." I turn. "Come."

"No."

I stop, glance back over my shoulder. "The sun will be up soon."

"I don't care."

"You will when you see it." He doesn't answer me. I go and sit beside him, put my arm around his shoulder. "Is it Pat? You can talk to her, you know, if you must. I just think it's a bad idea."

He shakes his head. "I cannot talk to her."

"Then what are you doing here?"

He stares at me. "I come here because I have nowhere else to grieve."

"Ray."

"I mean, I don't know where my father's buried." He turns away and shrugs. "It doesn't matter. It's all gone."

I take his hand; he barely lets me. "I can take you to where I buried your father. But it's just a hole in the ground, covered over. It will not help you."

He looks up at the stars. "Do you think there are vampires on other planets?"

"I don't know. Maybe. In some distant galaxy there might be a whole planet filled with vampires. This planet almost was."

He nods. "Except for Krishna."

"Yes. Except for him."

He continues to stare at the sky. "If there were such a planet, where there were only vampires, it would not survive long. They would destroy one another." He looks at me. "Do I do that to you? Destroy you?"

I shake my head sadly. "No. You give me a great deal. I just wish I knew what to give you in return, to help you forget."

He smiles gently. "I don't want to forget, Sita. And maybe that is my problem." He pauses. "Take me to his grave. We won't stay long."

"Are you sure?"

"Yes."

I stand, offer him my hand. "Very well."

We drive into the woods. I lead him through the trees. I remember the spot where I buried P.I. Michael Riley, of course—I remember everything. Also, I smell the faint fumes of his decaying body as they seep up from beneath six feet of earth. I fear Ray smells them as well. The life of a vampire is a life of many corpses; they do not invoke in me the strong emotions they do in most humans. Ray drops to his knees as we reach the spot, and I retreat a few dozen feet because I want him to be alone with his emotions—a caldron of sorrows. I am still too weak to let them wash over me. Or else I am too guilty. I hear Ray weep dry tears on a missing tombstone.

My two most recent wounds have completely healed, but my chest continues to burn. I remember the night Ray pulled the stake from my heart while my house burned nearby. Barely conscious, I didn't know if I would live or die, and for the next three days Ray didn't, either. Because even though my wound closed quickly, I remained unconscious. All that time I had the most extraordinary dream.

I was in a starship flying through space. Ray was beside me and our destination was the Pleiades star cluster, the Seven Sisters, as it is often called by astronomers. Outside our forward portals, we could see the blue-white stars growing steadily in size and brilliance, and although our journey was long, we were filled with excitement the whole time. Because we knew we were finally returning home to where we belonged, where we weren't vampires, but angels of light who lived on the radiance of the stars alone. The dream was painful to awaken from, and I still pray each time I lie down to sleep that it will return. The color of the stars reminded me of Krishna's eyes.

Ray spills his grief quickly. We are back in the car and headed for home as the eastern sky begins to lighten. My lover sits silently beside me, staring at nothing, and my own dark thoughts keep my lips closed. My energy is at a low, but I know I mustn't rest, not until I have formulated a plan to stop the black plague spreading six hundred miles south of us. He of the wicked eyes will make more vampires the next night, I know. Replacements for the ones I destroyed. And they in turn will make their own. Each day, each hour, is crucial. The human race is in danger. Krishna, I pray, give me the strength to destroy this enemy. Give me the strength not to destroy myself.

As Ray lies down to rest, I let him drink from my veins, a

little, enough to get him through the day. Even that mouthful drains me more. Yet I do not lie down beside him as he closes his eyes to sleep. Let him dream of his father, I think. I will tell him of Los Angeles later.

I visit my friend Seymour Dorsten. Twice I have seen him since I destroyed the AIDS virus in his blood with a few drops of mine. His health is greatly improved. He has a girlfriend now and I tell him I am jealous, but he doesn't believe me. I climb in his window and wake him by shoving him off his bed and onto the floor. He grins as his head contacts the hard wood with a loud thud. Only my Seymour would welcome such treatment.

"I was dreaming about you," he says, his blankets half covering his face.

"Did I have my clothes on?" I ask.

"Of course not." He sits up and rubs the back of his head. "What the eyes have seen, the mind cannot forget."

"When did you ever see me naked?" I ask, although I know the answer.

He chuckles in response. I do not fool him, Seymour the Great, my personal biographer. Knowing our psychic bond, I wonder if he has spent the night writing about my trials, but he shakes his head when I ask. He watched a video with his new girl and went to bed early.

I tell him about Los Angeles, why I am bloody.

"Wow," he says when I am done.

I lean back on his bed, resting my back against the wall. He continues to sit on the floor. "You're going to have to do better than that," I say.

He nods. "You want me to help you figure out where they're coming from."

"They're coming from that monster. I have no doubt about that. I want to know where he came from." I shake my head. "I thought about it all the way here, and I have no explanation."

"There is always an explanation. Do you remember the famous Sherlock Holmes quote? 'When you have eliminated the impossible, whatever remains, no matter how improbable, must be the truth.'" Seymour thinks, his palms pressed together. "A vampire that strong could only have been created by Yaksha."

"Yaksha is dead. Also, Yaksha would not have created a vampire. He was bound by the vow he made to Krishna. He spent the last five thousand years destroying them."

"How do you know Yaksha is dead? Maybe he survived the blast."

"Highly unlikely."

"But not impossible. That's my point. Yaksha was the only one besides you who could make another vampire. Unless you want to bring in the possibility that another yakshini has been accidentally invoked into the corpse of a pregnant woman."

"Don't remind me of that night," I growl.

"You're in a bad mood. But I suppose being stabbed twice in the same night, with your own knife, would do that to anybody."

I smile thinly. "Are you making fun of me? You know, I'm thirsty. I could open your veins right now and drink my fill and there would be nothing you could do about it."

Seymour is interested. "Sounds kinky. Should I take off my clothes?"

I throw a pillow at him, hard. It almost takes off his head. "Haven't you been able to get that girl of yours into bed? What's wrong with you? With my blood in your veins, you should be able to have who you want when you want."

He rubs his head again, probably thinking it is going to be sore for the rest of the day. "How do you know I haven't slept with her yet?"

"I can spot a male virgin a mile away. They walk like they've been riding a horse too long. Let's return to our problem. Yaksha would not have made this guy. It's out of the question. Yet you are right—Yaksha is the only one who could have made him. A paradox. How do I solve it? And how do I destroy this creature that clearly has at least twice my strength and speed? Tell me, young author, and I might let you live long enough to enjoy carnal pleasure with this silly girl you have foolishly chosen over me."

"I'm sorry, I can't answer your questions. But I can tell you where you must look to find the answers."

"Where?"

"Where you left the trail last. Where you last saw Yaksha. He went up in the blast you set at your house, but even dynamite leaves remains. Find out what became of those remains, and you might find out how your new enemy came to be."

I nod. His reasoning is sound, as always. "But even if I learn how he came to be, I still have to learn how to destroy him."

"You will. Yaksha was a more difficult foe. He knew at least as much as you about what a vampire could or could not do. The way this guy is carrying on, he must be newborn. He is still learning what he is. He doesn't know where he is weak. Find him, strike at that weak point, and he will fall."

I slip down onto the floor and kneel to kiss Seymour on the lips. Gently I toss up his hair. "You are so confident in me," I say. "Why is that?"

He starts to say something funny, but his expression falters. He trembles slightly beneath my touch. "Is he really that bad?" he asks softly.

"Yes. You are wrong when you say Yaksha was a more difficult foe. In his own way, Yaksha was a protector of mankind. This guy is a psychopath. He is bent on destroying all humanity. And he could succeed. If I don't stop him soon, nothing will."

"But you saw him only briefly."

"I looked deep into his eyes. I saw enough. Believe what I tell you."

Seymour touches my face, admiration, and love, in his eyes. "I have confidence in you because when you met me I was as good as dead and you saved me. You're the hero in my story. Find him, Sita, corner him. Then kick his ass. It will make for a great sequel." He adds seriously, "God will help you."

I squeeze his hand carefully, feeling once more my weakness, my pain. It will not leave me, I am certain, until I leave this world. The temptation is there before me for the first time. To just run and hide in oblivion. Yet I know I must not, I cannot. Like Yaksha, I have one last duty to perform before I die and return to the starry heaven of my dream.

Or to a cold hell. But I do not like the cold.

No vampire does. Like snakes, it slows us down.

"I fear the devil will help him," I say. "And I'm not sure who's stronger."

THREE

*T*he sun is firmly in the sky as I sit in my office to sort out what to do next. Three types of profession-als arrived after my house blew up six weeks earlier: firefighters, police officers, and paramedics. Ray told me this. They didn't talk to Ray, who had dragged me out of sight into the woods, but I contacted them later once I had regained consciousness. I pleaded innocent to any knowledge of the explosion: its cause or the reason it was rigged. At that time they didn't tell me of any human remains found in the vicinity. That, of course, doesn't mean a body wasn't found. The police could have withheld that information from me. For all I know I am still under investigation for the explosion and whatever was discovered in the area.

I need a contact with the local police and I need it immediately. The paramedics and the hospital would have the remains of Yaksha, but if I do not go through the proper channels and authorities, they will show me nothing. With my extensive contacts and wealth, I can develop a contact, but it will take time. As I sit at my desk, thinking, a light on my phone begins to blink. It is an out-of-state call. I pick it up.

"Yes?" I say.

"Alisa?"

"Yes. Agent Joel Drake—how nice of you to call." I make a decision immediately, figuring it is a sign from Krishna that the FBI man has phoned at this precise instant. Of course, I do not believe in signs, I am just desperate. I add, "I've been meaning to call you. There are some things we should discuss that I failed to bring up last night."

He is interested. "Such as?"

"I have a lead on who is behind the murders."

He takes a moment. "Are you serious?"

"Yes. I have a very good lead."

"What is it?"

"I will only tell you in person. Fly into Portland this afternoon and I'll pick you up at the airport. I guarantee you'll be glad you came."

"I thought you said you wouldn't be leaving town for a few days?"

"I lied. Call the airlines. Book your flight."

He chuckles. "Hold on a second. I can't fly up to Oregon

in the middle of an investigation. Tell me what you know and then we can talk."

"No," I say firmly. "You must come here."

"Why?"

"The murderer is from here."

"How do you know that?"

I pitch my voice in my most beguiling manner. "I know many things, Agent Drake. That one of the guys you found in the Coliseum had a javelin through his chest, the other had his skull stabbed open, and every bone in the neck of the third was shattered. Don't ask me how I know these things and don't tell your FBI pals about me. Not if you want to solve this case *and* get all the credit. Think about it, Joel, you can be the big hero."

My knowledge stuns him. He considers. "You misunderstand me, Alisa. I don't need to be a hero. I just want to stop the killing."

He is being sincere. I like that.

"It will stop if you come here," I say softly.

He closes his eyes; I hear them close. My voice will not leave his mind. He wonders if I am some kind of witch. "Who are you?" he asks.

"It doesn't matter. I will hold while you book your flight. Take the earliest one."

"I will have to tell my partners where I'm going."

"No. Just the two of us are going to work on this. That's my condition."

He chuckles again, this time without mirth. "You're pretty gutsy for a young woman."

I think of the knife that stabbed me in the belly less than twelve hours ago. "I have strong guts," I agree.

Joel puts me on hold. A few minutes later he returns. His plane will land in three hours. I agree to meet him at the gate. After setting down the phone, I leave my office and crawl into bed beside Ray. He stirs and turns his back to me but doesn't wake. Portland is an hour and a half away. I have only ninety minutes to rest before I must take on the enemy.

Joel looks tired when I pick him up at the airport. I don't imagine he got much sleep the previous night. He immediately starts with his questions, but I ask him to wait until we are in my car. Once inside I put on music, a tape of my playing the piano. We drive toward Mayfair. I am still thinking how I should approach this matter. Since we are dealing with evidence that points toward a mysterious agency, I am not worried about staying conservative.

"Who is the pianist?" he asks finally.

"Do you like it?"

"The music is haunting, and the pianist is wonderful."

An appropriate choice of words. "It's me."

"Are you serious?"

"You have asked me that twice today. I am always serious, Agent Drake."

"Joel, please. Is Alisa your real name?"

"Why? Have you been researching me?"

"A bit. I haven't turned up much."

"You mean, you haven't turned up an Alisa Perne in your computers?"

"That's correct. What's your real name and who taught you to play such exquisite piano?"

"I am self-taught. And I like to be called Alisa."

"You haven't answered my question."

"I answered one of them."

He stares at me. For a few sentences I forgot to be careful how I pitched my voice, and the echo of my age creeps into it. My words and voice, I know, can throb like living ghosts. My music is not the only thing that is haunting.

"How old did you say you were?" he asks.

"Older than I look. You want to know how I know about the murders."

"Among other things. You lied to me last night when you said you had not been in the Coliseum."

"That is correct. I was there. I saw the three young men in the field killed."

"Did you get a good look at the killer?"

"Good enough."

He pauses. "Do you know him?"

"No. But he is associated with a man I once knew. That man died in an explosion at my house six weeks ago. The reason I have brought you here is to help me trace the remains of that man. We are driving to the Mayfair Police Station now. I want you to ask them to open their files to you."

He shakes his head. "No way. You're going to answer my questions before I do anything to help you."

"Or you will arrest me?"

"Yes."

I smile thinly. "That will not happen. And I am not going to answer all your questions, just the ones I choose to answer. You have no choice but to cooperate with me. Like you said last night—you have no leads. And you are more in the dark than you admit. You have several people who seem to have been killed by a person of extraordinary strength. A person so strong, in fact, that he seems superhuman."

"I wouldn't go that far."

I snort softly. "It takes a great deal of strength to snap every cervical in a man's neck. Isn't that what the autopsy showed?"

Joel shifts uneasily, but I have his full attention. "The autopsy isn't complete on any of the victims."

"But the LAPD medical examiner has told you about the guy's neck. It makes you wonder, doesn't it?"

He speaks carefully. "Yes. It makes me wonder how you know these things."

I reach over and touch his leg. I have a very sensual touch, when I wish to flaunt it, and I must admit I find myself attracted to Joel. Not that I love him as I do Ray, but I wouldn't mind seducing him, as long as Ray wouldn't know. Having had ten thousand lovers, I don't share most mortals' illusions of the sacredness of fidelity. Yet I will not risk hurting Ray for sex, and I will not lie to him anymore. Joel feels the electricity of my fingers and shifts all the more. I like my boys fidgety.

"You want to say something?" I ask, my hand still on his thigh.

He clears his throat, "You are very alluring, Alisa. Particularly when you are being vague, or trying to be persuasive." He stares down at my hand as if trying to decide whether it is a priceless jewel or a spider that has crawled into his lap. "But I am beginning to see through your facade."

I remove my hand, not insulted. "Is that all it is? A facade?"

He shakes his head. "Where did you grow up?"

I burst out laughing. "In the jungle! A place not unlike where these murders are happening. I watched as that young man's neck was snapped. A normal person couldn't do that. The person you are looking for is not normal. Nor was my friend who died when my house blew up. If we can find what became of him, his remains, then we can find your murderer— I hope. But don't ask me how these people are not normal, how they have such strength, or even why my house was blown up. I won't tell you."

He keeps looking at me. "Are you normal, Alisa?" he asks.

"What do you think?"

"No."

I pat his leg. "It's all right. You go on thinking that way."

Yet, I think, he knows too much about me already.

When all this is over, I am going to have to kill Joel Drake.

FOUR

On the drive to Mayfair Joel tells me about his life. Maybe I pry the information out of him a bit. Maybe he has nothing to hide. I listen attentively and grow to like him more with each passing mile, much to my disquiet. Maybe that's his intention—to be open with me. Already, I think, he knows I am more dangerous than I appear.

"I grew up on a farm in Kansas. I wanted to be an FBI agent from the first time I saw that old series, *The F.B.I.*, that starred Efrem Zimbalist, Jr. Do you remember that show? It was great. I suppose I did have dreams of being a hero: catching bank robbers, finding kidnapped kids, stopping serial murderers. But when I graduated from the academy in Quantico, Virginia, I was assigned to white-collar crime in Cedar Rapids, Iowa. I spent twelve months chasing accountants. Then I got a big break. My landlady was murdered. Stabbed with a knife and buried in a cornfield. That was at the end of summer. The local police were called in, and they found the body pretty quick. They were sure her boyfriend did it. They even had the guy arrested and ready to stand trial. But I kept telling them he loved his woman and wouldn't have hurt her for the world. They wouldn't listen to me. There is an old rivalry between the FBI and police. Even in Los Angeles, working on this case, the LAPD constantly withholds information from me.

"Anyway, privately, I went after another suspect—the woman's sixteen-year-old son. I know, he sounds like an unlikely candidate—the woman's only child. But I knew her son as well as the boyfriend, and the kid was bad news. An addict ready to steal the change from a homeless person. I was their tenant and I caught him breaking into my car once to steal my radio. He was into speed. When he was high, he was manic—either the nicest guy in the world or ready to poke your eyes out. He had lost all sense of reality. At his mother's funeral he began to sing "Whole Lot of Love." Yet, at the same time, he was cunning. His bizarre behavior hid his guilt. But I knew he'd done it, and, as you're fond of saying, don't ask me why. There was something in his eyes when I talked to him about his mother—like he was thinking about how nice it was finally to have the house all to himself.

"The problem was, I didn't have a shred of evidence that linked him to the crime. But I kept watching him, hoping he'd reveal something. I was anxious to move to another place, but during my off hours, I told myself, I was on stakeout. I felt in my gut something would turn up.

"Then Halloween came, and that evening the sonofabitch was out on his front porch carving a huge jack-o'-lantern. He flashed me a nauseatingly sweet smile as I walked to my car, and something about his expression made me pause to look closer at his knife. By this time the victim's boyfriend was in the middle of his trial, and losing. As I mentioned, the woman had been stabbed, and as I studied her son and the pumpkin on his lap, I remembered how the autopsy report noted the unusual spacing of the metal teeth marks on the victim's skin. This knife was weird—the cutting edge had irregularly spaced ridges.

"I hid my interest in the knife with a nonchalant wave, but the next day I got a warrant to search the house. I obtained the knife, and its cutting edge was compared to the photographs taken by the coroner. There was a match. To make a long story short, the son was eventually convicted. He is serving a life sentence in Iowa as we speak." Joel adds, "All because of one jack-o'-lantern."

"All because of one sharp agent," I say. "Was your success on the case your ticket to bigger and better things?"

"Yes. My boss was pleased by my persistence, and I was put on a couple of old unsolved murder cases. I solved one of them and was promoted. I have been working difficult murder cases in L.A. ever since." He nods. "Persistence is the key to solving most mysteries."

"And imagination. Why did you tell me this story?"

He shrugs. "Just trying to make casual conversation with a potential witness."

"Not true. You want to see how I react to your tales of insight and intrigue."

He has to laugh. "What do you want with me, Alisa? To make me into a hero or a goat? I did as you requested—I told no one where I was going. But I'll have to call in some time today. And if I tell them I'm in Oregon riding around with a cute blond, it's not going to look good on my record."

"So you think I'm cute?" I ask.

"You catch the operative words, don't you?"

"Yes." I add, "I think you're cute as well."

"Thank you. Do you have a boyfriend?"

"Yes."

"Is he normal?"

I feel a pang in my chest. "He is wonderful."

"Can he verify where you were the last two days?"

"That's not necessary. I already told you I was in the Coliseum watching necks being broken and chests pierced. If there is guilt by association, then I'm guilty as sin."

"Aren't you worried about telling that to an FBI agent?"

"Do I look worried?"

"No. That's what worries me." His tone becomes business-like again. "How did this abnormal person break the young man's neck?"

"With his bare hands."

"But that's impossible."

"I told you not to ask me these questions. Let's wait till we get to Mayfair, see what we find out from the local police. Then perhaps I'll tell you more."

"I will have to call the local office of the FBI and have them notify the police that I'm coming. They won't open their files to me just because I walk in the front door."

I hand him my cell phone. "Notify whoever you have to, Joel."

The Mayfair police give us scant information, and yet it is crucial. While I wait in the car and listen to the conversation that takes place inside the station, Joel learns that there was a body recovered from the explosion at my house, not just pieces of flesh as I expected. I have to wonder—how did Yaksha's form survive the blast? He was more powerful than any creature that walked the earth, but even he should have had to bow to several crates of dynamite. The police tell Joel that the body was taken to a morgue in Seaside, seventy miles south of Mayfair, the city where I combated the people Yaksha sent after me, Slim and his partners.

"Please! I don't want to die."

"Then you should never have been born."

Slim's blood was bitter tasting, as was his end. So be it.

Joel returns to my car and I give him every chance to lie to me about what the police have told him. But he gives me the straight facts.

"We're going to Seaside," I say, handing him the phone again. "Tell them we're on our way."

"What was the name of your friend who died?"

"Yaksha."

"What kind of name is that?"

"It's Sanskrit." I glance over. "It's the name of a demonic being."

He dials the Seaside morgue. "Love the company you keep."

I can't resist—I give him a wink. "It's improving by the hour."

Joel is big-time FBI. The morgue is only too happy to show him whatever bodies they have on ice. The problem is, when we get there—this time I go inside with Joel—the body we are looking for is missing. Now I know what the Mayfair police were holding back. Joel looks irritated. I feel dizzy. Is Yaksha still alive? Did he create the monster who attacked me? If that is the case, then we are all doomed. Seymour can have all the confidence in the world in me, but I will not be able to stop my creator if he is bent on spreading our black blood. Yet it makes no sense. Yaksha was looking forward to his end, secure in the knowledge that he was going to his death having done the Lord's bidding.

"What do you mean, it's missing?" Joel demands. "What happened to it?"

The bespeckled coroner shakes at Joel's question. He is the kid who has been caught with his fingers in the cookie jar. Only this guy's fingers look as if they have been dipped in formaldehyde every morning for the last twenty years. The jaundice virus could be oozing out of his big ears. Here I am a vampire, but even I can't understand why anyone would want to be a coroner and work with corpses all day, even fresh ones filled with nice blood. Morticians are an even stranger lot. I once buried a mortician alive—in France after World War II—in his most expensive coffin. He made the mistake of saying all Americans were pigs, which annoyed me. He kicked like a pig as I shoveled the dirt on top of him. I enjoy a little mischief.

"We don't know for sure," the coroner replies. "But we believe it was stolen."

"Well, that's just great," Joel growls. "How long was the body here before it disappeared?"

"A week."

"Excuse me," I interrupt. "I am Special Agent Perne and an expert when it comes to forensic evidence. Are you absolutely sure the body we are discussing was in fact a body? That the person was dead?"

The coroner blinks as if he has tissue sample in his eyes. "What are you suggesting?"

"That the guy simply got up and walked out," I say.

"That would have been quite impossible."

"Why?" I ask.

"Both his legs had been blown off," the coroner says. "He was dead. We had him in the freezer all the time he was here."

"Do you know who might have stolen the body?" Joel asks.

The coroner straightens. "Yes. We had an employee here, an Eddie Fender, who vanished the same time as the body. He took off without even collecting his final paycheck. He worked the night shift and was often unsupervised."

"What was his position?" Joel asks.

"He was an orderly, of sorts."

I snort. "He helped prepare the bodies for dissection."

The coroner is insulted. "We do not dissect people, Agent Perne."

Joel raises his hand as a call for peace. "Do you have a résumé on this guy? A job application?"

The coroner nods. "We handed over copies of those items to the Seaside police. But you are welcome to see the originals. If you'll come into my office, I'll dig them out of our files."

"Go ahead," I say to Joel. "I want to browse, check out the sights."

He rolls his eyes. "Don't disturb the dead."

I check the individual freezer lockers in the back. My keen sense of smell brings me quickly to the one Yaksha occupied. The aroma of the venom—still there even in death, in ice. Yet the odor is not precisely as I remember it, even from six weeks or five thousand years ago. There is something wrong with the faint traces of his blood that remain in the cold locker. Somehow it has been polluted. Grotesque vibrations linger over the hollow space. If Yaksha is in fact dead, he did not leave the world thinking about Krishna, as he hoped. My disquiet deepens.

While Joel stays with the coroner, I wander deeper into the morgue and find an office space with a secretary with her feet up on her desk, doing her nails. I like a woman who doesn't take her job too seriously. This gal doesn't even bother to sit up as I walk in. Of course, to some, I look like a teenager. About thirty, she has a *National Enquirer* and a two-liter bottle of Diet Pepsi sitting on her desk beside a computer screen that keeps flashing: TEMPORARY MALFUNCTION! Her lips swim in red paint; her hair stands up like an antique wig. Twenty pounds overweight, she looks jovial, a little slutty.

"Wow," she says when she sees me. "Aren't you a pretty little thing! What are you doing in this haunted house?"

I smile. "I am with Special Agent Joel Drake. My name is Alisa Perne. We are investigating a murder."

Now she sits up. "You're FBI? You look like a cheer-leader."

I sit down. "Thank you. You look like an executive secretary."

She pulls out a cigarette and waves her hand. "Yeah, right. And this is the executive suite. What can I do for you?"

"Did you know Eddie Fender?"

"The guy who stole the stiff?"

"Did he steal it?"

She lights her cigarette. "Sure. He was in love with that corpse." She chuckles. "It did more for him than I ever did."

"Did you see Eddie socially?"

She leans forward and blows smoke. "You mean, did I screw him? Listen, sister, I would just as soon blow my brains out as do it with Eddie Fender, if you get my meaning."

I nod. "What's your name?"

"Sally Diedrich. I'm not German, just got the name. Is Eddie a suspect in a murder case?"

"We're just gathering background information at this point. I would appreciate anything you could tell me about him."

Sally whistles. "I could give you background on that guy that would make you want to turn your back and run the other way. Listen, you got a minute? Let me tell you a story about Eddie and his relationship to reality."

I cross my legs. "I have many minutes. Tell me everything you know."

"This happened three months ago. We had a temp in here helping me search through some of our oldest files for missing x-rays. Don't believe what the cops and the papers tell you— none of that forensic evidence should hold up in court. We're forever mixing autopsy reports together. We had a dead guy who stayed here a few days, and it says on his death certificate that he croaked because of a tubal pregnancy. Anyway, the temp's name was Heather Longston and she was pretty as pie, if a bit slow. Eddie flirted with her and asked her out, and she said sure before I could warn her. By the time I did talk to her, she felt 'committed.' That's an example of how stupid she was. A guy compliments her on her dress and offers to take her to dinner and she feels committed. Heather was the kind of girl who felt obligated to buy everything that gets sold over the phone. I visited her home once, and she had two sets of those carving knives that they say can be used as dowsing rods to find water and oil.

"So Heather went out with Eddie, and let me tell you, that was one date for Ripley's Believe It or Not! First, he took her to McDonald's for dinner. She told me he had three hamburgers, nothing else. No drink, no fries, no nothing. He ate the hamburgers plain—meat on a bun. Then he took her for a walk. Guess where he took her?"

"The cemetery," I say.

"You got it! He wolfed down his burgers and took her hand and they went tombstone sighting. Heather said he got all giddy when they got to the graves. He wanted to lie down on top of them and make out. Said it would give her a rush like she wouldn't believe. Well, she believed it. They made out six feet above some rotting corpse. Heather said he wasn't a bad kisser. He swiped some flowers off a grave and gave them to her as a present. The gesture touched her, I swear." Sally shook her head. "Isn't it just lovely when two loonies get together?"

"As lovely as when two uglies get together," I say.

"I hear you. Anyway, here comes the sick part. Eddie takes her back to his apartment to watch movies, and guess what he pulls out of his drawer?"

"Pornographic films?"

Sally leans farther forward. Her big breasts crush last week's work and push her bottle of Diet Pepsi aside. "Snuff films. Do you know what those are?"

"Yes. Movies made where people—usually women—are supposedly killed."

"Sick, huh? Eddie had a whole set of them. He showed Heather three or four—they're usually pretty short, I understand—before she figured out she wasn't watching the latest Disney releases. Then she got up and wanted to leave. The only problem was, Eddie wouldn't let her."

"Did he threaten to harm her?"

Sally scratched her head. "I'm not sure. I don't think so. But what he did do was tie Heather up in his bedroom closet, standing up and wearing his high school jacket—and nothing else—and force her to suck on Popsicles all night."

"How did he force her?"

"He would tickle her if she stopped. Heather was very ticklish. She worked those Popsicles until the sun came up. Said when she got home she felt as if she had gargled a whole pint of novocaine."

"But he didn't hurt her in any way?"

"Her wrists had rope burns on them, but other than that she was fine. I tried to get her to talk to the police about what had happened, but she wouldn't. She wanted to go out with him again! I said no way. I went to Eddie and told him if he saw Heather again, I would personally speak to the police about his collection of snuff films. They're illegal, you know. Of course you know that! You work for the FBI. Sorry, I forgot that for a moment, with you just sitting there looking so young and everything. Anyway, Eddie backed off 'cause he didn't want to lose his job. Jesus, I tell you, that guy was born to work with the dead. You'd think they were his Barbie dolls."

"You said he loved the corpse that was stolen. What do you mean?"

"He was always fooling with it."

"Exactly how did he fool with it?"

"I don't know. He just always had it out is all."

"Didn't anyone tell him to stop fooling with it?"

Sally giggled. "No! The corpse never complained."

I pause a moment to take this all in. Fooling with Yaksha's remains might mean fooling with his blood. Could the blood of a dead vampire make a living vampire? I didn't know.

"He didn't bother Heather again?" I ask.

"No."

"Did he take any revenge on you for threatening him?"

Sally hesitated; her natural gaiety faltered. "I don't know for sure. I had an old cat, Sibyl, that I'd owned since she was born. I was very fond of her. Two days after I spoke to Eddie, I found her dead in my backyard."

"How did she die?"

"Don't know. There wasn't a mark on her. I didn't bring her to a vet for an autopsy." Sally shivered. "I get enough of that here. You understand."

"I do. I'm sorry about your cat. Tell me—did Eddie have startling green eyes, bony hands, and an acne-scarred face?"

Sally nods. "That's him. Has he killed anybody?"

I stand. I feel no relief that I have found my man. He is worse than I feared.

"Yes," I say. "He is making his own snuff films now."

FIVE

We are the only ones sitting at the end of Water Cove Pier, where Slim and his people came for me with their many guns and unbreakable handcuffs. It is too cold for most people to eat outside, but we are bundled up. We eat fish and chips and feed the birds. The sun is bright and reflects off the calm water, and the chilly air is heavy with the smell of salt. I wear dark sunglasses and a hat. I like hats, red and black ones.

The first time I ever saw the sea I was already a vampire. So I don't know what it looks like to a mortal. The many fish, the seaweed, and the shells—I see them even in murky water. For me the ocean is a huge aquarium, teeming with visible life, food. In moments of extreme thirst I have drunk the blood of fish, of sharks even. Once, in the seventeenth century, off the coast of what is now Big Sur, I even killed a great white shark, but not for food. The thing tried to bite off my legs.

I think of Yaksha without his legs.

And I ask myself the impossible question.

Could he still be alive?

Joel holds in his hand the papers he obtained from the coroner, the details on Edward Fender—Eddie. I will relieve him of the papers in a few minutes. But first I want to talk to him because I want to keep him from talking. Honestly, I do not want to kill him. He is a good man—I see that. More interested in helping humanity than in being applauded. But to convince him to keep his mouth shut, I have to tell him even more about the enemy, and myself. And then I will have even more reason to kill him. It is a paradox. Life is that way. God designed it that way. I believe I met him once. He was full of mischief.

I will say things I never should say to any mortal. Because I am hurt, I feel my own mortality. The feeling gives me reason to be reckless.

"Do you often come here?" Joel asks, referring to Water Cove, which is twenty miles south of Mayfair. "Or go down to Seaside?"

"No." My weakness haunts me like a second shadow. If I do not drink soon, and a lot, I will be in no shape to return to Los Angeles tonight. "Why do you ask?"

"I was just thinking how you told me your house exploded

six weeks ago. By strange coincidence there was a group of violent murders in Seaside at that same time. I believe they occurred a day before you said you lost your house, if my memory serves me correctly."

"You have a good memory."

He waits for me to elaborate, but I don't. "Were you and your friend connected with those murders as well?" he asks.

I peer at him through my dark lenses. "Why do you ask?"

"One of the people killed at a gas station in Seaside was a woman. Her skull was cracked open by an exceptionally strong person. The coroner told me about it. He said it would take a monster to do what had been done to her." He pauses, adds, "The manner of her death reminds me of what's happening in Los Angeles."

I offer a bird one of my french fries. Animals generally like me, if I'm not chasing them. "Do you think I'm a monster, Joel?"

"You cannot keep answering my questions with questions."

"But one answer always leads to another question." I shrug. "I'm not interested in discussing my life story with you."

"Were you there that night those people died in Seaside?"

I pause. "Yes."

He sucks in a breath. "Did your friend kill that woman?"

A white dove takes my fry. I wipe off my hands on my skirt. "No. My friend sent that woman to kill me."

"Some friend."

"He had his reasons."

Joel sighs. "I'm getting nowhere with you. Just tell me what you're trying to tell me and be done with it."

"Eddie Fender is our man."

"You don't know that."

"I do. To me, it's a fact. And the other thing is—I like you and I don't want you to get hurt. You have to leave Eddie to me."

He snorts. "Right. Thank you, Alisa, but I can take care of myself."

I touch his arm, hold his eyes, even through my dark glasses. "You don't understand what you're up against. You don't understand me." I let the tips of my fingers slide over the sleeve of his jacket. I hold his hand. Despite my weakness, his proximity is stimulating. Even without trying, my gaze weakens him. Better to kiss him, I think, than to kill him. But then I think of Ray, whom I love. He will be waking soon. The sun nears the horizon. The orange glow lights Joel's face as if he were sitting in a desolate purgatory, where the judgment of the damned and the saved had already been completed, five thousand years ago. He sits so close to me, but I cannot welcome him too far into my world without devouring his, as I did Ray's. But I do have to scare him, yes, and deeply. I add, "I was the one who killed that woman."

He smiles nervously. "Sure. How did you do it? With your bare hands?"

I take his hand. "Yes."

"You must be very strong?"

"Yes."

"Alisa."

"Sita. My name is Sita."

"Why do you go by Alisa?"

I shrug. "It's a name. Only those I care about call me Sita."

"What do you want me to call you?"

I smile sadly. "What would you prefer to call a murderer?"

He takes his hand from mine and stares at the ocean a moment. "Sometimes when I talk to you I feel like I'm talking to a mental case. Only you're too together to be labeled unstable."

"Thank you."

"You weren't serious about having killed that woman, were you?"

I speak in a flat voice. "It happened at the corner of Fryer and Tads. The woman was found on the floor of the women's room. Her brains were on the floor as well. Like you said, her head had been cracked open, the front of it. That was because I grabbed her from behind when I rammed her face into the wall." I sip my Coke. "Did the coroner give you these details?"

I see from Joel's stunned face that the coroner must have

enlightened him on some of the facts. He can't quit staring at me. For him, I know, it is as if my eyes are as big as the sea, as black as the deepest subterranean crevasse. Beneath the ocean is molten bedrock. Beneath my eyes I believe he senses an ageless fire. Yet he shivers and I understand why. My words are so cold.

"It's true," he whispers.

"Yes. I am not normal." Standing, I pluck the papers from his hand before he can blink. My eyes bore down on him. "Go home, Joel, to wherever home is. Don't try to follow me. Don't talk about me. If you do, I will know about it and I will have to come after you. You don't want that, any more than you want to take on this murderer. He is like me, and at the same time he is not like me. We are both cruel, but his cruelty is without reason, without kindness. Yes, I did kill that woman, but I didn't do so out of malice. I can be very kind, when it suits me. But when I am cornered, I am as dangerous as this Eddie. I have to corner him, you see, in a special place, under special circumstances. It's the only way to stop him. But you can't be there. If you are, you will die. You will die anyway, if you don't leave me alone. Do you understand?"

He stares at me as if I am a distorted apparition trying to materialize from a realm he never knew existed. "No," he mumbles.

I take a step back. "Try to arrest me."

"Huh?"

"Arrest me. I have admitted to killing a woman with my bare hands. I know details of the crime only the killer could know. It's your responsibility as an FBI agent to bring me in. Take out your gun and read me my rights. Now!"

My pounding gaze has short-circuited his brain synapses. But he does stand, and he does pull out his gun and point it at me. "You're under arrest," he says.

I slap the gun away. It lands a hundred yards off in the water. But for him it is just gone. His stunned expression, even in the ruby light, goes pale.

"You see," I say softly. "You can't play this game with me. You don't have the proper equipment. Your gun is on the bottom of the sea. Believe me, Joel, trust me—or you will end up in the bottom of a grave." I pat his shoulder as I step past him. "There will be a bus along soon. There is a stop at the entrance to the pier. Goodbye."

SIX

Ray should *not* come with me to Los Angeles. I feel this in my heart. But after the sun sets, and he awakens, and I explain to him what is happening in L.A., he insists on joining me. How he shudders at the thought of more vampires! How his horror breaks my heart, even though intellectually I share his opinion. Truly, he still sees us as evil. But, he says, two are stronger than one, and I know his math makes sense. I might very well need him at a critical moment. Also, unless I take him with me, I know he will go another night without feeding. How many nights he can survive, I don't know. I can endure for as long as six months without drinking blood. As long as I don't have other vampires throwing knives in me, that is.

Anxious to get down to Los Angeles, we fly south in my Learjet without feeding. But once on the ground, before we do anything else, I tell Ray we are going hunting. He agrees reluctantly, and I have to promise him we will not hurt anybody. It is a promise I make reluctantly. Opening large veins, I never know what complications might result.

We go to Zuma Beach, north of Malibu. The beaches have always been a favorite den of victims for me. Plenty of out-of-state travelers, homeless people, drunks—portions of the population who are not immediately missed. Of course, I seldom kill my meal tickets these days, since I have begun to believe in miracles, or since I have fallen in love with my reluctant Count Dracula, whichever came first. Actually, I once met Vlad the Impaler, the real man Count Dracula was based on, in the fifteenth century in Transylvania during the war with the Ottoman Turks. Forget those stories about his mean-looking canines. Now, there was a fellow who needed modern dentistry. His teeth were rotting out of his mouth, and he had the worst breath. He was no vampire, just a Catholic zealot with a fetish for decapitation. He asked me out, though, for a ride in his carriage. I attract unusual men. I told him where to stuff it. I believe I invented the phrase.

Driving north on the Coast Highway, I spot a young couple on the beach making out on their sleeping bags. Up and down the beach, for at least half a mile, there isn't another soul. Looks like dinner to me, but Ray has his doubts. He always does. I swear, if we were a normal couple going out to a restaurant, he would never be satisfied with the menu. Being a vampire, you can't be a picky eater, it just doesn't work. Yet you might wonder—what about blood-borne diseases? What about AIDS? None of them matters. None of them can touch us. Our blood is a fermented black soup—it strips to the bone whatever we sink our teeth into. This particular young couple looks healthy and happy to me, a blood type I prefer. It is true I am sensitive to the "life vibration" of those I feed upon. Once I drank the blood of a well-known rap singer and had a head-ache for a week.

"What is wrong with them?" I ask Ray as we park a hundred yards north of them. They are behind and below us, not far from the reach of the surf. The waves are big, the tide high.

"They're not much older than I am," he says.

"Yes? Would it be better if they were both in their eighties?"

"You don't understand."

"I do understand. They remind you of the life you left behind. But I need blood. I shouldn't have to explain that to you. I suffered two serious wounds last night, and then I had to feed you when I returned home."

"I didn't ask you to feed me."

I throw up my hands. "And I didn't ask to have to watch you die. Please, Ray, let's do this quick so that we can take care of what we came for."

"How are we going to approach them?"

I open my car door. "There's going to be no approach. We are simply going to rush them and grab them and start drink-ing their blood."

Ray grabs my arm. "No. They'll be terrified. They'll run to the police."

"The police in this town have more important matters to deal with than a couple of hysterical twenty-year-olds."

Ray is stubborn. "It will take you only a few moments to put them at ease and hypnotize them. Then they won't suffer."

I stand up outside the car and scowl at him. "You would rather I suffer."

Ray wearily climbs out of his side of the car. "No, Sita. I would prefer to fast."

I walk around and take his hand—a handsome young couple out for an innocent stroll. But my mood is foul. "You would rather I suffer," I repeat.

The blond couple doesn't even look up as we approach, so entranced are they in each other's anatomy. I throw Ray another unpleasant glance. I am supposed to hypnotize these two? He shrugs—he would prefer I anesthetize them before pinching their veins. My patience has reached its limit. Striding over to the hot-blooded boy and girl, I reach down and grab their sleeping bag and pull it out from under them. They fly three feet in the air—literally. They look up at me as if I might bite them. Imagine.

"You are about to be mugged," I say. "It will be a novelty mugging. You will not be hurt and you will not lose any money. But you are going to perform us a great service. Stay calm and we'll be done in ten minutes."

They do *not* remain calm. I don't care. I grab the girl and throw her to Ray, and then I am on the guy. Pulling his arms behind his back and pinning them there with one hand, I don't worry when he opens his mouth and screams for help. With the pounding surf, no one will hear him. Not that it would make much difference if someone did. In L.A. the earth could shake and people would think it was the Harmonic Convergence. A little screaming on Zuma Beach never worried anyone. Yet I do end up clamping the guy's mouth shut with my free hand.

"I prefer to dine in silence," I say. Glancing over at Ray who is struggling with the girl—for no reason—I remark in his direction, "You make it worse by dragging it out."

"I do things my own way," he says.

"Hmm," I grunt. Closing my eyes, using my long thumb-nail to open a neck vein, I press my lips on the torn flesh and suck hard. I have cut the carotid artery. The blood gushes into my mouth like hot chocolate poured over ice cream. My young man goes limp in my arms and begins to enjoy the sensation. For me and my victim, feeding can be intensely sensual. I know he feels as if every nerve in his body is being caressed by a thousand fingers. And for me the blood is a warm pulsing river. But if I wish, feeding can be terrifying for my victim. By the time I finished with Slim, for example, he felt as if hell would be a welcome respite.

None of my victims, of course, becomes a vampire simply by being bitten. There has to be a massive exchange of blood to bring about that transformation. I wonder if Eddie Fender has needles and syringes.

So caught up am I in replenishing my strength that I don't immediately notice that we are three when we should be four. Opening my eyes, I see that Ray's girl has escaped. She is running down the beach at high speed, soundlessly, in the direction of concrete steps that will lead her past the beach boulders and back up onto the Coast Highway.

"What the hell!" I say to Ray.

He shrugs. "She bit my hand."

"Go get her. No, I'll get her." I hand over my happy boy. "Finish with this guy. He's good for another pint."

Ray accepts the young man reluctantly. "His strength is ebbing."

"You worry about your own strength," I call over my shoulder as I chase after the girl. She's a hundred yards away, on the verge of leaping onto the steps—it is a wonder that she hasn't started screaming yet. I have to assume she is in shock. She is ten feet from the highway when I pounce on her and drag her back down the steps. There is more fight in her than I expect, however. Whirling, she punches me hard in the chest. To my great surprise, the blow hurts. She has hit me exactly where the stake penetrated my heart. But my grip on her does not falter. "This is going to hurt, sister," I tell her as she stares at me in horror.

My right hand pins her arms, my left closes her mouth. Again, the thumbnail opens her big neck vein. But I am even more eager than before and suck her red stream as if I am drinking from the elixir of immortality itself, as indeed I am. Yet it is not the matter, the fluids or elements in the blood, that grant the vampire his or her longevity. It is the *life*—that essence that no scientist has ever been able to replicate in his laboratory—that makes any other source of nourishment pale by comparison. But this feeding with this girl is not erotic—it is ravenous. Feeling as if I am trying to drown my pain and weariness in one gulp, I drink from this girl as if her life is my reward for all the evildoers I have been forced to bring to justice.

Yet my thirst deludes even my sense of right and wrong. My vast experience fails me. Suddenly I feel Ray shaking me, telling me to let go. Opening my eyes, I notice the boy lying lazily on the beach, still a hundred yards away, sleeping off his unexpected encounter with the creatures of the night. He will wake with a bad headache, nothing more. The girl in my arms is another matter. Desperately pale, cold as the sand we stand on, she wheezes. Her heart flutters inside her chest. Crouching down, I lay her on her back on the beach. Ray kneels across from me and shakes his head. My guilt is a bitter-tasting dessert.

"I didn't mean to do this," I say. "I got carried away."

"Is she going to make it?" Ray asks.

Placing my hand over her chest, I take a pulse reading that tells me more than an intensive care unit filled with modern equipment could. It is only then that I note the girl's heart is scarred—the right aorta; possibly from a childhood disease. It is not as though I have drained her completely. Yet I have taken more from her than I should have, and in combination with her anatomical weakness, I know she is not going to make it.

"It doesn't look good," I say.

Ray takes her hand. He has not reached for my hand in over a month. "Can't you do something for her?" he asks, pain in his voice.

I spread my hands. "What can I do? I cannot put the blood I have taken back inside her. It's done—let's get out of here."

"No! We can't just leave her. Use your power. Save her. You saved me."

I briefly close my eyes. "I saved you by changing you. I cannot change her."

"But she'll die."

I stare at him across my handiwork. "Yes. Everyone who is born dies."

He refuses to accept the situation. "We have to get her to a hospital." He goes to lift her. "They can give her a transfusion. She might make it."

I stop him, gently, slowly removing his hands from the girl's body. Folding her hands across her chest, I listen as her heart begins to skip inside. Yet I continue to look at my lover, searching his expression for signs of hatred or the realization that this being he is to spend the rest of eternity with is really a witch. But Ray only looks grieved, and somehow that makes it worse for me.

"She is not going to live," I say. "She would never make it to a hospital. Her heart is weak. I failed to notice that at the start. I was so thirsty—I got carried away. It happens sometimes. I am not perfect. This is not a perfect creation. But if it is any consolation, I am sorry that this has happened. If I could heal her, I would. But Krishna did not give me that ability." I add, "I can only kill."

Ray follows the girl's breathing for a minute. That is all the time it lasts. The girl gives a soft strangled sound and her back arches off the sandy floor. Then she lies still. Standing, I silently take Ray by the hand and lead him back to the car. Long ago I learned that death cannot be discussed. It is like talking about darkness. Both topics bring only confusion—especially to us, who have to go on living through the night. All who are born die, I think, remembering Krishna's words. All who die will be reborn. In his profound wisdom he spoke the words to comfort all those born in Kali Yuga, the age in which we now live, the dark age. Yet it's strange, as we get in the car and drive away from the beach, I cannot remember his eyes, exactly what they looked like. The sky is covered with haze. The stars, the moon—they are not out. I cannot think what it means to be young. All is indeed dark.

SEVEN

When I met Private Investigator Michael Riley, Ray's father, he talked to me about my previous residence. Trying to impress me with how much he knew about my wealth.

"Prior to moving to Mayfair, you lived in Los Angeles—in Beverly Hills, in fact—at Two-Five-Six Grove Street. Your home was a four-thousand-square-foot mansion, with two swimming pools, a tennis court, a sauna, and a small observatory. The property is valued at six-point-five million. To this day you are listed as the sole owner, Miss Perne."

I was very impressed with Riley's knowledge. That was one of the main reasons I killed him. It is to this house we go after Zuma Beach. Mr. Riley forgot to mention the mansion's deep basement. It is here I keep a stockpile of sophisticated weapons: Uzis, grenade launchers, high-powered laser-assisted

sniper rifles, 10-millimeter pistols equipped with silencers—
toys easily purchased on any Middle Eastern black market.
Loading up my car, I feel like Rambo, who must have been
a vampire in a previous incarnation. Loved the way that guy
snapped people's necks. Ray watches me pile on the weapons
with a bewildered expression.

"You know," he says, "I've never even fired a gun."

That concerns me. Just because he's a vampire he's not necessarily a crack shot, although he could quickly become one
with a couple of lessons. Myself, I have practiced with every
weapon I own. My skill is such that I use every gun to its full
capacity.

"Just don't shoot yourself in the foot," I say.

"I thought you were going to say, just don't shoot me."

"That, too," I say, feeling uneasy.

Edward Fender's job application and résumé contain only
one permanent address, which is his mother's. It is my belief
that the lead is valid. Mrs. Fender's house is located only four
miles west of the Coliseum, in the city of Inglewood, a suburb
of Los Angeles. It is a quarter after nine by the time we park
in front of her place. Rolling down the window and bidding
Ray to sit silently, I listen carefully to what's going on inside
the residence. The TV is on to "Wheel of Fortune." An elderly
woman sits in a rocking chair reading a magazine. Her lungs
are weak; she has a slight dry cough. A front window of the
house is half open. The interior is dusty and damp. It smells

of poor health and of human serpents. A vampire has recently been in the house, but he is no longer there. Now I am absolutely certain of the identity of the monster I pursue.

"He was here less than two hours ago," I whisper to Ray.

"Is he in the area?"

"No. But he can come into the area swiftly. He has at least twice my speed. I am going to speak to the woman alone. I want you to park out of sight down the street. If you see someone approach the house, don't try to warn me. Drive off. I will know he is coming. I will deal with him. Do you understand?"

Ray is amused. "Am I in the army? Do I have to take your orders?"

I take his hand. "Seriously, Ray. In a situation like this you can't help me. You can only hurt me." I let go of him and slip a small revolver into my coat pocket. "I just have to put a couple of bullets in his brain, and he will not be making any more vampires. Then we can go after the others. They will be a piece of cake."

"Do you like cake, Sita?"

I have to smile. "Yes, of course. With ice cream, especially."

"You never told me when your birthday is. Do you know?"

"Yes." I lean over and kiss him. "It is the day I met you. I was reborn on that day."

He kisses me back, grabs my arm as I go to leave. "I don't blame you, you know."

I nod, although I don't completely believe him. "I know."

The woman answers the door a moment after I knock and remains behind the torn screen door. Her hair is white, her face in ruins. Her hands are arthritic; the fingers claw at the air like hungry rats' paws. She has flat gray eyes that look as if they have watched black-and-white television for decades. There is little feeling in them, except perhaps a sense of cynical contempt. Her bathrobe is a tattered gown of food and blood-stains. Some of the latter look fresh. There are red marks on her neck, still healing.

Her son has been drinking her blood.

I smile quickly. "Hello. Mrs. Fender? I'm Kathy Gibson, a friend of your son's. Is he at home?"

My beauty, my smooth bearing throw her off balance. I shudder to think of the women Eddie usually brings home to Mother. "No. He works the graveyard shift. He won't be home till late." She pauses, gives me a critical examination. "What did you say your name is?"

"Kathy." My voice goes sweet and soft, strangely persuasive. "I didn't mean to stop by so late. I hope I'm not disturbing you?"

She shrugs. "Just watching TV. How come I've never heard Eddie mention you before?"

I stare at her. "We only just met a few days ago. My brother introduced us." I add, "He works with Eddie."

"At the clinic?"

The woman is trying to trick me. I frown. "Eddie doesn't work at a clinic."

The woman relaxes slightly. "At the warehouse?"

"Yes. At the warehouse." My smile broadens. My gaze penetrates deeper. This woman is mentally unstable. She has secret perversions. My eyes do not cause her to flinch. She is fond of young women, I know, little girls even. I wonder about Mr. Fender. I add, "May I come in?"

"Pardon?"

"I have to make a call. May I use your phone?" I add, "Don't worry, I don't bite."

I have pushed the right button. She enjoys being bitten. Her son drinks her blood with her consent. Even I, an immoral beast, have never been drawn to incestuous relationships. Of course, in the literal sense of the word, we are not talking about incest. Still, the Brady Bunch would never survive in this house. She opens the screen door for me.

"Of course," she says. "Please come in. Who do you have to call?"

"My brother."

"Oh."

I step inside, my sense of smell on alert. Eddie has recently slept in this house. She must let him sleep away the days, not questioning his aversion to the sun. My ability to handle the sun is hopefully my ace in the hole against this creature. Even Yaksha, many times more powerful than myself, was far less comfortable in the sun than I am. Secretly I pray Eddie can't even leave the house in the daylight hours without wearing sunscreen with an SPF of 100 or better, like Ray. Although my senses study the interior of the house, my ears never leave the exterior. I cannot be taken unaware, like before. Mrs. Fender leads me to the phone beside her rocking chair. Her reading material lies partially hidden beneath a dirty dishrag—a back issue of *Mad Magazine*. Actually, I kind of like *Mad Magazine*.

I dial a phony number and speak to no one. I'm at Eddie's house. He's not here. I'll be a few minutes late. Goodbye. Setting down the phone, I stare at the woman again.

"Has Eddie called here tonight?" I ask.

"No. Why would he call? He just left a couple of hours ago."

I take a step toward her. "No one's called?"

"No."

She's lying. The FBI has called, probably Joel himself. Yet Joel, or anyone else for that matter—with the exception of Eddie—has not been in the house recently. I would smell their visit. Yet that situation will soon change. The authorities will converge on this place sooner or later. That fact may not be as crucial as it appears. Eddie would not easily walk into a trap, and clearly he does not meet with his cohorts in this house. The warehouse is the key. I need the address. Taking another step forward, I force the woman to back against a divider that separates the meager living room from the messy kitchen. My eyes are all over her, all she sees. There is no time for subtlety. Fear blossoms inside her chest but also awe. Her will is weird but weak. I stop only a foot away.

"I am going to visit Eddie now," I say softly. "Tell me the best way to the warehouse from here."

She speaks like a puppet. "Take Hawthorne Boulevard east to Washington. Turn right and go down to Winston." She blinks and coughs. "It's there."

I press my face to her face. She breathes my air, my intoxicating scent. "You will not remember that I was here. There is no Kathy Gibson. There is no pretty blond girl. No visitor stopped by. The FBI didn't even call. But if they should call again, tell them you haven't heard from your son in a long time." I put my palm on the woman's forehead, whisper in her ear. "You understand?"

She stares into space. "Yes."

"Good." My lips brush her neck, but I don't bite. But if Eddie pisses me off again, I swear, I am going to strangle his mother in front of him. "Goodbye, Mrs. Fender."

Yet as I leave the house I note a cold draft from the back rooms. I feel the vibration of an electric motor and smell coolant. The house has a large freezer next to one of the back bedrooms. I almost turn to explore more. I have planted my suggestions, however, and to return may upset the woman's delicate state of illusion. Also, I have the location of the warehouse, and finding Eddie is my first priority. If need be, I can return later and search the rest of the house.

EIGHT

*T*ell me about your husband Rama?" Ray asks as we drive toward the warehouse. "And your daughter, Lalita?"

The question takes me by surprise. "It was a long time ago."

"But you remember everything?"

"Yes." I sit silently for a moment. "I was almost twenty when we met. Three or four times a year merchants used to pass by that portion of India that is now known as Rajastan. We lived between the desert and the jungle. The merchants would sell us hats to keep off the sun, herb potions to drive away the bugs. Rama was the son of a merchant. I first saw him by the river that flowed beside our village. He was teaching a small child how to fly a kite. We had kites in those days. We invented them, not the Chinese." I shake my head. "When I saw him, I just knew."

Ray understands but asks anyway, anxious to dwell on my humanity in the light of what happened at the beach. "What did you know?"

"That I loved him. That we belonged together." I smile at the memory. "He was named after an earlier incarnation of Lord Vishnu—the eighth avatar, or incarnation of God. Lord Rama was married to the Goddess Sita. Krishna was supposed to be the ninth avatar. I worshipped Lord Vishnu from the time I was born. Maybe that's why I got to meet Krishna. Anyway, you can see how Rama's and my names went together. Maybe our union was destined to be. Rama was like you in a lot of ways. Quiet, given to thoughtful pauses." I glance over. "He even had your eyes."

"They were the same?"

"They did not look the same. But they were the same. You understand?"

"Yes. Tell me about Lalita?"

"Lalita is one of the names of the Goddess as well. It means 'She who plays.' She was up to mischief the moment she came out of my womb. Ten months old and she would climb out of her cradle and crawl and walk all the way to the river." I chuckle. "I remember once I found her sitting with a snake in one of the small boats our people had. Fortunately the snake was asleep. It was poisonous! I remember how frightened I was." I sigh. "You wouldn't have known me in those days."

"I wish I had known you then."

His remark is sweet—he means it that way—yet it stings. My hands fidget on the steering wheel. "I wish many things," I whisper.

"Do you believe in reincarnation?" he asks suddenly.

"Why do you ask?"

"Just curious. Do you?"

I consider. "I know Krishna said it was a reality. Looking back, I believe he always spoke the truth. But I never talked to him about it. I scarcely talked to him at all."

"If reincarnation is a reality, then what about us? Are we evolving toward God? Or are we stuck because we're afraid to die?"

"I have asked myself the same questions, many times. But I've never been able to answer them."

"Can't you at least answer one of them?"

"Which one is that?" I ask.

"Are you afraid?"

I reach over and take his hand. "I don't fear death for myself."

"But to fear it at all—isn't it the same difference? If you trust Krishna, then you must trust that there is no death."

I force a smile. "We're a philosopher tonight."

He smiles. "Don't be anxious. I'm not thinking of suicide. I just think we have to look at the bigger picture."

I squeeze his hand and let go. "I believe Krishna saw all of life as nothing more than a motion picture projected onto a vast screen. Certainly nothing in this world daunted him. Even when I held his companion, Radha, in my clutches, he never lost his serenity."

Ray nods. "I would like to have such peace of mind."

"Yes. So would I."

His hand reaches over and touches my long hair. "Do you think I am Rama?"

I have to take a breath. My eyes moisten. My words come out weak. "I don't understand."

"Yes, you do. Did I come back for you?"

There are tears on my face. They are five thousand years old. I remember them. After Yaksha changed me, I saw neither my husband nor my daughter again. How I hated him for doing that to me. Yet, had I never become a vampire, I never would have met Ray. But I shake my head at his questions.

"I don't know," I say.

"Sita—"

"When I met you," I interrupt, "I felt as if Krishna had led me to you." I reach up and press his hand to the side of my face. "You feel like Rama. You smell like him."

He leans over and kisses my ear. "You're great."

"You're wonderful."

He brushes away my tears. "They always paint Krishna as blue. I know you explained that it's symbolic. That he is blue like the vast sky—unbounded. But I dream about him sometimes, when you lie beside me. And when I do, his eyes are always blue, like shining stars." He pauses. "Have you ever had such a dream?"

I nod.

"Tell me about it?"

"Maybe later."

"All right. But didn't your husband die before he could have met Krishna?"

"Yes."

"So I can't be remembering a past life?"

"I don't know. I wouldn't think so."

Ray lets go of me and sits back, seemingly disappointed. He adds casually, "I never dream of blood. Do you?"

Often, I think. Maybe once, five thousand years ago, we had more in common. Yet I lie to him, even though I hate to lie to those I love. Even though I have promised myself and him that I would stop.

"No," I say. "Never."

We park two blocks away from the warehouse, a gray rectangular structure as long as a football field, as tall as a lighthouse. But no light emanates from this building. The exterior walls are rotting wood, moldy plaster, panes of glass so drenched in dust they could be squares etched on the walls of a coal mine. The surrounding fence is tall, barbed—a good stretch of wire on which to hang fresh corpses. Yet the occupants are more subtle than that, but not a lot more. Even from this distance I smell the decaying bodies they have ravaged inside, and I know the police and the FBI are seriously underestimating Los Angeles's recent violent crime wave. The odor of the yakshini, the snakes from beyond the black vault of the universe, also wafts from the building. I estimate a dozen vampires inside. But is Eddie one of them? And how many of his partners presently walk the streets? Vicious dogs wander the perimeter. They look well fed.

"Do you have a plan?" Ray asks.

"Always."

"I want to be part of it."

I nod. "You realize the danger."

"I just have to look in the mirror, sister."

I smile. "We have to burn this building down with all of them inside. To do that we need large quantities of gasoline, and the only way we are going to get that is to steal a couple of gasoline trucks from a nearby refinery."

"With our good looks and biting wit, that shouldn't be too hard."

"Indeed. The hard part will come when we try to plant our trucks at either end of the building and ignite them. First we'll have to cut the fence, so we can drive in unobstructed, and to do that we will have to silently kill all the dogs. But I think I can take them out from this distance using a silencer on one of my rifles."

Ray winces. "Is that necessary?"

"Yes. Better a few dead dogs than the end of humanity. The main thing is, we must attack *after* dawn, when they're all back inside and feeling sleepy. That includes our prize policymaker—Eddie."

"I like to take a nap at that time myself," Ray remarks.

I speak seriously. "You are going to have to be strong with the sun in the sky, and drive one of the trucks. I know that won't be easy for you. But if all goes well, you can seek shelter immediately afterward."

He nods. "Sounds like a piece of cake."

"No. It's a baked Alaska." I study the structure and nod. "They'll burn."

Yet my confidence is a costume. The previous night, when I stared into Eddie's eyes, he seemed insane, but also shrewd. The ease with which we have found him and his people disturbs me. The stage is set for a snuff film, big time. But I have to wonder who is directing the show. Whether it will go straight onto the front pages of the *Los Angeles Times*. Or end up buried in film, in Eddie's private collection.

NINE

We crouch in the shadows two blocks down the street from the warehouse as I load my high-powered rifle, especially equipped with laser-guided scope and fat silencer. At our backs are two gasoline trucks, with two huge tankers hooked on to each one. We didn't even have to go to a refinery to steal them. Leaving the ghetto, we just spotted the blasted things heading toward the freeway. I *accidentally* pulled in front of one and got my car slightly damaged. Both drivers climbed out, and I started screaming at them. How dare you ruin my brand-new car! I just bought it! Man, you are going to pay big time!

Then I smacked their heads together and took the keys. I figure they should be waking up soon, in the Dumpster where I dropped them. Ray helped me drive one of the tankers back to the warehouse. For once, he seemed to be enjoying himself—the thrill of the hunt. Then the sun came up. Since that time, fifteen minutes ago, he has been hiding under a blanket and wiping at his burning eyes. He doesn't complain, though. He never does.

I finish loading the rifle and prop my left elbow on one knee, steadying the barrel in the direction of the big black dog closest to our end of the lot. Not only do I have to shoot each animal cleanly in the head, I must shoot between the holes in the wire fence. A stray bullet could ruin the whole plan. The dog growls as if sensing my attention, and I notice the blood that trickles from its saliva and the way it shakes when the sun catches in its eyes. Another Eddie Fender surprise.

An hour before dawn Eddie returned with a dozen partners. All together there are twenty-one vampires inside, all powerfully built males. With them they have two terrified Caucasian couples—breakfast. The four people started screaming the moment they were taken inside and didn't stop until their throats were ripped open. Ray paced miserably the whole time, insisting that we attack right then.

But I refused to risk the human race for the lives of four people.

"I would almost rather you were shooting people," Ray mumbles, hiding beneath the dirty orange covering. His blanket is a gift from a local homeless person. I gave the guy five hundred dollars for it and told him to flee the area. Although we are well shaded by a nearby brick wall, Ray's brow is covered by a film of sweat and he can't stop blinking. His bloodshot eyes look as if they have been sprayed with kerosene.

"If it's any consolation," I say, "these dogs are worse than rabid."

"What do you mean?"

"He has given them his blood."

"No way. Vampire dogs?"

"It could be worse. It could be vampire fish. Think of a school of those swimming the ocean. We'd never be able to find them all."

Ray chuckles weakly. "Can we go fishing up north after this is all over?"

"Sure. We can go salmon fishing in the streams in Washington. And you'll be pleased to know you won't need a fishing rod to catch them."

"I might still use a rod." He adds, "I used to go fishing with my dad."

"I did the same with my father," I say truthfully. Before Yaksha killed my father. Yaksha—where can his body be? And what shape is it in? Doubt continues to plague me, but I push it aside. Fixing my aim on the first dog, I whisper to Ray, "I'm going to do them quickly. Don't speak to me for a moment."

"Fine."

I peer into the dog's cruel eye through my scope. Pressing the trigger, there is a gentle *swish* of air. My caliber is small; nevertheless, the top of the dog's head comes off. Silently it topples over. Its partners hardly notice. But they will soon enough. They will smell the blood, and being infected with Eddie's blood, they may go crazy. But I don't give them the chance. Scarcely pausing between shots, I move from one beast to the next, killing all nine in less than a minute. I set the rifle down and pick up my wire cutters.

"Stay here until I return," I say. "Then be ready to move. If all goes according to plan, we'll be out of here in ten minutes."

Barefoot, soundlessly, I scurry toward the tall fence. Fortune continues to favor us. The hour is early and the street remains deserted. We are not all that far from the Coliseum, perhaps two miles, in a rundown industrial section of town. Cutting a hole in the fence would be unnecessary if I just wanted to ram the warehouse with our trucks and take a flying leap to safety. I have vetoed this idea for two reasons. I worry that Ray, in his weakened condition, would end up getting killed. Also, I believe a more deft approach will ensure we get all the vampires. My sensitive nose has determined that the warehouse was previously used as storage for foam rubber, and that there are still a large number of polyurethane sheets inside. Polyurethane is extremely flammable. It is our intention to quietly park our trucks at either end of the building, light the ten-second fuses attached to the explosive caps I have brought from my L.A. home, and dash for safety. The occupants will be caught between two crushing waves of expanding flame. Behind the warehouse stands the tall brick wall of another abandoned building. The fire will smash against that wall and cut off any chance of a rear escape. And if by chance any of the vampires do manage to get out of the inferno, I will be waiting for them beyond the perimeter of the fence with my rifle. They will go down as easily as the dogs. It is a good plan and it should work.

Still, I worry.

Kneeling by the fence, I quickly begin to cut the wires, searching for guards, or a head appearing at one of the filthy windows, or any sign of movement inside. All is silent and calm. Eddie's newly made vampires are undoubtedly sensitive to the sun and probably can't stand guard after dawn. He may be overconfident of his powers—that is my real hope. My cutters click like sharp electronic pulses over a telephone line. Soon I am laying the wire down on the broken asphalt ground. In less than five minutes I have opened a hole large enough to drive our trucks through. I retreat to Ray and the tankers. Huddling under his blanket, he peers up at me with feverish eyes.

"Wish it were a cloudy day," he mutters.

I nod. "An eclipse would be even better." I offer him my hand. "Are you ready to rock?"

He gets up slowly, his blanket still wrapped around his head, and studies my handiwork from afar. "Are they all asleep?"

"They seem to be."

"Are you sure Eddie's still inside?"

"I saw him go in. I never saw him come out. But he could have sneaked out the back way." I shrug. "We may never get this good a chance. We have to strike now and we have to strike hard."

He nods. "Agreed." He limps toward his truck, and I help him into the driver's seat. "You know, Sita, I don't have a license to drive this big a rig. What we're doing is against the law."

"There are human laws and there are God's laws. We may not be the most lovable creatures in creation, but we are doing the best we can."

He studies me seriously, his entire face now flushed red, soaked in sweat. "Is that true? Is there anything good we can give to the world?"

I hug him. "If we can stop these creatures, our being here will have been justified a thousand times over." I kiss him. "I'm sorry I let the girl die."

He wraps his arm around me. "It wasn't your fault."

"I'm sorry I killed your father."

"Sita." He holds me at arm's length. "You're five thousand years old. You have too much history. You have to learn to live in the present."

I smile, feeling like a foolish child. It is not a bad feeling. Despite all I have seen and done, he is the wise one. Reaching up, I brush his hair aside, out of his eyes, and then all at once I am kissing him again.

"You do remind me of Rama," I whisper in his ear. "So

much so that you must be him. Promise me, Ray, and I will promise you. We will stay together—always."

He doesn't answer right away, and I pull back slightly to see what the matter is. He has dropped his blanket and is staring in the direction of the sun, although not directly, since we are still in the shade. But I would think the move would just hurt his eyes more.

"The sky is so blue," he says thoughtfully. "So vast." He turns back to me and chuckles softly. "We're like those vampire fish, lost in that ocean."

I frown. "Ray?"

"I was just thinking of Krishna." He squeezes my hands. "I promise our love will survive." He glances at the warehouse. "You want me to go to the south side?"

"Yes, to the left. Follow me in. Stay close. Drive up with your door slightly ajar. Don't let it bang. Kill the engine as you pass the gate and coast in. Park as close as you can to the building. Don't close your door when you get out. As soon as you can, light the fuse and run. I will hear it burning and light mine. If they try to escape, I will cut them down. We will meet here when it's over. Then we can go fishing." I pause, wanting to add something else, not knowing what it is. "Be careful, Ray."

"You, too, Sita." He touches his heart. "Love you."

I touch mine. The pain is back; it is hard to breathe.

Maybe it is a sign from God.

"Love you," I say.

We cruise toward the warehouse, me first. The hole in the gate easily accommodates the tankers. The head of a dead dog flattens as the front wheel of the rig rolls over it. Turning off the engine, I allow my momentum to carry me toward the rear of the building. My maneuver is trickier than his, and for that reason I have chosen it. I have to swing around the side of the building rather than slide straight in. But there are few human devices I am not master of, and I have drunk the blood of so many long-distance truckers over the years that one could say the skill is deep in my veins. I complete the turn smoothly and park and climb out. My two tankers stand less than five feet from the wall of the building. Out the corner of my eye I notice an ice-cream truck parked down the block.

Still, all is calm, all is quiet. Even to my acute hearing.

Ray's truck, on the far side of the building, has also halted. I hear him climb out of his rig and walk toward the rear of the tanks where I have set the fuse. Yet I hear him stop in midstride, and I don't hear the fuse burning. I count my heartbeats and wait for him to complete his task.

But all is quiet. The fuse stays unlit.

My heart begins to pound.

My rifle over my shoulder, I walk toward the rear of my truck, moving in Ray's direction. Something is wrong, I fear. I cannot ignite my tankers without knowing what the problem is. Yet I cannot explode my gasoline from a distance—at least not easily. A bullet may or may not accomplish the feat. Yet I cannot check on Ray without leaving the fuel. It is a paradox once again—my whole life is. After a moment to consider, I reach out and unscrew the cap at the bottom of the rear tanker. The gasoline gushes out. The warehouse rests on an incline, my end higher than Ray's. Stepping around the corner of the building, the volatile fuel follows me in a bubbling stream, soaking my bare feet. I fear the fumes will alert whoever is inside, yet feel I have no choice. The gasoline runs ahead of me, down toward the other truck. Our bombs will become one.

Now I see Ray's truck, but I do not see him, nor his feet standing behind one of the tankers. Moving slowly, my rifle at the ready, I let my hearing precede me. Inside the building the status remains. Twenty-one vampires sleeping peacefully, their bellies full, their dreams dripping red. There is someone behind the truck, however. Two people, maybe,

Two vampires, maybe.

Faintly I hear their breathing. One is calm and easy. The other gasping, struggling, perhaps against a hand clamped over his mouth. In an instant I know what has happened. Eddie was lying in wait for us. He has caught Ray and is holding him hostage on the passenger side of the rig, standing on the step that leads up into the cab. Eddie is waiting for me to come for Ray, to poke my head out. Then he will pounce. I have made the mistake I swore I would not make. I have underestimated an enemy.

It was all a setup. Eddie wanted to trap me.

Yet I do not panic. I don't have time and the day may yet be saved. My hearing has grown more acute over the centuries. I suspect that, even though Eddie is stronger than I, his senses are not as keen. He may not be aware that I am aware of him. The element of surprise may still be mine.

Once again I consider quickly. I can come at him from the left or the right. Or I can come at him from above. The latter seems the most dangerous move, and therefore probably carries with it the greatest element of surprise. I favor it. But I will not simply leap onto the roof of the rig. I will fly right over it. Holding my rifle firmly in my hands, I take several long strides before the truck and then kick up vigorously, as long jumpers do. Floating over a respectable chunk of the lot, over the truck cabin, I turn in midair, bringing the muzzle to bear where I calculate Eddie will be. But I am moving fast, very fast, and when I reach the other side of the truck, near the end of my downward arc, they are not there.

Damn.

So startled am I by their disappearance that I almost lose my footing as I hit the ground. It takes me a moment to get my bearings. And in that time Eddie casually walks out from behind the front of the truck, standing behind Ray, using him as a shield, his bony hands wrapped around my lover's neck. Eddie's speed continues to amaze. In the short time I was in the air, he managed to move out of harm's way. Yet it is not only his superior reflexes that shock me, but his ability to anticipate my moves. He reads me like an open book. But is that so amazing? After all, we are both predators. He shakes Ray to let me know his grip is deadly. For his part Ray appears calm. He believes I will save him. I wish I shared his belief.

Eddie grins. "Hello, Sita. So we meet again."

Yaksha must be alive for him to know my name. Yet I cannot believe Yaksha would betray me to this monster, even though we had been mortal enemies. Keeping my gun level and circling slowly, I study Eddie's expression. He appears to be more sedate than the previous night, slightly weary. Absorbing six bullets must have taken something out of him. Yet his eyes remain chilling. I wonder about his mother, his upbringing, what it takes to create a man who watches snuff films for pleasure. I understand that he has always felt an outcast, and that he spent the majority of his lonely nights imagining what he would do if he had unlimited power. Then it just fell into his lap. Like a gift from God. There is a bit of the fanatic in his eyes. He believes he is on a holy mission and has elected himself the main deity. That disturbs me even more. A prophet is more dangerous than a criminal. At least a criminal's needs are simple. A prophet requires constant stimulation. The false ones, at least. Eddie has not killed Ray yet because he wants to play with us. This is all right, I decide. I know many games.

The sun bothers Eddie, but he can bear it. He squints.

"Hello, Eddie," I say pleasantly. "You look well."

"Thank you. You've made a nice recovery yourself. Congratulations on finding me so quickly. I thought it would take you at least a week to locate the warehouse." He adds, "How did you find me?"

His voice is a strange brew—crafty and eager, easy and sick. There is no depth to his tone, however, and I wonder if he is susceptible to my gentle words. Trying to shoot him while he holds Ray is out of the question. At any one instant he barely shows an inch of himself.

He knew I was in the area because he was waiting to ambush us. But his remarks show that he does not know I visited his mother, or how I probed his past.

"You leave a unique trail," I say softly. "I just had to follow the *red* brick road."

He is amused. And annoyed. He is a pile of contradictions, I see. He shakes Ray hard and my lover gasps. "Answer my question," he orders.

"What will you give me in return?" I continue to circle at a distance of thirty feet. So far there is no movement from inside the warehouse. I do not believe he has an accomplice who can help him. The gasoline from my draining tanker puddles nearby, although none of us is standing directly in it. Once again I try to plant my words in his mind. But the ground there is not fertile.

"I will let your boyfriend live," Eddie says.

"Why don't we do this? Let my friend go and I will answer

all your questions. I will even set aside this shiny new gun."

"Set it aside first and I will consider your suggestion," Eddie replies.

My voice has yet to affect his mind. Still, I continue to try. "It is clear we don't trust each other. We can remain stalemated for a long time. Neither of us wants that. Let me offer you something in exchange for my friend's release. You're a newborn vampire. I am very old. There are many secrets to using your powers that I could teach you. Alone, it would take you several centuries to discover those secrets. To be what you want to be, you need me."

"But how do I know you will give me these secrets?" he asks. "How do I know that the moment I release your friend you won't open fire on me?"

"Because I need you," I lie, but persuasively. "Your blood is more powerful than my own. We can have an even exchange— your power for my knowledge."

Eddie considers. "Give me an example of one of your secrets."

"You have already seen an example. I am here today, right now. You do not know how I got here so quickly. A secret led me to you. I can give you that secret, and others, if you will release my friend."

"You have an interesting voice."

"Thank you."

Eddie's voice hardens. "Is that one of your secrets? The manner in which you manipulate people?"

His question stuns me. He misses nothing, and if that is the case he is not going to release Ray because he must know I will kill him. I consider a dangerous alternative.

"I manipulate mortals like puppets," I reply. "It is not so easy to manipulate *powerful* vampires. But weaker ones—like many of your followers—I could show you how to control them. You know, Eddie, the more you make, and the more they make, the less control you will have."

"I don't believe that."

"You will. Listen to me with an open mind. This is a rare opportunity for you. If you do not take it, you will regret it. You will also die. You're so young. You feel so powerful. But you have made a big mistake confronting me unarmed. This rifle can fire many bullets before having to be reloaded. Your body cannot withstand what I will do to you. If you kill my friend, I will kill you. It's that simple."

He is undaunted. "You may be old and full of secrets, but you have made the big mistake. This guy is important to you. I have his life in my hands. If you do not put down your rifle, I will kill him." His grip tightens and suddenly Ray is unable to breathe. "Put it down now."

"You dare to threaten me, punk." I raise my rifle and point it at Ray's chest. "Release him now."

Eddie remains determined. "Did they play poker thousands of years ago? I don't think so. You don't know how to bluff. Put it down, I say. Your friend is already turning blue."

"Blue is better than red," I reply. "But a little red does not frighten me. I am going to shoot now unless you do as *I* say. This is a sniper rifle. The bullets leave the barrel at high velocity. I am going to shoot my friend in the chest, through one of his lungs, and that same bullet will probably go into one of your lungs. You will have trouble holding on to my friend with a hole in such a vital spot. True, you will start to heal immediately, but before you do, I will put another bullet in my friend, and in you. How many bullets do you think you can take before you have to let go? How many bullets can you take before you die?" I pause. "I don't make many mistakes, Eddie."

My audacity shakes him. It shakes Ray as well; he turns a bit green. He continues to choke. Eddie reconsiders. "You will not shoot your friend," he says.

"Why not? You're about to kill him anyway." I settle on a spot on Ray's belly, just below the rib cage. They are roughly the same height; the wounds should be identical, less serious than holes in the lungs. "I am going to count to three. One—two—"

"Wait," Eddie says quickly. "I'll make you a counter proposal."

I keep my aim fast. "Yes?"

"I will tell you where your other friend is—as a sign of good faith—and you will allow me to leave with your boyfriend as far as the other end of the warehouse. There I will release him."

He's lying. He will break Ray's neck as soon as he puts some distance between us. "First tell me where Yaksha is, then I will consider your proposal."

Eddie snorts. "You are one cunning bitch."

"Thank you. Where is Yaksha?"

"He's not far."

"I tire of this." I put four pounds on a five-pound trigger. "Ray," I say gently, "after I shoot, I want you to fight to shake free. He will try to hold on to you, of course, but remember he will be bleeding as badly as you are. And even though he is stronger than both of us, he is alone. Even if I have to put two or three bullets in you, I promise, you will not die." My tone becomes bitter. "But you, Eddie, will die screaming. Like those people you tortured last night."

He is a cruel devil. "I look forward to hearing *your* screams."

I fire. The bullet hits where I intend and penetrates both of them, exiting Eddie's back and striking the passenger door of the gasoline truck. Red blossoms on Ray's midsection and he gasps in pain. But Eddie does not try to defend himself by continuing to use Ray as a shield. The guy is totally unpredictable. Instead, he throws Ray at me, momentarily knocking me off balance. Then he is on me. Yes, even though I hold the rifle in my hands and there are thirty feet between us, Eddie is able to get to me before I can get off another shot. He is like black lightning. Crashing into me with tremendous force, he knocks me onto my back. The rear of my skull smacks the ground and my grip on the rifle falters, although I have not let go of it. For a moment I see stars, and they are not Krishna blue but hellish red and threatening to explode. Stunned himself, Eddie slowly climbs to his knees beside me. He regains his concentration swiftly, however. His eyes focus on the rifle, the only thing that gives me an advantage over him. I try to bring it up, to put a bullet in his face, but once again he is too fast. Lashing out in a sharp karatelike motion with his right hand, he actually *bends* the barrel of the rifle, rendering it useless. He is bleeding badly from his stomach, but he grins as he stares at my broken toy. He thinks he has me now.

"I can take a lot before I die," he says, answering my previous question.

"Really?" I kick him in the belly, in his wound, and he momentarily doubles up. But my blow is not decisive. Before I can fully climb to my knees, he strikes with his left fist, and I feel as if my head almost leaves its place on top of my shoulders. Again, I topple backward, blood pouring from my mouth. I land dizzily in a pile of gravel. Pain throbs through my entire body from my face. He has broken my jaw, several of my teeth, at least. And he is not done. Out the side of a drooping eye, I see him climb to his feet and ready his sharp black boots to kick me to death. Out the other eye I see Ray also stand. Eddie has momentarily forgotten my lover, probably considering him small game.

Uncertain, Ray makes a move to attack Eddie that will

lengthen my life by all of five seconds. Shaking my head minutely, I raise my bleeding arm in the direction of the truck. A look passes between us. Ray understands. Light the fuse, I am saying, detonate our bomb. Save the human race. Save yourself. I will keep Eddie busy for ten seconds. Ray turns in the direction of the truck, the gasoline from the other tanker puddling around the wheels. Of course Eddie also sees him turn for the truck. He moves to stop him. In that moment, summoning the last of my strength, I launch myself off the ground at Eddie's midsection.

We crash and fall into another painful pile. As we once more struggle to stand, he reaches over and grabs me by the hair, pulling my face close to his. His breath is foul; I believe he not only sucks his victims dry, but eats them as well. He looks as if he would like to take a bite out of me. His eyes are crazed: excited and furious at the same time. Prozac would not help him. He yanks at my hair and a thousand roots come out.

"That hurts," I say.

He grins, cocking his fist back. "Try this on for size, Sita."

I close my eyes and wait for the blow. This one, I am sure, will send me into the promised land. I just hope I have bought Ray enough time. What I do not understand is that Ray is still trying to buy me time. The blow never arrives. Ray's voice comes to me as if from far away.

"Eddie," he says firmly.

I open my eyes. Eddie and I both look over and discover that rather than follow my last instruction and light the fuse, Ray has chosen to punch a hole in the tanker with his fist. The gasoline pours out beside him like a gusher from a cracking dam. Of greater note, he has already struck a single wooden match and holds the flame above his head like a miniature torch that will lead us safely past the valley of the shadow of death. Or else straight into it. I am fully aware that the fumes of gasoline are more volatile than the actual liquid itself. And Ray stands in a cloud of petroleum fog. Not that Eddie and I loiter at a safe distance. Gasoline soaks both sets of our feet.

"I only have one match," Ray says to Eddie. "If you do not let Sita go, I will have to drop this one. What do you say?"

Eddie just won't learn. "You're bluffing," he says.

I catch Ray's eye. "No," I plead.

Ray smiles faintly in my direction. "Run, Sita. Fly. Return and fight him another day. In the end you'll win. Remember, you have Krishna's grace." His fingers move.

"Ray!" I scream.

He lets go of the burning match. Eddie lets go of me, in a hurry. For a moment I stare transfixed as the little orange flame topples toward the waterfall of gasoline. Despite my endless years, the countless deaths I have witnessed, it strikes me as inconceivable that such a tiny flame has the potential to scorch my universe, to burn everything I love and cherish. Yet my state of denial does not last forever. The match is halfway to the ground when I bolt toward Ray. But even I, Yaksha's prime pupil, am too slow for gravity. Before I can reach Ray's hands, which he holds up to ward me off, the match kisses the flowing river of fuel.

"No!" I cry.

Combustion is immediate. The gasoline at his feet ignites. The flames race up his soaked clothes. In an instant my beautiful boy is transformed into a living torch. For a moment I see his eyes through the flames. Perhaps it is a trick of the light, but his brown eyes suddenly appear blue to me, shining with the light of stars I have never seen, or stars I no longer remember. There is no pain on his face; he has made his choice willingly, to save me, to save us all. He stands for a moment like a candle fit to be offered to the Lord. But the flames are not idle; they rush toward me while at the same time they leap toward the truck that stands behind Ray. The truck is closer. Before my own legs begin to burn, before I can reach Ray and pull him free of the holocaust, the fire snakes into the opening Ray had punched in the tanker. The stream of fire is not a fuse we planned, but it is an effective one nevertheless.

The gasoline truck explodes.

An angry red hand slaps the entire front of my body. I have a last glimpse of Ray's fiery form disintegrating under the hammer of the shock wave. Then I am flying through the air, shooting through the smoke. A blur of a wall appears and I hit it hard and feel every bone in my body break. I slump to the ground, falling into a well of despair. My clothes are on fire, but they fail to light this black well because it is bottomless.

My last conscious awareness is of a sport coat being thrown over me.

Then I am blackness.

TEN

I stand on a vast grass field of many gently sloping hills. It is night, yet the sky is bright. There is no sun, but a hundred blazing blue stars, each shimmering in a long river of nebulous cloud. The air is warm, pleasant, fragrant with the perfume of a thousand invisible flowers. In the distance a stream of people walk toward a large vessel of some type, nestled between the hills. The ship is violet, glowing; the bright rays that stab forth from it seem to reach to the stars. Somehow I know that it is about to leave and that I am supposed to be on it. Yet, before I depart, there is something I have to discuss with Lord Krishna.

He stands beside me on the wide plain, his gold flute in his right hand, a red lotus flower in his left. His dress is simple, as is mine—long blue gowns that reach to the ground. Only he wears a single jewel around his neck—the brilliant Kaustubha gem, in which the destiny of every soul can be seen. He does not look at me but toward the vast ship, and the stars beyond. He seems to be waiting for me to speak, but for some reason I cannot remember what he said last. I only know that I am a special case. Because I do not know what to ask, I say what is most on my mind.

"When will I see you again, my Lord?"

He gestures to the vast plain, the thousands of people leaving. "The earth is a place of time and dimension. Moments here can seem like an eternity there. It all depends on your heart. When you remember me, I am there in the blink of an eye."

"Even on earth?"

He nods. "Especially there. It is a unique place. Even the gods pray to take birth there."

"Why is that, my Lord?"

He smiles faintly. His smile is bewitching. It has been said, I know, that the smile of the Lord has bewildered the minds of the angels. It has bewildered mine.

"One question always leads to another question. Some things are better to wonder about." He turns toward me finally, his long black hair blowing in the soft night breeze. The stars reflect in his black pupils; the whole universe is there. The love that flows from him is the sweetest ambrosia in all the heavens. Yet it breaks my heart to feel because I know it will soon be gone. "It is all *maya*," he says. "Illusion."

"Will I get lost in this illusion, my Lord?"

"Of course. It is to be expected. You will be lost for a long time."

"I will forget you?"

"Yes."

I feel tears on my face. "Why does it have to be that way?"

He considers. "There was this great god who was master of a vast ocean. This ocean—you may not know its name, but it is very near to here. This god had three wives. You know how hard it is to please one wife? You can imagine how difficult it was to keep all three happy. Not long after he married the three, two of them came to him and asked for gifts. The first one said, 'O great Lord. We are the finest of your wives, the most beautiful. Reward us with special presents and we will be most pleased.' And the second one said, 'We have served you faithfully and love none other than you. Give us treasures and we will stay with you for the rest of your life.' The god laughed at their requests, but because he was pleased with them, he fulfilled their wishes. To the first he gave all the jewels in his ocean: the diamonds, the emeralds, the sapphires. To the second he gave all the colored coral, all the beautiful seashells. The third wife, of course, asked for nothing in particular. So he gave her the salt."

"The salt, my Lord? Is that all?"

"Yes. Because she asked nothing from him, he gave her the salt, which she spread out in the ocean. All the bright jewels became invisible, and all the pretty seashells were covered over.

And the first two wives were unable to find their treasure and so were left with nothing. So you see the salt was the greatest of the gifts, or at least the most powerful." Krishna pauses. "You understand this story, Sita?"

I hesitate. There are always many meanings in his stories. "Yes. This nearby ocean is the creation we are about to enter. The salt is the *maya*, the illusion, that covers its treasures."

Krishna nods. "Yes. But understand that these treasures are not evil, and the goddesses who own them are not simply vain. Dive deep into this ocean and they will cause currents to stir that will lead you to things you cannot imagine." He pauses and then continues in a softer voice, once more looking at the sky. "I dreamed of the earth, and that is how it came to be. In my dream I saw you there." He reaches out and his hand touches my hair and I feel I will swoon. "You go there to learn things that only earth can teach. That is true but it is also false. All of truth is paradoxical. With me, there is never any coming or going. Do you understand?"

"No, my Lord."

He removes his hand. "It doesn't matter. You are like the earth, unique. But unlike the others you see before you, you will not come and go there many times. In your dream, and mine, you will go there and stay."

"For how long, my Lord?"

"You will be born at the beginning of one age. You will not leave until the next age comes."

My tears return. "And in all that time I am never to see you?"

"You will see me not long after you are changed. Then, it is possible, you may see me again before you leave the earth." Krishna smiles. "It is all up to you."

I do not understand what he means by changed, but have more pressing concerns. "But I don't want to go at all!"

He laughs so easily. "You say that now. You will not say that . . . later." His eyes hold mine for what seems a moment, but perhaps is much longer. In that brief span I see many faces, many stars. It is as if the whole universe spins below and completes an entire revolution. But I have not left the hilltop. I continue to stare into Krishna's eyes. Or are they really eyes and not windows into a portion of myself that I have striven so hard to reclaim? A tiny globe of light emerges from his eyes and floats into mine, a living world of many forms and shapes. He speaks to me in a whisper. "How do you feel now, Sita?"

I raise my hand to my head. "Dizzy. I feel somehow as if I have just lived . . ." I stop. "I feel as if I have already been to earth and been married and had a child! It is all so strange. I feel as if I have been something other than human. Is that possible?"

He nods. "You will be human for only a short time. And, yes, it has all happened already. You see, that is the *maya*. You think what you have to do, to accomplish, to perfect yourself to reach me. But there is no doer-ship. You are always with me, and I am always with you. Still, it is deep in your heart to be different from the rest, to try to do in one long life what it takes others thousands of lives to accomplish. So be it. You are an angel, but you wish to be like me. But I am both angel and demon, good and evil. Yet I am above all these things. Dive deep into the ocean, Sita, and you will find that the greatest treasures you find are the illusions you leave behind."

"I do not understand."

"It doesn't matter." He raises his flute to his lips. "Now I will play you a song made up of the seven notes of humanity. All the emotions you will feel as a human and as a vampire. Remember this song and you will remember me. Sing this song and I will be there."

"Wait! What is a vampire?"

But Krishna has already started to play. As I strive to listen a sudden wind comes up on the plain and the notes are drowned out. The dust rises and I am blinded, and I can't see Krishna anymore. I can't feel him near. The light of the stars fades and all goes dark. And my sorrow is great.

Yet I have to wonder if I have lost the song because I have become the song. If I have lost my Lord because I do indeed desire to be what I will become. A lover who hates, a saint who sins, and an angel who kills.

I awake to a world I don't want. There is no transition for me. I am in paradise, I am in hell.

"Hello?" a voice says.

Actually, I am in a cheap motel. Looking around, I see a chipped chest of drawers, a dusty mirror that reflects bare walls, a dumpy mattress. It is on this mattress that I lay, naked, covered with a sheet. In this reflection I also see Special Agent Joel Drake, who sits on a chair near the window and waits anxiously for me to respond to his query. But I say nothing at first.

Ray is dead. I know this, I feel this. Yet, at the same time I hurt too much to feel anything. I hear my heart pump inside my chest. It cannot belong to me, however. In my long life I have drunk the blood of thousands, but now I am an empty vessel. I shiver even though the room is warm.

"Yes?" I say finally.

"Sita." In the mirror I watch the reflection of Joel come and sit on the bed beside me. The soggy springs respond to the weight, and my body sags in the middle. "Are you all right?" he asks.

"Yes."

"You're in a motel. I took you here after the explosion at the warehouse. That was twelve hours ago. You have slept away the entire day."

"Yes."

He speaks without believing his own words. "I followed in your footsteps. I went to see the mother. She was in a strange state, incoherent, like a broken record. She kept repeating the location of the warehouse that blew up. She said little else."

"Yes." Clearly I pushed the mother's brain too hard, etched my suggestion in her psyche, set up an echo. I have done this in the past, and the effect is seldom permanent. The woman will probably be all right in a day or two. Not that I care.

"I immediately drove to the warehouse," Joel continues. "When I got there you and your partner were confronting that guy. I was running over just as the explosion happened." He pauses. "You were thrown free, but I was sure you were dead. You hit a brick wall with incredible force, and your clothes were all on fire. I covered you with my coat and put out the flames. Then I saw that you were still breathing. I loaded you in my car and was taking you to the hospital when I noticed . . . I saw with my own eyes." He has trouble speaking. "You started to heal, right there in front of me. The cuts on your face closed, and your back—it had to be broken in a hundred places—just knit back together. I thought to myself, This is impossible. I can't take her to a hospital. They'll want to lock her away for the next ten years for observation." He stops. "So I brought you here. Are you following this?"

"Yes."

He is getting desperate. "Tell me what's happening here. Who are you?"

I continue to stare in the mirror. I don't want to ask the questions. Simply to ask is to be weak, and I am always strong. It is not as though I have any hope. Yet I ask anyway.

"The young man near the truck . . . ," I begin.

"Your partner? The guy who was on fire?"

"Yes." I swallow. My throat is dry. "Was he thrown free?"

Joel softens. "No."

"Are you sure?"

"Yes."

"But is he dead?"

Joel understands what I am saying. My partner was like me, not normal. Even severely injured, he could have healed. But Joel shakes his head, and I know Ray was blown to pieces.

"He's dead," Joel says.

"I understand." I sit up and cough weakly. Joel brings me a glass of water. As I touch the rim of the glass to my lips, a drop of red stains the clear liquid. But the color does not come from my mouth or nose. It is a bloody tear. Seldom have I ever cried. This must be a special occasion.

Joel hesitates. "Was he your boyfriend?"

I nod.

"I'm sorry."

The words really do not help me. "Did both tankers, at both ends of the warehouse, blow?"

"Yes."

"Did you see anyone run out of the warehouse after the explosion?"

"No. That would have been impossible. It was an inferno. The police are still going through the mess, picking out the charred bodies. They've cordoned off the whole area." He pauses. "Did you set those tankers to blow?"

"Yes."

"Why?"

"To kill those inside. They were your killers. But I don't want to talk about that now. What about the other man? The one who was with my boyfriend and me? Did he get away?"

"I don't know where he went. He was just gone."

"Oh." That means he got away.

"Who was that man?" Joel asks.

"I'm sure you can guess."

"Edward Fender?"

I nod. "Eddie."

Joel sits back and stares at me. At this young woman whose body was crushed twelve hours ago, and who now appears completely well except for a few bloody tears. I note the dark sky through the cracked window, the glow of neon signaling the beginning of another long night. He wants me to tell him *why*. But I am asking myself the same question. Why did it take five thousand years to find someone to love again? Why was he then taken from me after only six weeks?

Why time and space, Krishna? You erect these walls around us and then close us in. Especially when those we love leave us. Then the walls are too high, and no matter how hard we jump, we cannot see beyond them. Then all we have are walls falling in on us.

I do not believe my dream. Life is not a song. Life is a curse, and no one's life has been longer than mine.

"How did you heal so fast?" Joel asks me.

"I told you, I am not normal."

He trembles. "Are you a human being?"

Wiping away my bloody tears, I chuckle bitterly. What was that in my dream? That part about me wanting to be different? How ironic—and foolish. It was as if I were a child going to sleep at night and asking my mother if I could please have a horrible nightmare.

"Ordinarily I would say no," I reply. "But since I'm crying, and that's a thing humans often do, then maybe I should say yes." I stare down at my red-stained hands and feel his eyes on them as well. "What do you think?"

He takes my hands in his and studies them closer. He is still trying to convince himself that reality has not suddenly developed a pronounced rip.

"You're bleeding. You must still be injured."

I take my hand back and wave away his question. "I am this way. It is normal for me." I have to wipe my cheeks again. These tears—I cannot stop them. "Everywhere I go, everything I touch . . . there is blood."

"Sita?"

I sit up sharply. "Don't call me that! I am not her, do you understand? She died a long time ago. I am this thing you see before you! This . . . this bloody thing!" Not minding my nakedness, I stand and walk to the window, stepping over my burnt clothes, lying on the floor in a pile. He must have peeled them off me; the material is sticky with charred flesh. Pulling the curtain farther aside, I stare out at a landscape that looks as foreign from the world of my dream as another galaxy. We cannot be far from the warehouse. We are still in the ghetto, still on the enemy's turf. "I wonder what he's doing right now," I mutter.

Joel stands at my back. "While you rested, I went out and bought you some clothes." He gestures to a bag sitting on a chair in the corner. "I don't know if they will fit."

"Thank you." I go to the corner and put them on: blue jeans, a gray sweatshirt. They fit fine. There are no shoes, but I don't need them. I notice my knife sitting on the chair beneath the bag. However, the leather strap that I used to secure it to my leg is not there. I put it in my back pocket instead. It sticks out a few inches. Joel follows my moves with fear in his eyes.

"What are you going to do?" he asks.

"Find him. Kill him."

Joel takes a step toward me. "You have to talk to me."

I shake my head. "I cannot. I tried to talk to you on the pier, and you still followed me. I suspect you will try to follow me again. But I understand that. You're just trying to do your job. I'm just trying to do mine." I turn toward the door. "It will be over soon enough, one way or the other."

He stops me as I reach for the knob. Even after all he has

seen of me. He is a brave man. I do not shake his hand from my arm. Instead, I stare into his eyes, but without the intention of manipulation, the desire to control. I stare at him so that he can stare at me. Without Ray, for the first time in a long time, I feel so lonely. So human. He sees my pain.

"What would you like me to call you?" he asks gently.

I make a face. Without the mirror I don't know if it is very pleasant. "You may call me Sita if you wish . . . Joel."

"I want to help you, Sita."

"You cannot help me. I've explained to you why, and now you've seen why." I add, "I don't want you to get killed."

He is anxious. It must mean he likes me, this bloody thing. "I don't want *you* to get killed. I may not have your special attributes, but I am an experienced law enforcement officer. We should go after him together."

"A gun won't stop him."

"I have more to offer than a gun."

I smile faintly and reach up to touch his cheek. Once again I think what a fine man he is. Consumed with doubts and questions, he still wants to do his duty. He still wants to be with me.

"I can make you forget," I say to him. "You saw how I affected the mother's mind. I can do that kind of thing. But I don't want to do it to you, even now. I want you just to get away from here, get away from me. And forget any of this ever happened." I take my hand back. "That is the most human thing I can tell you, Joel."

He finally lets go of my arm. "Will I see you again?" he asks.

I am sad. "I hope not. And I don't mean that cruelly. Goodbye."

"Goodbye."

I walk out the door and close it behind me. The night is not as warm as I like it, nor is it cold, as I hate. It is cool and dark, a fine time for a vampire to go hunting. Later, I tell myself, I will grieve for Ray. Now there is too much to do.

ELEVEN

On foot I return to the vicinity of the warehouse. But as Joel said, the entire area is cordoned off by numerous police officers. From several blocks away I study the remains of the warehouse with my acute vision, perhaps subconsciously searching for the remains of Ray. The investigative crew, however, is working the ruins. Whatever was lying around outside has already been picked up and deposited into plastic bags with white labels on them. With the many flashing red lights, the mounds of ash, and the ruined bodies, the scene depresses me. Still, I do not turn away from it. I am thinking.

"But what he did do was tie Heather up in his bedroom closet, standing up and wearing his high school letter jacket—and nothing else—and force her to suck on Popsicles all night."

The night I met the newborn vampires, I heard an ice-cream

truck in the vicinity, its repetitive jingle playing loudly. In the middle of December in the middle of the night. Then, when I visited Mrs. Fender, I learned she had a large freezer in her house. Finally, after parking my tanker outside the warehouse, I saw out of the corner of my eye an ice-cream truck. From where I stand now, I cannot see that same spot to tell if the truck is still there. But with the security in the area I think that it might be there, and I believe that it might be important.

What kind of thing did Eddie have about Popsicles?

What kind of fetish did he have about frozen corpses?

Were the fetishes related?

If Eddie did get his hands on Yaksha's remains and Yaksha was still alive, Eddie would have been forced to keep Yaksha in a weakened state to control him. There are two ways to do that—at least, only two that I know of. One is to keep Yaksha impaled with a number of sharp objects that his skin cannot heal around. The other is more subtle and deals with the nature of vampires themselves. Yaksha was the incarnation of a yakshini, a demonic serpent being. Snakes are cold-blooded and do not like the cold. In the same way vampires hate the cold, although we can withstand it. Yet ice thwarts us as much as the sun, slowing down our mental processes, hampering our ability to recover from serious wounds. Going by Eddie's obvious strength and knowledge of my identity, I hypothesize that he has indeed gotten a hold of Yaksha *alive* and is keeping him in an extremely weak state while he continues to drink his blood. I suspect Eddie keeps him impaled *and* half frozen.

But where?

At home with Mom?

Doubtful. Mom is crazy and Yaksha is a treasure too dangerous to leave lying around. Eddie would keep his blood supply close. He would even take it with him when he went out hunting at night.

I find a phone booth nearby and call Sally Diedrich. Before leaving the coroner's office, I had obtained her home and work number. I am not in the mood for idle gossip, so I come right to the point. Before going into the stiff business, did Eddie used to be an ice-cream man? As a matter of fact, yes, Sally replies. He and his mom owned a small ice-cream truck business in the Los Angeles area. That's all I wanted to know.

Next I call Pat McQueen, Ray's old girlfriend.

I don't know why I do it. She is not someone I can share my grief with, and besides, I do not believe such a thing should be shared. Yet, on this darkest of all nights, I feel an affinity with her. I stole her love and now fate has stolen mine. Maybe it is justice. Dialing the number, I wonder if I call to apologize or to antagonize her. I remind myself that she thinks Ray perished six weeks ago. My call will not be welcome. I may just open wounds that have already begun to close. Still, I do not hang up when she answers after a couple of rings.

"Hello?"

"Hello, Pat. This is Alisa. I'm sure you remember me?"

She gasps, then falls into a wary silence. She hates me, I know, and wants to hang up. But she is curious. "What do you want?" she asks.

"I don't know. I stand here asking myself the same question. I guess I just wanted to talk to someone who knew Ray well."

There is a long silence. "I thought you were dead."

"So did I."

An even longer pause. I know what she will ask. "He is, isn't he?"

I bow my head. "Yes. But his death was not just an accident. He died bravely, by his own choice, trying to protect what he believed in."

She begins to weep. "Did he believe in you?" she asks bitterly.

"Yes. I like to think so. He believed in you as well. His feelings for you went very deep. He did not leave you willingly. I forced him."

"Why? Why couldn't you just leave us alone?"

"I loved him."

"But you killed him! He would be alive now if you had never spoken to him!"

I sigh. "I know that. But I did not know what would happen. Had I known, I would have done things completely different. Please believe me, Pat, I did not want to hurt you or him. It just worked out that way."

She continues to cry. "You're a monster."

The pain in my chest is great. "Yes."

"I can't forget him. I can't forget this. I hate you."

"You can hate me. That's all right. But you don't need to forget him. You won't be able to anyway. Nor will I be able to. Pat, maybe I do know why I called you. I think it was to tell you that his death does not necessarily mean the end of him. You see, I think I met Ray long ago, in another place, another dimension. And that day at school when we all introduced ourselves, it was like magic. He was gone, but he came back. He can come back again, I think, or at least we can go to him, to the stars."

She begins to quiet. "I don't know what you're talking about."

I force a smile, for myself. "It doesn't matter. We both loved him and he's gone, and who knows if there is anything else? No one knows. Have a good night, Pat. Have sweet dreams. Dream about him. I know I will for a long time."

She hesitates. "Goodbye, Alisa."

Hanging up, I stare at the ground. It is closer than the sky, and at least I know it is real. Clouds hang overhead anyway, and there are no stars tonight. I call my old friend Seymour. He answers quickly, and I tell him everything that has happened. He listens without interrupting. That's what I like about him. In this world of gossip a good listener is rarer than a great orator. He is silent when I finish. He knows he cannot console me and he doesn't really try. I respect that as well. But he does acknowledge the loss.

"Too bad about Ray," he says.

"Yeah. Real bad."

"Are you all right?"

"Yes."

His voice is firm. "Good. You have to stop this bastard. I agree with you—Yaksha is probably in that ice-cream truck. All the signs point in that direction. Why didn't you wait until you checked it out before calling me?"

"Because if he is in there, and I get him away from Eddie and the cops, I won't be of a mind to make phone calls."

"Good. Get Yaksha. He'll heal quickly and then the two of you go after Eddie."

"I don't think it will be that easy."

Seymour pauses. "His legs won't grow back?"

"This might surprise you, but I don't have a lot of experience in such matters. But I doubt it."

"That's not good. You'll have to face Eddie alone."

"And I didn't do so well last time."

"You did well. You destroyed his partners. But you have to act fast or he will make more, and this time he will not allow them to gather in one place and be so easily wiped out."

"But I cannot beat him by force. I have proved that to myself already. He is just too fast, too strong. He's also smart. But you're smart, too. Just tell me what to do and I'll do it."

"I can only give you some hints. You have to place him in a situation where your advantages are magnified. He probably cannot see and hear as well as you. He is probably more sensitive to the sun."

"The sun didn't slow him down much."

"Well, he may be more sensitive to cold than you. I suspect that he is and doesn't know it. He certainly seems sensitive when it comes to his mother. He's what? Thirty years old? And he's a vampire and he's still living at home? The guy can't be that fearsome."

"I appreciate the humor. But give me something specific."

"Take her hostage. Threaten to kill her. He'll come a-running."

"I have thought of that."

"Then do it. But get Yaksha away from him first. I think it's Yaksha who can give you the secret of how to stop him."

"You read and write too many books. Do you really think there is a magical secret?"

"You are magic, Sita. You are full of secrets you don't even know. Krishna let you live for a reason. You have to find that reason, and this situation will resolve itself automatically."

His words move me. I had not told him of my dream. Still, my doubts and my pain are too heavy for words alone to wash away.

"Krishna is full of mischief," I say. "Sometimes, so the stories went, he did things for no reason at all. Just because he wanted to."

"Then you be mischievous. Trick Eddie. The football players at our school are all bigger and stronger than I am. But they're all a bunch of fools. I could whip their asses any day."

"If I survive this night, and tomorrow night, I will hold you to that proud boast. I might tell your football team exactly what you said about them."

"Fair enough." He softens. "Ray was enough. Don't die on me, Sita."

I am close to tears again. "I will call you the first chance I get."

"Promise?"

"Cross my heart and hope to die."

He groans but he is frightened for me. "Take care."

"Sure," I say.

Sneaking into the secured area is not difficult. I simply leap from one rooftop to the next when no one is looking. But getting out with an ice-cream truck in tow will not be so easy. There are police cars parked crossways at every exit. Nevertheless, that is the least of my worries. Moving silently a hundred feet above the ground, I see that the ice-cream truck is still in place. A palpable aura of pain surrounds it like a swarm of black insects above a body that has lain unburied. Dread weighs heavily on me as I leap from my high perch and land on the concrete sidewalk beside the truck. I feel as if I have just jumped into a black well filled with squirming snakes. No one stands in the immediate vicinity, but the odor of venom is thick in the air. Even before I pull aside the locked door to the refrigerated compartment, I know that Yaksha is inside and in poor condition.

I open the door.

"Yaksha?" I whisper.

There is movement at the back of the cold box.

A strange shape speaks.

"What flavor would you like, little girl?" Yaksha asks in a tired voice.

My reaction is a surprise to me. Probably because I feared him for so long, it is difficult for me even to approach him without hesitation—even while seeking him out as an ally. Yet, with his silly question, a wave of warmth sweeps over me. Still, I do not stare too hard at what he has become. I do not want to know, at least not yet.

"I will get you out of here," I say. "Give me ten minutes."

"You can take fifteen if you need, Sita."

I close the compartment door. Only police cars are allowed in and out of the area. Not even the press has gotten through the roadblocks, which is understandable. It is not every day twenty-plus bodies are incinerated in Los Angeles, although, on the other hand, it is not that unusual an occurrence in this part of town.

My course is clear. I will get myself a police car, maybe a navy blue police cap to cover my blond hair. I walk casually in the direction of the warehouse, when who do I run into but the two cops who stopped me outside the Coliseum: Detective Doughnut and his young prodigy. They blink when they see me, and I have to refrain from laughing. A box of doughnuts is set out on the hood of their black-and-white unit, and they are casually sipping coffee from Styrofoam cups. We are still a block from where all the action is going on, relatively isolated from view. The situation appeals to my devilish nature.

"Fancy meeting you here," I say.

They scramble to set down their nourishment. "What are you doing here?" the older cop asks politely. "This is a restricted area."

I am bold. "You make this place sound like a nuclear submarine."

"We're serious," the young one says. "You'd best get out of here quick."

I move closer. "I will leave as soon as you give me your car keys."

They exchange a smile. The older one nods in my direction. "Haven't you seen the news? Don't you know what's happened here?"

"Yeah, I heard an atomic bomb went off." I stick out my hand. "But give me the keys, really. I'm in a big hurry."

The young one puts his hand on his nightstick. Like he would really need it with a ninety-eight-pound young woman who looks all of twenty. Of course, he would need a Bradley

Tank to stop me. The guy has a phony prep school demeanor, and I peg him for a rich dropout who couldn't get into law school and so joined the force to annoy Daddy.

"We're running out of patience," Preppy says, acting the tough guy. "Leave immediately or we're hauling your tight ass in."

"My tight ass? What about the rest of me? That sounds like a sexist statement if I ever heard one." I move within two feet of Preppy and stare him in the eye, trying hard not to burn it out of its socket. "You know I have nothing against good cops, but I can't stand sexist pigs. They piss me off, and when I get pissed off there's no stopping me." I poke the guy in the chest, hard. "You apologize to me right now or I'm going to whip your ass."

To my surprise—I could pass, after all, for a high school senior—he pulls his gun on me. Backing off a pace as if shocked, I raise my arms over my head. The older cop takes a tentative step in our direction. He is more experienced; he knows it is always a bad idea to go looking for trouble where trouble does not exist. Yet he does not know that trouble is my middle name.

"Hey, Gary," he says. "Leave the girl alone. She's just flirting with you is all. Put away your gun."

Gary does not listen. "She's got a pretty dirty mouth for a flirt. How do we know she's not a prostitute? Yeah, that's right, maybe she is. Maybe we should haul her tight ass in on a charge of soliciting sexual favors for money."

"I haven't offered you any money," I say.

That angers Gary. He shakes his gun at my belly. "You get up against that wall and spread your legs."

"Gary," the old cop complains. "Stop it."

"Better stop now, Gary," I warn him. "I can tell you for sure you won't be able to finish it."

Gary grabs me by the arm and throws me against the wall. I let him. When I am upset, I like to hunt. Actually, when I feel any strong emotion, I like to hunt, to drink blood, to kill even. As Gary begins to frisk me, I debate whether to kill him. He is way over the line as he pats down my tight ass. He is not wearing a wedding band; he will not be missed much, except perhaps by his partner, who is soon headed for a heart attack anyway, with his diet of greasy doughnuts and black coffee. Yes, I think as Gary digs into my pockets and discovers my knife, his blood will taste good, and the world can do with one less creep. He holds the weapon up to his partner as if he has found the key to a treasure. In his mind it is that way. Now, because I am a certifiable criminal, he can do what he wants with me, as long as no one is videotaping the proceedings. No wonder the people in this neighborhood riot from time to time.

"Well, look at what we have here!" Gary exclaims. "Bill, when was the last time you saw a knife like this on a college coed?" He taps me on the shoulder with the flat of the blade. "Who gave this to you, honey? Your pimp?"

"Actually," I reply, "I took that knife off the body of a

French nobleman who had the audacity to touch my ass without asking my permission." I slowly turn and catch his eye. "Like you."

Officer Bill reaches out and takes the knife away from Officer Gary, who tries to stare me down. He would have more luck staring down an oncoming train. Carefully I allow a little heat to enter my gaze and watch with pleasure as Gary begins to perspire heavily. He still grips his gun but has trouble keeping it steady.

"You're under arrest," he mutters.

"What is the charge?"

He swallows. "Carrying a concealed weapon."

I ease up on Gary for a moment, glance at Bill. "Are you arresting me as well?"

He is doubtful. "What are you doing with this kind of knife?"

"I carry it for protection," I reply.

Bill looks at Gary. "Let her go. If I lived around here, I'd carry a knife, too."

"Are you forgetting that this is the same girl we ran into outside the Coliseum?" Gary asks, annoyed. "She was there the night of the murders. Now she's here at the burned-out warehouse." With his free hand he takes out his handcuffs. "Stick out your hands, please."

I do so. "Since you said please."

After holstering his gun, Gary slaps on the cuffs. He grabs

me by the arm again and pulls me toward the patrol car. "You have the right to remain silent. If you choose to give up that right, anything you say may be used as evidence against you. You have the right to the presence of an attorney, either retained or appointed—"

"Just a second," I interrupt as Gary starts to force my head into the rear seat.

"What is it?" Gary growls.

I turn my head in Bill's direction and catch his eye. "I want Bill to sit down and take a nap."

"Huh?" Gary says. But Bill does not say anything. Too many doughnuts have made him gullible. Already he is under my spell. I continue to bore into his eyes.

"I want Bill to sit down and go to sleep," I say. "Sleep and forget, Bill. You never met me. You don't know what happened to Gary. He just vanished tonight. It's not your fault."

Bill sits down, closes his eyes like a small boy who has just been tucked in by his mother, then goes to sleep. His snores startle his partner, who quickly takes out his gun again and points it at me. Poor Gary. I know I am no role model for the war against violence, but they should never have let this guy out of the academy with live ammunition.

"What have you done to him?" he demands.

I shrug. "What can I do? I'm handcuffed." To illustrate my helplessness, I hold my chained hands up before his eyes. Then, smiling wickedly, I snap them apart. When I flex my wrists, the remains of the metal bonds fall to the concrete, clattering like loose change falling from torn pockets. "You know what that French nobleman said before I slit his throat with his own knife?"

Gary takes a stunned step back. "Don't move. I'll shoot."

I step toward him. "He said, 'Don't come a step closer. I'll kill you.' Of course, he didn't have your advantage. He didn't have a gun. As a matter of fact, there were no guns in those days." I pause and my eyes must be so big to him. Bigger than moons that burn with primordial volcanoes. "Do you know what he said as my fingers went around his throat?"

Gary, trembling, cocks the hammer on his revolver. "You are evil," he whispers.

"Close." Lashing out with my left foot, I kick the gun out of his hand. Much to his dismay it goes skidding down the block. I continue in a sweet voice, "What he said was, 'You are a witch.' You see, they believed in witches in those days." Slowly, deliberately, I reach over and grab my pale white victim by the collar and pull him toward me. "Do you believe in witches, Gary?"

He is a mask of fear, a bodysuit of twitches. "No," he mumbles.

I grin and lick his throat. "Do you believe in vampires?"

Incredibly he starts to cry. "No."

"There, there," I say as I stroke his head. "You must believe in something scary or you wouldn't be so upset. Tell me, what kind of monster do you think I am?"

"Please let me go."

I shake my head sadly. "I'm afraid I can't do that, even though you did say please. Your fellow cops are just around the block. If I let you go, you'll run to them and tell them that I'm a prostitute who carries a concealed weapon. By the way, that wasn't a very flattering description. No one has ever paid me for sex, at least not with money." I choke him a little. "But they have paid me with their blood."

His tears are a river. "Oh, God."

I nod. "You go right ahead and pray to God. This might surprise you, but I met him once. He probably wouldn't approve of the torture I'm putting you through, but since he let me live, he must have known I would eventually meet you and kill you. Anyway, since he just killed my lover, I don't know if I care what he thinks." I scratch Gary with my thumbnail, and he begins to bleed. The red liquid sinks into his clean starched shirt collar like a line of angry graffiti. Leaning toward his neck, I open my mouth. "I am going to enjoy this," I mutter.

He clenches his eyes shut and cries, "I have a girlfriend!"

I pause. "Gary," I say patiently. "The line is 'I have a wife and two children.' Sometimes I listen to such pleas. Sometimes not. The French nobleman had ten kids, but since he had three wives at the same time, I was not inclined to be lenient." His blood smells good, especially after my hard day and night, but something holds me at bay. "How long have you known this girl?" I ask.

"Six months."

"Do you love her?"

"Yes."

"What's her name?"

He opens his eyes and peers at me. "Lori."

I smile. "Does she believe in vampires?"

"Lori believes in everything."

I have to laugh. "Then you must make such a pair! Listen, Gary, this is your lucky night. I am going to drink some of your blood, just until you pass out, but I promise you that I won't let you die. How does that sound?"

He doesn't exactly relax. I suppose he's had better offers in his days. "Are you really a vampire?" he asks.

"Yes. But you don't want to go telling your fellow cops that. You'll lose your job—and, maybe your girlfriend, too. Just tell them some punk stole your car when you weren't watching. That's what I'm going to do as soon as you black out. Trust me, I need it." I squeeze him a little just to let him know I am still a strong little bitch. "Does this sound fair?"

He begins to see he has no choice in the matter. "Will it hurt?"

"Yes, but it will be a good hurt, Gary."

With that I open his veins farther and close my hungry lips over his flesh. I am, after all, in a terrible hurry. But only as I drink do I realize that his having a girlfriend has nothing to do with my letting him live. For the first time in my life the blood does not satisfy me. Just the feel of it in my mouth, the smell of it in my nostrils, revolts me. I do not kill him because I am tired of killing—finally. My prattle with the cops was a diversion for myself. The weight of knowing that I am the only one who can stop Eddie, the pain of my loss—they send sharp stakes into my heart that I cannot pull free. For once I cannot drown my trials in blood as I have drowned so many other difficult times over the centuries. I wish that I were not a vampire, but a normal human being who could take solace in the arms of someone who does not kill to live. My dream haunts me, my soul desire. The red tears return, I no longer want to be different.

Gary barely starts to moan in pleasure and pain when I release him. As he slumps to the ground, dazed, I reach over and grab his keys and cap and get in the patrol car. My plan is simple. I will put what is left of Yaksha in the car and then slip through the barricade with a tip of my cap and a hard stare at whoever is in charge of security. I will take Yaksha to a lonely spot. There we will talk, of magic perhaps. Of death, certainly.

TWELVE

I drive to the sea, not far from where I killed the woman the previous night. On the way there Yaksha rests on the seat beside me, what is left of him—a ruined torso shrouded at the base in an oily canvas sack that protrudes with the steel stakes Eddie has driven into him to keep him in pain. We do not talk. As I loaded him into the patrol car, I tried to pull off this hideous sack and remove the spikes, but he stopped me. He did not want me to see what had become of him. His dark eyes, still beautiful despite everything that has happened, held mine. The words passed unspoken between us. *I want you to remember me the way I was.* And I prefer to.

The surf has quieted from the night before. The sea is almost as calm as a lake, and I remember a time Yaksha took me to a huge lake in southern India only a month before we met Krishna. It was at night, naturally. He wanted to show me a treasure he'd found under the water. Yaksha had a special gift for locating precious jewels and gold. He was simply drawn to them: secret caves, buried mines—they grabbed him like a magnet. Yet, when he found these things, he never kept them. It was as if he just wanted to see what beauty the past had left behind for us to discover.

He told me, however, that this particular lake had a whole city beneath it, and that no one knew. He believed it was over a hundred thousand years old, the last remnant of a great civilization that history had forgotten. Taking me by the hand, he led me into the water. Then we were diving deep. In those days I could go for half an hour without having to take a breath. Yaksha, I think, could last for hours without air. Being vampires, we could see fairly well, even in the dark and murky water. We went down over a hundred feet, and then the city was upon us: pillared halls, marble paths, sculpted fountains, all inlaid with silver and gold, now flooded with so many drops of water that they would never again sparkle in the sun. The city awed me, that it could simply exist completely unknown, so beautiful, so timeless. It also saddened me, for the same reasons.

Yaksha led me into what must have been a temple. Tall stained-glass windows, many still sound, surrounded the vast interior, which rose step by step in concentric circles, a series of pews that climbed all the way up the wall to a stone ceiling. The temple was unique in that there were no paintings, no statues. I understood that this was a race that worshiped the formless God, and I had to wonder if that was why they went the way they did, into extinction. But as Yaksha floated beside me, there was a joy in his eyes I had never seen before. He came from the abyss, I thought, and maybe it was as if he had finally found his people. Not that they were demons like him, certainly, but they seemed to come from beyond the world. I, too, in that moment felt as if I belonged, and it made me wonder where I had come from. Yaksha must have sensed the thoughts in me because he nodded, as if we had accomplished our purpose in coming, and brought me back to the surface. I remember how bright the stars looked as we emerged from that lost city. For some reason, from then on, the stars always shone with a special luster when I was near a large body of water.

In the present moment the clouds have fled and the stars are bright as I lay him on his back not far from the water, although the light of nearby Los Angeles dims the definition of the Milky Way. How much modern civilization has lost, I think, when they lost the awareness of the billions of stars overhead. Unfortunately, my awareness is also rooted to the earth this night. Eddie has actually sewn the canvas bag covering Yaksha *into his flesh.* The unseen spikes twitch under the material, or maybe it is the dissected muscles that shake. A wave of nausea passes through me as I think of the torture he has endured. Reaching out, I touch my hand to his still cold forehead.

"Yaksha," I say.

His head rolls to one side. His lustrous dark eyes stare at the water with such longing. I know somehow that, like myself, he thinks of the lost city. That afternoon had been our last intimate moment together, before Krishna came on the scene and put a halt to the spread of the vampires by making Yaksha swear to destroy them all, if he wished to die with Krishna's grace.

"Sita," he says in a weak voice.

"There must be many hidden cities beneath the ocean."

"There are."

"You've seen them?"

"Yes. Under this ocean and the others."

"Where do you think all these people went?" I ask.

"They did not go to a place. Time is a larger dimension. Their time came, their time went. It is that way."

We allow some time to pass. The lapping of the small waves on the sand rhythmically echoes my breathing. For a minute they seem as one: each inhalation is a foam wave pushing up on the sand, each exhalation the pull of the receding tide. Over the last five thousand years the waves have reworked this coast, worn it down, carved out fresh bays. But even though my breath has moved in and out of my lungs all that time, I have not changed, not really. The ocean and the earth have known more peace than I have. They have been willing to change, while I have resisted it. My time went and I did not go with it. Yaksha is telling me that.

"That night," I say. "What happened?"

He sighs, so much feeling in the sound. "The moment you ran out the front door, I had the urge to walk to the window. I wanted to get a better view of the ocean. It reminds me of Krishna, you know, and I wanted it to be my last sight before I left this world. When the bomb went off, I was blown out of the house and into the woods, in two pieces. Landing, I felt myself burning, and I thought, surely I will die now." He stops.

"But you didn't die," I say.

"No. I slipped into a mysterious void. I felt as if I drifted forever on a black lagoon. The next ice age could have arrived. I felt bitter cold, like an iceberg drifting without purpose in a subterranean space. Finally, though, I became aware of my body again. Someone was shaking me, poking me. But I still couldn't see and I wasn't completely conscious. Sounds came to me out of a black sky. Some might have been my own thoughts, my own voice. But the others—they seemed so alien."

"It was Eddie asking you questions."

"Is that his name?"

"Yes."

"He never told me his name."

"He is not exactly a warm and fuzzy kind of guy."

Yaksha grimaces. "I know."

I touch him again. "Sorry."

He nods faintly. "I don't even know what I told him, but it

must have been a lot. When I finally did regain full awareness and found myself in his ice-cream truck, I also found myself the captive of a madman who knew a great deal of my history, and consequently yours."

"Did he withdraw your blood and inject himself with it?"

"Yes. When I was in the morgue, he must have noticed what was left of me trying to heal. He has kept me alive so that he can keep getting more of my blood. He has taken so much, he must be very powerful."

"He is. I have tried twice to stop him and have failed. If I fail a third time he will kill me."

Yaksha hesitates, and I know what he is going to ask. His vow to Krishna, to destroy all the vampires, is in jeopardy.

"Has he made more vampires?" he asks.

"Yes. As far as I can tell he made twenty-one new ones. But I was able to destroy them all this morning." I pause. "I had help from my friend."

Yaksha studies my face. "Your friend was killed."

I nod. Another tear. Another red drop to pour into the ocean of time and space, which collects them, it seems, with no thought of how much it costs our supposedly immortal souls.

"He died to save me," I say.

"Your face has changed, Sita."

I look at the ocean, searching for its elusive peace. "It was a great loss for me."

"But we have both lost much over the centuries. This loss

has but uncovered the change that was already there."

I nod weakly and put a hand over my heart. "The night of the explosion, I took a wooden stake through the heart. For some reason that wound never really healed. I am in constant pain. Sometimes it is not so bad. Other times I can hardly bear it." I look at him. "Why hasn't it healed?"

"You know. The wound was supposed to kill you. We were supposed to die together."

"What went wrong?"

"I stood and walked to the window. You probably beheld your beloved's face as you passed out and prayed to Krishna to give you more time to be with him."

"I did just that."

"Then he has given you that time. You have his grace. I suspect you always get what you want."

I shake my head bitterly. "What I wanted more than anything was for Ray to be by my side for the next five thousand years. But your precious God didn't even give me one year with him." I bow my head. "He just took him."

"He is your God as well, Sita."

I continue to shake my head. "I hate him."

"Mortals have always exaggerated the difference between hate and love. Both come from the heart. You can never hate strongly unless you have loved strongly. The reverse is also true. But now you say your heart is broken. I don't know if it can be healed." He stops and takes my hand. "I told you this before. Our time has passed, Sita. We don't belong here anymore."

I wince and squeeze his hand. "I am beginning to believe you." I remember my dream. "Do you think if we do leave here that I will see Ray again?"

"You will see Krishna. He is in all beings. If you look for Ray there, you will find him."

I bite my lower lip, drink my own blood. It tastes better than the cop's. "I want to believe that," I whisper.

"Sita."

"Can you help me stop this monster?"

"No." His eyes glance over his ruined body. "My wounds are too deep. You will have to stop him alone."

His statement deflates what strength I have left. "I don't think I can."

"I have never heard you say you couldn't do something."

I have to chuckle. "That's because we've been out of touch for five thousand years." I quiet. "He has no weak spot. I don't know where to strike."

"He is not invincible."

I speak seriously. "He might very well be. At least in a fight with any creature walking this earth." I feel a sudden wave of longing for Ray, for love, for Krishna. "I wish Krishna would return now. He could stop him easily enough. Do you think that's possible? That he will come again soon?"

"Yes. He may already be here and we don't know it.

Certainly, when he returns, few will recognize him. It is always that way. Did you know I saw him again?"

"You did? Before he left the earth?"

"Yes."

"You never told me."

"I never saw you."

"Yes, I know, for five thousand years. When and where did you see him?"

"It was not long before he left the earth and Kali Yuga began. I was walking in the woods in northern India and he was just there. He was alone, sitting by a pool, washing his feet. He smiled as I approached and gestured for me to sit beside him. His whole demeanor was different from when we saw him the first time. His power was all about, of course, but at the same time he seemed much gentler, more an angel than a god. He was eating a mango and he offered me one. When he looked at me, I felt no need to explain how I had been doing everything in my power to keep my vow to him. We just sat in the sun and soaked our feet in the water and everything was fine. Everything was perfect. Our past battle was forgotten. I felt so happy right then I could have died. I wanted to die, to leave the earth with him. I asked him if I could, and he shook his head and told me this story. When he was finished, I didn't even know why he told it to me." Yaksha pauses. "Not until this night."

"What do you mean?" I ask.

"I believe he told me this story so that I could now tell it to you."

I am interested. "Tell me."

"Lord Krishna said that there was once this demon, Mahisha, who performed a great austerity to gain the favor of Lord Shiva, who as you know is really no different from Krishna. Because there can be only one God. Mahisha kept his mind fixed on Shiva and meditated on him and his six-syllable mantra—*Om Namah Shivaya*—for five thousand years. But Shiva did not appear before him, and so Mahisha thought to build a huge fire and offer everything he possessed to Shiva, believing this would surely bring him. Mahisha put his clothing and jewels and weapons—even his fifty wives—into the fire. And still Shiva did not come to him. Then Mahisha thought, what have I left to offer? I have renounced everything I own. But then he realized he still had his body, and he decided that he would put that in the fire as well, piece by little piece. First he cut off his toes, and then his ears, and then his nose. All these things he threw into the fire. Seeing this from his high mountaintop in the blessed realm of Kailasha, Shiva was horrified. He didn't want any devotee, even a demonic one such as Mahisha, cutting himself up like that. Just when the demon was about to carve out his heart, Shiva appeared before him.

"He said, 'You have performed a great and difficult austerity, Mahisha, and proved your devotion to me. Ask anything of me and I will grant it.'

"Then Mahisha smiled to himself because it was for this very reason that he had undertaken his austerity. He said, 'O Lord Shiva, I ask for but two boons. That I should be unkillable and that whoever I should touch on the top of the head should in turn be killed.'

"As you can imagine, Shiva was not too happy with the request. He tried to talk Mahisha into something more benign: a nice palace, divine realization, or even a few nymphs from the heavens. But Mahisha would not be swayed, and Shiva was bound by his word, to grant anything asked of him. So in the end he said, 'So be it.' And then he quickly returned to Kailasha lest Mahisha tried to touch him on the head.

"As you can imagine, Mahisha immediately started to cause all kinds of trouble. Gathering the hosts of demons together, he assaulted Indra, the king of paradise, and his realm. None of the gods could stop him because he was invincible, and, of course, every time they got near him, he would put his hand on the top of their heads and they would be killed. You understand that even a god can lose his divine form. In the end all the gods were driven from heaven and had to go into hiding to keep from being destroyed. Mahisha was crowned lord of paradise, and the whole cosmos was in disarray, with demons running wild, knocking down mountains, and raising up volcanoes."

"Were there people on the earth at this time?" I ask.

"I don't know. Krishna never said. I think there were. I

think the ruins of the races I have found might have been from those times. Or maybe in the realms we speak of there is no time as we understand it. It doesn't matter. The situation was desperate and there was no relief in sight. But at the bequest of his wife, the beautiful Indrani, Indra performed a long austerity himself, with his mind fixed on Krishna and his twelve-syllable mantra—*Om Namo Bhagavate Vasudevaya*. Indra was hiding in a deep cave on earth at the time, and he had to meditate for five thousand years before Krishna finally appeared and offered him any boon he wished. Of course Krishna realized what was happening in heaven and on earth, but he did not intervene until after there had been great suffering."

"Why?" I ask.

"He is that way. There is no use in asking him why. I know, I have tried. It is like asking nature the same question about itself. Why is fire hot? Why do the eyes see and not hear? Why is there birth and death? These things just are the way they are. But since Krishna had offered Indra a boon, Indra was wise enough to jump at the opportunity. Indra asked Krishna to kill the unkillable Mahisha.

"It was an interesting problem for Krishna. As I have already said, in essence he is the same as Shiva, and he could not very well undo a boon he had freely granted. But Krishna is beyond all pairs of opposites, all paradoxes. What he did decide to do was appear before Mahisha as a beautiful goddess. The form he took was so ravishing that the demon immediately forgot about all the nymphs of the firmament and began to chase after her. But she—who was really a he, if the Lord can be said to have a particular sex—danced away from him, moving through the celestial forest, her hips swaying, waving her veils, dropping them along hidden paths so that Mahisha would not lose her, yet always staying out of arm's reach. Mahisha was beside himself with passion. And you know what happens when your mind becomes totally fixed on one person. You become like that person. Krishna told me that was how even the demons can become enlightened and realize him. They hate him so much they can't stop thinking about him."

I force a smile. "So it is all right if I hate him."

"Yes. The opposite of love is not hate. It is indifference. That is why so few people find God. They go to church and talk about him and that sort of thing. They may even go out and evangelize and try to win converts. But in their hearts, if they are honest with themselves, they are indifferent to him because they cannot see him. God is too abstract for people. God is a word without meaning. If Jesus came back today, nothing he said would make any sense to those who wait for him. They would be the first ones to kill him again."

"Did you ever meet Jesus?" I ask.

"No. Did you?"

"No. But I heard about him while he was still alive."

Yaksha draws in a difficult breath. "I don't even know if Jesus could heal me now."

"You would not ask him to even if he could."

"That is true. But let me continue with my story. In the form of the beautiful goddess, God was not too abstract for Mahisha. Because she danced, he in turn began to dance. He mimicked her movements exactly. He did so spontaneously, of his own free will, not imagining for a moment that he was in danger. He was fearless because he knew that he could not be killed. But the paradox of the boons granted to him was also the solution to the paradox. He had asked for two gifts, not one. But which one was stronger? The first one because it was asked for first? Or the second one because it was asked for second? Or was neither one stronger than the other? Maybe they could cancel each other out.

"As the goddess danced before Mahisha, in a subtle manner, at first almost too swift for the eye to see, she began to brush her hand close to the top of her head. She did this a number of times, slowing down a little bit on each occasion. Then, finally, she actually touched her head, and because Mahisha was so absorbed in her, he did likewise."

"And in that moment he was killed," I say, having enjoyed the story but not understood the purpose of it.

"Yes," Yaksha says. "The invincible demon was destroyed, and both heaven and earth were saved."

"I understand the moral of the story, but I do not understand the practicality of it. Krishna could not have given you this story to give to me. It does not help me. The only way I could bewitch Eddie would be to show him a snuff film. The guy is not interested in my body, unless it happened to assume the form of a corpse."

"That is not true. He is very interested in what is inside your body."

I nod. "He wants my blood."

"Of course. Next to mine, your blood is the most powerful substance on earth. He must have figured out that the two of us have grown in different ways over the centuries. He wants your unique abilities, and he can only absorb them by absorbing your blood into his system. For that reason I do not believe he will simply kill you outright when he sees you next."

"The first time we met he had a chance to kill me and didn't."

"Then you see the truth of what I say."

I speak with emotion, for all this talk does nothing to soothe my torment. Ray is dead and my old mentor is dying and God takes five thousand years to respond to a prayer. I feel as if *I* drift on the icy lagoon, hearing only gibberish whispered down to me from a black sky. I know Eddie will kill me the next time we meet. He will slowly peel off my flesh, and when I scream in pain, I know Krishna will not heed my pleas for help. How many times must Yaksha have cried out to Krishna to save him while Eddie pushed the steel spikes deeper into his torn body? I ask Yaksha this very question, but he is staring at the ocean again.

"Faith is a mysterious quality," he says. "On the surface it seems foolhardy—to trust so completely in something you don't know is true. But I think that trust, for most people, vanishes when death stands at the doorstep. Because death is bigger than human beliefs. It wipes them all away. If you study a dead Jew or a dead Christian or a dead Hindu or a dead Buddhist—they all look the same. They all smell the same, after a while. For that reason I think true faith is a gift. You cannot decide to have it. God gives it to you or he doesn't give it to you. When I was trapped in the truck these last few weeks, I didn't pray to Krishna to save me. I just prayed that he would give me faith in him. Then I realized it was all accomplished for me. I saw that I already had that faith."

"I don't understand," I say.

Yaksha looks at me once more. Reaching up, he touches my cheek where my red tear has left a tragic stain. Yet he smiles as he feels my blood, this creature who has just been put through such incredible pain. How can he smile? I wonder. There is a glow about him even in the midst of his ruin, and I realize that he is like the sea he loves so much, at peace with the waves that wash over him. Truly, we do become what we love, or what we hate. I wish that I still hated him and could therefore share a portion of his peace. With all I have lost, I fear to approach him with a feeling of love.

Yet I lie even to myself. I love him as much as I love Krishna. He is still my demon, my lover, my enchanter. I bow my head before him and let him stroke my hair. His touch does not kill me but brings me a small measure of comfort.

"What I mean is," he says, "I knew you would come for me. I knew you would deliver me from my torment. And you see, you have. In the same way, even as he stuck his long needles into me and then injected himself in front of me and laughed and told me the world was now his, I knew that after you found me and heard Krishna's story, you would destroy him. You would save the world and fulfill my vow for me. I have that faith, Sita. God has given it to me. Please trust in it as I trust in you."

I am all emotion. I, the cold vampire. I shake before him like a lost little girl. I was young when I met him, so long ago, and in all that time I have failed to mature. At least in the way Krishna probably wanted me to. I know I am about to lose Yaksha, that he is going to ask me to kill him, and the thought devastates me.

"I do not know what the story means," I whisper. "Can't you tell me?"

"No. I don't know what it means, either."

I raise my head. "Then we're damned!"

Gently he takes a handful of my long hair. "Many in the past have called us that. But tonight you will make them repent those words because you will be their savior. Find him, Sita, bewitch him. I was every bit as powerful as he when I came for you that night I made you what you are. I did not come back willingly. You had bewitched me—yes, even then—and I was a monster every bit as corrupt as this Eddie."

I take his hand. "But I never really wanted to destroy you." He goes to speak and I quickly shake my head. "Don't say it, please."

"It must be done. You will need the strength of my blood. It is the least I can give you."

I hold his hand to my trembling mouth, but I am careful with his fingers, keeping them from my teeth. I do not want to bite them, even scratch them. How, then, can I drain him dry?

"No," I say.

His eyes wander back to the sea. "Yes, Sita. This way is the only way. And I am closer to it this time. I can see it." He closes his eyes. "I can remember him as if I saw him only yesterday. As if I see him now." He nods to himself. "It is not such a bad way to die."

I have had the same thought, and yet lived on. I do not deny him his last request, however. He has suffered greatly, and to make him go on as he is would be too cruel. Lowering my head and opening his veins, I press my lips to the flesh that brought my own flesh to this mysterious moment, which has sadly become a paradox of powers and weaknesses, of hopeless characters lost in time and space, where the stars turn overhead and shine down upon us like boons from the almighty Lord, or else curses from an indifferent universe. Yet the flavor of his blood adds color to my soul, and drinking it I feel an unlooked-for spark of hope, of faith. As he takes his last breath, I whisper in his ear that I will not do likewise until the enemy is dead. It is a vow I make to Yaksha as well as to Krishna.

THIRTEEN

Once again I sit outside the house of the mother of Edward Fender. The time is eleven-thirty at night. Christmas is ten days away. Up and down the block cheap-colored lights, like so many out-of-season Easter eggs that have been soaked in Day-Glo paint, add false gaiety to a neighborhood that should have been on the late Soviet Union's first-strike priority list. Sitting in Gary and Bill's patrol car, I allow my senses to spread out, in and outside of the Fender home, around the block. My hearing is my greatest ally. Even the movements of worms through the soil a quarter of a mile away come to my sensitive ears. Mrs. Fender is still awake, sitting in her rocking chair and reading her magazines, watching a save-your-soul-before-Armageddon Jesus program. She is definitely alone in the house, and I am pretty sure Eddie is not in the immediate neighborhood.

This puzzles me. With the police security near the warehouse and his confidence in the cleverness of his Yaksha hiding place, I can understand why Eddie left the ice-cream truck unguarded. But I cannot understand why he has left his mother wide open for me to take hostage. By now he must have figured out that I found the warehouse through her. Again, I am wary of a trap.

With Yaksha's blood in my system, my strength is back to a hundred percent, maybe even at a hundred and twenty percent, although I know I am still no match for Eddie, who drew upon Yaksha's blood many times over several weeks. Unfortunately, my state of mind is shaky. After Yaksha drew his last breath, I weighted the canvas bag that covered his lower portion with stones and waded out into the water and sank him. I made certain his remains are now safe from harm. He will never be found. Yet he has left me with a riddle I can't solve. Krishna told him his story five thousand years ago. Why was Yaksha so sure Krishna gave it to him to give to me for this particular emergency? For the life of me—and my life is very large—I can't see how I am going to destroy Eddie by dancing for him. For me, the word *faith* is as abstract as the word *God*. I trust that everything is going to work out for the best about as much as I trust that Santa Claus is going to bring me a bottle of blood for Christmas.

What can I do? I have no real plan except the obvious. Take Mrs. Fender hostage and force Eddie to come running, and then put a bullet in his brain when I get the chance. On my lap rests Officer Gary's revolver. Or is it Officer Bill's? It doesn't matter. It was in their car and it has six bullets in it. After tucking it in the front of my pants under my shirt, I get out of the car and walk toward the house.

I don't knock. Why bother? She will not open the door for me. Grabbing the knob, I break the lock and am on her before she can reach for the remote control on her TV. Modern Americans are so into their remotes. They treat them as if they were hand phasers or something, capable of leveling any obstacles. Fear and loathing distort her already twisted features. Yet the emotions are a sign that her brain has cleared. I am so happy for her, really. Grabbing her by the throat, I shove her up against the wall and breathe cold vampire air in her ugly face. Before burying Yaksha in the sea, I stripped down to nothing, but I was still wet when I put my clothes back on. The pants Joel bought for me drip on the wood floor as I tighten my grip on the old lady. Her weird gray eyes peer into mine, and as they do her expression changes. The bondage scares her but excites her as well. What a family.

"Where's your son?" I ask.

She coughs. "Who are you?"

"One of the good guys. Your son's one of the bad guys." I throttle her a bit. "Do you know where he is?'

She shakes her head minutely, turning a little blue. "No."

She is telling me the truth. "Have you seen him tonight?"

"No."

Another genuine reply. Odd. I allow a grim smile. "What did Eddie do as a kid for fun? Did he stick firecrackers in frogs' mouths and blow their heads off? Did he pour gasoline on cats and light them on fire? Did you buy him the gasoline? Did you buy him the cats? Really, I want to know what kind of mother it takes to make that kind of son."

She momentarily masters her fear and grins. The expression is like a crack in swamp mud, and smells just as foul.

"My Eddie is a good boy. He knows what to do with girls like you."

"Your boy has never met a girl like me before." I throw her back in her chair. "Sit there and keep your mouth shut." Taking the chair across from her, I sit down. "We are going to wait for Eddie."

"What are you going to do to him?"

I pull out my revolver. "Kill him."

She hardly blinks. In fact, on the whole she is remarkably accepting of my extraordinary strength. Her boy must have enlightened her on the new kids in town. Her fear continues to remain strong, but there is a cockiness to her as well. She nods as if to herself, her arthritic neck creaking like a termite-infested board.

"My boy is smarter than you. I think you'll be the one killed."

Turning off the TV with the remote, I cross my legs. "If

he's so smart, then why didn't he run away from home the day he learned to walk?"

She doesn't like that. "You're going to be sorry you said that."

I am already bored with her. "We shall see."

An hour later the phone rings. Since I hope to scare Eddie into rushing to the house, there is no point in having the mother answer and pretending that I am not here. Eddie will not fall for so simple a ruse anyway. I pick up the phone.

"Hello?" I say.

"Sita."

It is Joel and he is in serious trouble. In an instant I realize that after I left him, he went to this house, where he was abducted by Eddie. Eddie was here while I was rescuing Yaksha, probably outside hiding, probably confident I would return here the first chance I got. But when I didn't show, he took the man who rescued me from the flames, no doubt thinking he could use him as leverage with me. In a moment I understand that the chances of Joel living through the night are less than one in a hundred.

"He is nearby," I say.

Joel is scared but still in control. "Yes."

"He has made his point as far as you are concerned. Put him on the line."

"I am expendable," Joel says. "You understand that?"

"We're both expendable," I reply.

Eddie comes on the line a moment later. His voice is liquid grease. He sounds confident, as well he should.

"Hello, Sita. How's my mother?"

"She's fine, busy boasting about her son."

"Have you hurt her?"

"Thinking about it. Have you hurt Joel?"

"Just broke his arms is all. Is he another boyfriend of yours? That last one of yours didn't last so long."

I strain to sound casual. "You win some, you lose some. When you're as old as I am, one is as good as another."

Eddie giggles. "I don't know about that. Right now I don't think you could do any better than me."

I want to antagonize him, make him act foolishly. "Are you making a pass at me, Eddie? Is that what this is all about? You want to rule the world so you can be sure to have a date for Friday night? You know, I talked to your old employer and heard what your idea of a good time is. I swear, with your social graces, I wouldn't be surprised if you're still a virgin."

He does not like that. It is good, I think, to find sensitive nerves before we again meet in battle. For all of Eddie's intelligence, he seems to have a fundamental immaturity when it comes to dealing with people, and I don't mean that he is simply psychotic. Many psychotics I have known have had excellent interpersonal skills—when they weren't murdering people. Eddie is a sorrier case. He was the nerd in the high school library at lunch picking at his zits and fantasizing about rape every time a cheerleader walked by. His tone turns mean and nasty.

"Let's cut to the chase," he says. "I want you to meet me at Santa Monica Pier in thirty minutes. If you are not there by then, I will begin to kill your friend. I will do so slowly just in case a flat tire has delayed your arrival. It's possible you still might be able to recognize him if you're less than twenty minutes late. My mother, of course, is to be left in her home unharmed." He pauses for effect. "Do you understand these instructions?"

I snort. "Oh, gimme a break. I don't jump when you say jump. You have nothing with which to threaten me. Such a thing does not exist on this planet. You want to talk to me, *you* get here within thirty minutes. If not, I will hang your mother's head on the front door in place of a Christmas wreath. The red color will be in keeping with the holiday spirit." I pause. "Do you understand my instructions, you foul-mouthed pervert?"

He is angry. "You're bluffing!"

"Eddie, you should know me better than that by now."

With that I hang up the phone. He will come, I am sure of it. But I have to wonder if I want him to bring Joel, if another standoff with an important life hanging in the balance will not cause me to falter again. Almost, I pray that he kills Joel before I am forced to kill him.

FOURTEEN

A thousand years ago, in the Scottish Highlands, I was faced with a situation similar to the one that now confronts me. At the time I had a royal lover, the Thane of Welson, my Harold. We lived in a moderate-size castle on the northwestern coast of Scotland, where the biting winter winds blew off the foaming ocean water like ice daggers carved by frigid mermaids. They were enough to make me dream of Hawaiian vacations, even though Hawaii had yet to be discovered. I liked Harold. More than any other mortal I had met, he reminded me of Cleo, my old Greek friend. They had a similar sense of humor and they were both leches. I like horny men; I feel they are true to their inner natures.

Harold was not a doctor, however, like Cleo, but an artist, and a great one at that. He painted me in a number of poses, many times nude. One of these paintings now hangs in the

Louvre in Paris, and is attributed to an artist who never even existed. Once I visited the museum and found a skilled art student painting a copy of the work. Coming up at his side, I just stood there for the longest time, and he kept glancing at me and getting more curious. Indeed, looking a little closer he even acted kind of scared. He wanted to say something to me but didn't know what. Before leaving I just smiled at him and nodded. Harold had caught my likeness perfectly.

At that time in Scotland there was an arrogant authority figure in the area, a certain Lord Tensley, who had a much bigger castle and ego than my Harold, but not the great object of his desire, which just happened to be me. Lord Tensley wanted me in the worst way and did everything in his power to woo me away from Harold. He sent me flowers and horses and carriages and jewels—the usual Middle Ages fluff. But I will take a sense of humor over power and money any day. Besides, Lord Tensley was cruel, and even though I have been known to bite a few necks in my day—and crush a few skulls—I have never thought of myself as one who enjoys pain at another's expense. One story had it that Lord Tensley had beheaded his first wife when she refused to smother their slightly handicapped female firstborn. All of Lord Tensley's subsequent lovers had stiff necks from checking their backs constantly.

While I was with Harold, I was going through one of my reckless periods. Usually I go to great lengths to keep my true identity secret, and it wasn't as if I romped around the Scottish

Highlands biting the neck of every MacFarland and Scottie Boy who walked by in the dark. But during that time, perhaps because I was lazy and tired of arguing with people, I used the power of my eyes and voice to quickly get what I wanted. Naturally, after a time, I developed the reputation of being a witch. This did not bother Harold, as it had not bothered Cleo before him. Both were progressive thinkers. But unlike Cleo, Harold actually knew that I was a vampire, and that I often drank human blood. It really turned him on to have such a girlfriend. When he painted me, I often had blood on my face. Harold occasionally asked me to make him a vampire so that he wouldn't have to grow old and die, but he knew of Krishna and the vow I'd made to him and so he didn't press me. Once Harold painted a picture of Krishna for me from my description, and that was a work I treasured above all others, until it was destroyed in England in a German bombing raid during World War II.

Because I had shunned Lord Tensley, and had developed the reputation of being a witch, the good man of God felt it was his duty to have me tried and burned at the stake, a practice that was later to come into vogue during the Inquisition. In a sense Lord Tensley was a man ahead of his time. He dispatched a dozen armed men to bring me in, and because Harold's entire security force consisted of maids, butlers, and mule boys, I met the contingent myself before they reached our castle and sent their heads back to Lord Tensley with a note attached: *The answer is still no.* I thought that would scare him off, at least for a while, but Lord Tensley was more determined than I realized. A week later he kidnapped my Harold and sent a note to me stating that unless I surrendered myself promptly, he would be sending me Harold's head. Storming Lord Tensley's heavily fortified castle would have been a difficult proposition, even for a creature such as I, and besides, I thought a little feigned cooperation would bring Harold back to me all the sooner. I sent another note back: *The answer is yes, but you have to come get me. Bring Harold.*

Lord Tensley brought Harold and twenty of his best knights. Hearing them approach, I sent my people off. None were fighters and I didn't want them to get killed. Alone, I stood atop my castle gate that cold dark night with a bow and arrow in hand as the witch-squad rode up on their horses. The nervous exhalations of the men and animals shone like dragon's breath in the orange glow of the flickering torches. Lord Tensley carried Harold before him on his own horse, a jagged knife held tight at my lover's throat. He called up to me to surrender or he would kill my boyfriend before my eyes. The interesting thing about Lord Tensley was that he didn't underestimate me in the slightest. Naturally, one would expect the ten heads I sent back to him to make him cautious. But the way he maintained his distance, keeping Harold directly in front of him, and even the manner in which he avoided looking in my direction made me think he honestly believed I was a witch.

That was a problem. Generally in the past, before the advent of modern weapons, I could extricate myself from most situations by sheer speed and strength. An arrow or spear shot in my direction—I could just duck aside or catch it in midair. There was never a chance someone could defeat me in a sword fight, even when I didn't have a sword. It wasn't until guns were developed that I had to move more carefully and use my head first before my feet or hands.

For a long moment I licked the tip of the arrow in my hand and considered taking my best shot at Lord Tensley. The chances were excellent that I would be able to kill him without harming Harold. The problem was I would not be able to stop the other men from quickly chopping up my lover.

"I will surrender," I called down. "But first you must let him go."

Lord Tensley laughed. He was an intensely handsome man, but his face somehow reminded me of a fox that dreamed of being a wolf. What I mean is he was sly and proud at the same time, and didn't care if he got his snout bloody, as long as it was at mealtime. Harold, on the other hand, was as ugly as a man could be and still have all his basic features in the right places. He had broken his nose on three occasions, each time while drunk, and the sad thing was that each shattered cartilage actually improved his appearance. But he could make me laugh and he could make love all night and what did the rest of it matter? I would do my best to save him, I knew, even at the risk of my own life. Cowards I have always despised above all else.

"You surrender first," Lord Tensley called back. "And then we will let him go."

"I am all alone here," I said. "A frail woman. Why don't your knights come get me?"

"We will not debate with you, witch," Lord Tensley replied. And with that he stabbed his knife through Harold's upper right arm, a serious injury to receive in those days without modern surgical techniques and drugs. Even in the cold wind, I could smell the amount of blood pouring out of Harold. By bartering, I had made a mistake. I had to get to him soon.

"I will come down now," I called, setting aside my bow and arrow.

Yet I hung behind the castle gate even as I peered my head out at the wicked gang. Knowing they were coming, I had placed a fresh horse and supplies just beyond a nearby bluff. If Harold could get to the animal, I knew he would ride to a cave two miles distant that only the two of us knew about. There he could hide until his girlfriend extraordinaire figured out a way to wipe out the enemy. Harold had the utmost confidence in me. Even at that moment, bound and bleeding as he was, he smiled at me as if to say, give 'em hell. I was not worried about that part. It was keeping him alive at the same time that concerned me. But to that end I sought to focus my gaze on Lord

Tensley as I looked out from behind the gate. He continued to avoid my eyes, however.

"Let him go," I called, pitching my voice as powerfully as I could, knowing, if given the chance, that eye contact would magnify my subtle influence tenfold.

"Come out now, witch, or I stab his other arm," Lord Tensley called back. "Then your heathen lover will be doing no more of those corrupt paintings of your filthy body."

Harold was in fact left-handed. I had to restrain myself from replying that if I was burned at the stake, then Harold wouldn't be doing any more paintings of me in either case. And as far as my filthy body was concerned—he hadn't minded the look and smell of it until I had told him to take a hike. Another phrase, by the way, that I think I invented. There is a place for sarcasm and this was not one of them. I stepped into the open and spoke steadily.

"Now you keep your word and release him," I said.

Lord Tensley did as requested, but it was a feint. I knew the moment he had me bound and gagged he would chase after Harold and either cut him down or recapture him to be tried as a witch alongside me. Still, Lord Tensley could not know about the horse I had waiting nearby, and for that reason I exchanged a long stare with Harold as they untied him and let him climb to the ground. Harold and I had a deep telepathic bond; it was another special element in our relationship. Even with the pain of his wound and the pressure of the situation, he was able to sense my mind. Common sense also came to his aid; he knew I would want him to get to the cave. He nodded slightly before turning and fleeing into the night. Sadly, he left behind a trail of blood that I could smell only too clearly.

When he was out of sight, I turned my attention to Lord Tensley's son, who had no reservations about looking at me. The young man was barely sixteen but large as an ox. He had one of those cheerful blank expressions that made me think that if his karma remained constant, then in his next life he would be a lineman for a professional football team and make two million dollars a year. Never mind that at that time there was no football, or even dollars for that matter. Some faces and things I just have a feeling for. It was my intention to send him on to his great destiny as quickly as possible, but I knew subtle suggestion would not work on his primitive brain. Stepping forward and focusing my eyes deep into his head, I said in a calm clear voice:

"Your father is the witch. Kill him while you still can."

The boy spun and shoved his sword into his father's gut. A look of immense surprise shone on Lord Tensley's face. He turned to me just before he fell off his horse. Of course I was smiling.

"I know you've kept one of Harold's paintings of me in your closet," I said. "I look pretty good for a witch, don't I?"

He tried to answer, but a glob of blood came out of his mouth instead of words. Toppling forward, Lord Tensley was dead before he hit the ground. Half the knights fled right then, including the athletic son, the other half stayed to fight. I dealt with them quickly, without mercy, largely because I was in a hurry to get to Harold.

But I was too late. I found him lying on his back beside the horse I had left for him. The wound in the arm had punctured an artery, and he had bled to death. My Harold—I was to miss him for a long time. To this day I have never returned to Scotland.

What was the moral of the story? It was painfully simple. One cannot argue with evil men. They are too unpredictable. Waiting for Eddie, with his mother firmly in hand, I know he will do something weird.

Still, I do not know what the moral of Krishna's story is.

FIFTEEN

The smell of Eddie, even from four blocks away, is clear to me. Not that he makes any effort to sneak up on me. I assume this is because he values his mother's life as much as his own. His car stays at the speed limit. He parks out front. Two sets of feet come up the porch steps. Eddie actually pays me the courtesy of knocking. Standing on the far end of the living room with my gun to Mom's head, I call for them to come in.

The door opens.

Eddie has broken both of Joel's arms. They hang uselessly by the agent's side. Despite his intense pain, Joel strives to appear calm, and I admire him for it. He has many fine qualities— I really do care for the guy. Again, I have to tell myself that I cannot risk all of humanity for this one life. Joel flashes me a wan smile—almost in apology—as he is shoved through the door before Eddie. But he has no need to apologize to me, even though he has done exactly what I told him not to do. True courage, in the face of almost certain death, is the rarest quality on earth.

Eddie has found himself a gun, a 10-millimeter affair—standard FBI issue. He keeps it close to Joel's head and Joel's body close to his own. Eddie really does have a serious complexion problem. It looks as if when he was an adolescent he tried to treat his problem acne with razor blades. The experiment was a distinct failure. But it is his eyes that are the scariest. The green centers look like cheap emeralds that have been dipped in sulfuric acid and left out to dry in a radioactive dust storm. The whites are more red than white; his eyes are not merely bloodshot but hemorrhaging. Perhaps a local pollen irritates them. Maybe it's the sun I dragged him out into earlier. He looks happy enough to see me, though, and his mother. He flashes us both a toothy smile. Mom doesn't reply, not with my fingernails around her throat, but she does appear relieved to see her darling boy.

"Hi, Mom," Eddie says. "Hi, Sita." He kicks the door closed behind him.

"I'm glad you were able to make it on time," I say. "But I didn't mind waiting. It's been pleasant talking to your mother, getting to know what Edward Fender was like as a young man growing up in troubled times."

Eddie scowls. "You're a bitch, you know that? Here I try to

be friendly in a difficult situation, and you try to insult me."

"I don't consider your trying to kill my boyfriend and myself an act of friendship," I say.

"You drew first blood," Eddie says.

"Only because I was quicker than your friends. Drop the B.S., Eddie, please. Neither of us is here to kiss and make up."

"Why are we here?" Eddie asks. "To play standoff again? That didn't work so well for you last time."

"I don't know. I destroyed your silly gang."

Eddie snickers. "You're not sure of that."

I smile. "Now I am sure. You see, I can tell when someone lies. It's one of those great gifts I possess that you don't. There is only you left, and we both know it."

"What of it? I can make more whenever I feel the need."

"Why do you feel the need? So that you can always have someone to order about? And while we're on the subject, what is your ultimate goal? To replace all of humanity with a race of vampires? If you study the situation logically, you'll see that it won't work. You cannot make everyone a hunter. There will be nothing left to hunt."

Eddie appears momentarily puzzled. He is intelligent but not wise. His vision is sharp but also myopic; he does not look beyond next week. Then, just like that, he is angry again. His temper comes and goes like flares in a lava pit. Logic is not going to work on him.

"You're just trying to confuse me with that witchy voice

of yours," he says. "I'm having a good time and that's all I care about."

I snort. "Well, at least now we understand your priorities."

He grows impatient. Pulling Joel tighter, he digs his thumbnail into Joel's neck, coming close to breaking the skin. "Let my mother go," he orders.

I act casual, even as I dig my nail into his mother's neck. "You have a problem here, Eddie. I hardly know this guy. You can kill him and I won't bat an eye. You're in no position to give me orders."

He tries to stare me down. There is power in his gaze but no control. "I don't believe you will just kill an innocent woman," he says.

"She bore you," I say. "She's not innocent."

In response Eddie pricks Joel's neck. The ice-cream man has a good feel for deep-rooted veins. The flow of blood is immediate and thick. Joel shifts uneasily but does not try to shake free, which he probably knows is impossible anyway. So far he has allowed me to play the game, probably hoping I have a card up my sleeve that I'm not showing. All I have is Krishna's abstract tale. But as Joel feels his life draining away, soaking his white shirt a tragic red, I understand his need to speak. Yet he has finally begun to grasp the stakes of this particular pot and is not afraid to die.

"He's not going to let me walk out of here alive, Sita," Joel says. "You know that. Take your best shot and be done with it."

The advice is sound. Using Mom as a shield, I can simply open fire. The only trouble is Joel is not Ray. He will not heal in a matter of minutes. He will certainly die, and still I won't be sure of killing Eddie. This problem—it is age old. To do what is right and save the day without destroying the very thing the day is lived for. I hesitate a moment, then dig my nail deep into Mom's neck. The woman lets out a terrified gasp. Warm blood spurts over my fingers. Which pump will run out sooner? I honestly don't know. Mom shakes visibly in my arms and Eddie's face darkens.

"What do you want?" he demands.

"Let Joel go," I say. "I will let your mother go. Then it will just be between the two of us, the way it should be."

"I will beat you to the draw," Eddie says.

I am grim. "Maybe."

"There is no maybe about it and you know it. You're not going to release my mother. You're not here to negotiate. You just want me dead."

"Well," I say.

"Just use your gun," Joel says with feeling. His blood drips off his shirt and onto his pants. Eddie has opened the jugular. I estimate Joel has three minutes to live. He will be conscious for only half that. Slumping slightly, he leans back into Eddie, who has no trouble supporting him. Although Joel struggles to remain calm, his color is white. It is not easy to watch yourself bleed to death. And what makes it worse is with his broken arms he can't even raise a hand to press over his wound. Naturally, Mom tries to stop the bleeding, scratching me in the process with her clawlike fingers, but I keep the red juice coming. They will both die about the same time, unless I do something quick, or Eddie does.

But I do not know what to do.

"Release him," I say.

"No," Eddie says. "Release my mother."

I do not reply. I begin to panic instead. I cannot stand by and watch Joel die. Yes, I, ancient Sita, the scourge of Krishna, who has killed thousands. But maybe my unchanging nature has finally been rattled. I am not who I was two days ago. Perhaps it is because of the loss of Ray and Yaksha, but the thought of another death on my hands chills me to the core. A wave of nausea sweeps over me, and I see a red that is not there, a deeper red than even the color of blood. A blotted sun sinking below the horizon at the end of the world. It will be the end of humanity, I know, to surrender to this maniac, but the mathematics of human life suddenly won't add up. I cannot spend one life to protect five billion. Not when that one life begins to wobble and sink before my eyes. Joel's blood now drips off the hem of his pants, onto the dusty floor. Mom's blood does likewise, through her frumpy nightgown. What is wrong with Eddie? Can't he see the seconds ticking by? His mother cries in my arms, and I actually feel sorry for her. Yeah, I know, I picked a wonderful time to turn into a softy.

"In less than a minute your mother will be beyond help," I explain. "But if you act now, I will heal her neck and let her go."

Eddie sneers. "You can't heal. You can only kill."

I harden my voice. "I can do both. I can show you. Just let him go. I will do the same with your mother. We can do it together, simultaneously."

Eddie shakes his head. "You're lying."

"Maybe, maybe not. But your mother is dying. That's a certainty." I pause. "Can't you see that?"

Eddie's cheek twitches, but his will doesn't. "No," he says.

Joel sags dangerously to one side and now has to be completely supported. There are two pints of blood on his shirt, two on the floor. His eyes are the color of baking soda. He tries to tell me to be strong and he can hardly get the words out.

"Just shoot," he begs.

God, do I want to. A bullet in the brain to put Joel out of his misery, then another five bullets in Eddie, in more choice spots than at the Coliseum. With his mother's life still in balance, I am confident I can get off all six shots without taking a bullet myself. But the balance is on the verge of tripping; the scale is about to break. Mom sags in my arms. There is no longer enough blood in her veins to keep her heart from skipping. She has strength left for her tears, however. Why do they affect me so? She is a terrible person. Krishna will not be waiting to welcome her on the other side, if there really is such a place.

Yet, ironically, it is her very wretchedness that makes me pity her so. I don't know what's wrong with me.

I don't know what to do!

"Joel," I say, showing Eddie just how lousy my hand is by letting pain enter my voice. "I didn't want any of this."

"I know . . ." He tries to smile, fails. "You warned me."

"Eddie," I say.

He likes to hear the weakness in my voice. "Yes, Sita?"

"You are a fool."

"You are a bitch."

I sigh. "What do you want? Really? You can tell me that much at least."

He considers. "Just what I have coming to me."

"Christ." I want to throw up. "They'll kill you. This planet is only so big. There are only so many places to hide. The human race will hunt you down and kill you."

He is cocky. "Before they know what's happening, there won't be many of them left to do the hunting."

Joel's dripping blood is like a river, a torrential current I cannot free myself of no matter how hard I try. Once upon a time I enjoyed such red floods, but that was when I believed they flowed into an ocean. The endless sea of Krishna's grace. But where is he now? This great God who promised me his protection if I but obeyed his command? He is dead, drowned by the indifference of time and space like the rest of us.

"Krishna," I whisper to myself. "Krishna."

He does not appear before me in a vision and explain to me why I suddenly release my grip on Eddie's mother. The surrender is not an act of faith. The despair I feel in this moment crushes the breath of either possibility. The woman stands at death's door but somehow manages to stagger toward her son, with a twisted grin on her face that reminds me of a wind-up doll's. Her darling son, she believes, has conquered again. A sticky red trail follows her across the wood floor. Bereft of my mortal shield, I stand helpless, waiting for the shots that never come. Of course, time is on Eddie's side, and he probably has worse things planned for me. He waits while his mother comes to him.

"Butterfly," she says sweetly, raising her bloodless arms to embrace him. Shifting Joel into one arm, Eddie acts as if he is ready to hug her.

"Sunshine," Eddie replies.

Yet he grabs his mother with his free hand. Hard.

He yanks her head around. All the way.

The touch of the demon. Every bone in her neck breaks.

Hitting the floor dead, her eccentric grin is still plastered on her face.

Guess he wasn't that crazy about Mom, after all.

"She was always telling me what to do," Eddie explains.

The next minutes are a blur. I am told to surrender my gun, which I do. Joel is deposited on the couch, where he stares glassy-eyed at the two of us, still alive, still aware of what is happening, but unable to do anything about it. Eddie does allow me to stop Joel's bleeding, however, with a drop of blood from my own finger. Eddie probably just wanted to see how it was done. On the whole, as Yaksha predicted, he is very interested in my blood. By remarkable coincidence he has a syringe and plastic tubing in his pocket—don't leave home without them. The modern medical devices no doubt facilitated his manufacture of other vampires. Pointing his gun at me, Eddie has me take a seat at the dining room table. He also has a tourniquet, which he instructs me to tie around my upper left arm. I am a role model of cooperation. My veins pop up beneath my soft white skin. It is odd that I should notice a mole on my elbow right then, one which I never knew I had, even though it must have been there for the last five thousand years.

I cannot believe that I am about to die.

Not taking his eyes or his aim off me, Eddie fetches a couple of glasses, and ice, from the kitchen. Clearly he wishes to celebrate his conquest with several toasts. I do not flinch as he sticks the needle in my largest vein and my blood traces a clear plastic loop into his glass. I'll have a Bloody Sita—on the rocks. The glass fills steadily. We look at each other across the dining room table. Joel is lying semiconscious ten feet off to my left, his breathing labored. From vast experience I know a large blood loss can cause a person to smother. In a few minutes I may even know it from personal experience. The grin on Eddie's face is most annoying.

"So I win," he says.

"What do you win? You're a miserable creature, and when I'm gone you'll still be miserable. Power, wealth, even immortality—they don't bring happiness. You will never know what the word means."

Eddie laughs. "You don't look so happy right now."

I nod. "That's true. But I don't fool myself that I am. I am what I am. You are just a caricature of a hero in one of your perverted fantasies. One morning, one night I should say, you'll wake up and look at yourself in the mirror and wish the person staring back at you weren't so ugly."

"You're just a lousy loser."

I shake my head. "I am not just talking about your ugly face. If you live long enough, you're going to eventually see what you are. It's inevitable. If I do fail to kill you tonight, I predict you will eventually kill yourself. Out of sheer loathing. One thing for sure, you're never going to change. You'll always be something sick that the creation just happened to vomit forth when God was looking the other way."

He snorts. "I don't believe in God."

I nod sadly. "I don't know if I do, either."

A wave of dizziness sweeps over me.

My blood, my immortal blood, is leaving me.

It will not be long now.

Yet I cannot stop thinking of Krishna, even when the tall glass is full and Eddie raises it to his lips and toasts my good health and drinks it down in one guttural swallow. It is as if my dream of Krishna and the story he gave to Yaksha have become superimposed over each other in my mind. Actually, it is as if I have two minds, one in this hell I can't block out, the other in a heaven I can't really remember. But the duality of consciousness does not comfort me. The memory of the bliss of my imagined conversation with Krishna on the enchanted hilltop just makes this bitter end that much more difficult to accept. Of course, I do not accept it. Even though I have surrendered, I have lived too long to lie down and be sucked dry like this. Krishna beat the demon by playing the enchantress. How may I play this same role? What is the key? If only he would appear before me now and tell me. Another glass fills and Eddie drinks it down.

"Now I will play you a song made up of the seven notes of humanity. All the emotions you will feel as a human and as a vampire. Remember this song and you will remember me. Sing this song and I will be there."

Why did he tell me that? Or did he tell me anything at all? Did I not just dream the whole thing? I had just lost Ray. My subconscious must have been starving for comfort. Surely I created the whole thing. Yet, if I did, the joy of the creation brought me more joy than anything in this world has. I cannot forget the beauty of Krishna's eyes—the blue stars wherein the whole of the creation shines. It is as if I trust in his beauty more than in his words. His love was a thing that never needed to be understood. The day we met, it was just there, like the endless sky.

The day we met.

What did he do that remarkable day?

He played his song on his flute. Yaksha had challenged him to a contest. Together they went into a large pit filled with cobras, and it was agreed that whoever came out alive would be the victor. Both carried flutes and played songs to enchant the serpents and keep them from striking. But in the end Krishna won because he knew the secret notes that moved the different emotions inside all of us who were present. With his song Krishna struck deep into Yaksha's heart and brought forth love, hate, and fear—in that order. And it was this last emotion that defeated Yaksha because a serpent only strikes when it senses fear. His body oozed venom by the time Krishna had Yaksha carried from the pit.

I have no flute on which to play that song.

Yet I remember it well. Yes.

"Sing this song and I will be there."

From that day, and that time outside of time, before there even were days, I remember it. My dream was more than a dream. It was a key.

Staring Eddie straight in the eye, I begin to whistle.

He pays me no heed, at first.

He drinks down a third glass of my blood.

My strength begins to fail. There is no time for love, even

for hate. I sing the last song Krishna sang to us, the one of fear. The note, the tone, the pitch—they are engraved in my soul. My lips fold into the perfect lines of Krishna's flute. I do not see him, of course, and I doubt that I even feel his divine presence. Yet I feel something remarkable. My fear is great, it is true, and that emotion goes deep into my blood, which Eddie continues to drink. Anxiety crosses his face as he takes another sip, and for that I am glad. Yet beyond this I sense the true significance of my body, the instrument through which this song of life and death is continually playing for all of us. The realization even gives me a sense of the player, my true self, the *I* that existed before I stepped on this wicked stage and donned the costume of the vampire.

Again, I remember wanting to be different.

Eddie pauses with the bloody glass in his hand. He looks at me strangely. "What are you doing?" he asks.

I do not answer him with words. The tune continues to pour from my lips, a poisonous note with which I hope to save the world. The influence of it spreads throughout the room. Joel's breathing becomes painful—my song is killing him as well. It is irritating Eddie, that's for sure. He suddenly drops his glass and shakes his gun at me.

"Stop that!" he orders.

I know I have to stop, at least this melody. If I don't he will shoot me and I will be dead. But another note comes to me, and it is odd because it is not one that Krishna played the day he dueled with Yaksha. Yet I know it, and once again I believe that the dream must have been a genuine vision. Before I entered the creation, Krishna gave me all the notes of life, all the keys to all the emotions a human being, and a monster, could experience.

I sing the note of the second center in the body—the sex center. Here, when the life energy flows, there are experienced two states of mind. Intense creativity when the energy goes up, intense lust when it goes down. Leaning toward Eddie, holding his eye as if it were his pleasure button, I pierce that secret note through his ears and into his nervous system and I send it *down*. Down even into the ground where I wish to bury his stinking body. It does not matter that I do not lust for him myself. It only matters that I have finally understood the meaning of Krishna's fable. *I am the enchantress.* The gun in Eddie's hand wavers and he stares at me in a new light. No longer does he just want my blood. He wants the container as well—my flesh. I pause long enough to give him a nasty grin. He resisted my suggestions before and my lover died. He will not resist me now and he will die.

I am that cheerleader he never had in high school.

"You have never had someone like me," I say softly.

Another note. Another inhuman caress.

Eddie licks his lips.

"You will never have someone like me," I whisper.

I do not sing the note. It sings itself.

Eddie fidgets, beside himself with passion.

"Never." I form the word with my wet lips.

One more note. I barely get it out.

Eddie drops his gun and grabs me. We kiss.

Hmm. Yuck.

I pull back slightly to let him adore the whole of me.

"I like it cold," I say.

Eddie understands. He is an ice-cream man, a connoisseur of frozen corpses. It is his thing and we should not judge him too harshly. Especially when he falls for my suggestion and drags me in the direction of the rear of the house. Toward the huge freezer where he used to go searching for Popsicles in the middle of the night. I am so weak—Eddie drags me by my hair. Yanking the fat white door open, he throws me inside, into the foggy frost, the cold dark, where his eyes are not as sharp as mine, and both our aversions to cold will stand or fall in critical balance. Landing on my ass, I quickly stand and find Eddie staring at me in that special way. I do believe he is not even going to give me a chance to fully undress. Tossing my head and hair to the side, I raise my right hand and place it on my left breast. One last time, just before I speak, I whistle the note.

"I do so prefer the dark," I say. "For me, it makes it that much more dirty."

Eddie—he has many buttons. This one makes his leg lash out. Behind him, the door shuts. The overhead light either doesn't work or doesn't exist. All is dark, all is cold.

I hear him coming toward me.

More than that I can distinguish a faint outline of him, even in the total absence of light. And I can tell by the lack of focus in his movements that he cannot see me at all. Also, already I can tell the cold has dulled his vampiric blood. This is both good and bad. The slower he is, the easier he will be to handle. Yet the same effect applies to me as well. My only advantage is that I know the dullness is coming. Unfortunately, snakes never mate on a winter night. The freezer puts a hold on his reckless passion just when I need it most. Before I can sing another note, he pauses in midstride, and I see that he realizes he has been tricked. In a flash he turns for the door.

I trip him. He falls to the floor.

In the event a large freezer door gets jammed and a person is locked inside, it is required by law that an ax be kept inside at all times. That way, if need be, the unfortunate individual can chop his way out. In Eddie's freezer the ax is strapped to the inside of the door, which is normal. As Eddie falls, I leap onto his back and over his head and grab that ax. It is a big sucker. Raising it over my head, feeling the weight of its sharp steel blade, I know true happiness.

"What's your favorite flavor, little boy?" I ask.

Eddie quickly goes up onto his knees, searching for me in the dark, feeling with his hands, knowing I'm near but not realizing what I have in my hands.

"Huh?" he says.

"Cherry red?" I shout.

I bring the ax down hard. Cut off his goddamn head. Black blood gushes out and I kick his amputated coconut into what could be a box of ice-cream sandwiches. Dropping the ax, I fumble in the dark with the door, barely getting it open. My strength is now finished. Even with the ax, even being a vampire, I would not have had the energy to chop my way out.

I find Joel dying on the couch. He has a minute more, maybe two. Kneeling before him, I lift up his sunken head. He opens his eyes and tries to smile at me.

"You stopped him?" he whispers.

"Yes. He is dead." I pause and glance at the needle still in my arm, the tourniquet and the plastic tubing. I twist the latter to keep it from leaking my blood onto the floor. Searching Joel's face, I feel such guilt. "Do you know what I am?" I ask.

The word comes hard. "Yes."

"Do you want to be like me?"

He closes his eyes. "No."

I grab him, shake him. "But you will die, Joel."

"Yes." His head falls on his chest. His breath is a thing of resignation, a settling of ripples on a mountain pond that prepares for a winter's frost. Yet he speaks once more, one sweet word that pierces my heart and makes me feel he is my responsibility: "Sita."

The seconds tick. They always do. The power of an entire sun cannot stop them even for a moment, and so death comes between the moments, like a thief of light in the dark. Eddie had brought a spare syringe. It sits on the dining room table like a needle that waits for me to poke in the eye of God. Krishna made me promise to make no other vampires, and in return he would grant me his grace, his protection. And even though I did make another when I changed Ray, Yaksha believed I still lived in that grace because I gave Ray my blood to save him, only because I loved him.

"Where there is love, there is my grace."

I believe I can save Joel. I feel it is my duty to do so.

But do I love him?

God help me, I don't know.

Stumbling into the dining room, I fetch the extra syringe. It fits snugly onto the end of the plastic tubing. Because I still wear the tourniquet, the pressure is on my veins and my blood will flow into his. Like Ray, six weeks ago, Joel will be forever altered. But staring down at his unconscious face, I wonder if any creature, mortal or immortal, has the right to make decisions that last forever. I only know I will miss him if he dies.

Sitting beside him, cradling him in my arms, I stick the needle in his vein. My blood—it goes into him. But where will it stop? As I sink into the couch and begin to pass out, I realize that he may hate me in the morning, which from now on will always come at night for him. He told me not to do it. He may even kill me for what I have done. Yet I am so weary, I don't know if I even care. Let him carry on the story, I think.

Let him be the last vampire.

RED DICE

For Rene

ONE

I am a vampire. Blood does not bother me. I like blood. Even seeing my own blood does not frighten me. But what my blood can do to others—to the whole world for that matter—terrifies me. Once God made me take a vow to create no more vampires. Once I believed in God. But my belief, like my vow, has been shattered too many times in my long life. I am Alisa Perne, the now-forgotten Sita, child of a demon. I am the oldest living creature on earth.

I awake in a living room smelling of death. I watch as my blood trickles through a thin plastic tube into the arm of Special Agent Joel Drake, FBI. He now lives as a vampire instead of the human being he was when he closed his eyes. I have broken my promise to Lord Krishna—Joel did not ask me to make him a vampire. Indeed, he told me not to, to let him die in peace. But I did not listen. Therefore, Krishna's protection, his grace, no longer applies to me. Perhaps it is good. Perhaps I will die soon. Perhaps not.

I do not die easily.

I remove the tubing from my arm and stand. At my feet lies the body of Mrs. Fender, mother of Eddie Fender, who also lies dead, in a freezer at the end of the hall. Eddie had been a vampire, a very powerful one, before I cut off his head. I step over his mother's body to search for a clock. Somehow, fighting the forces of darkness, I have misplaced my watch. A clock ticks in the kitchen above the stove. Ten minutes to twelve. It is dark outside.

I have been unconscious for almost twenty-four hours.

Joel will awaken soon, I know, and then we must go. But I do not wish to leave the evidence of my struggle with Eddie for the FBI to examine. Having seen how Eddie stole and used the blood of my creator, Yaksha, I know I must vaporize this sick house. My sense of smell is acute, as is my hearing. The pump that cools the large freezer in the back is not electric but powered by gasoline. I smell large amounts of fuel on the back porch. After I toss the gasoline all over the house, and wake Joel, I will strike a match. Fire pleases me, although it has the power to destroy me. Had I not been a vampire, I might have become a pyromaniac.

The gasoline is stored in two twenty-gallon steel tanks. Because I have the strength of many men, I have no trouble lifting them both at once. Yet even I am surprised by how light they feel. Before I passed out, I was like Joel, on the verge of death. Now I am stronger than I can ever remember being. There is a reason. Yaksha gave me what blood he had left in his veins before I buried him in the sea. He gave me his power, and I never realized how great it was until this moment. It is a wonder I was able to defeat Eddie, who also drank from Yaksha. Perhaps Krishna came to my aid, one last time.

I take the drums into the living room. From the freezer, I remove Eddie's body, severed head, and even the hard blood on the freezer floor. I pick them all up and place them on my living room barbecue. Next I begin to break up the couch and tables into easy-to-burn pieces. The noise causes Joel to stir but he does not waken. Newborn vampires sleep deep and wake up hungry. I wonder if Joel will be like my beloved Ray, reluctant to drink from the living. I hope not. I loved Ray above all things, but as a vampire, he was a pain in the ass.

I think of Ray.

He has been dead less than two days.

"My love," I whisper. "My sorrow."

There is no time for grief; there never is. There is no time for joy, I think bitterly. Only for life, pain, death. God did not plan this creation. It was a joke to him, a dream. Once, in a dream, Krishna told me many secrets. But he may have lied to me. It would have been like him.

I am almost done throwing the fuel around and tearing up the house when I hear the sound of approaching cars. There are no sirens but I know these are police cruisers. Police drive differently from normal people, worse actually. They drive faster and the officers in these squad cars are anxious to get here. I have incredibly sensitive hearing—I count at least twenty vehicles. What brings them here?

I glance at Joel.

"Are they coming for Eddie?" I ask him. "Or for me? What did you tell your superiors?"

But perhaps I am too quick to judge, too harsh. Los Angeles has seen many strange sights lately, many bodies killed by superhumans. Perhaps Joel has not betrayed me, at least not intentionally. Perhaps I have betrayed myself. I have gotten sloppy in my old age. I hurry to Joel's side and shake him roughly.

"Wake up," I say. "We have to get out of here."

He opens his drowsy eyes. "You look different." he whispers. "Your eyes are different."

Realization crosses his face. "Did you change me?"

"Yes."

He swallows weakly. "Am I still human?"

I sigh. "You're a vampire."

"Sita."

I put a finger to his lips. "Later. We must leave here quickly. Many cops are coming." I pull him to his feet and he groans. "You will feel stronger in a few minutes. Stronger than you have ever felt before."

I find a Bic lighter in the kitchen, and we head for the front door. But before we can reach it I hear three cruisers skid to a halt outside. We hurry to the back, but the situation is the same. Cops, weapons drawn, have jumped out of their cars with whirling blue and red lights cutting paths in the night sky. More vehicles appear, armored monstrosities with SWAT teams inside. Searchlights flash on and light up the house. We are surrounded. I do not do well in such situations, or else, one might say, I do very well—for a vampire. What I mean is, being trapped brings out my most vicious side. I push aside my recently acquired revulsion for violence. Once, in the Middle Ages, surrounded by an angry mob, I killed over a hundred men and women.

Of course, they didn't have guns.

A bullet in the head could probably kill me, I think.

"Am I really a vampire?" Joel asks, still trying to catch up with reality.

"You're not an FBI agent anymore," I mutter.

He shakes himself as he straightens up. "But I am. Or at least they think I am. Let me talk to them."

"Wait." I stop him, thinking. "I can't have them examine Eddie's remains. I don't trust what will happen to his blood. I don't trust what his blood can still do. I must destroy it, and to do that I must burn down this house."

Outside, through a bullhorn, a gruff-voiced man calls for us to come out with our hands in the air. Such an unimaginative way of asking us to surrender.

Joel knew what Eddie had been capable of. "I was wondering why everything smelled like gasoline," he remarks. "You light the place on fire—I have no problem with that. But then what are you going to do? You can't fight this army."

"Can't I?" I peer out the front window and raise my eyes to the rhythmic thrumming in the sky. They have a helicopter. Why? All to catch the feared serial killer? Yes, such a beast would demand heavy forces. Yet I sense a curious undercurrent in the assembled men and women. It reminds me of when Slim, Yaksha's assassin, came looking for me. Slim's people had been warned that I was not normal. As a result, I barely escaped. In the same way, these people know that there is something unusual about me.

I can almost read their thoughts.

This strikes me as strange.

I have always been able to sense emotions. Now, can I read thoughts, too?

What power has Yaksha's blood given me?

"Alisa," Joel says, calling me by my modern name. "Even you cannot break free of this circle." He notices I'm lost in thought. "Alisa?"

"They think there is a monster in here," I whisper. "I *hear* their minds." I grip Joel. "What did you tell them about me?"

He shakes his head. "Some things."

"Did you tell them I was powerful? Fast?"

He hesitates, then sighs. "I told them too much. But they

don't know you're a vampire." He, too, peers through the curtains. "They were getting suspicious about how the others died, torn to pieces. They had my file on Eddie Fender, including where his mother lived. They must have tracked us here that way."

I shake my head. "I cannot surrender. It is against my nature."

He takes my hands. "You can't fight them all. You'll die."

I have to smile. "More of them would die." I lose my smile. "But if I do make a stand here, you will die also." I am indecisive. His advice is logical. Yet my heart betrays me. I feel doom closing in. I speak reluctantly. "Talk to them. Say what you think best. But I tell you—I will not leave this house without setting it ablaze. There will be no more Eddie Fenders."

"I understand." He turns for the door, then stops. He speaks with his back to me. "I understand why you did it."

"Do you forgive me?"

"Would I have died?" he asks.

"Yes."

He smiles gently, not turning to look at me. I feel the smile. "Then I must forgive you," he says. He raises one hand above his head, and with the other reaches for the doorknob. "I hope my boss is out there."

Through a crack in the curtains I follow his progress. Joel calls out his identity and a group of FBI agents step forward. I can tell they're FBI by their suits. Joel is one of them. He looks the same as he did yesterday. Yet they don't greet him as a friend. In an instant I grasp the full extent of their suspicions. They know that whatever plague of death has been sweeping L.A. is communicable. Eddie and I left too many bodies behind. Also, I remember the cop I freed. The one whose blood I sampled. The one I told I was a vampire. The authorities may not have believed that man, but they will think I am some kind of demon from hell.

Joel is handcuffed and dragged into an armored vehicle. He casts me a despairing glance before he vanishes. I curse the fact that I listened to him. Now I, too, must be taken into the vehicle. Above all, I must stay close to Joel. I don't know what he'll tell them. I don't know what they'll do with his blood.

Many of them are going to die, I realize.

The SWAT team cocks their weapons.

They call again for me to surrender.

I twirl the striker on the lighter and touch it to the wood I have gathered around Eddie's body. I say goodbye to his ugly head. Hope the Popsicles you suck in hell cool your cracked and bleeding lips. Casually, while the inferno spreads behind me, I step out the front door.

They are on me in an instant. Before I can reach the curb, my arms are pulled behind me and I am handcuffed. They don't even read me my rights. You have the right to a pint of blood. If you cannot afford one, the court will bleed a little for you. Yeah, I think sarcastically as they shove me into the back of the armored vehicle where they threw Joel, I will be given all my rights as an American citizen. Behind me I see them trying to put out the fire. Too bad they brought the firepower but forgot the fire engines. The house is a funeral pyre. Eddie Fender will leave no legacy to haunt mankind.

But what about me? Joel?

Our legs are chained to the floor of the vehicle. Three men with automatic weapons and ghostly faces lit from a single overhead light sit on a metal bench across from us, weapons trained on us. No one speaks. Another two armed men sit up front, beside the driver. One carries a shotgun, the other a machine gun. They are separated from us by what I know is bulletproof glass. It also acts as soundproofing. I can break it with my little finger.

But what about the miniature army around us? They won't break so easily. As the door is closed and we roll forward, I hear a dozen cars move into position around us. The chopper follows overhead, a spotlight aimed down on our car. Their precautions border on the fanatical. They know I am capable of extraordinary feats of strength. This realization sinks deep into my consciousness. For five thousand years, except for a few isolated incidents, I have moved unknown through human history. Now I am exposed. Now I am the enemy. No matter what happens, whether we escape or die trying, my life will never be the same.

I'll have to tear up my credit cards.

"Where are you taking us?" I ask.

"You are to remain silent," the middle one says. He has the face of a drill sergeant, leathery skin, deeply etched lines cut in from years of barking commands. Like his partners, he wears a flak jacket. I think I would look nice in one. I catch his eye and smile faintly.

"What's the matter?" I ask. "Are you afraid of a young woman?"

"Silence," he snaps, shaking his weapon, shifting uncomfortably. My stare is strong medicine. It can burn holes in brain neurons. My voice is hypnotic, when I wish it to be. I could sing a grizzly to sleep. I let my smile widen.

"'May I have a cigarette?" I ask.

"No," he says flatly.

I lean forward as far as I can. These men, for all their plans, have not come as well prepared as Slim's people did. Yaksha had them bring cuffs made of a special alloy that I could not break. I can snap these like paper. Yet they are seated close together, these SWAT experts, and they have three separate weapons leveled directly at me. They could conceivably kill me before I could take out all of them. For that reason I have to take a subtle approach.

Relatively speaking.

"I don't know what you've been told about me," I continue. "But I think it's way out of line. I have done nothing wrong. Also, my friend here is an FBI agent. He shouldn't be treated this way. You should let him go." I stare deep into the man's eyes, and I know all he sees are my widening black pupils, growing as large as the dark sides of twin moons. I speak softly. "You should let him go *now*."

The man reaches for his keys, then hesitates. The hesitation is a problem. Pushing a person's will is always a hit-or-miss proposition. His partners are watching him now, afraid to look at me. The youngest one rises half off his bench. He is suddenly scared and threatens me with his weapon.

"You shut your goddamn mouth!" he yells.

I lean back and chuckle. As I do, I catch his eye. Fear has made him vulnerable; he is an easy mark. "What are you afraid of?" I ask. "That your commander will let me go? Or that you'll turn around and shoot him?" I bore my gaze into his head. "Yeah, you could shoot him. Yeah, that might be fun."

"Alisa," Joel whispers, not enjoying my game.

The young man and the commander exchange worried glances. The third guy has sat up, panting, not really understanding what is happening. Out of the corner of my eye, I see Joel shaking his head. Let him see me at my worst, I think. It is the best way to begin our new relationship, without illusions. My eyes dart from the commander to the young one. The temperature inside their craniums is increasing. Ever so slightly, each weapon begins to veer toward the other man's chest. Yet I know I'll have to push them a lot harder to get them to let me go or kill each other. It is not necessary. I can do it on my own. Really, I just want to distract them a bit—

Before I break them in two.

With their guns aimed away from me, they are vulnerable when I suddenly shoot my legs up, snapping my ankle chains. The third man, the one I have left untouched, reacts quickly, by human standards. But he is moving in slow motion compared to a five-thousand-year-old vampire. As he reaches for the trigger on his gun, my right foot lashes out and my big toe crushes his flak jacket, his breastbone, and the beating heart beneath the two. The heart beats no more. The man crumples and falls into a pitiful ball.

"Should have given me the cigarette," I say to the commander as I snap my handcuffs and reach over to take his head between my palms. His eyes grow round. His lips move. He wants to tell me something, maybe apologize. I'm not in the mood. He is putty in my hands, Silly Putty once I squeeze my palms together and crack his skull. Now his mouth falls open as his eyes slowly close. His brains leak out the back, over his starched collar. I don't want his flak jacket.

I glance over at the young one.

He's more scared than before.

I just stare at him. He has forgotten his weapon.

"Die," I whisper intently. My will is poisonous, when I am mad, and now, with Yaksha's blood in my veins, the poison is worse than the venom of a cobra. The young man falls to the floor.

His breathing stops.

Joel looks as if he will be sick.

"Kill me," he swears. "I cannot stand this."

"I am what I am." I break his chains. "You will become what I am."

He is bitter. He has no illusions. "Never."

I nod. "I said the same thing to Yaksha." I soften, touch his arm. "I cannot let them take you or me into custody. We could have a thousand Eddies running around."

"They just want to talk to us," he says.

I shake my head as I glance at the men up front, unaware, so far, of what has happened to their comrades. "They know we are not normal," I whisper.

Joel pleads. "You can escape far more easily without me. Fewer people will have to die. Leave me behind. Let them catch me in a shower of bullets. My blood will soak the pavement, nothing more."

"You are a brave man, Joel Drake."

He grimaces as he glances at what I have done to the others. "I have spent my life trying to help people. Not destroy them."

I stare softly into his eyes. "I can't just let you die. You don't know what I have sacrificed to keep you alive."

He pauses. "What did you sacrifice?"

I sigh. "The love of God." I turn toward the men at the front. "We will discuss this later."

Joel stops me one last time. "Don't kill when you don't have to."

"I will do what I can," I promise.

The bulletproof glass is two inches thick. Although the ceiling of the van forces me to crouch, I am able to leap far enough off the floor to plant two swift kicks onto the barrier. I have exceptionally strong legs. The glass shatters into thousands of little pellets. Before the two armed men can turn, I reach forward and knock their heads together. They collapse in a mangled heap. They are unconscious, not dead. I remove the revolver from the hip holster of the driver and place the barrel to his head.

"The men in the back are dead," I whisper in his ear. "If you glance in your rearview mirror you will see it is true. But I have allowed your partners up front to live. That is because I am a nice girl. I am nice and I am nasty. If you tell me where we are headed, I will be nice to you. If you don't, if you try to alert your partners on the road ahead of us or behind us, I will tear out your eyes and swallow them." I pause. "Where are you taking us?"

He has trouble speaking. "C-Fourteen."

"Is that a police station?"

"No."

"What is it? Quickly!"

He coughs, frightened. "A high-security facility."

"Who runs it?"

He swallows. "The government."

"Are there labs there?"

"I don't know. I've only heard stories. I think so."

"Interesting." I tap his head lightly with his gun. "What's your name?"

"Lenny Treber." He throws me a nervous glance. Sweat pours off him in a river. "What's your name?"

"I have many names, Lenny. We are in a tight fix here. You and I and my friend. How do we get out of it?"

He can't stop shaking. "I don't understand."

"I don't want to go to C-Fourteen. I want you to help me escape this dragnet. It is to your advantage to help, and to the advantage of your fellow cops. I don't want to leave several dozen women widowed." I pause. "Are you married, Lenny?"

He tries to calm himself with deep breaths. "Yes."

"Do you have children?"

"Yes."

"You don't want your children to grow up without a father, do you?"

"No."

"What can you do to help me and my friend?"

It is hard for him to concentrate. "I don't know."

"You will have to do better than that. What happens if you radio ahead and say you need to take a bathroom break?"

"They won't believe it. They'll know you have escaped."

"Is this van bulletproof?"

"Yes."

"What did they tell you about me?"

"That you were dangerous."

"Anything else?" I ask.

He is near tears. "They said you can kill with your bare hands." He catches a clear view of the brain tissue dripping out of the commander's skull. It is a gruesome sight, even by my flexible standards. A shudder runs through Lenny's body. "Oh God," he gasps.

I pat him sweetly on the back. "I do have my bad side," I admit. "But you cannot judge me by a few dead bodies. I don't want to kill you, Lenny, now that we're on a first-name basis. Think of another way for us to escape the escorts."

He struggles. "There isn't one. This job has the highest security imaginable. They'll open fire if I try to get away from them."

"Those were the orders?"

"Yes. Under no circumstances were you to be allowed to escape."

I ponder this. They must know me, even better than Lenny thinks. How's that possible? Have I left that much evidence behind? I think of the Coliseum, the necks I broke, the javelins I threw. It's possible, I suppose.

"I am going to escape," I tell Lenny, picking up the dropped machine gun and shotgun from the front seats. I also yank a flak jacket off one of the men. "One way or the other."

"They'll open fire," Lenny protests.

"Let them." I take ammunition for both weapons from the

unconscious men. I gesture to Joel, who is still getting adjusted to his vampire senses. He's staring around the interior of the van as if he's stoned. "Put on one of those flak jackets," I tell him.

"Does there have to be shooting?" he asks.

"There will be a lot of shooting." I speak to Lenny. "What's the top speed of this van?"

"Eighty miles an hour."

I groan. "I need a cop car."

"There are a lot of them behind and in front of us," Lenny says.

I peer at the chopper in the sky. "They hang close to the ground."

"They're heavily armed," Lenny says. "They won't let you escape."

I climb in the front seat beside him, shoving the men aside. The flak jacket is a little large on me. "You think I should surrender?"

"Yes." He adds quickly, "That's just my opinion."

"You just follow my orders if you want to live," I say, studying the cruisers in front, in back. Sixteen altogether—two officers in each, I know. Plus there are at least three unmarked cars—FBI agents. It continues to amaze me how quickly they took Joel into custody. They hardly gave him a chance to speak. I call back to him, "Come up here. We're going to switch vehicles in a few minutes."

Joel pokes his head close to my shoulder, flak jacket in

place. "The chopper is a problem," he says. "It doesn't matter how good a driver you are or how many cop cars you disable. It'll stay with us, lighting us up."

"Maybe. Put on a seat belt." I brace a foot on the dashboard and point to an approaching alley. "There, Lenny, I want you to take a hard left. Floor it as soon as you come out of the turn."

Lenny sweats. "Okay."

I start to hand Joel Lenny's revolver. "Don't be afraid to cover my back." I pause and catch his eye. "You are on my side, aren't you?"

Joel hesitates. "I won't kill anybody."

"Will you try to kill me?"

"No."

I give him the revolver. "All right." The alley closes. "Get ready, Lenny. No tricks. Just put as much distance between us and the procession as you can."

Lenny veers to the left. The alley is narrow; the van shoots through it at high speed, knocking over garbage cans and crates. The response from the cops is immediate. Half the cars jam into the alley in pursuit. But half is better than all, and locked in behind us as they are, the cops can't fire at us so easily.

Unfortunately, the alley crosses several streets. Fortunately, it's midnight, with almost no traffic. At the first street we're lucky. But we lose two police cars to a collision. At the second crossing we're also fortunate. But as we drive into the third cross street we smash sideways into the only vehicle on the street, an open produce truck loaded with oranges. The fruit spills over the van. Lenny has bumped his head on the steering wheel and appears to be dazed. He gets another bump on his head when a squad car smashes into us from behind. This is what I wanted—a pileup.

"Come on!" I call to Joel.

I jump out of the side of the van and raise the machine gun and fire a spray of bullets at the cars piled up behind us. They are pinned down, but I know it won't be long before a herd of fresh cars comes around the block. The suddenness of my attack causes them to scramble from their vehicles. Overhead, the chopper swoops dangerously low, the spotlight momentarily focused straight on me. I look through the glare of the light and see a marksman stand in the open doorway and raise a high-powered rifle. Pumping the shotgun, I take aim at him and pull the trigger.

The man loses the top of his head.

His lifeless body falls onto the roof of a nearby building.

I am not finished.

My next shot takes out the spotlight. My third hits the small vertical rotor at the rear. The blade sputters but continues to spin. Pumping the shotgun, I put another round in it, and this time the propeller dies. It is the vertical rotor that prevents fuselage rotation and also provides rudder control. In other words, it gives stability to the helicopter. Immediately the flying machine veers out of control. To the horror of the watching police officers, it crash-lands in the midst of their line of cars. The explosion is violent, crushing several officers, setting a few ablaze. I use the distraction to reach in and pull Joel out of the van. We run down the block, faster than any human could.

All this has happened in ten seconds.

So far, not a single shot has been fired at us.

A second line of cop cars comes around the block.

I jump into the middle of the street and pour two shotgun rounds into the window of the first one, killing both officers inside. The vehicle loses control and crashes into a parked car. The police cars behind it slam on their brakes. A spray of bullets from my machine gun makes them scramble out of their vehicles in search of cover. I run toward the second car, shielding Joel with my body. To the police, I know, my movements appear as nothing more than a blur. They can't get a lock on me. Nevertheless, they do open fire and a hail of bullets flies around me. My flak jacket takes several rounds, causing no damage. But one bullet catches me in the leg above my left knee and I stumble, although I don't fall. Another shot hits me in my right upper arm. Somehow, I reach the second police car and shove Joel inside. I want to drive. I am bleeding, and the pain is intense, but I am in too much of a hurry to acknowledge it.

"Keep your head down!" I snap at Joel as I throw the car

in gear. Peeling out, we are treated to another shower of bullets. I take my own advice and duck. Both the front and rear windshields shatter. Glass pellets litter my long blond hair. It will take a special brand of shampoo to get them out.

We escape, but are a marked couple in a highly visible car. I jump on the Harbor Freeway, heading north, hoping to put as much distance between us and our pursuers as quickly as possible. I keep the accelerator floored, weaving in and out of the few cars. But I have two police cars on my tail. Worse, another helicopter has appeared in the sky. This pilot has learned from his predecessor. He keeps the chopper up high, but not so high that he can't track us.

"We can't hide from a chopper," Joel says again.

"This is a big city," I reply. "There are many places to hide."

He sees I am bloody. "How bad are your injuries?"

It is an interesting question because already—in the space of a few minutes—they have completely healed. Yaksha's blood—it is an amazing potion.

"I am all right," I say. "Are you injured?"

"No." He pauses. "How many men have died since this started?"

"At least ten. Try not to count."

"Is that what you did after a few thousand years? You stopped counting?"

"I stopped thinking."

I have a goal. Because I know we cannot stay on the freeway long, I decide that the only way we can escape the helicopters is to get into one ourselves. Atop several of the high-rises in downtown Los Angeles there are helicopter pads with choppers waiting to whisk executives to high-level meetings. I can fly a helicopter. I can operate any piece of machinery humankind has developed.

I exit the freeway on Third Street. By now I have ten black-and-whites on my tail. Coming down the off ramp, I see several cop cars struggling to block the road in front of me. Switching to the wrong side of the street, I bypass them and head east in the direction of the tallest buildings. But my way is quickly blocked by another set of black-and-whites. We must have half the LAPD after us. I am forced to swerve into the basement garage of a building I don't know. A wooden bar swings down to block my way, but I don't stop to press the green button and collect my ticket. Nor does the herd of law enforcement behind me. We all barrel through the barricade. A sign for an elevator calls my attention and I slam the car to a halt inches from the door. We jump out and push the button. While we wait for our ride to higher floors, I open fire on our pursuers. More people die. I lied to Joel. I do count—three men and a woman take bullets in the face. I am a very good shot.

The elevator comes and we pile inside.

I press the top button. Number twenty-nine.

"Can they halt the elevator from the basement?" I ask as I reload.

"Yes. But it'll take them a few minutes to figure out how to do it." He shrugs. "But does it matter? They'll surround this building with an army. We're trapped."

"You're wrong," I say.

We exit onto the top floor. Here there are expensive suites, for law firms, plastic surgeons, and investment counselors. But there is too much high-priced real estate in Los Angeles—several of the suites are empty. Kicking in the door of the nearest vacancy, I stride up and down beside the wide windows, studying the neighboring buildings. I will have to cross the block and move over a few buildings to reach a high-rise that has a helicopter pad. I curse the fact that I am not a mythic vampire from films, capable of flying.

Yet I am able to leap tall buildings in a single bound.

Joel moves to my side. Below us, we watch the forces of righteousness gather. Two more helicopters have appeared in the night sky. Their bright beams rake the sides of the building.

"They won't come up the elevator after us," Joel says. "They will only come when they have us surrounded top and bottom." He pauses. "What are we going to do?"

"*I* am going to set a new Olympic record." I point to the building across the street. Its roof is only three stories below where we are. "I am going to jump over to it."

He is impressed. "That's far. Can you really do it?"

"If I get a running start. I'll come back for you in a few minutes, in a helicopter. I will land it on the roof of this building. Be waiting for me."

"What if you miss the roof of that building?"

I shrug. "It's a long way down."

"Could you survive the fall?"

"I think so. But it would take me time to recover."

"You shouldn't come back for me," Joel says. "Steal a helicopter and escape."

"That is not a consideration."

He speaks seriously. "Too many people have died. Even if we escape, I can't live with this slaughter on my conscience."

I am impatient. "Don't you see how dangerous you are to the human race? Even dead. They could take your blood, inject it into animals, into themselves—just as Eddie did. And they will do that, after witnessing what we can do. Believe me, I only kill tonight so that the world can wake safely in the morning."

"Is that true, Sita? You would die to save all these men and women?"

I turn away. "I would die to save you."

He speaks gently. "What did you sacrifice to keep me alive?"

I would weep, I think, if I could. "I told you."

"I didn't understand."

"It doesn't matter. It's done." I turn back to him. "There will be time later for these discussions."

He touches my hair—pieces of glass fall to the floor. "You miss him."

"Yes."

"I didn't know what he meant to you when I watched him die."

I smile sadly. "Nothing is really known about a person until he or she is gone."

"I cannot take his place."

I nod weakly. "I know." Then I shake my head. "I need to go."

He wants to hug me. "This could be goodbye."

"It is not over yet."

Before launching my daring leap, I kick out the window that blocks my way. This alerts the buzzing choppers but I don't give them time to zero in on me. I back away from the windows, taking only the shotgun with me, giving the machine gun to Joel.

"Are you afraid of heights?" he asks.

I kiss him. "You don't know me. I am afraid of nothing."

Taking a deep breath, I begin my hard approach. I can accelerate sharply and be at full speed in less than ten strides. My balance and ability to judge distance are flawless. I hit the shattered bottom edge of the window perfectly and all at once I am airborne.

The flight across the gap between the buildings is breathtaking, even for me. It seems as if I'll float forever, moving horizontally, in defiance of gravity. The searchlights on the helicopters are too slow to catch me. I soar in darkness, a huge bat, the cool air on my face. Below, the tiny figures raise their heads skyward, blinking at the impossible. I almost laugh. They thought they had me trapped, silly mortals. They thought wrong.

My landing is not entirely smooth because I have such momentum. I am forced into a roll as I skitter across the rooftop. I am bleeding as I finally come to a halt and jump up. Overhead the choppers are frantically maneuvering to open fire. I am not given a chance to catch my breath before moving. Leaping for the next rooftop, I watch as a line of bullets rips a path in front of me.

The ensuing jumps between buildings are all on the same side of the street and not so dramatic as the first one. Yet the last leap, to the skyscraper with the helicopter pad, is to be the most dramatic of all. Because I cannot jump to the top of a building twenty stories up, I do not plan to land on top of the skyscraper. I will jump *into* it, through its wall of windows. I only hope that I don't hit the steel and concrete between floors.

Once again, the choppers approach, their machine guns blasting.

Once again, I take a running start.

The windows of the skyscraper rush toward me like a hard black wall. An instant before contact, I lean back and kick out with my feet. My timing is perfect; the glass shatters around the lower part of my body, sparing my face and arms. Unfortunately, I land awkwardly on a row of secretarial desks. The shock is incredible, even for me. Coming to a halt in a pile of ruined PCs and paper clips, I lie still for a whole minute, trying to catch my breath. I am now covered with blood from head to toe. Yet even as I grimace in pain my flesh wounds begin to close and my broken bones begin to mend.

I have company on the outside. One of the helicopter pilots has taken it upon himself to come level with the hole I have punched into the side of the skyscraper. The chopper floats just outside the shattered window, scanning the office with its bright searchlight. There are three men, including the pilot, aboard the craft. Peering through the wreckage, I notice that the machine gunner has an itchy finger. I think to myself how much more I would prefer to have a police chopper than a civilian one. But the pilot is not reckless. He keeps the chopper constantly moving a little from side to side. For me to try to leap onto it would be risky. I opt for the more conservative plan.

I get up slowly, limping. My right shinbone is still fractured, but it will be all right in another minute—God bless Yaksha's blood. Ducking behind the desks, the beam from the searchlight stretching long, stark shadows across the office, I move away from the broken window. The helicopter swoops in a narrow arc, sometimes onto the far side of the hole, sometimes closer to where I'm hidden. The windows are tinted; it is easier for me to follow their movements than for them to follow mine, unless their light were to hit me directly. Yet they seem obsessed with the space just beyond the hole. They must feel that I am in the wreckage somewhere near it, injured and dying.

"Come to me, baby," I whisper.

On their third swing toward my side, I punch out the window in front of me and open fire. I take out the machine gunner first; I don't like his looks. The searchlight goes next. I take aim on the fuel tank. As I said, I enjoy fireworks, wicked explosions. When I pull the trigger on the shotgun, the chopper detonates in a huge fireball. The pilot screams, the flames engulfing his body. The other man is blown out the side door, in pieces. The life goes out of the machine and it sinks to the ground. Far below I hear people crying. Far above, to my right, I hear the other two helicopters veer away. They have lost enthusiasm for the fight.

On the way to the elevator, I pass a custodian. He hardly looks up. Despite my blood and artillery, he wishes me a good evening. I smile at him.

"You have a good night," I say.

The elevator takes me to the top floor, and from there it is not hard to find a private access ladder onto the roof. Not one but two helicopters wait to fly us to freedom. Both are jet powered and I am pleased. They will at least be as fast as the cops' choppers, if not faster. Unfortunately there's a security guard on duty. An old guy, obviously working the night shift to supplement a meager retirement, he takes one look at me and hurries over. He has a handgun but doesn't draw it. His glasses are remarkably thick; he squints through the lenses as he looks me up and down.

"Are you a cop?" he asks.

I don't have the heart to lie to him. "No. I'm the bad guy. I'm the one who just blew that chopper out of the sky."

He is awestruck. "I watched you jumping from building to building. How do you do that?"

"Steroids."

He slaps his leg. "I knew it! The drugs young people are taking these days. What do you want? One of these choppers?"

I point my shotgun at him. "Yes. Please give me the keys. I don't want to have to kill you."

He quickly raises his hands. "You don't have to do that. The keys are in the ignitions. Do you know how to fly a helicopter?"

I turn my weapon aside. "Yes. I've been taking lessons. Don't worry about me."

He walks me to the closest chopper, a Bell 230. "This baby has a range of over three hundred miles. You want to get far out of town. The radio and TV are babbling about you, calling you a band of terrorists."

I laugh as I climb into the cockpit. "You do nothing to destroy their illusions. Just tell them you were overwhelmed by superior forces. You don't want people to know a young woman stole a helicopter out from under your nose."

"And a blond one at that," he agrees. "You take care!"

He closes the door for me and I'm off.

Picking up Joel proves to be the easiest part of the night. The police helicopters are holding back—over a mile away. They aren't used to being blown out of the sky. The fire from the last downed chopper spreads over the front of the skyscraper. In the distance I see smoke from the first chopper. Joel shakes his head as he climbs in.

"They'll never stop hunting us after this," he says.

"I don't know," I jest. "They might be afraid to come after me."

We head northeast. I'm anxious to get out of the suburban sprawl and into the wild, somewhere we can disappear. The nearby mountains are a possibility. Our chopper is fast, capable of going two hundred miles an hour. To my surprise, the police helicopters don't really pursue us. It's not just because we're faster than they are—a fact I have to question. They allow the gap to grow between us to at least twenty miles. The length of the space doesn't reassure me because I know they still have us under visual observation. Nothing will be gained by plunging low to the ground, below the radar. They are waiting for something, biding their time.

"Reinforcements," I mutter as we swoop over the sleeping city at an elevation of a thousand feet.

Joel nods. "They've called for bigger guns."

"Army helicopters?"

"Probably."

"Which direction will they come from?"

"There is a large base south of here. You might want to head north."

"I was planning to do so after I reached the Cajon Pass." The pass cuts into the desert, also a nice place to hide. Highway 15 runs through the pass, and if followed far enough, leads to Las Vegas.

"You might not want to wait that long," Joel advises.

"I understand." Yet the temptation to put more distance between us and our pursuers is great. It gives me the illusion of safety, a dangerous illusion. But the farther we go, the more the desert beckons me. Being winter, the mountains are covered with snow, and even though I am highly resistant to cold, I don't like it. At our present speed Cajon Pass is not far ahead. Once over it, we will be clear of the city, able to roam free.

I ask the question I have been waiting to ask.

"Are you thirsty?"

He is guarded. "What do you mean?"

I glance over. "How do you feel?"

He takes a deep breath "Feverish. Cramping."

I nod. "You need blood."

He takes time to absorb my words. "Do you really drink people's blood? Like in the stories?"

"The stories have germs of truth in them, but can't be taken literally. As a vampire, you do need blood to survive. Yet you do not need to kill the person you drink from, and your contact with them will not change them into vampires. You can also live off the blood of animals, although you will find it unsatisfying."

"Do I need blood every day?"

"No. Every few days. But at first, you will crave it every day."

"What happens if I don't drink it?"

"You will die horribly," I say.

"Oh. Do I still need to eat regular food?"

"Yes. You will get hungry as before. But if need be, you will be able to survive for a long time without food. You will also be able to hold your breath for incredible lengths of time."

"But what about the sun? You sat out in the sun with me."

"Yes. But that is not something you want to try yet. The sun won't kill you, but it will irritate you, at least for the first few centuries. Even now, after five thousand years, I'm not nearly so strong while the sun is up. But forget everything else you've heard about vampires. Crucifixes and white roses and running water—none of those will bother you. Bram Stoker was just spicing up his novel when he wrote that stuff." I pause. "Did you know I met him once?"

"Did you tell him you were a vampire?"

"No, but he knew there was something special about me. He autographed my copy of *Dracula* and tried to get my address. But I didn't give it to him." I raise my wrist to my mouth. "I am going to open my vein. I want you to suck my blood for a few minutes."

He fidgets. "Sounds kinky."

"You'll enjoy it. I taste wonderful."

A moment later Joel reluctantly accepts my bleeding wrist, but he is no Ray. He has seen plenty of blood in his line of work and it doesn't make him sick to his stomach. Indeed, after a couple of minutes he is sucking hungrily on my wrist. I have to stop him before he is sated. I cannot allow my strength to wane.

"How do you feel?" I ask as I take back my arm.

"Powerful. Aroused."

I have to laugh. "Not every girl you meet will be able to do that for you."

"Can we be killed with a stake through the heart?"

The laughter dies in my throat. His question brings back the agony of the wound I suffered when my house exploded and Yaksha supposedly died. The chest pain is still there—yet, since drinking Yaksha's blood, it has receded. I wonder what Yaksha would think of me now that I have broken Krishna's vow against creating more vampires. After I have killed so many innocent people. No doubt he would say I am damned.

I miss Yaksha. And Ray. And Krishna.

"You can be killed that way," I say quietly.

Ten minutes later we reach the gap in the mountains and I veer north, climbing in altitude. The pass is almost a mile above sea level. The police helicopters are now thirty miles behind us, blinking red and white dots in the night sky. We have at most four hours of night left. Before then, I must find shelter for Joel and a place to sit quietly and plot my next moves. Scanning left and right, I consider dumping the helicopter. The cliffs of the pass offer more hiding places than the desert will. Yet I don't want to set down so soon. Another idea has come to me, one that may throw our pursuers off.

What if I were to crash the helicopter into a lake?

It would sink and hopefully leave no sign behind.

The plan is a good one. Fuel dictates I choose the closest lake, Big Bear or Arrowhead. But once again I resist heading into the snowy mountains. As a newborn, Joel will not fare well there. I remember how sensitive I was to the cold after Yaksha changed me. Vampires, serpents, the offspring of yakshinis— we prefer warmth.

I need a sand dune oasis with a lake in the center of it.

We plunge over the pass and into the desert.

The bleak landscape sweeps beneath us.

Time passes. I cannot see anyone following.

"We can't stay up here forever," Joel says finally.

"I know."

"What are you waiting for?"

"Lake Mead." Hoover Dam—it is only twenty minutes away, I estimate.

But I have waited too long.

Five minutes later I catch sight of two military helicopters, coming at us from the west, not the south. Because my eyes are so sharp, I see them far off—sixty miles away. I feel it is still possible to reach the lake. Yet I know they have spotted us, that they are tracking us on their radar. When I alter course slightly, they do likewise. Joel sees my concern but doesn't understand it at first. Even changed, his sight is no match for mine.

"What is it?" he asks.

"We have company," I say.

He looks around. "Can we reach the lake?"

"Possibly." I ask in jest, "Can we fight two Apache helicopters?"

"No way."

I guess at the type of craft that pursues us, but a few minutes later I see that I was right. My knowledge of the Apache isn't extensive, but I have read enough to know that we are facing the most lethal attack helicopter on earth. The two choppers move close to each other, on a direct intercept course with us. Black as the desert sky, with wide hypnotic propellers—they are clearly faster than we are. Their machine-gun turret and rocket launchers hang from the sides like dangerous fists. They sweep toward us for a knockout punch. Joel sees them.

"Maybe we should surrender," he suggests.

"I never surrender."

They catch us three miles short of the lake. The wide flat expanse of water is clearly visible, but it could be on the other side of the moon for all the good it can do us now. That's what I think at first. Yet the Apaches do not immediately lock on their weapons. They swoop above and below us, dangerously close, ordering us to land.

"Somebody has told them to take us alive," Joel observes.

"Who?"

Joel shrugs. "The order could have come from the President of the United States. But I suspect the commander of the base where these helicopters originated has given the order."

"We only need to get to the water," I say. "They couldn't imagine that we'd try to vanish underwater."

"I can't imagine it. Can we really hold our breath a long time?"

"I can go an hour."

"But what about me?"

I pat his leg. "Have faith. We should have died a dozen times tonight and we're still alive. Maybe Krishna hasn't deserted us after all."

"If they open fire in the next minute we might have a chance to ask him directly," Joel says dryly.

The Apaches buzz us a couple of times more, then grow tired of the cat-and-mouse game. They lay down a stream of bullets across our path and I have to slow sharply to avoid being torn to shreds. Still, they could blow us out of the sky whenever they wish. Yet they hold back, although they don't want me flying above the lake. They try blocking our path and I have to go into a steep dive to stay on course. We come within several feet of the ground and Joel almost has a heart attack.

"You are one mean pilot," he says when he catches his breath.

"I'm pretty good in bed as well," I reply.

"Of that I have no doubt."

These military men are not like the LAPD. They expect their orders to be obeyed. They may have instructions to take us alive, but they also have orders to prevent us from escaping. A quarter mile from the water, they open fire with surgical precision and suddenly our rotor blades are not a hundred percent intact. Our copter falters in the air, but stays up. The noise above us is deafening. Yet I continue on toward the lake. I have no choice.

"Get ready to jump," I tell Joel.

"I'm not leaving till you leave."

"Nice line. But you have to jump as soon as we cross over the water. Swim for the far shore, not the near one. Stay under water as long as possible."

Joel hesitates. "I don't know how to swim."

"What?"

"I said I don't know how to swim."

I can't believe it. "Why didn't you tell me that earlier?"

"I didn't know what you had planned. You didn't tell me."

"Joel!"

"Sita!"

I pound the chopper dashboard. "Damn! Damn! Well, you're just going to have to learn how to swim. You're a vampire. All vampires can swim."

"Says who?"

"Says me, and I'm the only authority on the subject. Now stop arguing with me and prepare to jump."

"You jump with me."

"No. I have to wait until they fire their lethal blow—that way they'll think I'm dead."

"That's crazy. You will be dead."

"Shut up and crack your door slightly. When you reach the far shore, run into the hills and hide. I'll find you. I can hear a vampire breathing ten miles away."

The Apaches are still determined to prevent us from reaching the water. One swoops overhead and literally drops itself directly into our path. I have to go into another steep dive to avoid it, which is easy to do because the craft is ready to crash anyway. The water is now only a hundred yards away. The Apache behind us opens fire. They mimic my earlier strategy. They blow off our tail rotor. I immediately lose control. We spin madly to the left. Yet the water is suddenly below us.

"Jump!" I scream at Joel.

He casts me one last glance—his expression curiously sad. Then he is gone.

Pulling back hard on the steering bar, I try to gain altitude, partly to distract them from Joel and partly to stay alive. It is my hope they didn't see him jump. My chopper swings farther out over the water. A mile away I see Hoover Dam. There is no way I can make it that far. The chopper bucks like a hyperactive horse on speed. Cracking my door, I take hold of the shotgun and blast at one of the Apaches as it swings nearby. I hit the top blades, but these suckers are tough. The military chopper banks sharply. Then the two helicopters regroup, hovering behind me, twin hornets studying a wounded butterfly. Over my shoulder I see one pilot nod to his gunner. The man reaches for a fresh set of controls, no doubt the firing mechanism for the rockets. As I throw my door open wide, an orange tongue of flame leaps out from the side of the Apache. My reflexes are fast, blinding by human standards, but even I cannot outrun a missile. I am barely free of my seat when the rocket hits.

My chopper vaporizes in midair.

The shock from the explosion hits with the power of an iron fist. A fragment of burning metal cuts into my skull above my hairline, sending waves of searing pain through my whole system. I topple like a helicopter without a stabilizing propeller.

Blood pours over my face and I am blinded. I do not see the cold water of the lake approaching, but I feel it when it slaps my broken side. The molten shrapnel in my head shudders as it contacts the dark liquid. A burst of steam almost causes my skull to explode. I feel myself spiraling down into a forsaken abyss. Consciousness flickers in and out. The lake is bottomless, my soul as empty as dice without numbers. As I start to black out, I wish that I didn't have to die this way—without Krishna's grace. How I would love to see him on the other side—his divine blue eyes. God forgive me, how I love him.

TWO

I awake with a pale wash of light panning across my face. Opening my eyes, I see it is the searchlights of hovering helicopters pointing down on me. Only they are high in the air, and I am many feet underwater, on my back, on the bottom of the lake. Even though unconscious, my mind must have had the wisdom to halt my breathing. I don't know how long I have been out. My head still hurts but the pain is bearable. It is obvious that the personnel in the helicopters cannot see me.

I wonder how Joel is, if he escaped.

My left leg is pinned under the wreckage of my chopper. It is good because otherwise I would be floating on the surface, probably with many bullet holes in me. Pulling my leg free, I roll over on my belly and begin to swim away from the lights, not sure at first if I am moving deeper into the lake or closer to the shore. My desire for breath is strong but not overwhelming. I know I can swim a long way before I'll have to surface. They can't scan every square inch of the lake. I am going to escape.

Yet there will be no freedom for me if Joel is not free.

Ten minutes later, when the lights are far behind me, I allow myself to swim to the surface and peek. I am far out in the center of the lake. Behind me, near the shore where my chopper was blown out of the sky, the helicopters still circle, their beams still focused on the water. Close to this spot, on the shore, are several trucks, many uniformed people, some cops, some army personnel. Joel stands in the middle of them, a dozen guns pointed at his head.

"Damn," I whisper. "He really couldn't swim."

I cannot rush in to save him. I know this yet I have to stop myself from making the attempt. It is my nature to act quickly. Patience has not come to me over the centuries. Floating in the center of the black lake, it seems to me the years have only brought grief.

Joel is ushered into an armored truck. Men on the shore are donning scuba gear. They want my body, they want to see it before they can rest. I know that I must act quickly if I am to track Joel. Yet I also know I have to stop killing. They'll be looking for any suspicious deaths in the area as a way to confirm I am still alive. A throbbing sensation in my forehead draws my attention. I reach up and pull away a chunk of shrapnel that has been working its way out of my skull. Before the infusion of Yaksha's blood, such an injury would have killed me.

I swim for the shore where Joel is being held, but a mile to the left, away from him and the dam. I am a better swimmer than most dolphins and reach land in a few minutes. No one sees me as I slip out of the water and dash into the rocky hills. My first impulse is to creep closer to the armed assembly. Yet I cannot steal one of their vehicles to follow Joel. Fretting about the growing gap between us, I turn away from the small army and run toward the campgrounds. Even in the winter, families come to Lake Mead to enjoy the nature. Overhead, an almost full moon shines down on me. Just what I don't need. If an Apache spots me again, I swear, I am going to jump up and grab its skids and take it over. My turn to fire the rockets.

The thoughts are idle, the mental chatter of a natural born predator.

I find a family of three asleep in a tent on the outskirts of the campground, their shiny new Ford Bronco parked nearby and waiting for me to steal. Silently, I break the lock and slip in behind the steering wheel. It takes me all of two seconds to hot-wire the vehicle. Then I am off, the window down.

Throughout my long life, hearing has always been my best sense. I can hear snowflakes as they emerge from a cloud two miles overhead. Indeed, I have no trouble hearing the army's motor parade start their engines and pull away from the lake. Probably the commander thinks he should get Joel to a secure place, even before the body of the blond witch is found. I use my ears to follow them as they move onto a road that leads away from the lake. Yet, with my nose in the air, it is my sense of smell that is the most acute. It startles me. I can smell Joel— even in the midst of the others—clearly, in fact. I suspect this is another gift of Yaksha, master yakshini, born of a demonic race of serpents. Snakes always have exceptional senses of smell.

I am grateful for this newfound sense because I can accurately trail the military parade from a great distance. These people are not stupid—they will check to see if they are being followed. Once again I am struck by my ability to sense their thoughts. I have always been able to discern emotions in mortals, but never ideas. Yaksha must have been an outright mind reader. He never told me. I know for sure the people up ahead are checking their backs. I allow the distance between us to grow to as much as fifteen miles. Naturally I drive with the lights out.

At first the group heads in the direction of Las Vegas. Then, five miles outside the City of Sin, they turn east onto a narrow paved road. The column stretches out and I have to stay even farther back. There are many signs: RESTRICTED AREA. I believe we are headed to some sort of government base.

My hunch is confirmed less than an hour later. Approximately fifty miles outside of Las Vegas, the armored vehicle carrying Joel disappears into an elaborately defended camp. I speed up and take my Bronco off the road, parking it behind a hill a mile from both the road and the camp. On foot, I scamper toward the installation, growing more amazed with every step at how complex and impenetrable it appears. The surrounding fence is over a hundred feet high, topped with billowy coils of barbed wire. Ordinarily I could jump such a barrier without breaking a sweat. Unfortunately, the place has manned towers equipped with machine guns and grenade launchers every two hundred feet. That's a lot of towers. The compound is huge, at least a half mile across. In addition to the towers and fence, there is a densely packed maze of three-foot high electronic devices—they resemble metal baseball bats—stretched along the perimeter. I suspect that if tripped they emit a paralyzing field. Vampires are sensitive to electricity. I was once hit by a bolt of lightning and spent the next three days recovering in a coffin. My boyfriend at the time wanted to bury me.

One side of the compound is devoted almost exclusively to a concrete runway. I remember reading about a top-secret government installation in the desert outside of Las Vegas that supposedly tests advanced fighter craft, nuclear weapons, and biological weapons. I have a sneaking suspicion that I am looking at it. The compound backs into a large barren hill, and I believe the military has mined deep into the natural slope to perform experiments best hidden from the eyes of spy satellites.

There are Sherman tanks and Apache helicopters parked close to barracklike structures. No doubt the weapons can be manned in ten seconds. One thing is immediately clear to me.

I will not be able to break into the compound.

Not and get out alive.

The armored vehicle carrying Joel has halted near the center of the compound. Armed soldiers scurry to line up around it, their weapons drawn and leveled. A cruel-faced general with a single star on his shoulder and death in his eyes approaches the vehicle. Behind him is a group of white-clad scientists—just what I don't want to see. The general signals to somebody out of view and the side door on the armored vehicle swings open. Heavily chained, his shoulders bowed down, Joel is brought into the open. The general approaches him, strangely unafraid, and searches him. Then he glances over his shoulder. Several of the scientists seem to nod. I don't understand the exchange. What are they approving? That Joel is a genuine vampire? They don't know about vampires.

"Or do they?" I whisper.

But it's not possible. For the last two thousand years or more, Yaksha and I were the only vampires on earth. Recently there have been others, of course. But Ray's conversion was short-lived, Eddie was a psychotic aberration, and I destroyed all of Eddie's offspring.

Or did I?

This general wanted us taken alive, I realize. He's the one who gave the order to the Apache pilots. They waited a long time before they used their rockets, and then only when they were forced to. In fact, the general is probably angry that they used them at all. The way he's studying Joel—it's almost as if he's gloating. The general wants something from Joel, and he knows what it is.

Joel is taken inside a building.

The general confers with one scientist and then they, too, go inside.

I sit back and groan. "Damn."

My objective is clear. I have to get Joel out of the compound before they can perform extensive tests on him—more specifically, before they can analyze his blood. I'm not even sure what they will find, but whatever they discover, it won't bode well for the long-term survival of the human race.

But I cannot force my way inside. Therefore, I must sneak in. How do I do that? Make friends with the guards? Seduce Mr. Machine Gun Mike? The idea may not be as farfetched as it seems with my magnetic personality and hypnotic eyes. But from what I can see, all the men live at the compound. This is unfortunate.

I glance in the direction of Las Vegas, neon fallout on the horizon.

"But the boys must leave the compound and go out on the town now and then," I mutter.

It is two hours before dawn. While I study the compound with my powerful eyes, searching for a vulnerable spot, I see the scientist whom the general conferred with climb into an ordinary car. He stops at a checkpoint before exiting the compound. By then I am running for my Bronco.

I want to talk to this scientist.

As I climb in my stolen vehicle, I notice that my arms and hands are glowing with a faint white light. The effect stuns me. My face is also glowing! In fact, all my exposed skin shines with the same iridescence as the full moon, which hangs low in the sky in the direction of Las Vegas.

"What kind of radiation are they fooling with out here?" I mutter.

I decide to worry about it later.

The scientist is a speed demon. He drives close to a hundred all the way to Las Vegas, or at least until he hits the public highway, five miles outside the town. I push the Bronco to keep up. I suppose no cop will give him a ticket on a government road. It is my hope he lives in Vegas, but when he goes straight to the Mirage Hotel, my hopes sink. He's probably just out for a few hours of fun.

I park near him in the lot and prepare to follow him inside.

Then I remember what I am wearing.

A ripped flak jacket and bloody clothes.

I do not panic. The people I stole the Bronco from are on vacation. They will have, I'm sure, ladies' clothes somewhere in the vehicle. Lo and behold, in the back I find a pair of blue jeans, two sizes too big, and a black Mickey Mouse sweatshirt that fits like a wet suit. Luckily, the blood and glass washed out of my hair while I slept beneath Lake Mead. Standing in a dark corner of the parking lot, I change quickly.

I find the scientist inside at the dice table.

He is an attractive man, perhaps forty-five, with thick black hair and large sensual lips. His face is sun dried, tanned and lined, yet on him the effect is not unpleasant. He looks like a man who has weathered many storms and come out ahead. His gray eyes are deep set, very alert, focused. He has discarded his white lab coat for a nicely tailored sports coat. He is holding a pair of red dice as I enter, and it seems to me that he is secretly willing them to obey his commands, as so many other gamblers do.

He fails to throw a pass, a seven, or an eleven. He loses his bet and the dice pass to another player. I note that he had a hundred-dollar chip on the table, not a small bet for a scientist on the government payroll. I am surprised when he lays down another hundred dollars. He loses that as well.

I observe the man for forty-five minutes. He is a regular—one of the pit bosses calls him Mr. Kane, another, Andy. Andrew Kane, I think. Because Andy continues to lose, at an alarming rate, he is forced to sign a slip to get more chips when the cash in his pockets is gone. But these black honeybees vanish rapidly, and his eagerness turns to frustration. I have been counting. Two thousand dollars gone—just like that. Sighing, he leaves the table and, after a double scotch at the bar, leaves the casino.

I follow him home. The place is modest.

He goes inside and prepares for bed. As the morning sun splashes the eastern sky, he turns out his own light. Obviously he works the night shift. Or else the general had called Andy into work because of Joel. I wonder if he will be working long hours in the days to come. Memorizing his address, I drive back toward the Mirage. If it is Andy's favorite hangout, it'll be mine as well.

I have no credit cards, money, or identification, but the woman at the reservation desk hands me a key to a luxury suite after staring hard into my beautiful blue eyes. Inside my room, I place a call to my primary business manager in New York City. His voice is unaffected—the government has not gotten to him yet. We do not talk long.

"Code red," I say. "Have the package delivered to the Mirage Hotel, Las Vegas. Room Two-One-Three-Four. Immediately."

"Understood," he says and hangs up.

The package will include everything I need to start a new life: passport, driver's license, cash, and credit cards. It will arrive at my door in the next hour. There will also be an elaborate makeup kit inside, wigs and different-colored contacts. Over the last fifty centuries, I have prepared for every eventuality, including this one. Tomorrow I will look like someone else, and Andrew Kane will meet a mysterious young woman, and fall in love.

THREE

The following evening a demure redhead with short bangs and green eyes waits outside Andrew Kane's house. Actually, I have been in the front seat of my newly purchased Jeep since noon, but the mad scientist has been fast asleep, as most normal people would be after staying up all night. I came to his house early because I am anxious to go through his things, learn exactly what he does before I make a move on him. The one fact that guides me as to his importance is that the general spoke only to him after Joel was brought inside the compound. Yet intuitively I sense Andy's value. There is something fascinating in his gray eyes, even though he is a degenerate gambler. This quality does not bother me, however, because I might be able to use his obvious casino debt against him. Of course, I plan to use Andy to get into the compound to rescue Joel.

Quickly. I feel the pressure of each passing hour.

Joel will be thirsty already, unless they happen to feed him.

A newborn's thirst is agonizing.

The papers are shouting about the barbaric terrorist attack in Los Angeles. Authorities estimate that there were at least three dozen Islamic fanatics involved, and that the local police were overwhelmed by superior forces and military equipment. The mayor has vowed that the city officials will not rest until the murderers are brought to justice.

The hot sun is draining for me after such an intense night. Yet I bear it better than I would have before drinking Yaksha's blood. I suspect, after five thousand years, the sun had no effect on Yaksha. I sure could use his power now. I pray he is finally at peace, in Krishna's blue abode. How often I pray to Krishna. How curious, since I am supposed to hate him. Oh well, the heart of a vampire is unfathomable. No wonder superstitious people are always trying to drive stakes through our hearts.

It is five in the evening before Andrew Kane emerges from his house and climbs in his car. He has no time for the casinos now. No doubt the general waits for him. Andy drives the five miles on Highway 15, then turns onto the government road, once again pushing his speed up to near a hundred. My Jeep has a powerful engine—I cruise five comfortable miles behind him. Actually, it is probably something of a waste to follow him all the way into work. He'll just drive inside and disappear into one of the buildings. But I want to see how long it takes him to pass through security, how many checks he goes through. Close to the compound, I veer off the road and tear across the desert, parking near the hill I hid behind before. On the seat beside me are high-powered binoculars. Even my supernatural sight can be improved by mechanical aids.

I am not given a chance to reach my vantage point before Andy gets to the front gate of the compound. Still, I can see well enough. He is stopped, naturally, but the guards know him well. He hardly has to flash his badge. The guards do not search his trunk. He parks his car in the same spot and enters the building where Joel was taken, the largest, most modern building in the whole complex. Chemical smells drift out from the building. It definitely has a lab inside.

I would like to examine the compound further but night is the time to do it. Plus I am anxious to get into Andy's house. I tear back to Las Vegas, not passing anyone on the road. I wonder if the scuba divers are still searching the bottom of Lake Mead for my body. I wonder if the general suspects I will try to rescue Joel. I doubt it.

Andy's house is a three-bedroom affair at the end of a quiet cul-de-sac. This being Las Vegas, there is the obligatory pool in the backyard. Leaving my Jeep on the adjoining street, I climb his wall and pick his back door lock. Inside it is cool; he left the air conditioning on. I shut the door and stand listening for a moment, smelling. Many aromas come to me then. They tell me much about the man, even though we have never been formally introduced.

He is a vegetarian. There is no smell of animal flesh. He doesn't smoke, but he does drink. I see as well as smell the bottles of liquor in a walnut cabinet. He does not use cologne, but there is a faint odor of various makeup products. Our Mr. Andrew Kane resents middle age.

He is a bachelor, there are no pictures of a wife or kids on the walls. I step into the kitchen. He eats out mostly; there is little food in the refrigerator. I riffle through his bills on the kitchen counter. There are a couple of envelopes from banks. He is up to his limit on three credit cards.

I walk into the bedroom he uses as an office.

I almost faint.

On his desk is a black and white and red plastic model of the double helix DNA molecule. That is not what staggers me. Beside it is a much more complex model of a different kind of DNA—one that has twelve strands of encoded information instead of two. It is not the first time I have seen it. Seven hundred years ago, the great Italian alchemist, Arturo Evola, created a similar model after spending six months in my company.

"It's not possible," I whisper.

Andrew Kane has already begun to crack the DNA of the vampire.

FOUR

*I*taly, during the thirteenth century, embodied all that was wonderful and horrible about the Middle Ages. The Catholic Church was the supreme power. Monarchs came and went. Kings and queens fought and died. But the Roman Pope wielded the true power over life and death.

Art was the gift of the Church to the people in those days. This was above and beyond the gift of their strict theology, which did nothing for the poor masses except keep them confused until the day they died. I say that with well-deserved bitterness. It would have been impossible to live in those days and not become angry at the Church. Today, however, I think the Church does much that is good, and much that is questionable. No religion is perfect, not after man gets through with it.

I lived in Florence from 1212 till 1245 and spent many months touring the churches where the finest paintings and sculptures were displayed. The Renaissance was, of course, a long way off, and Michelangelo and Da Vinci had yet to be born. Still, these earlier days were remarkable for their creativity. I remember well Bonaventura Berlinghieri's radiant *St. Francis* and Niccola Pisano's hypnotic sculpture *Annunciation to the Shepherds.*

The Inquisition was another gift of the Church. The boon of the devil in the minds of most people in those days. Two informants, whose identities could remain unknown to the victim, were all that was necessary to charge someone with being a heretic. The informants could be heretics themselves, or witches—not pleasant titles to earn in old Italy. A confession was necessary to convict anyone of being a heretic. A little stretching of the limbs, or burning with live coals, or torturing the victim on the *strappado*—the dreaded vertical rack—was usually enough to get an innocent person to confess. I remember going to the central city courtyard to watch the victims being burned alive at the stake. I used to think back over the barbarism of the Emperors of the Roman Empire, the Mongolian hordes, the Japanese shoguns—and yet their forms of torture all paled compared to the pain caused by the Church because the people who lit the pyres wore crosses. They chanted prayers while their victims screamed and died.

I observed only a few executions before I lost the stomach for them. Yet I thwarted the Inquisition in my own way, by secretly killing many of the inquisitors. I usually left their bodies in compromised places—houses of prostitution and the like—to discourage thorough investigations. As I drained the inquisitors' blood, sucking their large neck veins and arteries, I whispered in their ears that I was an angel of mercy. None of them died easily.

Yet the Church was bigger than a single vampire, the Inquisition an infection that spread and multiplied through its own mysterious madness. It could not be easily stopped. It cast a gloom over my stay in Florence, over my joy in the resurgence of mankind's creativity. I have hunted humans throughout time, and yet I am proud of them as well, when they do something bold, something unexpected. The best art always comes unbidden.

Arturo Evola was not known as an alchemist or else he would not have lasted a day in medieval Florence. He was a twenty-one-year-old Franciscan priest, and a devout one at that. He had entered the priesthood at the age of sixteen, which was not unusual at that time, because the easiest way to obtain the finest education was to become a priest. He was a brilliant man, undoubtedly the most inspired intellect of the thirteenth century. Yet history does not know him. Only I do, and my memories of him are filled with sorrow.

I met him after Mass one day. I despised the Church, but enjoyed the actual service. All the chanting, the choirs, and

I loved to hear the early organs played. Often I would go to communion, after attending confession. It was difficult for me to keep a straight face while I told of my sins. Once, for fun, I told a priest the *whole* truth of what I had done in my life. But he was drunk and just said to do five Hail Marys and to behave myself. I didn't have to kill him.

I received the Holy Eucharist from Arturo and met him after the service. I could tell he was attracted to me. In those days many priests had mistresses. I had gone out of my way to see Arturo because a gypsy healer had told me about him. He was an alchemist, she said, who could turn stone into gold, sunlight into ideas, moonlight into lust. The gypsy had a high opinion of Arturo. She warned me to approach him cautiously because his real work had to be kept from the Church. I understood.

Commonly, an alchemist is known as an esoteric chemist who attempts to convert base metals into gold. This is a crude understanding. Alchemy is a comprehensive physical and metaphysical system embracing cosmology as much as anthropology. Everything natural and supernatural can be found in it. The goal of alchemy is to experience the totality of the organism. It is a path of enlightenment. The gypsy said Arturo was a born alchemist. Knowledge came to him from inside. No one had to teach him his art.

"The only trouble with him is he's a Catholic," she said. "A fanatic."

"How does he merge the two disciplines?" I asked.

The gypsy blessed herself. She was superstitious of the Church as well. "God only knows," she said.

Arturo did not strike me as a fanatic when we first met. His demeanor was soft, like his lovely eyes. He had a special ability to listen totally to a person, a rare gift. His large hands were exceptionally fine; when he brushed my arm with his fingers I felt he was capable of touching my heart. And he was so young! That first afternoon we talked about astronomy—a midway subject, in my mind, to alchemy. He was delighted with my knowledge of the heavens. He invited me to share a meal and afterward we went for a walk around the city. When we said goodbye that night, I knew he was in love with me.

Why did I pursue him? For the same reason I have done many things in my life—I was curious. But that was only my initial reason. Soon I, too, was in love with him. I must say, the feeling was present before I began to probe his knowledge of alchemy. Before going that deep into his secret world, I knew he was unlike other priests of his day. He was a virgin, and his vow of celibacy was important to him.

I did not just spring the questions on him one day. Can you turn copper into gold? Can you heal lepers? Can you live forever? I showed him a glimpse of my knowledge first, to inspire him to share his. My understanding of the medical properties of herbs is extensive. An old friar in Arturo's church became ill with a lung infection, and it seemed as if he'd die. I brought

Arturo an herb concoction of echinacea and goldenseal and told him to give it to his superior. The friar recovered within twenty-four hours and Arturo wanted to know who had taught me how to make tea.

I laughed and told him about my Greek friend, Cleo, failing to mention how many centuries ago he had died. Arturo was impressed. It was only then he began to talk about his crystals and magnets and copper sheets—the secret elements of alchemy that have now passed from human understanding. That very day Arturo confessed his mission in life to me. To discover the elixirs of holiness and immortality—as if searching for the secret to one of these conditions was not enough. Arturo always thought big. He was determined to recreate nothing less than the blood of Jesus Christ.

"What makes you think you can do it?" I asked, shocked.

His eyes shone as he explained. Not with a mad light, but with a brilliance I had never seen before or since in a mortal man.

"Because I have found the spirit of man," he said. "I have proven that it exists. I can show you how to experience it, how to remove the veil of darkness that covers it."

Sounded interesting to me. Arturo took me to a secret chamber beneath the church where he lived. Apparently the elderly friar whose life I had saved knew of Arturo's hobby and looked the other way. He was the only one who knew of the master alchemist, besides the gypsy. I asked Arturo about her. Apparently she had nursed him back to health when he had fallen from a horse while riding in the countryside. They had shared many intimate conversations over late-night fires. Arturo was surprised, and a bit angry, that she had told me about him.

"Don't blame her," I said. "I can be most persuasive." It was true that I had used the power of my eyes on her, when I saw she was hiding something important.

Arturo took me down into his secret room and lit many candles. He asked me to lie on a huge copper sheet, as thin as modern paper. On adjacent shelves, I noted his collection of quartz crystals, amethysts, and precious stones—rubies, diamonds, and sapphires. He also had several powerful magnets, each cut into the shape of a cross. I had never seen a magnetic cross before.

"What are you going to do?" I asked as I lay down on the copper.

"You have heard of the human aura?" he asked.

"Yes. It is the energy field that surrounds the body."

"Very good. It is spoken of in ancient mythology and is present in art. We see the halos in paintings above the heads of members of the holy family, and in drawings of saints. Still, most people don't believe in the aura because they don't experience it. They are only conscious of their physical bodies. What I am going to do to you now is draw out your aura, allow your consciousness to expand into it, so that your spiritual body becomes the focus of your attention, and not the physical body."

"Do you not like my physical body?" I asked. I often flirted with him.

He paused and stared down at me. "It's very lovely," he whispered.

He told me to close my eyes. He didn't want me to see how he set up the crystals and magnets. I peeked, of course, and saw that crystals were placed above my head and magnets below my body, at angles. He was creating a grid of some kind, one that transmitted unseen energies. He prayed as he worked, Hail Marys and Our Fathers. I have always enjoyed those prayers. But for me, of course, they reminded me of Radha and Krishna.

When Arturo was done, he told me to keep my eyes closed and breathe naturally through my nose. The breath was important, he said. It was one of the secrets of experiencing the soul.

For the first few minutes not much happened. But then, slowly, I felt an energy rise from my body, from the base of my spine to the top of my head. Simultaneously, I felt my mind expand. I became as big as the secret chamber. A curious floating sensation enveloped me, a warm peacefulness. My breath went in and out, sometimes fast, sometimes slow. I had no control over it and wanted none. Time passed. I wasn't entirely awake, but I wasn't asleep either. It was a mystical experience.

When Arturo spoke next, he sounded many miles away. He wanted me to sit up, to come out of the state. I resisted—I liked where I was. But he took my arm and forced me to sit up, breaking the spell. I opened my eyes and gazed at him.

"Why did you stop it?" I asked.

He was perspiring. "You can get too much energy at once." He stared at me; he seemed out of breath. "You have an amazing aura."

I smiled. "What is special about it?"

He shook his head. "It is so powerful."

The experiment in consciousness raising was interesting, but I failed to see how his technique would allow him to transform human blood into Christ's blood. I quizzed him about it at length but he would divulge no more secrets. The power of my aura continued to puzzle him. As we said good night, I saw fear in his eyes, and deep fascination. He knew I was no ordinary woman. That was all right, I thought. No harm done. He would learn no more about my special qualities.

But that was not to be.

He was to learn everything about me.

Perhaps even more than I knew myself.

There was an altar boy, Ralphe, who lived with the priests. Twelve years old and possessed of an exceptional wit, he was a favorite of Arturo's. Often the two would go for long hikes in the hills outside Florence. I was fond of Ralphe myself. The three of us had picnics in the woods and I would teach Ralphe the flute, for which he had a talent. The instrument had been a favorite of mine since the day I met Krishna. Arturo used to love to watch us play together. But sometimes I would get carried away and weave a melody of love, of romantic enchantment and lost dreams, which would always leave Arturo quiet and shaken. How long we could go on like this, chaste and virtuous, I didn't know. My alchemist stirred ancient longings inside me. I wondered about the energies his crystals invoked.

One day while I was helping Ralphe repair a hole in the church roof, the boy decided to amuse me by doing a silly dance on the edge of the stone tiles. I told him to be careful but he never listened. He was having too much fun. That is the mysterious thing about tragedy—it often strikes at the happiest moment.

Ralphe slipped and fell. It was over a hundred feet to the ground. He fell on the base of his spine, crushing it. When I reached him, he was writhing in agony. I was shaken to the core, I who had seen so much pain in my life. But centuries of time have not made me insensitive. One moment he had been a vibrant young man, and now he would be crippled for the rest of his days, and those would not be long.

I loved Ralphe very much. He was like a son to me.

I suppose that's why I did what I did.

I did not need to make him a vampire to help him.

I opened the veins on my right wrist and let the blood splash where his shattered spinal column had pierced his skin.

The wound closed quickly, the bones mended. It seemed he would make a complete recovery. Best of all, he appeared unaware of why he had recovered so quickly. He thought he'd just been lucky.

But there is good luck and bad luck.

Arturo saw what I did for Ralphe. He saw everything.

He wanted to know who I was. What I was.

I find it hard to lie to those I love.

I told him everything. Even what Krishna had told me. The tale took an entire night. Arturo understood when I was through why I preferred to tell the story in the dark. But he didn't recoil in horror as I spoke. He was an enlightened priest, an alchemist who sought the answer to why God had created us in the first place. Indeed, he thought he knew the answer to that profound question. We were here to become like God. To live like his blessed son. We just needed a few pints of Christ's blood to do it.

Arturo believed Krishna had let me live for a purpose.

So that my blood could save mankind from itself.

From the start, I worried about him mixing Christ and vampires.

"But I will make no more vampires," I protested.

He eagerly took my hands and stared into my eyes. A fever burned in his brain; I could feel the heat of it on his fingertips, in his breath. Whose soul did I experience then? Mine or his? It seemed in that moment as if the two of us had merged. For that reason, his next words sounded inevitable to me.

"We will make no more vampires," he said. "I understand why Krishna made you take such a vow. What we will create with your blood is a new man. A hybrid of a human and a vampire. A being who can live forever, in the glory of light instead of the shadow of darkness." His eyes strayed to the wooden crucifix hung above his bed. "An immortal being."

He spoke with such power. And he was not insane.

I had to listen. To consider his words.

"Is it possible?" I whispered.

"Yes." He hugged me. "There is a secret I haven't told you. It is extraordinary. It is the secret to permanent transformation. If I have the right materials—your blood, for example—I can transform anything. If you wish, you can become such a hybrid. I can even make you human again." He paused, perhaps thinking of my ancient grief over the loss of Lalita, my daughter. He knew my sterile condition was the curse of my unending life. He must have known, since he added, "You could have a child, Sita."

FIVE

*A*round midnight I return to the compound, determined to learn its layout from the outside. Dressed totally in black, I have an Uzi strung over my back, a high-powered pair of binoculars in one hand, a Geiger counter in the other. The momentary phenomenon of my glowing skin continues to haunt me. I wonder if they are doing something weird to Joel—using radiation on him.

I have decided the ideal vantage point from which to study the compound is the top of the hill in which the base is dug. To get to it I have to take a long walk. Here the terrain is even too rough for my new Jeep. I move swiftly, my head down, like the mystical serpent I embody. A deep desire to plant my teeth in that general I saw the past night stays with me. He reminds me of Eddie—not of the psycho's warped nature but of his delusions of grandeur. I can tell a lot by a man's face. Perhaps I read his mind a little as well. The general wants to use Joel to get ahead in the world, maybe take it over. I don't know where the Pentagon gets these people.

At the top of the hill I scan each square foot of the compound. Once again I am stunned by the level of security. It is as if they are set up to ward off an attack from an alien race. While I watch, a sleek jet with the lines of a rocket lands on the runway. It is like no jet I have ever seen before, and I suspect it can do Mach 10—ten times the speed of sound—and that Congress has never heard of it.

My Geiger counter indicates the radiation here is three times what is normal, but still well within safety limits. I'm puzzled. Radiation couldn't have been responsible for my luminous skin. Yet the fact that the level is high confirms that there are nuclear warheads in the vicinity. I suspect I am sitting above them, that they are stored in the caves the military has dug into this hill. The caves are now an established fact. I watch as men and equipment ride a miniature railroad beneath me into and out of the hill. This is how the human race gets into trouble. The danger of renegade vampires is nothing compared to the folly of handing unlimited sums of money over to people who like to keep "secrets." Who have on their payroll physicists and chemists and genetic engineers who, as children, rooted for Pandora to open her box of evils.

How Andrew Kane has partially managed to duplicate

Arturo Evola's work continues to preoccupy me. I cannot imagine an explanation.

A black cart rides beneath me into the hill. Soldiers sit on it, smoking cigarettes and talking about babes. My Geiger counter momentarily jumps. The level is not high enough to harm the human body, but it does confirm that the boys in uniform are sitting next to a thermonuclear device. I know the famed fail-safe system is a joke, as do most people in the government. The President of the United States is not the only one who can order an American-made nuclear device to explode. In West Germany, before the Wall came down, the authority to fire a miniature neutron bomb was often in the hands of a lieutenant. Currently, *all* the nuclear submarine captains in the U.S. Navy have the authority to launch their missiles without the required presidential black box and secret codes. It is argued that the captains must have this authority because if the country is attacked the President would most likely be one of the first to die.

Still, it makes me nervous.

The general must have the authority to trigger these bombs if he wishes.

It is good to know.

I have finished my study of the compound and am walking back to my Jeep when I notice that my legs are glowing again, as are my hands and arms. Once more, every square inch of my exposed skin is faintly shining with the whiteness of the moon—not good here at a top-secret camp. It makes me that much more visible. I hurry to my Jeep, climb inside, and drive away.

But long before I reach Las Vegas, I pull over, far off the road.

A bizarre idea has occurred to me.

The problem is not radiation. It is not man-made.

Climbing out of the Jeep, I remove all my clothing and stand naked with my arms outstretched to the moon, as if I were worshipping the astronomical satellite, bowing to it, drinking up her rays. Slowly the skin on my chest and thighs begins to take on the milky radiance. And it seems the more I invite the moonlight onto my skin, *into* my heart, the brighter it becomes. Because if I will it to stop, my skin returns to normal.

"What does it mean, Yaksha?" I whisper to my dead creator.

My right arm, as the moonlight floods in, shines particularly bright. Holding it close to my eyes, *I can see through it*! I can actually see the ground through my flesh!

I put my clothes back on.

I can't look like a Christmas light when I try to seduce Andrew Kane.

SIX

I am Lara Adams as I enter the casino later that night and stand beside Andrew Kane at the dice table. I'm still a redhead, with a soft Southern accent and a prim and proper smile. The name is not new to me. I used it to enroll at Mayfair High in Oregon, where I met Ray and Seymour. It's hard to believe that was less than two months ago. How life can change when you're a vampire on the run.

Andy glances over at me and smiles. He has the dice in his hands. He has been in the casino five minutes but already he's had a couple of drinks.

"Do you want to place a bet?" he asks.

I smile. "Do you feel hot?"

He shakes the dice in his palm. "I *am* hot."

I remove a stack of black hundred-dollar chips from my

bag and place one on the pass line, his favorite bet—seven or eleven. Andy rolls the dice. They dance over the green felt. Coming to a halt, the numbers four and three smile up at us.

"Lucky seven," the croupier says and pays off our bets. Andy flashes me another smile.

"You must be good luck," he says.

I double my bet. "I have a feeling this is my night," I say.

By the time the dice come to me, Andy and I have lost a combined total of eight hundred dollars. That is about to change. With my supernatural balance and reflexes, with practice, I can roll any number I desire. I have been practicing in my suite since I returned from the compound. Carefully I set the dice upright in my left palm in the configuration: five and six. In a blur, I toss them out. They bounce happily, seemingly randomly to human eyes. But they come to a halt in the same position they started out. Andy and I each win a hundred dollars on the number eleven. Since I threw a pass, I am invited to throw another—which I do. The people at the table like me. Most bet on the pass line.

I throw ten passes in a row before I let the dice go. We mustn't get greedy. Andy appreciates my style.

"What's your name?" he asks.

"Lara Adams. What's yours?"

"Andrew Kane. Are you here alone?"

I pout. "I did come with a friend. But it seems I'll be going home alone."

Andy chuckles. "Not necessarily. The night's still young."

"It's five in the morning," I remind him.

He nods at the glass of water I sip. "Can I get you something stronger?"

I lean against the table. "I think I need something stronger."

We continue to play craps, winning better than honest wages when I am throwing the dice. The people at the table don't want me to surrender the designated high roller position, but I am careful not to appear superhuman, just damn lucky. Andy bets heavily and wins back all the money he lost the night before, and then some. We both drink too much. I have four margaritas, Andy five Scotches and water, on top of what he had drunk before I entered. The alcohol has no effect on me. My liver neutralizes it almost the instant it enters my system. I can take in all kinds of poisons and remain undisturbed. Andy, however, is now drunk, just the way the casinos like people. He is betting five hundred dollars a roll when I pull him away from the table.

"What's the matter?" he protests. "We're winning."

"You can be winning and courting disaster at the same time. Come on, let's have some coffee. I'm buying."

He stumbles as he walks beside me. "I've been at work all night. I'd like a steak."

"You shall have whatever you want."

The Mirage coffee shop is open twenty-four hours a day. The menu is flexible—Andy is able to get his steak. He orders it medium rare with a baked potato. He wants a beer, but I insist he have a glass of milk.

"You're going to destroy your stomach," I say as we wait for our food. I do have favorite foods, besides blood. I have ordered roast chicken with rice and vegetable. Surprisingly, for a vampire, I eat plenty of vegetables. Nothing is as good for the body as those fresh greens, except, perhaps, those dripping reds. Sitting with Andy, I become thirsty for blood as well. Before I rest, I will grab some male tourist off the streets, show him a good time. That is, if I don't spend the night—the day—sleeping beside Andy. His eyes shine as he looks me over.

"I can always have it removed," he replies.

"Why not just drink less?"

"I'm on vacation."

"Where are you from?"

He chuckles. "Here!" He is serious for a moment. "You know you are one beautiful young woman. But I suppose you know that."

"It's always nice to hear."

"Where are you from?"

"The South—Florida. I came with a boyfriend for a few days, but he got angry with me."

"Why?"

"I told him I wanted to break up." I add, "He's got a nasty temper." I sip my milk, wishing I could squeeze our waitress's veins into it, add a little flavor. "What about you? What do you do?"

"I'm a mad scientist."

"Really? What are you mad about?"

"You mean, what kind of scientist am I?"

"Yes. And do you work around here?"

His voice takes on a guarded note, even though he is still quite drunk. "I'm a genetic engineer. I work for the government. They have a lab—in town."

I mock him playfully. "Is it a top-secret lab?"

He sits back and shrugs. "They would like to keep it that way. They don't feel comfortable unless we're working outside the reach of mainstream scientists."

"Do I detect a note of resentment in your tone?"

"Not resentment—that's too strong a word. I love my job. It has provided me opportunities I couldn't get in the normal business world. I think what you sense is frustration. The opportunities presented in our lab are not being fully exploited. We need people of many disciplines involved, from all over the world."

"You would like the lab to be more open?"

"Precisely. But that doesn't mean I don't appreciate the need for security." He pauses. "Especially as of late."

"Interesting things are happening?"

He looks away and chuckles, but there is a note of sorrow in his voice. "Very interesting things." He turns back to me. "May I ask you a personal question, Lara?"

"By all means."

"How old are you?"

I flirt. "How old do you think I am?"

He is genuinely puzzled. "I don't know. When we were at the table, you seemed about thirty. But now that we're alone together you seem much younger."

I have designed my makeup and dress to appear older. My longish white dress is conservative; I have a strand of pearls around my neck. My lipstick is glossy, overdone. I wear a red scarf to match my red wig.

"I'm twenty-nine," I say, which is the age on my new driver's license and passport. "I appreciate your compliment, however. I take care of myself." I pause. "How old are you?"

He laughs, picking up his glass of milk. "Let's just say my liver would be a lot younger if this was all I drank."

"'Milk does a body good.'"

He sets the glass down and stares into it. "So do other things."

"Andy?"

He shakes his head. "Just something that's going on at work. I can't talk about it. It would bore you anyway." He changes the subject. "Where did you learn to throw dice like that?"

"Like what?"

"Come on. You always throw them the same way, resting the number you want to come up on your open palm. How do you do it? I've never seen anyone who could control the bounce of the dice."

I realize I went too far. He is a smart man, I remind myself. His powers of observation are keen, even when he is intoxicated. Yet, at the same time I don't mind that he sees something special in me. I have no time to cultivate his interest slowly. I must have him under my thumb by tomorrow night. It is then I plan to rescue Joel.

I answer his question carefully. "I have had many interesting teachers. Perhaps I could tell you about them sometime."

"How about now, tonight?"

"Tonight? The sun will be up in an hour."

"I don't have to be at work until it goes down." He reaches across the table and takes my hand. "I like you, Lara. I mean that." He pauses. "I feel like I've met you before."

I shake my head, wondering if he senses the similarities between Joel and myself. "We have never met," I tell him.

SEVEN

We go back to his place. He offers me a drink. When I decline, he has one himself—a Scotch on the rocks. The food in his stomach has sobered him up somewhat, but he quickly proceeds to get drunk again. He has a real problem, and now it is my problem as well. Granted, his intoxicated state makes his tongue loose and he tells me far more about his work than he should, although he has yet to mention Joel or vampires. Still, I will need him clear headed to help me. I have no time to repair his wounded psyche. I wonder what makes him drink so much. He lied when he said he didn't resent his boss. Obviously he hates the general. But I cannot read his mind, probably because he keeps it scrambled with booze. I sense only deep emotional conflicts, coupled with intellectual excitement. He is grateful to be working on Joel, analyzing his blood, and yet it bothers him that he is directly involved in the project. I have no doubt of this.

We sit on the couch in the living room. He riffles through his mail and then throws it on the floor. "Bills," he mutters, sipping his drink. "The hardest reality of life, besides death."

"The way you gamble, I hope the government pays you well."

He snorts softly, staring at the eastern sky, which has begun to brighten. "They don't pay me what I'm worth, that's for sure." He glances at my strand of pearls. "You look like you don't have to worry about money."

"Daddy made millions in oil before he died." I shrug. "I was his only child."

"He left it all to you?"

"Every last penny."

"Must be nice."

"It is very nice." I move closer to him on the sofa, touch his knee. I have an alluring touch. I swear sometimes I could seduce an evangelist's wife as easily as I could a horny Marine. Sex holds no mystery for me, and I have no scruples. I use my body as easily as any other weapon. I add, "What exactly do you do at your lab?"

He gestures to his office. "It's in there."

"What's in there?"

He takes another swallow of Scotch. "My greatest discovery. I keep a model of it at home to inspire me." He burps. "But right now a fat raise would inspire me more."

Even though I know what's in his office, I walk over and have a peep at the two models of the DNA, the human one and the vampiric molecule. "What are they?" I ask.

He is enjoying his drink too much to get up. "Have you heard of DNA?"

"Yes, of course. I graduated from college."

"What school did you go to?"

"Florida State." I return to my place on the couch, closer to him than before. "I graduated with honors."

"What was your major?"

"English lit, but I took several biology classes. I know that DNA is a double helix molecule that encodes all the information necessary for life to exist." I pause. "Are those models of human DNA?"

He sets his drink down. "One of them is."

"What's the other one?"

He stretches and yawns. "A project my partners and I have been working on for the last month."

My blood turns cold. It was in the last month that Eddie began to produce his horde of vampiric gangbangers. Andy has been able to duplicate Arturo's visions of vampire DNA because he has been analyzing the molecules for a while, long before Joel was captured. That can only mean one of Eddie's offspring escaped my slaughter.

"I don't know. I destroyed your silly gang."

"You're not sure of that."

"Now I am sure. You see, I can tell when someone lies. It's one of those great gifts I possess that you don't. There is only you left, and we both know it."

"What of it? I can make more whenever I feel the need."

Eddie admitted that there were no others. He couldn't have tricked me, yet perhaps he himself was tricked. Maybe one of *his* offspring had made another vampire and didn't tell him. It's the only explanation. That vampire must have been caught by the government and taken to the desert compound. I wonder if the mystery vampire is still in the place. My rescue effort has just been complicated.

I have to wonder if I'm already too late. Andy has—at the least—an outline of the DNA code of the vampire. How long will it be before he and his partners are able to create more bloodsuckers? The only thing that gives me hope is that the general struck me as a man who keeps everything under wraps, until it is time to make his move. Andy has said as much about him. Everything connected to vampires is still probably locked up in the compound.

In response to Andy's comment, I force a chuckle. Boy, do I force it. "Are you making a modern Frankenstein monster?" I ask, kidding, but not kidding.

My question hits a nerve, for obvious reasons, and Andy sits quietly for a moment, staring at his drink as if it were a crystal ball.

"We are playing a high-stakes game," he admits. "Altering

the DNA code of any species is like rolling the dice. You can win and you can lose."

"But it must be exciting to be playing such a game?"

He sighs. "We have the wrong pit boss in charge."

I put my hand on his shoulder. "What's his name?"

"General Havor. He's a hard ass—I don't think his mother gave him a first name. At least I don't know it. We call him 'General' or 'Sir.' He believes in order, performance, sacrifice, discipline, power." Andy shakes his head. "He definitely doesn't create an environment for free thinking and loving cooperation."

I am the understanding girlfriend. "You should quit then."

Andy flashes an amused, bitter grin. "If I quit now I'd be walking away from one of the greatest discoveries of modern time. Plus I need the job. I need the money."

I caress his hair. My voice is soft and seductive. "You need to relax, Andy, and not think of this stupid general. Tell you what—when you get off work tomorrow, come straight to my suite. I'm staying at the Mirage, Room Two-One-Three-Four. We can play the tables and have another late dinner together."

Gently he takes my hand. His eyes momentarily come into focus, and I see his intellect again, feel his warmth. He is a good man, working in a bad place.

"Do you have to go now?" he asks sadly.

I lean over and kiss him on the cheek. "Yes. But we'll see

each other tomorrow." I sit back and wink. "We'll have fun."

He is pleased. "You know what I like about you, Lara?"

"What?"

"You have a good heart. I feel I can trust you."

I nod. "You can trust me, Andy. You really can."

EIGHT

One of the saddest stories told in modern literature, to me at least, is Mary Shelley's *Frankenstein*. Because in a sense I am that monster. Knowingly or unknowingly, to much of history, I am the inspiration of nightmares. I am the primeval fear, something dead come to life, or better yet—and more accurate—something that refuses to die. Yet I consider myself more human than Shelley's creation, more humane than Arturo's offspring. I am a monster, but I can also love deeply. Yet even my love for Arturo could not spare him from plunging us into a nightmare from which there seemed to be no waking.

His secret of transformation was very simple, and profound beyond belief. It is fashionable among New Age adherents to use crystals to develop higher states of consciousness. What most of these people do not know is that a crystal is merely an amplifier, and that it has to be used very carefully. Whatever is present in the aura of the person, in the psychic field, gets magnified. Hate can be boosted as easily as compassion. In fact, cruel emotions expand more easily when given the chance. Arturo had an intuitive sense of the proper crystal to use with each person. Indeed, on most people he refused to use crystals at all. Few, he said, were ready for such high vibrations. How tragic it was that when he had a vial of my blood in his hand, his intuition deserted him. It is a pity his special genius did not leave him as well. It took a genius to take us as far as he did.

A mad one.

Using the magnets and copper sheets, in his secret geometric arrangements, the vibrations from whatever Arturo placed over the person were transmitted into the aura. For example, when he placed a clear quartz crystal above my head, a deep peaceful state settled in my mind. Yet if he used a similar crystal with young Ralphe, the boy would become irritated. Ralphe had too much going on in his mind and was not ready for crystals. Arturo understood that. He was an alchemist in the truest sense of the word. He could transform what could not be changed. Souls as well as bodies.

Arturo did not believe the body created the mind. He felt it was the other way around, and I believe he was correct. When he altered an aura, he changed the person's physiology as well. He just needed the proper materials, he said, to change anything. A flawed human into a glorious god. A sterile vampire into a loving mother.

It was, in the end, the chance to become human again that caused me to give him my blood. To hold *my* daughter in *my* hands again—what ecstasy! I was seduced by ancient griefs. Yaksha had made me pay dearly for my immortality, with the loss of Rama and Lalita. Arturo promised to give me back half of what had been stolen. It had been over four thousand years. Half seemed better than nothing. As I let my blood drip into a gold communion chalice for Arturo, I prayed to Krishna to bless it.

"I am not breaking my vow to you," I whispered, not believing my own words. "I am just trying to break this curse."

I did not know, as I prayed to my God, that Arturo was also praying to his. To allow him to convert human and vampiric blood into the saving fluid of Jesus Christ. Genius may make a person a fanatic, I don't know. But I do know that a fanatic will never listen to anything other than his own dreams. Arturo was soft and kind, warm and loving. Yet he was convinced he had a great destiny. Hitler thought the same. Both wanted something nature had never granted—the perfect being. And I, the ancient monster, just wanted a child. Arturo and I—we should never have met.

But perhaps our meeting was destined.

My blood looked so dark in the chalice.

The sacredness of the chalice did nothing to dispel my gloom.

Arturo wanted to place my blood above the head of select humans. To merge the vibration of my immortal pattern into that of a mortal. If he changed the aura, he said, the body would be transformed. He, of all people, should have known how potent my blood was. He had stared deep into my eyes. He should have known my will would not bend easily to the will of another.

"You will not put the blood in their veins?" I asked as I handed him the chalice. He shook his head.

"Never," he promised. "Your God and my God are the same. Your vow will remain unbroken."

"I'm not fooling myself," I said quietly. "I have broken a portion of it." I moved close to him. "I do this for you."

He touched me then—he rarely did, before that night. It was hard for him to feel my flesh and not burn. "You do this for yourself as well," he said.

I loved to stare deeply into his eyes. "That is true. But as I do this—for you as well as for myself—you must do likewise."

He wanted to draw back but he only came closer. "What do you mean?"

I kissed him then, for the first time, on the cheek. "You have to break your vow. You have to make love to me."

His eyes were round. "I can't. My life is dedicated to Christ."

I did not smile. His words were not funny, but tragic. The seed of all that was to follow was hidden inside them. But I did not see that then, at least not clearly. I just wanted him so badly. I kissed him again, on the lips.

"You believe my blood will lead you to Christ," I said. "I do not know about that. But I do know where I can take you." I set down the bloody chalice and my arms went around him, the wings of the vampire swallowing its prey. "Pretend I am your God, Arturo, at least for tonight. I will make it easy for you."

There was one last ingredient in Arturo's technique that I did not witness during my first session. While I was lying on the floor with all the paraphernalia around me, he had set a mirror above the crystals. This mirror was coordinated with an external mirror, which allowed moonlight to shine through the crystals. It was actually the light, altered by its passage through the quartz medium, that set in motion the higher vibration in the aura that altered the body. Arturo never focused the sun directly through the crystals, saying it would be much too powerful. Of course, Arturo understood that the light of the moon was identical to the light of the sun, only softened by cosmic reflection.

Arturo made with his own hands a crystal vial to hold my blood.

His first experiment was with a local child who had been retarded since birth. The boy lived on the streets and existed on the scraps of food tossed to him by strangers. It was my desire that Arturo first work on someone who couldn't turn him over to the Inquisition. Still, Arturo was taking a big risk experimenting on anyone. The Church would have burned him at the stake. How I hated its self-righteous dogma, its hypocrisy. Arturo never knew how many inquisitors I killed—a small detail that I forgot to mention in my confession to him.

I remember well how gently Arturo spoke to the child to get him to relax on the copper sheet. Normally the boy was filthy, but I had given him a bath before the beginning of the experiment. He was naturally distrustful of others, having been abused so many times during his life. But he liked us—I had been feeding him off and on and Arturo had a way with children. Soon enough, he was lying on the copper and breathing comfortably. The reflected moonlight, peering through the dark vial of my blood, cast a haunting red hue over the room. It reminded me of the end of twilight, of the time just before night falls.

"Something is happening," Arturo whispered as we watched the boy's breathing accelerate. For twenty minutes the child was in a state of hyperventilation, twitching and shaking. We would have stopped the process if the boy's face hadn't looked calm. Plus, we were watching history being made, maybe a miracle.

Finally the boy lay still. Arturo diverted the reflected moonlight and helped the boy to sit up. There was a new strangeness to his eyes—they were bright. He hugged me.

"Ti amo anch'io, Sita,*"* he said. *"I love you, Sita,"* I had never heard him say a whole sentence before. I was so overjoyed that I didn't stop to think I had never told him my real name. In all of Italy, only Arturo and Ralphe knew it. We were both happy for the child, that his brain seemed to be functioning normally. It was one of the few times in my life I cried, tears of water, not tears of blood.

The red tears would come later.

This first successful experiment gave Arturo tremendous confidence and weakened his caution. He had seen a mental change; he wanted to see a physical one. He went looking for a leper, and brought back a woman in her sixties whose toes and fingers had been eaten away by the dread disease. Over the centuries I had found it particularly painful to look upon lepers. In the second century, in Rome, I had a beautiful lover who developed leprosy. Toward the latter stages of his disease, he begged me to kill him, and I did, crushing his skull, with my eyes tightly clenched. Of course, now there is AIDS. Mother Nature gives each age its own special horror. She is like Lord Krishna, full of wicked surprises.

The woman was almost too far gone to notice what we were doing to her. But Arturo was able to get her breathing deeply, and soon the magic was happening again. She began to hyperventilate, twitching worse than the boy had. Yet her eyes and face remained calm. I was not sure what she felt; it was not as if she suddenly sprouted toes and fingers. When she was through, Arturo led her upstairs and had her lie down on a bed. But from the start she did seem stronger, more alert.

A few days later she began to grow toes and fingers.

Two weeks later there was no sign of her leprosy.

Arturo was ecstatic, but I was worried. We told the woman not to tell anyone what we had done for her. Of course she told *everyone*. The rumors started to fly. Wisely, Arturo passed her cure off to the grace of God. Yet, during these days of the Inquisition, it was more dangerous to be a saint than a sinner. A sinner, as long as he or she was not a heretic, could repent and escape with a flogging. A saint might be a witch. Better to burn a possible saint, the Church thought, than let a genuine witch escape. They had a weird sense of justice.

Arturo was not a complete fool, however. He did not heal more lepers, even though dozens came to his door seeking relief. Yet he continued to experiment on a few deaf and dumb people, a few who were actually retarded. Oh, but it was hard to turn away the lepers. The lone woman had given them such hope. Modern-day pundits often talk of the virtue of hope. To me, hope brings grief. The most content people are those who expect nothing, who have ceased to dream.

I had dreamed what it would be like to be Arturo's lover, and now that he was mine, he was unhappy. Oh, he loved to sleep with me, feel me close beside him. But he believed he had sinned and he couldn't stop. The timing of our affair was unfortunate. He was breaking his vow of celibacy just when he was on the verge of fulfilling his destiny. God would not know whether to curse or bless him. I told him not to worry about God. I had met the guy. He did what he wanted when he wanted, no matter how hard you tried. I told Arturo many stories of Krishna, and he listened, fascinated. Still, he would weep after we had sex. I told him to go to confession. But he refused—he would only confess to me. Only I could understand him, he said.

But I didn't understand. Not what he had planned.

He began to have visions during this period. He'd had them before—they didn't alarm me, at least not at first. It was a vision that had given him the mechanics of his transformative technique, long before we met. But now his visions were peculiar. He began to build models. Only seven hundred years later did I realize he was building models of DNA—human DNA, vampiric, and one other form. Yes, it is true, while we watched the people twitch on the floor under the influence of my bloody aura, Arturo saw more deeply than I did. He actually understood the specific molecule whose code defined the body. He saw the molecule in a vision, and he watched it change under the magnets, crystals, copper, and blood. He saw the double helix of normal DNA. He saw the twelve straight strands of my DNA. And he saw how the two could be conjoined.

"We need twelve helix strands," he confided in me. "Then we will have our perfect being."

"But the more people you experiment on, the more attention you will draw to yourself," I protested. "Your Church will not understand. They will kill you."

He nodded grimly. "I understand. And I cannot keep working on abnormal people. To make a leap toward the perfect being, I must work with a normal person."

I sensed what was in his mind. "You cannot experiment on yourself."

He turned away. "What if we try Ralphe?"

"No," I pleaded. "We love him the way he is. Let's not change him."

He continued to stare at the wall, his back to me. "You changed him, Sita."

"That was different. I knew what I was doing. I had experience. I healed his wounds. I altered his body, not his soul."

He turned to me. "Don't you see it's because I love Ralphe as much as you do that I want to give him this chance? If we can change him from the inside out, transform his blood, he will be like a child of Christ."

"Christ never knew of vampires," I warned. "You should not mix the two in your mind. It's blasphemy—even to me."

Arturo was passionate. "How do you know he didn't? You never met him."

I got angry. "Now you speak like a fool. If you want to experiment on anyone, use me. You promised me you would when we started this."

He stiffened. "I can't change you. Not now."

I understood what he was saying. Suddenly I felt the weight of shattered dreams. In my mind I had been playing with a daughter who had never been born, and who probably never would be.

"You need my blood first," I replied. "The pure vampire blood." It was true he had to replenish the blood in the crystal vial, not before each experiment, but often. Old blood did not work—it was too dead. I continued, "But what if your experiment does work and you do create a perfect being? I cannot give enough blood to alter everyone on this planet."

He shrugged. "Perhaps those who are altered can become the new donors."

"That is a huge *perhaps*. Also, I know people. This will be an exclusive club. It doesn't matter how good your intentions are now." I turned away and chuckled bitterly. "Who will be given a chance at perfection? The nobility? The clergy? The most corrupt will feel they are the most deserving. It is the oldest lesson of history. It never changes."

Arturo hugged me. "That will not happen, Sita. God has blessed this work. Only good can come from it."

"No one knows what God has blessed," I whispered. "And what he has cursed."

A few days went by during which Arturo and I hardly spoke. He would stay up late making models of molecules no one had seen, afraid to talk to me, to touch me. I never realized until then how he saw me as both a gift and a test from God. Of course I had given him my immortal perception on the matter, but he had seen me that way from the start. I brought him magic blood *and* delicious sensuality. He was supposed to take one and not the other, he thought. He lost his intuitive sense that kept him from mistakes, I believe, because he no longer thought he was worthy of having it. He stopped praying to God and started muttering to himself about the blood of Jesus Christ. He was more obsessed with blood than I was, and I had it for dinner every few days.

One evening I could find Ralphe nowhere. Arturo said he had no idea where he was. Arturo wasn't lying, but he wasn't telling the whole truth either. I didn't press him. I think I didn't want to know the truth. Yet had I insisted he tell me, I might have stopped the horror, before it got out of hand.

The screams started in the middle of night.

I was out for a walk at the time. It was my custom to go out late, disguised, find a homeless person, drink a pint of blood, whisper in his or her ear, and put the person back to sleep. Except for evil priests, I didn't often kill in those days. The cries that came to me that night chilled me through. I ran toward the sounds as fast as I could.

I found five bodies, horribly mangled, their limbs torn off. Obviously, only a being of supernatural strength could have committed these acts. One person, a woman with an arm lying beside her, was the last one still alive. I cradled her head in my lap.

"What happened?" I asked. "Who did this to you?"

"The demon," she whispered.

"What did this demon look like?" I demanded.

She gagged. "A hungry angel. The blood—" Her eyes strayed to her severed arm and she wept. "My blood."

I shook her. "Tell me what this demon looked like?"

Her eyes rolled up into her head. "A child," she whispered with her last breath and died in my arms.

Sick at heart, I knew who the child was.

Far away, on the far side of the town, I heard more screams.

I flew toward them but once again I was too late. There were more shredded bodies, and this time there were witnesses. An angry mob with burning torches was gathering. They had seen the demon child.

"It was heading for the woods!" they cried.

"We have to stop it!" others cried.

"Wait!" I yelled. "Look how many it has killed. We can't go after it without help."

"It killed my brother!" one man cried, pulling out a knife. "I'm going to kill it myself."

The mob followed the man. I had no choice but to tag along. As we wound through the dark streets, we found still more bodies. A few had had their heads ripped off. What was the mob thinking? I asked myself. They would fare no better against the monster. Of course mobs and rational thought are not complementary. I have seen too many mobs in my day.

When we reached the trees on the edge of town, I left the rabble to search for the monster myself. I could hear it, two miles ahead, laughing uproariously as it tore off the head of an animal. It was fast and strong, but I was a pure vampire, not a hybrid. It would be no match for me.

I came across it as it ducked from tree to tree, preparing to attack the mob.

"Ralphe," I whispered as I moved up behind him.

He whirled around, his face covered with blood, a wild light in his eyes. Or I should say, no light shone there. His eyes were snakelike. He was a serpent on the prowl, searching for the eggs of another reptile. Yet he recognized me—a faint flicker of affection crossed his face. If it was not for that, I would have killed him instantly. I had no hope he could be converted back to what he had been. I have intuition of my own. Some things I simply know. Usually the bitterest of things.

"Sita," he hissed. "Are you hungry? I am hungry."

I moved closer, not wanting to alert the mob, which was closing in. Ralphe had left a trail of blood. The stuff dripped off him; it was enough to make even me sick. My heart broke in my chest as he came within arm's reach.

"Ralphe," I said softly, all the time knowing it was hopeless. "I have to take you back to Arturo. You need help."

Terror disfigured his bloody expression. Obviously the transformation had not been pleasant for him. "I will not go back there!" he shouted. "He made me hungry!" Ralphe paused to stare down at his sticky hands. A portion of his humanity did indeed remain. His voice faltered on a lump of sorrow in his throat. "He made me do this."

"Oh, Ralphe." I took him in my arms. "I'm so sorry. This should never have happened."

"Sita," he whispered, nuzzling his face into my body. I could not kill him, I told myself. Not for the whole world. But just as I swore the vow inside, I leapt back in pain, barely stifling a cry. He had bitten me! His sorrow had vanished in a lick of his lips. I watched in horror as he chewed down a portion of my right arm, an insane grin on his face. "I like you, Sita," he said. "You taste good!"

"Would you like more?" I asked, offering him my other arm, tears filling my eyes. "You can have all you want. Come closer, Ralphe. I like you, too."

"Sita," he said lustfully as he grabbed my arm and started to take another bite. It was then I spun him around in my arms and gripped his skull from behind. With all the force I could muster and before my tears overwhelmed me, I yanked his head back and to the side. Every bone in his neck broke. His small body went limp in my arms—he had not felt any pain, I told myself.

"My Ralphe," I whispered, running my hands through his long fine hair.

I should have fled with his body then, buried it in the hills. But the execution was too much, even for a monster like me. The life went out of me and I wanted to collapse. When the mob found me, I was cradling Ralphe's body in my arms, weeping like a common mortal. My ancient daughter, my young son—God had stolen them both from me.

The mob surrounded me.

They wanted to know how I had stopped the demon child.

A few in the mob knew me.

"You take care of this boy!" they cried. "We saw you and the priest with him!"

I could have killed them right then, all fifty of them. But the night had seen too much death. I let them drag me back to the town, their torches burning in my bleary eyes. They threw me in a dungeon near the center of town, where the executions took place, taunting me that they were going to get to the bottom of how this abomination was created. Before the sun rose, I knew they would be pounding on Arturo's door, digging into his secret underground chamber, collecting the necessary evidence to show the feared inquisitors. There would be a trial and there would be a judge. The only problem was, there could be only one sentence.

Yet I was Sita, a vampire of incomparable power. Even the hard hand of the Church could not close around my throat unless I allowed it. But what about Arturo? I loved him but could not trust him. If he lived, he would continue his experiments. It was inevitable because he believed it was his destiny. He had enough of my blood left to make another Ralphe, or worse.

A few hours later they threw him in a cell across from me. I begged him to talk to me but he refused. Huddled up in a corner, staring at the wall with eyes as vacant as dusty mirrors, he gave no indication of what was going through his mind. His God did not come to save him. That was left for me to do.

I ended up testifying against him.

The inquisitor told me it was the only way to save my life. Even chained in the middle of the high court with soldiers surrounding me, I could have broken free and destroyed them all. How tempting it was for me to reach out and rip open the throat of the evil-faced priest, who conducted his investigation like a hungry dog on a battlefield searching for fresh meat. Yet I could not kill Arturo with my own hands. It would have been impossible. But I could not have him live and continue his search for the sacred blood of Jesus Christ. Jesus had died twelve hundred years ago, and the search would never end. It was a paradox—the only solution was agonizing. I could not stop Arturo so I had to let others stop him.

"Yes," I swore on the Holy Bible. "He created the abomination. I saw him do it with my own eyes. He *changed* that boy. Then he tried to seduce me with the black arts. He is a witch, Father, that fact is indisputable. God strike me down if I lie!"

The old friar at the church also testified against Arturo, although the inquisitor had to first stretch him on the *strappado* to get the words out of his mouth. It broke the friar's heart to condemn Arturo. He was not alone in his guilt.

Arturo never confessed, no matter how much they tortured him. He was too proud, his cause too noble, in his mind. After the trial, we never spoke. Indeed, I never saw him again. I didn't attend his execution. But I heard they burned him at the stake.

Like any witch.

NINE

I sit at a poker table trying to bluff a high roller from Texas into folding. The game has been going on awhile. There is one hundred thousand dollars in cash and chips on the table. His hand is better than mine. Yaksha's mind-reading gift has grown more powerful in me—I can now see the man's cards as if viewing them through his eyes. He has three aces, two jacks—a full house. I have three sixes—Satan's favorite number. He has the winning hand.

The Texan wears leather cowboy boots, a five-gallon hat. The smoke from his fat cigar does not irritate my eyes. He blows a smelly cloud my way as if to intimidate me. I smile and match his last bet, then raise him another fifty thousand. We are enjoying a private game, in a luxurious corner of the casino, where only fat cats hang out. Three other men sit with us at the table, but they have since folded. They follow the action closely—they all know each other. The Texan will not like to be humiliated in front of them.

"You must have a royal flush, honey child," he says. "Betting the way you do." He leans across the table. "Or else you got a sugar daddy paying your bills."

"Honey and sugar," I muse aloud. "Both are sweet—like me." I add, sharpening my tone, "But I pay my own bills."

He laughs and slaps his leg. "Are you trying to bluff me?"

"Maybe. Match my bet and find out."

He hesitates a moment, glancing at the pot. "The action is getting kind of heavy. What do you do, child, to have so much dough? Your daddy must have given it to you."

He is trying to ascertain how important the money is to me. If it means a lot, in my mind, then I will be betting heavily only if I have an unbeatable hand. Leaning across the table, I stare him in the eye, not strong enough to fry his synapses but hard enough to shake him. I don't like being called a child. I am five thousand years old after all.

"I earned every penny of it," I tell him. "The hard way. Where did you get your money, old man?"

He sits back quickly, ruffled by my tone, my laser vision. "I earned it by honest labor," he says, lying.

I sit back as well. "Then lose it honestly. Match my bet or fold. I don't care which. Just quit stalling."

He flushes. "I'm not stalling."

I shrug, cool as ice. "Whatever you want to call it, old man."

"Damn you," he swears, throwing his cards down. "I fold."

My arms reach out and rake in the money. They're all staring at me. "Oh," I say. "I bet you're wondering what I had? But you're all too professional to ask, aren't you?" I stand and start to stuff the cash and chips in my purse. "I think I'll call it a night."

"Wait right there," the Texan says, getting up. "I want to see those cards."

"Really? I thought you had to pay to see them. Are the rules different for Texans?"

"They are when you've got fifty grand of my money, bitch. Now show me."

I dislike being called a "bitch" more than a "child."

"Very well," I say, flipping over my cards. "You would have won. That's the last time I show a hand you didn't pay to see. Now do you feel better? You were bluffed out of your wrinkled skin, old man."

He slams the table with his fist. "Who are you anyway?"

I shake my head. "You're a sore loser, and I've wasted enough time on you." I turn away. One of his partners grabs my arm. That is a mistake.

"Hold on now, honey," he says. The others move closer.

I smile. "Yes?" Of course I am protected by the casino. I need only raise my voice and these men will be thrown out. But I dislike going to others for help when I am so capable of taking care of myself. Dinner will be a four-course meal tonight, I think. "What can I do for you?" I ask.

The man continues to hold on to my arm but doesn't respond. He glances at the Texan, who is clearly the boss. The Texan has regained his smile.

"We would just like to play some more, honey," he says. "That's only fair. We need a chance to win our money back."

My smile widens. "Why don't I just give you the money back?"

My offer confuses him. The Texan shrugs. "If you want. I'll be happy to accept it."

"Good," I say. "Meet me at the west end of the hotel parking lot in ten minutes. We'll go for a little drive. You'll get all your money back." I glance at the others. "The only condition is you must all come."

"Why do we have to go anywhere?" the Texan asks. "Just give it to us now."

I shake off the other's hold on me. "Surely you're not afraid of little old me, sugar daddy?" I say sweetly.

The men laugh together, a bit uneasily. The Texan points a finger at me.

"In ten minutes," he says. "Don't be late."

"I never am." I reply.

We meet as planned and drive a short distance from town, each in our own cars. Then I lead them off the road and into the desert a few miles, stopping near a low-lying hill. The time is eleven at night, the evening cool and clear, the almost full moon brilliant against the night sky. The men park beside me and climb out. They *are* afraid of me. I can smell their fear. Except for the big boss, they are armed. The bulges beneath their coats are noticeable. I smell the gunpowder in their bullets. They probably figure I am setting them up to be robbed. They study the terrain as they walk toward me, puzzled that I am alone. They are not very subtle. Two of them have their hands thrust in their coat pockets, their fingers wound around their handguns. The Texan steps in front and reaches out to me.

"Give us your bag," Tex orders.

"All right." I hand him my bag. The money is inside, much to his pleasure. His eyes are wide as he counts it. I know he had expected to find a gun in the bag. "Are you satisfied?" I ask.

Tex nods to a partner. I am frisked. Roughly.

"She's cool," the partner mumbles a moment later, backing away.

Tex stuffs the money in his pockets. "Yeah, I'm satisfied. But I don't get it. Why did you drag us all the way out here?"

"I'm hungry," I say.

He grins like the crooked oil baron that he is. "We would have been happy to have taken you to dinner, honey pie. We still can. What would you like?"

"Prime ribs," I say.

He slaps his leg again. Must be a nervous gesture with him. "Goddamn! That's my favorite. Ribs dripping with red juice.

We'll take you out and get you some right now." He adds with a phony wink, "Then maybe we can have a little fun afterward."

I shake my head as I take a step toward him. "We can eat here. We can have a picnic. Just the five of us."

He glances at my car. "Did you bring some goodies?"

"No. You did."

His impatience is never far away. "What are you talking about?"

I throw my head back and laugh. "You're such a fake! Your politeness only appears when it is useful to you. Now that you have stolen the money I won fair and square, you want to take me out for dinner."

Tex is indignant. "We did not steal this money. You offered to return it to us."

"After pressure from you. Let's call a spade a spade. You're a crook."

"No one calls me that and gets away with it!"

"Really? What are you going to do? Kill me?"

He steps forward and slaps me across the face with the back of his hand. "Bitch! You just be happy I'm not that kind of man."

I put a hand to my mouth. "Aren't you that kind of man?" I ask softly. "I see your heart, Mr. Money Bags. You have killed before. It's good we meet tonight, out here in the desert. If you lived, you would probably kill again."

He turns to leave. "Let's get out of here, boys."

"Wait," I say. "I have something else to give you."

He glances over his shoulder. "What?"

I take another step forward. "I have to tell you who I really am. You did ask, remember?"

Tex is in a hurry. "So, who are you? A Hollywood star?"

"Close. I am famous, in certain circles. Why just a few days ago the entire LAPD was chasing me around town. You read about it in the papers?"

A wary note enters his voice. Once again, his men glance around, this time looking for Arab backups. "You're not connected to that group of terrorists, are you?"

"There were no terrorists. That was just the cops trying to cover their asses, it was just me and my partner. We caused all the ruckus."

He snorts. "Right. You and your partner wasted twenty cops. You must be a terminator, huh?"

"Close. I'm a vampire. I'm five thousand years old."

He snickers. "You're a psycho, and you're wasting my time." He turns again. "Good night."

I grab him by the back of his collar and yank him close, pressing his cheek next to mine. He is so startled—he hardly reacts. But his men are better trained. Suddenly I have three revolvers pointed at me. Quickly, I shield myself with Tex. My grip on him tightens, cutting off his air. He gags loudly.

"I am in a generous mood," I say calmly to the others. "I

will give you men a chance to escape. Ordinarily I would not even consider it. But since my cover has been blown, I am not so picky about destroying every shred of evidence." I pause and catch each of their eyes, no doubt sending a shiver to the base of their spines. "I suggest you get in your cars and get out of here—out of Las Vegas completely. If you don't, you will die. It is that simple." I throttle Tex and he moans in pain. My voice takes on a mocking tone. "You can see how strong I am for a honey child."

"Shoot her," Tex gasps as I allow him a little air.

"That is a bad idea," I say. "To shoot me they have to shoot you first because you are standing in front of me. Really, Tex, you should think these things out before giving such orders." I glance at the others. "If you don't get out of here, I'll have you for dinner as well. I really am a vampire and, for me, prime ribs come in all shapes and forms." With one hand, I lift Tex two feet off the ground. "Do you want to see what I do to him? I guarantee it will make you sick to your stomach."

"God," one of the men whispers and turns to flee. He doesn't bother with the car. He just runs into the desert, any-where to get away from me. Another fellow edges toward the periphery. But the remaining man—the guy who grabbed me in the casino, the same one who frisked me—snaps at him.

"She's not a vampire," he says. "She's just some kind of freak."

"That's it," I agree. "I take steroids." I glance at the guy who wants to leave. "Get out of here while you still can. You will see neither of these men alive again. Believe me, you'll hear their screams echoing over the desert."

My tone is persuasive. The guy leaves, chasing after the first one. Now there are just the three of us. How cozy. In reality, I was not looking forward to having to dodge the bullets fired by three separate men. I allow Tex a little more air, let him say his last words. His tune has not changed.

"Shoot her," he croaks at his partner.

"You could try it and see what happens," I remark.

The hired hand is unsure. His gun wavers in the air. "I can't get a clear shot."

Tex tries to turn toward me. "We can make a deal. I have money."

I shake my head. "Too late. I don't want your money. I just want your blood."

Tex sees I am serious. My eyes and voice appear devilishly wicked when I am in the mood, and I'm starving right now. Tex turns deathly pale, matching the color of the moonlight that pours down on us.

"You can't kill me!" he cries.

I laugh. "Yes. It will be very easy to kill you. Do you want me to demonstrate?"

He trembles. "No!"

"I will give you a demonstration anyway. " I call over to

Tex's partner, who has begun to perspire heavily. "What is your name?"

"Go to hell," he swears, trying to circle around us, to get off a lucky shot.

"That cannot be your name," I say. "Your mother would never have called you that. It doesn't matter. You are going to be nobody in a minute. But before I kill you, is there anything you want to say?"

He pauses, angry. "Say to who?"

I shrug. "I don't know. God, maybe. Do you believe in God?"

I exasperate him. "You are one weird bitch."

I nod solemnly. "I am weird." The full power of my gaze locks into his eyes. With me boring into him, he is unable to look away. All he sees, I know, is my fathomless pupils, swelling in size like black holes. I speak very slowly, softly. "Now my dear man, you are going to take your gun and put it in your mouth."

The man freezes for a moment.

Then, as if in a dream, he opens his mouth and puts the gun between his lips.

"Chuck!" Tex screams. "Don't listen to her! She's trying to hypnotize you!"

"Now I want you to grasp the trigger," I continue in my penetrating voice. "I want you to place a certain amount of pressure on the trigger. Not enough to fire the bullet, mind you, but almost enough. There, that is perfect, you have done well. You are half an inch from death." I pause and turn down the power of my eyes. My voice returns to normal. "How does it feel?"

The man blinks and then notices the barrel in his mouth. He almost has a heart attack. He is so scared, he actually drops the gun. "Jesus Christ!" he cries.

"See," I say. "You must believe in God. And because I do as well, and I can only drink the blood of one of you at a time, I think I will let you go as well. Quick, join your partners out in the desert, before I change my mind."

The man nods. "No problem." He dashes away.

"Chuck!" Tex screams. "Come back here!"

"He is not coming back," I tell Tex seriously. "You cannot buy that kind of loyalty. You certainly cannot buy me. You can't even buy my dinner." I pause. "You must understand by now that you *are* dinner."

He weeps like a child. "Please! I don't want to die."

I pull him closer, whisper my favorite line.

"Then you should never have been born," I say.

I enjoy my meal.

When I am finished draining the Texan and have buried him far from his car, I go for a walk in the desert. My thirst is satisfied but my mind is restless. Andy will be off work in a few hours. I should be planning how I will convince him to help me, yet I cannot concentrate. I keep thinking I'm missing something important. I contemplate the last few days and somehow I know something is missing—a piece of the puzzle. This piece exists just beyond the edge of my vision. What it is, I cannot grasp.

Arturo's ghost haunts me. The world never knew what it had lost in him. What greater sorrow could there be? I ask myself how he would have been remembered if there had been no Inquisition. If there had been no Sita and no magical blood to poison his dreams. Perhaps his name would have been uttered in the same breath as that of Leonardo da Vinci, of Einstein. It tortures me to think of the lost possibilities. Arturo the alchemist—the founder of a secret science.

"What did you do to Ralphe?" I whisper aloud. "Why did you do it? Why did you refuse to talk to me when we were in jail?"

But his ghost has questions of its own.

Why were you so quick to kill Ralphe?

"I had to," I tell the night.

Why did you betray me, Sita?

"I had to," I say again. "You were out of control."

But I never accused you, Sita. And you were the real witch.

I sigh. "I know, Arturo. And I was not a good witch."

I have come far from where I started. A steep hill stands before me and I climb to the top of it. Twenty miles off to my left is Las Vegas, glowing with extravagance and decadence.

The almost full moon is high and to my right. The hike has left me hot and sweaty. After shedding my clothes, I once more bow to the lunar goddess. This time I feel the rays enter my body, a tingling coolness that is strangely comforting. My breathing becomes deep and expanded. I feel as if my lungs can draw in the whole atmosphere, as if my skin can soak up the entire night sky. My heart pounds in my chest, now circulating a milky white substance instead of sticky red blood. Without using my eyes, I know I am becoming transparent.

I feel extraordinarily light.

As if I could fly.

The thought comes from an unknown place. It is like a hissed whisper spoken to me from the eternal abyss. Perhaps Yaksha's soul returns to grant me one final lesson.

The soles of my feet leave the top of the hill.

But I have not jumped. No.

I am floating—a few inches above the cool sand.

TEN

When I return to my room, I call Seymour Dorsten, my friend and personal biographer, the young man I cured of AIDS with a few drops of my blood. Seymour is my psychic twin—he often writes about what I am experiencing, without my having to tell him what it is. Lately, I've been *broadcasting* him great material. I wake him up, but as soon as he hears my voice he is instantly alert.

"I knew you'd be calling me soon," he says. "Was that you down in Los Angeles?"

"Joel and I."

He takes a moment to absorb what I am saving, "Joel is a vampire now?"

"Yes. Eddie roughed him up bad. He was dying. I had no choice."

"You've broken your vow."

"Do you need to remind me?"

"Sorry." He pauses. "Can I become a vampire?"

"You don't want the headache. Let me tell you what's been happening."

For the next ninety minutes Seymour listens while I detail everything that has occurred since just before I rescued Yaksha and battled with Eddie. I mention Tex, sleeping in his shallow grave in the desert; and my levitating in the moonlight. Seymour ponders my words for a long time.

"Well?" I ask finally. "Have you been writing about all of this already?"

He hesitates. "I was writing a story about you. In it you were an angel."

"Did I have wings?"

"You were glowing white and flying high above a ruined landscape."

"Sounds like the end of the world," I remark.

Seymour is serious. "It will be the end of the world if you don't get Joel away from these people. You think they really have another vampire in addition to Joel?"

"Yes. Andy has constructed a model of vampire DNA. He wouldn't have had time to do it after Joel was brought to him."

"How do you know what vampire DNA looks like?"

I haven't told Seymour about Arturo. The story is too painful, and besides, I don't think it applies to the situation.

"Trust me, I have experience in the matter," I reply. "Andy's model is accurate. Anyway, whether I have to rescue one or two, my dilemma is the same. I have to get in there and then I have to get three of us out."

"It sounds like your best bet is Andy. Can't you stare him in the eye and make him do what you want?"

"That can backfire, if I push too hard, I'll scramble his brain, and the others will know there's something wrong with him. But if I'm careful I can plant a few suggestions deep in his mind."

"Money is a smart angle. Offer him millions. The fact that he hates his boss doesn't hurt either."

"I agree. But, Seymour, you're supposed to tell me what I'm missing."

"Do you feel you're missing something?" he asks.

"Yes. I can't explain, but I know it's there. It's just not evident to me."

Seymour considers. "I'll tell you a couple things you won't want to hear. When you get inside the compound, you can't go straight for Joel."

"Why not?"

"You have to get to the general. You have to be able to control him."

"He might be harder to get to than Joel."

"I doubt it. Joel will be locked in a cage even you wouldn't be able to escape from. Obviously they know how strong a vampire is."

"Joel is powerful, no doubt. But he is still a child next to me. They don't know that."

"They know more than you think, Sita. You're really not looking at the whole picture. They're probably still searching Lake Mead for your body. The fact that they haven't found it tells the general that you're still alive. And for you to have survived what they put you through means that you have to be handled with *extreme* care." Seymour pauses. "The general must have figured you'll come for Joel."

"You sound so certain," I say. "I'm not."

"Look at it logically. You had several chances to leave Joel during your fight with the LAPD—but you didn't. In fact, you showed tremendous loyalty to him. Believe me, they have constructed a psychological profile on you. They know you're coming for him. They'll be waiting for you. That's one of the reasons you have to go after the general first. Control him and his mind and you control the compound."

"His associates will know something is up."

"You need only control him for a short time. Also, you have no choice. You need the general for something other than rescue and escape."

"What?" I ask, knowing what he'll say.

"Samples of vampire blood will be spread all over the compound. I bet they have several labs there, and you won't be able to walk around and find all the samples. On top of that, they'll have the research that they've conducted in their computers. For these reasons the compound has to be completely destroyed. It's the only way. You're going to have to force the general to detonate a nuclear warhead."

"Just like that? Blow up all those people?"

"You killed plenty of people down in L.A."

My voice is cool. "I didn't enjoy that, Seymour."

He pauses. "I'm sorry, Sita. I didn't mean to imply that you did. And I don't mean to sound cold and cruel. I'm not, you know. I'm just a high school kid, and a lousy writer on top of that."

"You're too brilliant to be lousy at anything. Please continue with your analysis. How can I get Joel out alive and blow the place up?"

He hesitates. "You might not be able to do both."

I nod to myself. "This could be a suicide mission. I've thought of that." I add sadly, "Won't you miss me?"

He speaks with feeling. "Yes. Come here tonight. Make me a vampire. I'll help you."

"You're not vampire material."

"Why? I'm not sexy enough?"

"Oh, that's not the problem. If you were a vampire, I'm sure you'd be a sex machine. It's just that you're too special to be . . ." My voice falters as I think of Arturo. "To be contaminated by my blood."

"Sita? What's wrong?"

I swallow past my pain. "It's nothing—the past. That's the trouble with living for five thousand years—I have so much past.

It's hard to live in the present when all that history is inside you."

"Your blood saved my life," Seymour says gently.

"How are you feeling? Are the HIV tests still negative?"

"Yes, I'm fine. Don't worry about me. When do you see Andy next?"

"In a few hours, near dawn. Then, when he returns to work in the evening, I plan to stow away in the trunk of his car."

"You'll need his cooperation. You can't go searching the compound for Joel."

"Andy will cooperate, one way or the other." I pause. "Is there anything else you can tell me that might help?"

"Yeah. Practice that levitating trick. You never know when it'll come in handy."

"I don't know what's causing it."

"Obviously, Yaksha's blood. He must have developed the ability over the centuries. Could he fly when you knew him in India?"

"He never demonstrated that he could."

"You vampires are full of surprises."

I sigh. "You're so anxious to become like me. You envy my powers. But what you don't know is that I envy you more."

Seymour is surprised. "What do I have that you could possibly want?"

I think of Lalita, my daughter.

But I cannot talk about children, on this of all nights.

"You're human," is all I say.

ELEVEN

When Andy gets to my suite, he acts stressed out but excited. He is in the door only a minute when I give him a hard kiss on the lips. He wants more, and reaches for it, but I push him away.

"Later," I whisper. "The night is still young."

"It's almost morning," he says, recalling my line from the night before.

I turn away. "I want to gamble first."

For a degenerate gambler, I know, dice are better than sex.

"Now you're talking, Lara," he says.

We go down to the casino. It's only a few days before Christmas but the place is packed. The image of a nuclear bomb exploding on the Strip haunts me. Of course, that will never happen. Even if we set a nuclear warhead to go off at the compound, it would not affect Las Vegas, except for slight fallout—if the wind is blowing the wrong way. I wonder if Seymour's dream means I will succeed in my mission or fail.

A glowing angel, flying above the world?

We play craps, dice, and I am the designated roller. Without trying, I throw ten passes in a row and the table cheers me on. Andy bets heavily, wins plenty, and drinks even more. Before we leave the first table, he is drunk. I scold him.

"How can you be a scientist when you keep killing off your brain cells?" I ask.

He laughs, throwing an arm over my shoulder. "I'd rather be a lover than a scientist."

We walk down the Strip to another casino, the Excalibur. Here it is even more crowded. It is a fact that the town never sleeps. We play blackjack, twenty-one. I count cards, only betting heavily when the deck favors the player. But the advantage from even perfect counting is limited, and we don't win any money. Andy drags me back to the dice table—his favorite. The dice come to me, and again I throw another six passes in a row. But I don't want Andy to win too much and be free of debt. Just as the sun begins to color the sky, I drag him back to the Mirage, to my hotel suite. Once there, he falls on my bed, exhausted.

"I hate what I do," he mutters to the ceiling.

I hate that I can't read his mind. It must be the booze. I sit beside him. "Another hard night at work?"

"I shouldn't talk about it."

"You can. Don't worry—I'm good at keeping secrets."

"My boss is crazy."

"The general?"

"Yes. He's stark raving mad."

"What do you mean? What is he doing?"

Andy sits up and glances at me with bloodshot eyes. "Remember I told you we were working on an amazing discovery?"

"Yes. You said it was one of the greatest discoveries of modern time." I smile. "I thought you were trying to impress me."

He shakes his head. "I wasn't exaggerating. We're playing with explosive genetic material, and that's putting it mildly. This general has ordered us to artificially clone it. Do you know what that means?"

I nod. "You're going to make more of it—in a test tube."

"Yes. That's a layman's view, but it is essentially correct." He stares out the window, at the glitter that is the Strip. When he speaks again, his voice reflects the horror he feels. "We are going to try to duplicate something that, if it got out, could affect all of mankind."

It's worse than I thought. The charade must end.

He has given me an opening. I must seize it.

"Andy?" I whisper.

He looks at me. I catch his eye.

"Yes, Lara?" he says.

I do not push him, not yet, but I do not let him turn away

either. A narrow tunnel of whirling blue fog exists between us. He is at one end, chained to a hard wall, and I am steadily rushing toward him, shadows at my back. I hold his attention but slightly blur his focus. Since ingesting Yaksha's blood, my mind-altering abilities are more refined, more powerful. I have to be careful I don't destroy his brain.

"My name is not Lara."

He tries to blink, fails. "What is it?"

"It doesn't matter. I am not who I appear to be." I pause. "I know what you are working on."

He hesitates. "How?"

"I know your prisoner. He is a friend of mine."

"No."

"Yes. I lied to you last night, and I'm sorry. I won't lie to you anymore. I came to Las Vegas for the purpose of freeing my friend." I touch his knee. "But I didn't come to hurt you. I didn't know I would end up caring for you."

He has to take a breath. "I don't understand what you're saying?"

I have to relax my hold on him. The pressure inside his skull is building. Sweat stands out on his forehead. Standing, I turn my back to him and walk to the window to look out at the Strip. The Christmas decorations glitter even amid the neon in the faint light of the dawn.

"But you do understand," I say. "You are holding a prisoner, Joel Drake. He is an FBI agent, but since you have begun to examine him you have come to see that he's much more than that. His blood is different from that of most humans, and this difference makes him very strong, very quick. That's why you keep him locked up in a special cell. Your general tells you he is dangerous. Yet this same general makes you and your partners work night and day so that you can change more people's blood to match that of the supposedly dangerous prisoner." I pause. "Is this not accurate, Andy?"

He is a long time answering. His voice comes out hesitantly.

"How do you know these things?"

I turn to face him. "I told you. I am his friend. I am here to rescue him. I need your help."

Andy can't stop staring at me. It's as if I'm a ghost.

"They said there was another," he mumbles.

"Yes."

"Are you the one?"

"Yes."

He winces. "Are you like him?"

"Yes."

He puts a hand to his head. "Oh God."

Once more, I sit beside him on the bed.

"We are not evil," I say. "I know what you must have been told, but it is not true. We only fight when threatened. The men and woman who died in L.A. trying to arrest us—we didn't want to harm them. But they came after us, they cornered us. We had no choice but to defend ourselves."

His head is buried in his hands. He is close to weeping. "But you killed many others before that night."

"That is not true. The one who did the killing—he was an aberration. His name was Eddie Fender. He accidentally got ahold of our blood. I stopped him, but Eddie is a perfect example of what can happen if this blood gets out. You said it yourself a moment ago—it could affect all of humanity. Worse, it would destroy all of humanity. I am here to stop that. I am here to help you."

He peers up at me, his fingers still covering much of his face. "That's why you can throw the dice the way you do?"

"Yes."

"What else can you do?"

I shake my head. "It doesn't matter. All that matters is that more people are not allowed to become like me and my friend."

"How many are there of you?" he asks.

"I thought there were just two of us left. But I suspect you have another at the compound." I pause. "Do you?"

He turns away. "I can't tell you. I don't know who you are."

"Yes, you know me better than anyone. You've seen what my DNA is like."

He stands and walks to the far wall. He puts a hand on it for support, breathing rapidly. "The man you speak of—Joel—he's ill. He has fever, severe cramps. We don't know what to do with him." Andy struggles. My revelation is too much for him. "Do you know?" he asks.

"Yes. Have you kept him out of the sunlight?"

"Yes. He's in a cell, in a basement. There is no sun." He pauses. "Is he allergic to the sun?"

"Yes."

Andy frowns. "But how does it make him ill? I told you, he doesn't see it."

"The sun is not what makes him ill. I was only ruling out a possibility. He is sick because he is hungry."

"But we have fed him. It doesn't help."

"You are not feeding him what he needs."

"What is that?"

"Blood."

Andy almost crumbles. "No," he moans. "You're like vampires."

I stand and approach him cautiously, not wishing to scare him worse than I already have. "We *are* vampires, Andy. Joel has been one only a few days. I changed him in order to prevent him from dying. Eddie had mortally wounded him. Believe me, I don't go around making vampires. It's against my—principles."

Andy struggles to get a grip on himself. "Who made you?"

"A vampire by the name of Yaksha. He was the first of our kind."

"When was this?"

"A long time ago."

"When?" he demands.

"Five thousand years ago."

My revealing my age does not help the situation. The strength goes out of Andy; he slides to the floor. Rolling into a ball, he recoils as I come closer. I halt in midstride.

"What do you want from me?" he mumbles.

"Your help. I need to get into your compound and get my friend out before the world is destroyed. It is that simple. The danger is that great. And you know I'm not exaggerating. Our blood in the hands of your general is more dangerous than plutonium in the hands of terrorists."

Andy nods weakly. "Oh, I believe that."

"Then you will help me?"

My question startles him. "What? How can I help you? You're some kind of monster. You're the source of this danger."

I speak firmly. "I have walked this world since the dawn of history. In all that time, there have been only myths and rumors of my existence, and the existence of others like me. And those myths and rumors weren't based on fact. They were just stories. Because in all this time none of us has set out to destroy humanity. Yet your general will do this, whether he wants to or not. Listen to me, Andy! He has to be stopped and you have to help me stop him."

"No."

"Yes! Do you want him to clone Joel's blood? Do you want

that material shipped to a weapons plant in the heart of the Pentagon?"

Anger shakes Andy. "No! I want to destroy the blood! I don't need your lectures. I know what it can do. I have studied it inside out."

I move closer, kneel on the floor beside him. "Look at me, Andy."

He lowers his head. "You might cast a spell on me."

"I don't need spells to convince you of the truth. I am not the enemy. Without my assistance, you won't be able to stop this thing from progressing to the next level. Try to imagine a society where everyone has our vampire strength and appetites."

The visions I conjure make him sick. "You really drink human blood?"

"Yes. I need it to live. But I do not need to kill or even harm the person I drink from. Usually, they don't even know what has happened. They just wake up the next day with a headache."

My remark causes him to smile unexpectedly. "I woke up with a headache this evening. Did you drink some of my blood without my knowing?"

I chuckle softly. "No. Your headaches are your problem. Unless you cut down on the booze, your liver is going to give out. Listen to the advice of a five-thousand-year-old doctor."

He finally looks at me. "You're not really that old, are you?"

"I was alive when Krishna walked the earth. I met him in fact."

"What was he like?"

"Cool."

"Krishna was cool?"

"Yes. He didn't kill me. He mustn't have thought I was a monster."

Andy is calming down. "I'm sorry I called you that. It's just—well, I've never met a vampire before. I mean, I was never in a hotel room with one."

"Aren't you glad you didn't sleep with me last night?"

He obviously forgot that small point. "Would I have been changed into a vampire?"

"It takes more than sex with an immortal to make you immortal." I speak delicately. "But you may know that."

He is grim. "There has to be a blood transfer to bring about the change. I imagine a lot of blood is involved."

"Yes, that is correct. Have your experiments established that?"

"We have established a few things. But the human immune system reacts violently to this kind of blood. It embraces it and at the same time tries to destroy it. We have postulated that a large infusion of this DNA code would transform the entire system. Actually, we think your DNA would just take over, and replicate itself throughout every cell in the body." He pauses. "Is that what happened when *Yaksha* changed you?"

I hesitate. I don't want to give him information that could be used later.

"When he changed me, I was young. I cried through most of it."

"He is dead now?"

"Yes."

"When did he die?"

"A few days ago." I add, "He wanted to die."

"Why?"

I smile faintly, sadly. "He wanted to be with Krishna. That was all that mattered to him. He was evil when he changed me. But when he died—he was a saint. He loved God very much."

Andy stares at me, mystified. "You're telling me the truth."

I nod weakly. The thought of Krishna always shakes me.

"Yes. Maybe I should have told you from the beginning. You see, I was going to try to hypnotize you. I was going to seduce you and offer you money and set your head spinning—until you didn't know what you were doing." I touch his leg gently. "But none of that is necessary now. You are a true scientist. You seek the truth. You don't want to harm people. And you know that this blood can harm many people. Give it back to me. I know how to care for it, to keep it out of harm's way."

"If I help you into the compound, they will lock me away for the rest of my life."

"Vehicles go in and out of the compound all day. I've observed them from a distance. You can bring me inside in your trunk. When no one is looking, I will climb out, and no one will blame you."

Andy's not convinced. "Your friend is in a cell in the basement of our main lab. The walls of the cell are made of a special metal alloy—even you couldn't break through. I know for a fact your partner can't. I've watched him try. Also, your friend is under constant surveillance. Cameras watch him twenty-four hours a day. Then, there is the security of the camp itself. It is surrounded by towers. The soldiers inside these towers are well armed. The place is a fortress. There are tanks and missiles behind every building." He pauses. "You won't be able to break him out."

"This special cell where Joel is being held—how does the door to it open?"

"There is a button on a control panel just outside the cell. Push it and the door swings aside. But it is a long way from my car trunk to that button. It is a longer way back outside the compound. To escape with your friend, you'll have to become invisible."

I nod. "We can go over, point by point, the security of the camp. But for now, answer my earlier question. Is there another vampire in the place?"

He hesitates, lowers his head. "Yes."

"How long has he been there? A month?"

"Yes."

"Was he captured in Los Angeles?"

"Yes. He's a black youth. He lived in South Central L.A. before he was changed." Andy looks up. "But he never said anything about an Eddie. The person who changed him was someone else. I forget the name right now."

My theory was correct. "That other person was changed by Eddie. Trust me—I know the ultimate source of this other vampire. Where is he located in relation to Joel?"

"In the cell beside Joel's. But he's virtually comatose. He has the same disease as your friend—cramps and fever." Andy shakes his head. "We didn't know what to do for him. He never asked for blood."

"Your people must have captured him right after he was changed. No one told him what he is now." It isn't pleasant to contemplate the pain this poor soul is going through. "I'll have to take him out as well."

"You'll have to carry him then."

"I can do that, if I have to."

Andy studies me. "You say you are so old. That must mean you're smarter than we short-lived mortals. If you are, you must know how the odds are stacked against you."

"I have always managed to beat the odds. Look how well I do at the dice tables."

"You will probably die if you do this."

"I'm not afraid to die."

He is impressed. "You really aren't a monster. You're much braver than I am."

I take his hand. "I was wrong a minute ago when I said your helping me would not put you at risk. It will take a brave man to sneak me inside the compound in the trunk of his car."

He squeezes my hand. "What's your real name?"

"Sita." I add. "Few people have known me by that name."

He touches my red hair. "I was wrong only to say your blood scares me. It fascinates me as well." He pauses and a sly grin crosses his face. "Sex is not enough to make me immortal?"

"It hasn't worked in the past. But these days are filled with mysterious portents." An unexpected warmth for him flows over me. His eyes—they have *me* hypnotized, with their uncanny depth, their gentle kindness. Smiling, I lean over and hug him and whisper in his ear, "The dawn is at hand. In ancient times, it was considered a time of transformation, of alchemy. I'll stay with you, for now." I pause. "Who knows what may happen?"

TWELVE

I dream a dream I've had before. A dream that seems to go on forever. It takes place in eternity, at least, my idea of such a place.

I stand on a vast grassy plain with a few gently sloping hills in the far distance. It is night, yet the sky is bright. There is no sun, but a hundred blue stars blaze overhead, shimmering in a long nebulous river. The place feels familiar to me. The air is warm, saturated with sweet aromas. Miles away a large number of people walk into a vessel—a violet-colored spaceship of gigantic proportions. The vessel shines from the inside with divine radiance, almost blinding in its brilliance. I know it is about to depart and that I am supposed to be on it. Yet I cannot leave until I have finished speaking with Lord Krishna.

He stands beside me on the wide plain, his gold flute in his right hand, a red lotus flower in his left. We both have on long blue gowns. He wears an exquisite jewel around his neck—the Kaustubha gem, in which the destiny of every soul can be seen. He stares up at the sky, waiting for me to speak. But I can not remember what we were discussing.

"My Lord," I whisper. "I feel lost."

His eyes remain fixed on the stars. "You feel separate from me."

"Yes. I don't want to leave you. I don't want to go to earth."

"No. You misunderstand. You are not lost. The entire creation belongs to me—it is a part of me. How can you be lost? Your feeling of separation gives rise to your confusion." He glances my way, finally, his long black hair blowing in the soft wind. The stars shimmer in the depths of his dark eyes. The entire creation *is* there. His smile is kind, the feeling of love that pours from him overwhelming. "You have already been to earth. You are home now."

"Is this possible?" I whisper, straining to remember. Faint recollections of being on earth come to me. I recall a husband, a daughter—I can see her smile. Yet a dark film covers them. I view them from a peculiar perspective, from a mind I can scarcely believe is connected to me. In front of them many centuries stretch out, choked with endless days and nights, suffering people, all awash in blood. Blood that I have spilled. I have to force the question from my lips. "What did I do on earth, my Lord?"

"You wanted to be different—you were different. It doesn't matter. This creation is a stage, and we all play roles as heroes and villains alike. It is all *maya*—illusion."

"But did I—sin?"

My question amuses him. "It is not possible."

I glance toward the waiting vessel. It is almost full. "Then I don't have to leave you?"

He laughs. "Sita. You have not heard me. You cannot leave me. I am always with you, even when you think you are on earth." He changes his tone—he becomes more of a friend than a master. "Would you like to hear a story?"

I have to smile, although I am more confused than ever.

"Yes, my Lord," I say.

He considers. "There was once a fisherman and his wife, who lived in a small town by the ocean. Every day the fisherman would go out to sea in his boat, and his wife would stay behind and care for the house. Their life was simple, but happy. They loved each other very much.

"The wife had only one complaint about her husband—he would eat only fish. For breakfast, lunch, and dinner, he would eat only what he caught. It didn't matter what she cooked and baked: bread or pastries, rice or potatoes—he would have none of it. Fish was his food, he said, and that was the way it had to be. From an early age, he had been this way, he had taken a vow his wife could not understand.

"It came to pass one day that his wife finally got fed up

with his limited diet. She decided to trick him, to mix a piece of cooked lamb in with his fish. She did this cleverly, so that from the outside the fish looked as if it had come straight from the sea. But hidden beneath the scales of the fish was the red meat. When he returned home that evening and sat down at the table, the fish was waiting for him.

"At first he ate his meal with great relish, noticing nothing amiss. His wife sat beside him, eating the same food. But when he was halfway through, he began to cough and choke. He couldn't catch his breath. It was only then he smelled something odd on his plate. He turned to his wife, eyes blazing with anger.

"'What have you done?' he demanded. 'What is in this fish?'

"The wife sat back, scared. 'Only a little lamb. I thought you might enjoy the change.'

"At these words the fisherman wiped the plate from the table and onto the floor. His anger knew no bounds. Still, he could not catch his breath. It was as if the lamb had caught in his windpipe and refused to shake loose.

"'You've poisoned me!' he cried. 'My own wife has poisoned me!'

"'No! I only wanted to feed you something different.' She stood and slapped him on the back, but it did not help. 'Why are you choking like this?'

"The fisherman fell onto the floor, turning blue. 'Don't you know?' he gasped. 'Don't you know who I am?'

"'You are my husband,' the wife cried, kneeling beside him.

"'I am . . . ,' the fisherman whispered. 'I am what I am.'

"Those were his last words. The fisherman died, and as he did, his body changed. His legs turned into a large flipper. His skin became covered with silver scales. His face bulged out and his eyes became blank and cold. Because, you see, he was not a person. He was a fish, which is what he had been all along. As a big fish, he could eat only smaller fish. Everything else was poison to him." Krishna paused. "Do you understand, Sita?"

"No, my Lord."

"It doesn't matter. You are what you are. I am what I am. We are the same—when you take the time to remember me." Krishna raises his flute to his lips. "Would you like to hear a song?"

"Very much, my Lord."

"Close your eyes, listen closely. The song is always the same, Sita. But it is always changing, too. That is the mystery, that is the paradox. The truth is always simpler than you can imagine."

I close my eyes and Lord Krishna begins to play his magical flute. For a time, outside of time, that is all that matters. The music of his enchanted notes floats on a wind that blows from the heart of the galaxy. Overhead the stars shine down on us as the universe slowly revolves and the ages pass. I do not need to see my Lord to know that he is present everywhere. I do not need to touch him to feel his hand on my heart. I do not need anything, except his love. After a while, that is all there is—his divine love pouring through the center of my divine being. Truly, we are one and the same.

THIRTEEN

I lie flat on my back in the trunk of Andy's car. My hearing is acute—up ahead I hear the noises of the compound, the guards talking at the gate. The blackness in the trunk is not totally dark to me. I clearly see the white lab coat I have donned, the fake security badge pinned to my breast pocket. The badge is an old one of Andy's. I have cleverly put my picture over his, and changed the name. I am Lieutenant Lara Adams, Ph.D., a microbiologist on loan from the Pentagon. Andy says a large number of scientists have arrived from Back East. My makeup makes me look older. I should be able to blend in.

We stop at the security gate. I hear Andy speak to the guards.

"Another long night, Harry?" Andy asks.

"Looks like it," the guard replies. "Are you working till dawn?"

"Close. This night shift is a bear—I don't know whether

I'm coming or going." Andy hands something to the guard, a pass that must be electronically scanned. He has to have one to leave the compound as well. I have one in my back pocket. Andy continues in a natural voice, "I just wish I could do a little better at the tables, and quit this stupid job."

"I hear you," the guard says. "How's your luck been holding out?"

"I won a couple of grand last night."

The guard laughs. "Yeah, but how much did you lose?"

Andy laughs with him. "Three grand!"

The guard hands the pass back. "Have a good night. Don't piss off the man."

I hear Andy nod. "It's a little late for that."

We drive into the compound. Andy has promised he'll park between two sheds, out of sight of the manned towers. From my earlier examination of the place, I am familiar with the spot. As the car moves, I feel confident we are heading straight for it. Especially when Andy turns to the left, stops, and turns off the engine. He climbs out of his car, shutting the door behind him, and walks away. I listen to his steps as he enters the main lab. So far so good.

I pop open the trunk and carefully peer out.

The car sits in shadow. No one is around. After slipping out of the car, I silently close the trunk. I smooth my lab coat over my slim body, adjust my red hair. My thick glasses make me look almost nerdy but smart.

"Lara Adams from Back East," I whisper. *Back East* means the Pentagon, Andy said. They never called the place by name.

"You have to get to the general. You have to control him."

Seymour's advice remains with me. Resisting the temptation to follow Andy into the main lab—where I know Joel is being held captive—I turn instead in the direction of a small house located behind the lab. This is the general's private quarters. I move onto his front steps, then pause. I don't press the doorbell; I know without knocking that there is no one at home. Andy warned me of this. In fact, he said the general was seldom at home. Andy wants me to get Joel and get the hell out of the place, as quickly as I can. He doesn't, of course, know I need to control the general in order to blow the place up. But I have warned him that when the fireworks start, he should get out of the compound as quickly as possible.

For a moment, I stand undecided.

"The general knows you'll come for Joel."

Seymour is wise, but I still think he overestimates the intelligence of the man. For example, I tell myself, look how easily I entered the compound. The general couldn't know that I was on my way. Certainly, I can't search the entire compound for him.

I decide to have a peek at Joel. After seeing exactly where he is, I'll be in a better position to figure out what to do next. I head back to the front entrance of the lab, where Andy disappeared.

The interior of the lab is a complex maze of halls and offices. It seems clear the real work of dissecting and analyzing is done downstairs. Men and women in lab coats mill about. There is an occasional armed soldier. No one pays any attention to me. Listening for an elevator, I hear the sound of people going up and down steps. I prefer a stairway to an elevator. The latter can be a death trap for an invading vampire.

I find the stairs and go down a couple of flights. Andy told me Joel is being held two stories below the surface, and that his cell is at the east end of the building, farthest from the main gate. On this lower floor there are fewer people. They speak in soft tones. Moving like the sharp professional I'm supposed to be, I make my way down a narrow hall toward the rear of the building. Faintly, I smell Joel's scent. But I cannot hear his heart beating, his breathing. The walls of his cell must be thick. The scent is my compass and I follow it carefully, sensitive to the way it is spread by the ventilation ducts, the passage of people.

I come to a security center, equipped with monitors and two armed soldiers. I hear everything inside the closed room. Cracking the door, I peer inside and see Joel on one of the screens. He sits in the corner of a brightly lit cage, pinned to the corner by a metallic wrist chain.

I do not see another vampire on a separate monitor. Odd.

I close the door and knock. One of the guards answers.

"Yes? Can I help you?"

"Yes. My name is Dr. Lara Adams." I nod to Joel on the screen. "I am here to talk to our patient."

The guard glances at his buddy, back to me. "You mean, over the speaker, right?"

"I would prefer to talk to him in person," I say.

The guard shakes his head. "I don't know what you've been told, but no one talks to the—to the patient directly. Only over the speaker." He pauses, glances at my badge, my breasts. Boys will be boys. "Who gave you clearance to interview this guy?"

"General Havor."

The guy raises an eyebrow. "He told you himself?"

"Yes. You can check with him if you like." I nod to the interior of the room. "May I come in?"

"Yes." The guard stands aside. "What did you say your name was?"

"Dr. Lara Adams." I gesture to the monitor. "I see this guy but where is he really? Nearby?"

"He's just around the corner," the other guard answers, while his buddy reaches for the phone. "He's in a box so thick an atomic bomb couldn't blast through it."

"Oh," I say. That is useful information.

My hands lash out, my fingers cutting the air like knives.

Both guards crumple on the floor, unconscious, not dead.

I hang up the phone. Around the corner I go.

I push the large red button to open the cage.

There is a hiss of air. A door as thick as a man's body swings aside.

"Joel," I cry softly, seeing him huddled in the corner, chained to the wall, burning like a dying coal as he shakes. I rush toward him. "I'm going to get you out of here."

"Sita," he gasps. "Don't!"

The door slams shut at my back. Locking me in.

Overhead, a TV monitor comes to life.

Andy stares down at me. Behind him stands the cruel-faced General Havor, wearing a barely disguised smirk. Yet there is no joy in Andy's expression as he slowly shakes his head and sighs. It is strange, but it is only then that I see my adversary clearly. The many years have reshapen his face, dulled his eyes, bruised his soft voice. Yet it is no excuse, not for a vampire as supposedly careful as I am. Right from the start I should have known who it was I was dealing with.

"Sita," he says sadly with a faint Italian accent. *"E passato tanto tempo dall' Inquisizione."*

"Sita. It's been a long time since the Inquisition."

In a single horrifying instant, I understand everything.

"Arturo," I whisper.

FOURTEEN

Several hours have elapsed since my capture. I have spent the majority of it sitting on the floor with my eyes closed, like a meditating yogi. But I enjoy no blissful nirvana. Inside, I seethe with rage: at General Havor, at Arturo, and most of all at myself. Arturo left signs for me everywhere, and I missed them all. Again and again my mind forces me to review the list.

1. When Joel was captured, he was brought before Andy. It was Andy who confirmed the special nature of Joel to General Havor. But rather than stay to examine Joel, Andy left the compound and went gambling. What an odd thing to do right after the catch of the century! Of course Andy was not out for fun. He knew I would be watching. He knew I could be lured in.

2. I never saw Andy out in the sun, and it wasn't just because he worked the night shift. He was sensitive to the sun as a vampire should be. Yet he is not a pure vampire.

3. Andy talked about his highly classified work—to me, a total stranger. I hardly had to prod it out of him. He planted all the right clues for a person dissatisfied with his job—not enough pay, a totalitarian boss, a lousy work schedule. He tricked me in the most insidious way—by handing me all the ammunition I needed to think I could trick him.

4. He protested when I asked him to help me break into the compound. He put on a great show of defiance. But the fact that he helped me at all, without my having to manipulate his brain, was peculiar.

5. Andy had Arturo's model of vampire DNA. I passed it off, figuring he had already examined another vampire and broken the genetic code. The only problem was—there was no other vampire. I had destroyed all of Eddie's bastards. The only one the government had was Joel.

"Because, you see, he was not a person. He was a fish, which is what he had been all along. As a big fish, he could eat only smaller fish."

In my dream, Krishna had been trying to tell me that the hidden truth was the most obvious truth.

Andy was able to construct Arturo's model because he was Arturo!

Why did he leave it out for me to see? To taunt me, no doubt.

I open my eyes. "Damn," I whisper.

Joel looks over. I have broken his chains; he is no longer pinned to the wall, but is able to lie down properly and rest. The chains have accomplished their purpose, however. Had Joel been at the door, I would not have walked into the cage. I have tested the strength of the walls. The guard was right—a nuclear bomb couldn't blast through them.

The walls of the cell are a flat white color, metallic. The space is square—twenty feet by twenty feet. A seatless toilet is attached to one wall, a single cot to the opposite one. Joel lies on the thin mattress.

"We all make mistakes," he says.

"Some make more than others."

"I appreciate your trying to rescue me. You should have left me to die after Eddie opened my veins."

"You're probably right. But then I wouldn't have the pleasure of your company right now." I pause. "How are you feeling?"

The first thing I did after being captured, before sitting down to berate myself, was let Joel drink a pint of my blood. The transfusion alleviated his more severe symptoms but he still looked gaunt. Yet I am reluctant to give him more nourishment. We both know I need to be at full strength if we are to break out.

"I feel fine." He adds, "Better than I have in days."

I reach out and squeeze his hand. "It must have been hard for you. Have they been examining you inside out?"

"That's a literal way of putting the question." He gestures to the screen. I have told him nothing of Arturo. "I take it he is an old friend?"

I know our every word is being recorded. I don't know what can and will be used against me in a court of law. But I do know I don't have the right to remain silent. I wonder if they will try to torture information out of me. It will be a waste of their time. I doubt they're going to let me call a lawyer.

"We go way back," is all I say.

"How was Vegas?"

"Fine. Won a lot of money at craps."

"That's great. Where did you stay?"

"At the Mirage." I sigh. "I'm sorry, Joel. Neither of us should be in here. I messed up."

"Don't be so hard on yourself. After all, you stopped Eddie."

"Yeah. Only to set up a situation where there might be a thousand Eddies." I abruptly raise my voice and yell at the monitor. "Did you hear that, Arturo? A thousand Ralphes running loose! Is that what you want?" My voice sinks to a whisper. "That's what you're going to get."

I don't expect to get a response to my outburst, but a minute later the TV monitor comes back to life. Arturo is alone, sitting at a desk in the security room. Around the corner, as they say.

"Sita," he says. *"None oho mai pensato che ti avrei rivista."*

"I never thought I would see you again."

"Same here," I mutter.

"Are you comfortable?" he asks, switching languages effortlessly. When he wishes, he has no accent. He must have been living in America for a long time.

"No cage is ever comfortable." I pause. "Are you comfortable?"

He spreads his hands. I remember how large they were. Suddenly, I recall many details about him: the warm gray of his eyes, the strength of his jawline. Why didn't I recognize him? There are the obvious reasons. He has aged twenty-five years since we last met, and yet, his face has changed more than the two and a half decades warrant. Probably since it has, in reality, been over seven hundred years.

Yet none of that should have fooled me. I didn't recognize him for two sound reasons: I knew he couldn't possibly exist in our time, so I never even considered the idea; and the Andy I stalked did not possess the same soul as the Arturo I once loved. This man who stares down at me—I hardly know him, and I slept with him for months.

"What would you have me do?" he replies. "You had to be stopped."

My voice is filled with scorn. "Stopped from what?"

"There were the violent murders in Los Angeles. I knew that was you."

"You knew it was not me! You knew it was some other vampire! Don't start off our first conversation in seven centuries with a lie. You know I never killed for pleasure."

My wrath makes him pull back a step. "I apologize. I should say I knew you were indirectly involved." He pauses. "Who committed the killings?"

I forget my resolve to say as little as possible. The information cannot help them, anyway. My blood is all that matters.

"A psychotic vampire by the name of Eddie Fender started the murders. The LAPD and the FBI were doing everything they could to stop him. But it was I who put a halt to the killings. And what do I get for it? A medal? No, the entire police force comes after me."

"You killed two dozen of those officers."

"Because they were trying to kill me! I am not the villain here. You and the scum you are associated with are." I pause, settle down. "Why are you with these people?"

"I can help them. They can help me. We have vested interests. Isn't that the reason for most partnerships?"

"It is among people who have selfish goals. But I never remember you as selfish. Why are you working for the U.S. military machine?"

"Surely you must understand by now. I need to complete my experiments."

I laugh. "Are you still searching for the blood of Christ?"

"You say it as if it were a fool's errand."

"It's a blasphemous errand. You saw what happened last time."

"I made an error—that's all. I will not make the same error again."

"That's all? Just some error? What about Ralphe? I loved that boy. You loved him. And you turned him into a monster. You forced me to kill him. Do you know what that did to me?"

Arturo's voice goes cold. "It made you want to testify against me?"

"You had to be stopped. I didn't have the strength or the will to do it myself." I pause. "You had a chance to talk to me in the inquisitor's dungeon. You chose not to."

"I had nothing to say."

"Well, then, I have nothing to say to you now. Come, get your fresh supply of vampire blood. Send plenty of scientists and soldiers. Not all of them will be coming back to you."

"You present no danger to us as long as you are in your cell. And you will remain in there for the remainder of your life."

"We will see," I whisper faintly.

"Sita, I'm surprised at you. Aren't you curious how I'm still alive?"

I draw in a weary breath. "I have an idea as to how you

survived. Even when you swore to me you weren't experimenting on yourself, you were. That's why you began to have visions of DNA. You were seeing it through the eyes of your blessed hybrid state."

"I did experiment on myself. That is true. But I never reached the full hybrid status. That must be obvious to you."

I nod. "Because you have aged. Does it hurt, Arturo, that you're not the dashing young priest anymore?"

"I may yet achieve immortality."

"Hmm. And I always thought you wanted to die and go to heaven." He is right, of course; I am curious about those days. "What happened after the trial? How did you escape? I heard they burned you at the stake."

"The inquisitor granted me a private audience. He couldn't let me go, he said, but in exchange for my confession of witchcraft, he agreed to hang instead of burn me."

"And you recovered?"

"Yes."

"Were you surprised?"

"Yes. It was a calculated risk. I didn't have many options."

I hesitate. "What did you do to Ralphe?"

For once, Arturo looks ashamed. "I exposed him to the vial of your blood—with the midday sun pouring through it."

I was aghast. "But you said you'd never consider that. The vibration would destroy a man or woman."

"You saw how the word was spreading about me. I had

only a limited time to complete my experiments. Ralphe had been spying on us all along. Neither of us knew. He saw what we were up to. He wanted to try it."

Fury possesses me. "That's a ridiculous rationalization! He was a child! He didn't know what would happen to him! You did!"

"Sita."

"You were a coward! If your experiment was so precious to you, why didn't you perform it on yourself, with the midday sun pouring through my bloody vial?"

My words wound him, but he is still full of surprises. "But I did subject myself to the blood in the sunlight. That morning, when the mob approached the church, I heard them coming. I hurried down to the basement and let the full power of the vampire vibration wash over me. I believe that is why I have been able to live as long as I have. If the mob had not stopped me, maybe the transformation would have been complete, and I would have achieved the perfect state. I was never to know. The first thing the mob did was break the vial."

His words sober me. "Then what went wrong with Ralphe? Why did he turn into a monster?"

"There could be many factors that influenced his outcome. One was that I laid him on the copper sheets when the sun was high in the sky. Also—and I think this is the primary reason the experiment failed—Ralphe was ordinarily fearless by nature. But when the transformation started, he got scared. The power of the magnetic field magnified his fear, which in turn warped his DNA. When the process was complete, I couldn't control him. He had the strength of ten men. He was out the door before I could stop him."

"You should have told me. I could have stopped him before he killed anyone. We might have been able to change him back."

Arturo shook his head, "I don't think there was any going back." He adds, "I was too ashamed to tell you."

"Finally, the high priest confesses." I continue to sneer at him. "All your talk doesn't disguise the fact that you experimented on a child before yourself. And that you lied to me, after swearing on the name of your precious God that you would always tell me the truth."

"Everyone lies," he says.

"Guarda cosa sei diventata, Arturo," I say, reverting to the language of his youth, out of frustration, hope. *"Look what's become of you, Arturo."* "When we first met, you wouldn't have hurt a fly. That's why I gave you my blood. I trusted you."

Even on the monitor, I see his gaze is focused in the far distance. My words stir painful memories, for both of us. My hatred for him is matched only by my love. Yes, I still love him, and I hate that about myself. He seems to sense my thoughts for he suddenly glances back at me and smiles. It is a sad smile.

"I cannot defend my acts to you," he replies. "Except to say

I thought the rewards of success outweighed the possibility of failure. Yes, I should never have used Ralphe. Yes, I should never have lied to you. But if I had done these things—where would we be today? I'd be long dead in a forgotten grave and you'd be safe and secure in your own selfish universe. We wouldn't have your blood now so we could continue with our noble quest to finish what was started seven centuries ago."

I snicker. "I can't help but notice that you apply the word *selfish* to me. What sickness was magnified in your field when you lay beneath the vibration of my blood? You have become a megalomaniac. You were a priest, a good priest. You used to humble yourself before God. Now you want to be God. If Jesus were alive today, what would you say to him? Or would you give him a chance to explain himself before stealing his blood?"

"Do *you* want a chance to explain yourself?" Arturo asks gently.

"I answer to no man. My conscience is clear."

He raises his voice. I have finally hit a button. "I don't believe you, Sita. Why couldn't you look at me when you accused me of witchcraft?"

"You were a witch! And you haven't changed! Goddamn you, Arturo, can't you see how dangerous it is for me to be held captive by these people? I just have to look at General Havor to know he wants to rule the world."

"He's not the monster *Andy* led you to believe."

"You talk about beliefs. What do you believe in these days? I never met Jesus, it's true. But you must know as well as I that he would never condone your methods. Your lying and ambushing and torture. The means do not justify the end. You did not watch Ralphe chew on human flesh. If you had seen him, you'd know that this path you want to take stinks of the devil."

Arturo sits back from the screen. He is as tired as I am, perhaps shaken as well. In that moment, his face becomes much older than forty-five. He appears ready for the grave. Yet he is resolved, his destiny will be fulfilled. He shakes his head as he sighs.

"We can do this the hard way, Sita," he says. "Or we can do it the easy way. It is up to you. I need your blood and I am going to have it."

I smile grimly. "Then you'd better prepare yourself for a fight. Let me warn you, Arturo—I've shown you only a fraction of my powers. But if you come after me now, you will see all of them. There aren't enough soldiers and bullets in this compound to contain me for the remainder of my life. Tell your general that people will die if I'm not released. Their deaths will be on your conscience, Arturo. I swear in the name of my God, you will never get to heaven—in this world or the next."

The screen goes dead.

But not before I see the fear in his eyes.

FIFTEEN

*M*ore hours pass. Joel lies sleeping. Once again I sit silently on the floor, my legs crossed, my eyes closed. Yet this time my attention is turned outward. Through the wall, I can just hear the guards at the security station talk. There are three of them now. They discuss a football game.

"Those Forty-Niners are amazing," Guard One says. "Their offense works like a machine gun—it just keeps firing. I felt sorry for the Cowboys."

"You know, everybody looks at the quarterback," Guard Two says. "But I think when you got the receivers, you got all you need. Even a lousy pro quarterback can look good throwing to players who are wide open."

"I think it's the other way around," Guard Three says. "You got a great quarterback, he can hit a player who's totally covered. Not many teams win the Super Bowl with an average quarterback."

"Not many teams win the Super Bowl, period," Guard One says.

"Only one a year," Guard Two says.

"Wouldn't be a Super Bowl if everyone could win it," Guard Three says.

Beyond their chattering, I sense their thoughts. The gift of Yaksha's blood grows stronger the more still I become. Guard One is contemplating his sour stomach. He has an ulcer, and when he pulls an all-night shift, it always hurts. He wonders if he should go to his car on the next break and get his bottle of Maalox. But he needs to drink it in private. The other guys always kid him about having a stomachache like a little kid. Actually, Guard One has a lot of guts going into work in the pain he's in.

Guard Two's thoughts are dull. He is thinking about his wife, his current mistress, and a woman he just met in the cafeteria two hours earlier—all of them naked together in bed with him. He drank a large Coke before starting his last shift. He has to pee real bad.

Guard Three is interesting. Unknown to his buddies, he writes science-fiction in his spare time. His brother-in-law, who's a lawyer, just read his last book and told him to forget about becoming a writer. But Guard Three thinks that just because his brother-in-law has a law degree, it doesn't mean he can spot talent. And he's right—Guard Three's mind is rich in creative ideas.

I need to concentrate hard to sense their thoughts. I can only *read* one at a time. Since ancient times I have been able to influence people's thoughts by staring hard at them and whispering suggestions in their ears. But in here I am deprived of the power of my gaze, of the soothing allure of my velvety voice. Yet the longer I concentrate on these guys, the more certain I am that I can introduce thoughts into their minds. I focus in on Guard Three—he's the most sensitive. Creating a strong image in my mind, I send it through the wall.

"This girl is real dangerous. She can kill us all."

Guard Three is saying something that he suddenly breaks off in midsentence. I hear him shift uneasily in his chair. "Hey, guys," he says.

"What?" the other two ask.

"That chick in there is dangerous. We have to be careful with her. You saw what she did to Sam and Charlie."

"She knocked them out cold," Guard Two agrees. "But I'd like to see her try it on me. She wouldn't get far."

"I don't think you want to mess with her," Guard One says. "She's supposed to be super strong."

"Yeah, but they don't tell us why she's strong," Guard Three says. "They just tell us to watch her. But what if she gets out? She could kill us all."

"Yes," I whisper softly to myself.

"Relax," Guard One says. "There's no way she's getting out of that box."

"Even if she does break out," Guard Two says. "We can stop her. I don't care about orders, I'm opening fire."

"I hear bullets can't stop her," Guard Three says, continuing to dwell on how dangerous I am.

I shift my focus to Guard One and send out another suggestion.

"We mustn't lose sight of her."

"We'll keep an eye on her," Guard One says.

I place the same thought in Guard Three's mind.

"Yeah," Guard Three echoes. "We have to be alert, keep watching her."

I try to put the thought in Guard Two's mind.

"I've got to take a piss," Guard Two says.

"Oh, well," I whisper to myself. "Two out of three ain't bad."

Over the next thirty minutes—pausing only when Guard Two goes to the bathroom—I steadily build up their paranoia about how dangerous I am and how bad things will be if they don't keep me under constant surveillance. Pretty soon Guards One and Three are talking paranoid gibberish. Guard Two is not sure how to calm them down, or even *why* they need to be calmed down.

"If we don't watch her every second," Guard One says. "She'll escape."

"And if she escapes," Guard Three says. "She'll rip our hearts out and eat them."

"Stop!" Guard Two yells. "She's not going to escape."

"We know that," Guard One says. "If we don't blink, if we keep the lights on her, she won't escape."

"But if the lights go out, we're doomed," Guard Three says.

"Why would the lights go out?" Guard Two wants to know.

Taking a few deep breaths, I slowly ease out of my deep state of concentration. I reach over and gently shake Joel. He opens his eyes and smiles at me. In all the confusion I have forgotten how handsome he is. His dark blue eyes are filled with affection.

"What a pleasant sight to wake up to," he whispers.

"Thank you."

"Did you sleep?"

I lean over and whisper directly into his ear. "No. I've been planting the seeds of our escape. The guards outside are now terrified of losing sight of us."

He's curious. "You know this for a fact?"

"Yes. I'm going to break the lights in here, which will cause them to panic and call for help. I'm sure General Havor himself will come."

"Then what?"

"I have a plan of sorts, but it's not set in stone. Just follow my lead. Get up—get ready to act when I say the word."

Joel moves to the wall closest to the door. Standing in the center of the cell, staring at the overhead cameras, I give the guards on the other side of the wall one last thing to think about.

"I'm coming for you now," I say in a wicked voice. "You'd better run, you'd better hide." I lick my lips. "Because I'm *very* hungry."

Then, in a series of blindingly fast moves, I shatter every light on the ceiling and plunge the cell into darkness. I see perfectly, but Joel has to reach for the wall to get his bearings. At the security station, I hear Guard One and Guard Three screaming in terror. Guard Two fumbles for his weapon, yelling at his partners to stop. I suppress a giggle.

"Come to me, General." I whisper. "Come, Arturo."

Five minutes later I hear Arturo and Havor pounding down the narrow hall, speaking heatedly. Although I have not heard the general's voice before, I recognize it by the authority it commands. Arturo has influence within the confines of the compound, but the man with the star on his shoulder is in charge. I wonder about the details of their relationship. All about them, clutching machine guns and trying not to panic, are dozens of soldiers.

"She's not a danger as long as we keep the lock in place," Arturo says to the general. "This is a stunt she's pulling to get us to open the door."

"I don't like it that we can't see her," General Havor snaps back. "You heard what she told you. We don't know the full extent of her powers. For all we know she's cutting through a wall of the cell as we talk."

"She's a master of manipulation," Arturo counters. "She talked about her unknown powers to plant a seed of doubt in our minds—for just this occasion. If you open the door to check on her, she'll be on you in a second. You'll have to kill her to stop her and you can't kill her."

"We'll wait and see what she does next," General Havor says.

"What's happening?" Joel hisses in the dark.

I whisper softly so that only he can hear. "The general and Arturo are coming. They don't want to open the door, but I think I can do something to inspire them to relent. There will be a lot of noise in a few minutes. Besides creating the racket, I will be mentally projecting into the general's mind. Please don't speak to me during this time. I need to concentrate. Then, when they start to open the door, I need you to wedge yourself in the corner behind the door. But don't do it until I give the signal. There'll be gunfire, and the space behind the door will be the safest. Do you understand?"

"Yes. You really think they'll open the door?"

"Yes. I'll make them."

Once more I sit cross-legged on the floor, this time in the center of the room. Quieting my thoughts with several deep breaths, I project myself into the general's mind. It is easy to locate—the psychic energy that emanates from him is like molten lava from an erupting volcano. Yet his resolve will not be so easily manipulated with a few implanted thoughts. With a strong individual, even when I can look him in the eye and whisper in his ear, I have trouble getting him to do what I want. Now, I have neither of those options at my disposal. What I am attempting to do is set up several conditions that will work on the general and prompt him to give the order to open the door. Getting the guards nervous and knocking out the lights were the first of my conditional steps. The next ones will be more difficult.

I slip into General Havor's mind.

It is a black cavern, draped with the webs of poisonous spiders. When he does get my power, I see, General Havor fantasizes about raping me. He also plans to kill Arturo, as soon as the alchemist completes his experiments. There is no trust between the two. General Havor fears Arturo will alter his own DNA and then kill the general. But what Arturo thinks I cannot read. His mind is heavily cloaked—not unexpected in a partial hybrid. Anyway, I must concentrate on the man who gives the orders. General Havor must push the button that opens the door—this is all that matters.

I reach out with my mental claw.

"The witch will break down the door."

I hear the general speak to Arturo.

"Are you positive she cannot break down the door?" he asks.

"Even she cannot destroy this alloy," Arturo reassures him.

"The blood of a dead witch is as good as the blood of a living witch."

General Havor does not speak this thought aloud to Arturo. But I know he fantasizes about shooting me in the head, killing me, and immediately injecting my blood into his veins. It is an attractive idea to him. Arturo will not be able to stop him, or to come back at him later at an unexpected time, with an unseen dagger in his hand. It is this latter point that is the general's primary worry. My suggestion hits home, and I watch as my mental implant expands and warps. General Havor can almost feel what it will be like to have my blood flow through his veins in the next few minutes. I give the idea another nudge.

"Why wait for the witch's blood?"

Again, General Havor does not share this idea aloud with Arturo.

Still, he is not ready to open the door.

Stretching and breathing normally, I slowly come out of my trance. Enough for mental gymnastics. It is time for brutal force. Climbing to my feet, I study the supposedly impenetrable door, then launch my attack. I leap into the air and plant three extremely powerful kicks on the hard metal with my feet. In quick succession I leap again and again, alternately pounding the door with first my right then my left foot. The door doesn't give, but the noise I create is deafening. Outside I can hear them shouting to one another, and I know what the general is thinking. The witch is going to break out. I may as well open the door and kill her while I have her cornered. To hell with Arturo.

I keep up the pounding.

By this time, I am sure, Guard One and Guard Three have wet their pants.

After five minutes, I pause. Something is happening.

I strain to listen with my ears. General Havor and Arturo are arguing again.

"You are playing right into her hands!" Arturo yells. "The only protection we have from her is this cell. Open it and you open the door to death—both for yourself and your men."

"How long do you think that door can withstand that barrage?" General Havor asks. "See, there are cracks in the walls."

"The cracks are in the walls that hold the metal cage! The cage itself shows no sign of giving."

"I don't believe it!" General Havor snaps. "I say we face her now when we're armed and ready. Better she die than escape."

"But what about her blood? We need it."

"There'll be plenty of her blood lying around when I finish with her."

Arturo hesitates. He lowers his voice. "Plenty of blood for what?"

General Havor does not answer. He knows there will be only enough blood left in my body for him to inject into his own veins. The more I listen to the two, the clearer it becomes that General Havor is not interested in Arturo's hybrid. He wants to be a full-fledged vampire. That's where it's at in his mind.

I return to my pounding.

My feet ache. It doesn't matter.

The noise shakes the whole building.

I imagine even the men in the perimeter towers are trembling.

Outside the door, the guards shout to their general for orders.

General Havor and Arturo continue to argue. I hear them.

"We will die!" Arturo screams.

"She's only one!" General Havor yells. "She can't get us all!" He pauses, makes a decision, and shouts to his men. "Stand ready! We're going in!"

I relax for a moment and catch my breath. "They're coming," I whisper to Joel. "Get behind the door."

"Can't I help?" he asks, moving. "I am a vampire, after all. Not just FBI."

I chuckle softly. "Later, Joel."

Outside, I hear what sounds like a platoon of guards gathering around the red button. Each is more than a little reluctant to push it. The heavy metal door has become awfully comforting. But the general is shouting at them again to open it. Loaded magazines are popped onto M16s. Bullets are locked into firing chambers. Rifles are shouldered. I can smell the sweat of their fear.

Somebody gathers the courage to push the button.

The door begins to open.

I leap up and into a corner near the ceiling.

I don't need to use my newfound levitating abilities. I am able to wedge myself against the ceiling by pressing the back of my neck against one corner wall, and my feet against the other. Supernatural strength has its advantages. I leave my arms free—I am a black widow ready to swoop down and snatch her prey. They are going to rue the day they decided to lock me in a solid metal cage.

The door opens wider.

I hear them outside in the hall. Their frightened breathing.

You could hear a pin drop. Even without vampire ears.

"She's not there," someone whispers.

They aren't even worried about Joel. Just me, that damn witch.

"She's behind the door," General Havor snarls from farther down the hall.

It's good to know exactly where he is.

"What do we do?" someone croaks. Sounds like Guard Three.

"I'm not going in there," Guard One moans. His ulcer must be killing him.

"I don't like this," Guard Two agrees.

The door will not close again, no matter what happens. I will not let it. But now I am faced with a decision to make. There is only one hostage who will get me to where I want to go, and that is the kind-hearted General Havor. If I abduct Arturo, the general will tell his men to open fire on both of us. Certainly, any guard I would grab would be expendable in the general's mind. Friendly fire, they call it. Yet the general is maybe fifty feet up the hall. Between us are many soldiers. I am going to have to reduce the numbers. I need the men to panic and flee.

I know I will have to cause pain to make that happen.

In a move too swift for the soldiers to see, I slide onto the top of the door, reach outside the cage, grab one of the soldiers by the hair, and pull him back up into the corner with me. The man screams in my hands and I let him carry on for a bit. No doubt he feels like a victim in an *Alien* movie. Because he is crying so loudly, it takes me several seconds to recognize his voice.

It is Guard Three—the one who writes science-fiction in his spare time.

I am sure he has seen *all* the *Alien* movies.

I take his weapon and put my hand over his mouth.

"Shh," I whisper. "Things are not so bad as they seem. I am not going to kill you, not if you cooperate. I know about you and I like you. The problem is, I need to scare your friends out there. Now I know they are already pretty spooked, but I've got to get them to the point where they want to flee, no matter what your general orders. Do you understand?"

He nods, his eyes ready to burst out of his head.

I smile. "That's good. They are probably imagining that I am ripping your heart out right now. And with a little help from you, I can make them think that is *exactly* what I am doing. I will hardly have to hurt you at all. Oh, I see you notice I use the word *hurt*. To be honest, I will have to cut you enough so that I can blow the stream of your warm blood out into the hall. Splashing blood always creates a wonderful effect, especially when vampires are involved. While I do that, I want you to scream bloody murder. Can you do that?"

He nods.

I pinch him. "Are you sure?"

"Yes," he croaks. "I don't want to die. I have a wife and two kids."

"I know, and your brother-in-law is a lawyer. By the way, don't listen to a thing he tells you. He is like all lawyers—envious of those who do honest work for a living. You just keep writing your stories. If you want, you can even write one about me. But make me a blond—this red hair is store-bought."

"What's your name?" he asks, relaxing slightly.

I don't want him too relaxed. "I am Mrs. Satan." I scratch him on the inside of his right arm, tearing his flesh and drawing plenty of blood. "Start screaming, buddy."

Guard Three does as he's told. His performance is admirable—he believes half of it. *"Oh God! Stop it! Save me! She's ripping my heart out!"* Actually, he didn't have to get so specific, but I let it pass. While he cries to his fellow soldiers, I purse my lips and blow on the blood that trickles from his arm. I have quite the set of lungs. The blood splatters over the exterior of the wall, and onto the floor outside. I hear the men moaning in horror. This is worse than 'Nam, many think.

They haven't seen anything yet.

"Now let out a real loud death scream," I tell Guard Three. "Trail off into silence. Then, I'll drop you behind the door where my friend is hiding. You might want to stay there when the shooting starts. I warn you ahead of time, I am going to have to kill many of your friends. When I am through, you may leave this building. Get out as fast as you can. Steal a truck if you have to. Things are going to get awfully hot here. Do you understand?"

"Yes. You're not going to kill me?"

"No. Not tonight. You can relax, after you do exactly what I say."

The guard lets out the death scream. I spray an especially wide shower of blood through the doorway. Then I drop the guy down beside Joel, who pats him on the back and tells him to relax. I hand Joel the man's weapon and order him to keep it handy. Several guards outside the door are crying. They have backed away, but not far enough to be safe. I reach out and grab another. He carries a high-powered machine gun, which I wedge between the door and frame. He smells of hamburger and fries. His food is probably not digesting well.

I don't know this soldier, which doesn't bode well for him.

"You're going to die now," I tell his horrified face. "I am sorry it has to be this way."

I kill him slowly, painfully, so that his throat-tearing screams and red blood mingle to create an image so ghastly that many of the soldiers feel they are trapped in a nightmare from which they cannot awaken. When I am done, I throw what is left of his body into the hall. It is very messy—the terror in the air is as palpable as the hard metal door that can no longer be closed.

This last execution has disturbed me. If I am forced to kill, I prefer to do so efficiently and painlessly. I will not make another example—I don't have the stomach for it. It is time to leave the building, with Joel and General Havor in hand. To grab the machine gun the soldier brought in, I drop from my position on the ceiling and immediately retrieve it and open fire. The men outside the door stand frozen in place. They fall to their deaths like tenpins.

I kill eight of them before I step into the hall.

Arturo and General Havor are at the far end. They are a hundred feet away and backing up fast. Between us there are many soldiers. I cannot allow the big boss to leave the building without me. But the bloody examples I made of the first two men have had an effect. The soldiers are pushing and crowding behind General Havor and Arturo, slowing them down, preventing them from simply leaving. Also, General

Havor has lost control of his men. I stand a clear and easy target in the hallway, but no order to fire comes. In their hearts, the men do not believe this witch can be killed with mere bullets.

They wish they hadn't opened the door.

"Drop your weapons and I will let you live!" I yell.

Most in front of me surrender right then. The few who don't, who take aim, I shoot in the head. The sheer number of deaths does not numb me. I look in the eyes of each one I destroy, and wonder about his life and who he leaves behind. If it was just my life—honestly, if there was no danger of my blood falling into the wrong hands, I would let them cut me down. But I have a responsibility to mankind. I know that is the rationale of every great man or woman, of every merciless monster. The smell of blood is too thick even for my taste.

Arturo and General Havor disappear around the corner.

I call to Joel to join me in the hallway.

He cautiously peeks out. He groans.

"Nothing can be worth this," he whispers.

"You may be right," I say. "Still, we have to get out of here. To do that, we need General Havor."

"Where is he?"

"On the second floor." I grab Joel with my free arm and shield the top of his head with my palm. "Let's join him."

I leap straight up and smash through the ceiling. Again, Yaksha's blood comes to my aid. Without it, such a move would have given me a righteous headache. This time the ceiling barely slows me down. Pulling Joel through the hole I have created, we stand up on the floor of the basement, level one. I see soldiers down the hall jamming the stairs, frantic to exit. Arturo and General Havor struggle in the midst of the human flood. Raising the machine gun to my shoulder, I take aim at General Havor's right thigh. For a split second it is clearly visible. I put a bullet in it. The general stumbles and lets out a cry. No one stops to help him, least of all Arturo. I grab Joel's arm.

"Come," I say.

As I wade into the crowd, they scream and scatter. I guess my red hair does not suit me. Or perhaps it is the fact that I am soaked from head to toe in blood. I must look like a beast that has climbed from the depths of hell. Arturo is already out of sight, but General Havor lies helpless at the side of the stairway. He is lucky that he was not trampled to death. But he is not lucky that it is me who reaches out to help him to his feet.

"General Havor," I say. "Pleased to meet you face to face. Sorry I have to ask a favor so soon after saying hello. But I need you to take me and my friend into the cave behind this compound. I need one of those thermonuclear warheads you keep there. I have a thing about fire, you see, about explosions. For me, the bigger the better."

SIXTEEN

The cave turns into another prison. We reach it without excessive bloodshed, but once inside I am forced to kill all the soldiers. The endless slaughter weighs heavily on me. Joel's broken expression begs me to stop. But I can't stop until it is over, one way or the other. It is my nature never to quit.

We are scarcely inside when the remaining soldiers close the door on us. The metal is as thick as the door on the cell— it cuts in half the miniature rail tracks that run between the compound and the depths of the hill. They also turn off our lights, but there are emergency lanterns. For Joel's sake, and the general's, I turn on several. The stark rays cast ghastly shadows over the carnage I have inflicted. There is blood everywhere. The red blurs in the silent gloom, in my racing mind; it is as if the walls of the cave bleed. I try not to count the dead.

"I didn't want this," I say, pointing my weapon at the general, who sits on the edge of the small railroad car that carries supplies into this place of secrets. His leg continues to bleed but he doesn't complain. He is a horrible human being, but he is not without strength. A hard man with a blunt face, he wears his hair as if it were a disease growing on top of his head. I add, "It's your fault."

My accusation does not faze him. "You can always surrender."

I kneel beside him. To my left Joel sits on the ground, looking weary beyond belief. "But you see that is not an option," I tell the general. "When history started, I was there. And the only reason mankind has been able to move steadily forward is because I have chosen to stand apart from history. I watch what happens. I have no desire to have important roles. Do you understand that I tell you the truth?"

General Havor shrugs. "You've changed your style today."

My voice hardens. "You made me change." I gesture to the dead men who lie around us. "All this is because of you. Look at them. Don't you care about them?"

He is bored. "What do you want? A nuclear bomb?"

I stand and look down at him. "Yes. That's exactly what I want. And after you show it to me, I want you to arm it."

He snorts. "Do you think I'm crazy?"

"I know you're crazy. I have seen inside your mind. I know what you planned to do once you had my blood in your veins. You were going to murder Arturo and rape me."

He's cocky. "You flatter yourself."

I slap him in the face, hard enough to break his nose. "And you sicken me. I don't know how Arturo ever teamed up with you. He must have been desperate. He and I are not alike, by the way. I never beg for anything, but I know how to make you beg. Give me the warhead and arm it or I will subject you to such physical and mental torture you will think that soldier I ripped apart inside the cell died peacefully." I raise my hand to strike again. "Yes?"

He holds his nose; the blood leaks through his thick fingers. "May I ask what you plan to do with the warhead?" he asks.

I catch his eye, push hard enough to make him cower.

"I am going to clean up your mess," I reply.

General Havor agrees to furnish me with a bomb. He digs it out of the back, and wheels it into view on the railroad cart. A black squat affair with a pointed tip and an elaborate control box on the side, it looks like something from an old sci-fi movie. The general informs us that it is rated ten megatons— ten million tons of TNT.

I point to the color-coded buttons on the side.

"Can it be rigged to go off at a specific time?" I ask.

"Yes. It can be set to detonate in ten minutes, or in ten years."

"Ten years is a little long for my tastes. But your men may escape, if they listen to me. You will want to argue my position to them, once we get back outside. Which leads me to my next point." I gesture to the metal wall that blocks the exit. "How do we open this door?"

"It can't be opened from the inside. They've cut our power."

"Is there a radio in here?" Joel asks. "Can you talk to them?"

General Havor shrugs. "I have nothing to say to them."

I grab the general by the collar.

It doesn't take much for him to piss me off.

"You will tell them that we have an armed warhead in here set to detonate in fifteen minutes," I say. "That will be, by the way, the literal truth. You will also inform them that if they wish to prevent the bomb from exploding, they are to let us out. Finally, you will mention that I am willing to negotiate."

He laughs at me. "You can do what you want to me, I am not going to arm this warhead."

I let him go, take a step back. "You think you can play with me, General. You think the worst I can do is kill you. Arturo never told you of the power of my eyes. How my gaze can permanently fry your brain." I pause. "If in the next ten seconds you don't tell me the code to arm this warhead, I will stab such a needle into your forehead that you will have the IQ of a chimpanzee for the rest of your life—however long that may be."

He lowers his head. "I cannot allow you to set off this bomb."

"Very well." I step forward and grab him by the jaw, thrusting his head up, forcing him to stare at me. "Look deep, General! Into the eyes of the witch you thought to control. See where I have prepared a piece of fire for you to burn."

SEVENTEEN

*T*en minutes later the door is opened by the highest ranking commander on the outside and we wheel a fully armed warhead into the nighttime air. The detonator clicks off the seconds. Fifteen minutes to Armageddon. Driving at high speed should give us and the soldiers time to get clear of the blast. Overhead, the full moon shines down on our heads, bathing the entire desert with a milky white radiance. The setting is dreamlike, as if there has already been a nuclear explosion thousands of years ago and the radioactive fallout remains.

A small army aims a line of high-tech weapons at us.

On all sides, from the guard towers to the rocks in the hill, we are surrounded.

A minute before, a mumbling General Havor had ordered them to let us go.

But they're not listening.

The highest ranking commander on the outside is now Arturo.

He steps forward as we move out of the cave.

"Sita," he says. "This is madness."

"You tell me about madness, Arturo." I hold a pistol to General Havor's head, shielding myself and Joel with his wobbly figure. He wept as I bored into his brains but he resisted me as well. I had to destroy most of his mind to get what I wanted. Gesturing to the bomb, I add, "This warhead is set to detonate in less than fifteen minutes. That gives you and your men barely enough time to get clear."

Arturo shakes his head. "We cannot let you escape. An order has come from the President of the United States. At all costs, you are to be stopped." He gestures to the men around us. "We are expendable."

I force a chuckle. "You will not sacrifice all these people."

"It is not my decision to make."

"That's nonsense! They look to you to command them now. Command them to drop their weapons and get the hell out of here." I pause. "You are bluffing."

Arturo looks me in the eye. He is not intimidated by my gaze.

"I pray that you are the one who is bluffing," he says softly.

The timer on the detonator goes to fourteen minutes.

I meet his gaze. "When was the last time you prayed, Arturo? Was it before the inquisitor's court? The day they hanged you? I did what I did then because I know the danger my blood poses for the world. Tonight, I killed all these people for the same reason—to protect humanity."

Arturo challenges me. "To protect us from what? A chance to evolve into something greater? Into creatures that need never grow old, that need never hurt one another? Earlier you laughed at my mission. Seven hundred years ago you also laughed at me. But mine is still the noblest quest on earth—to perfect humanity, to allow it to become godlike."

"You do not become godlike by merging with a monster!"

My words surprise him. "You're not a monster, Sita."

"I am not an angel, either. Or if I am, I am an angel of death—as far as humanity is concerned. True, I have the right to live. Krishna granted me that right. But only if I lived alone, and made no more of my kind. Now I have broken that sacred vow. Krishna will probably judge me harshly. Perhaps he has already judged me, and that is why I am being forced to suffer in this place, to hurt all these people. But what is done is done. I am what I am. Humanity is what it is. We can never join. Don't you see that?"

"Don't you see me, Sita? I am an example of what can be accomplished with a merger of our DNAs. And I am only an incomplete example because I never got to complete the process. Think what mankind can change into if you'll just let me experiment with your blood for the next few weeks. Even a few days would be enough. That's all I'm asking. Then, when I'm finished, I promise to let you go. I will arrange it so that you can go free."

I speak with sorrow. "Arturo, I *can* see you. I see what's become of you. As a young man, you were the ideal person: devout, loving, brilliant. But your brilliance was perverted the day you received my blood. Your love was twisted. For the sake of your experiments, you even sacrificed a boy you loved. You sacrificed us—the love we had for each other. You lied to me, and I think you lie to me again. Your devotion is no longer to Christ—it is to yourself. And even though I have also lied to my God, I still love Krishna and pray he will forgive me for my sins. I still love you, and I pray you will order these people to let us go. But because of both of these loves, I cannot surrender. You cannot have my blood." I pause. "No man can have it."

Arturo knows me.

He knows I'm not bluffing, not when it comes to matters of life and death.

The timer goes to thirteen minutes. Unlucky thirteen.

His face and voice show his resignation. "I cannot let you go," he says quietly.

I nod. "Then we will stand here until the bomb goes off."

Joel looks at me. I stare silently at Joel. There are no words left.

Arturo stands still as a statue. The moon shines down.

Twelve. Eleven. Ten.

Ten minutes might be long enough to get clear of the blast.

"Arturo, ti prego," I say suddenly. *"Arturo, please."* "At least warn your men. Let them flee. I have enough blood on my conscience."

"The blast will leave no blood," he says, turning his eyes upward, toward the sky. "We will be like dust, floating on the wind."

"That is fine for you and me. We have lived long lives. But most of these men are young. They have families. Give the order—enough will remain to prevent Joel and me from escaping."

Arturo sighs and turns. He raises his arms and shouts. "Units G and H are free to go! Hurry! A nuclear bomb is about to detonate!"

There is a great commotion. I suspect more than units G and H want to leave. The men pour into their trucks. Engines roar to life. Tires burn rubber. The front gate is thrown open. The vehicles roar out of sight. Driving at a hundred miles an hour, they can put at least twelve miles between themselves and the blast in the time they have left. They should survive. Yet many remain behind who will not survive. Too many men still stand guard over us. If we try to escape, we will be cut down. It is better to go out like this, I think. Standing on our feet. Disintegrating in an all-consuming wave of fire.

Then I remember something.

"He's in a box so thick an atomic bomb couldn't blast through it."

But if we move and try to flee toward the lab basement, they'll open fire.

For the first time in my long life, I can see no way out.

Time creeps by.

Eight. Seven. Six. Five.

"I don't even know if the warhead can be deactivated once it's armed," I mutter.

"It can't be." General Havor mumbles with what is left of his mind.

"Oh," I say.

Then I begin to feel a peculiar sensation, a subtle but constant vibration inside my body. The moon is directly overhead, of course. It has been shining down on us since we left the cave. But what I didn't realize—with all that was going on around me—was that the moonlight has been filling my body all the time we have been out in the open. It has become more and more transparent. I feel as if I am made of glass. Interesting, I think—and I didn't even have to take my clothes off. It is Arturo who is the first one other than myself to notice the effect.

"Sita!" he cries. "What's happening to you?"

Standing beside me, Joel gasps. "I can see through you!"

I let go of the general. Staring down at my hands, I glimpse the ground through my open palms, through my fingers. Yet I can still see the blood pulsing in my veins, the tiny capillaries glowing like a complex web of fiber optics. A cool energy sweeps over me, yet my heart is strangely warmed.

It warms even as it starts to break.

The white glow spreads around me.

I realize I can just lift off and fly away.

Yaksha's blood, maybe Krishna's grace, gives me another chance.

Do I want it? I feel myself leave the earth.

I reach out to hug Joel, to carry him away with me.

My arms go right through him!

"Joel," I cry. "Can you hear me?"

He squints. "Yes, but it's hard to focus on you. What's going on? Is this a special vampire power?"

My luminous body floats a foot off the ground now.

"It is a gift," I say. Despite my unusual physical state, I feel tears on my face, white diamonds that sparkle with a red sheen as they roll over my transparent cheeks. Once more, I have to say goodbye to those whom I love. "It is a curse, Joel."

He smiles. "Fly away, Sita, far away. Your time is not over."

"I love you," I say.

"I love you. The grace of God is still with you."

The ground is two feet below me now. Arturo tries to grab me, but can't. He stands back and shakes his head, resigned.

"You are probably right," he says. "Mankind is not ready for this." He adds, "Everything you require is in my basement. It is your choice."

I don't understand. But I smile at him as I float higher.

"*Ti amo,*" I whisper.

"*Ti amo anch'io,* Sita."

A wind takes hold of me. Suddenly I am soaring. The stars shine around me. The moon beats down on the top of my head like an alien sun spawned in the center of a distant galaxy. It is so bright! My now-invisible eyes can hardly bear the glare, and I am forced to close them. As I do an even greater light ignites beneath me. The fiery rays of it rise up and pierce through my etheric body. There is tremendous heat and noise. A shock wave as thick as a granite mountain strikes me. Yet I feel no pain—just swept away, on currents of destruction and tidal waves of death. The compound is gone, the stolen blood is vapor. The world is safe once again. But I, Sita, I am lost in the night.

EPILOGUE

There is, to my utter amazement, a basement in Arturo's Las Vegas home. The afternoon after the atomic blast, I peer through the carefully hidden trapdoor and discover sheets of copper, magnetic crosses arranged in odd angles, and, most important of all, an empty crystal vial, waiting to be filled with blood. A mirror rests above the vial. It can reflect either the sun or the moon, depending on how much you want to wager.

I call Seymour Dorsten, explain the possibilities to him.

Wait, he cautions. He is on his way.

I sit down and wait. Time passes slowly.

"Everything you require is in the basement."

Do I still want a daughter? Do I still crave immortality?

Deep questions. I have no answers.

Seymour arrives and tries to talk me out of it.

Being human is not so great, he says.

Being a vampire gets old, I counter.

I know that I will attempt the transformation.

But I need some of his blood.

Make me a vampire first, he pleads.

That will not work, I remind him.

But, he protests.

The answer is no, I say firmly.

I take his blood, fill the vial to the brim, then tell him to get lost.

When the sun is at its peak, I lie down on the copper sheets.

The magnets draw out my aura. The magic begins.

When I awake, I feel weak and disoriented. Someone is knocking at the door. I have to struggle up the steps to answer it. There is a spongy texture to my skin I have never noticed before, and my vision is blurred. I am not even sure where I am—only that it is dark. Blood pounds in my head, and I feel I will be sick.

I reach the front door.

A shadow moves outside the glazed side window panel.

Just before I open the door, I remember everything.

"Am I human?" I whisper to myself.

Yet I am not given a chance to know.

The knocking continues.

"Who is it?" I call in a hoarse voice.

"It's your darling," the person replies.

Odd. It doesn't sound like Seymour.

Yet the voice is familiar. From long ago.

But the tone is a little demanding. Sort of impatient.

"Open the door," the person calls.

I wonder if I should.

Staring down at my trembling hands, I wonder many things.

Turn the page for a sneak peek
at the conclusion of Sita's story in:

THIRST

NO. 2

INCLUDES
PHANTOM
EVIL THIRST
CREATURES OF FOREVER

By Christopher Pike

Someone knocks at the door of the Las Vegas home where I stand. It is late evening; the living room is dimly lit, four walls of blurred shadows. I don't know who this person is. For that matter, I'm not sure who I am. I have just awakened from a dead alchemist's experiment. My mind is foggy and my nerves are shot. But before I embarked on the experiment, only hours ago, I was a steel-willed vampire—the last vampire on earth. Now I fear—and hope—that I may once again be human. That I may be a young woman named Alisa, the humble offspring of a five-thousand-year-old monster called Sita.

The person continues to knock.

"Open the door," he says impatiently. "It's me."

Who is me? I wonder. I do not recognize the voice, although it does sound familiar. Yet I hesitate to obey, even to respond.

Of those few I call friends, only Seymour Dorsten is supposed to know I am in this Las Vegas home. My other friends—well, a couple recently perished in the Nevada desert, in a nuclear blast. A lot has been happening in the last few days, and most of it has been my doing.

"Sita," the person outside the door says. "I know you're in there."

Curious, I think. He knows my ancient name. He even says it like he knows me. But why doesn't he tell me his name? I could ask him, but some emotion stops me. It is one I have seldom known in my five thousand years.

Fear. I stare down at my hands.

I tremble with fear. If I am human, I know, I am practically defenseless. That is why I do not want to open the door. I do not want to die before I have had a chance to taste mortality. Before I have had the opportunity to have a child. That is perhaps the primary reason I employed Arturo's alchemetic tools to reverse my vampirism—to become a mother. Yet I am still not a hundred percent sure the experiment has succeeded. I reach down with the nails of my right hand and pinch my left palm. The flesh breaks; there is a line of blood. I stare at it.

The wound does not immediately heal.

I must be human. Lord Krishna save me.

The knocking stops. The person outside takes a step back from the door. I hear his movements, even with my mediocre human ears. He seems to chuckle to himself.

"I understand, Sita," he says. "It's all right. I'll return soon."

I hear him walk away. Only then do I realize I have been standing in the dark with my breath held. Almost collapsing from relief, I sag against the door and try to calm my thumping heart. I am both confused and exalted.

"I am human," I whisper to myself.

Tears roll over my face. I touch them with my quivering tongue. They are clear and salty, not dark and bloody. Another sign that I am human. Moving slowly, striving to maintain my balance, I step to the living room couch and sit down. Looking around, I marvel at how blurred everything is, and wonder if the experiment has damaged my eyesight. But then I realize I must be seeing things as a human sees, which means to see so little. Why, I can't even distinguish the grain in the wood panel on the far wall. Nor can I hear the voices of the people in the cars that pass outside. I am virtually blind and deaf.

"I am human," I repeat in wonder. Then I begin to laugh, to cry some more, and to wonder what the hell I'm going to do next. Always, as a vampire, I could do anything I wished. Now I doubt if I will ever leave the house.

I pick up the remote and turn on the TV. The news—they are talking about the hydrogen bomb that exploded in the desert the previous night. They say it destroyed a top-secret military base. The wind was blowing away from Las Vegas so the fallout should be almost nonexistent. They don't say anything about me, however, even though I was there and witnessed the whole thing. The experts wonder if it was an accident. They don't connect it to the mass police killings I committed in Los Angeles a few days earlier. They are not very imaginative, I think. They don't believe in vampires.

And now there are no more vampires to believe in.

"I beat you, Yaksha," I say aloud to my dead creator, the vampire who sucked my blood five thousand years ago and replaced it with his own mysterious fluids. "It took me a long time but now I can go back to an ordinary life."

Yet my memories are not ordinary. My mind is not either, although I suddenly realize I am having trouble remembering many things that hours ago were clear. Has my identity changed with my body? What percentage of personal ego is constructed from memory? True, I still remember Krishna, but I can no longer see him in my mind's eye as I could before. I forget even the blue of his eyes—that unfathomable blue, as dear as the most polished star in the black heavens. The realization saddens me. My long life has been littered with pain, but also much joy. I do not want it to be forgotten, especially by me.

"Joel," I whisper. "Arturo."

I will not forget them. Joel was an FBI agent, a friend I made into a vampire in order to save his life. An alteration that caused him to die from a nuclear bomb. And Arturo, another friend, a hybrid of humanity and vampires from the Middle Ages, my personal priest, my passionate lover, and the greatest alchemist in history. It was Arturo who forced me to detonate the bomb, and destroy him and Joel, but my love for him is still warm and near. I only wish he were with me now to see what miracle his esoteric knowledge has wrought. But would the vampire blood–obsessed Arturo have still loved my human body? Yes, dear Arturo, I believe so. I still believe in you.

Then there was Ray, my Rama reincarnated. My memories of him will never fade, I swear, even if my human brain eventually grows forgetful. My love for Ray is not a human or vampire creation. It is beyond understanding, eternal, even though he himself is dead. Killed trying to kill a demon, the malignant Eddie Fender. There are worse reasons to die, I suppose. I still remember more than a few of them.

Yet, at the moment, I do not want to dwell on the past.

I just want to be human again. And live.

There comes another knock at the front door.

I become very still. How quickly frightened a human can become.

"Sita," this person calls. "It's me, Seymour. Can I come in?"

This voice I definitely recognize. Standing with effort, I walk to the front door and undo the lock and chain. Seymour stands on the porch and stares at me. He wears the same thick glasses and hopelessly mismatched clothes of the high school nerd I met in a stupid PE class only a few months before. His face changes as he studies me; his expression turns to one of alarm. He has trouble speaking.

"It worked," he gasps.

I smile and open the door all the way. "It worked. Now I am like you. Now I am free of the curse."

Seymour shakes his head as he steps in the house and I close the door. He liked me as a vampire, I know. He wanted me to make him a vampire, to poison him through the metamorphosis, an act that was strictly forbidden by Krishna five thousand years ago. Now Seymour is upset. Unable to sit, he paces in front of me. There are unshed tears in his eyes.

"Why did you do it?" he demands. "I didn't think you would really do it."

I force my smile wider and spread my arms. "But you knew I would. And I want you to be happy for me." I gesture for him to come to me. "Give me a hug, and this time I won't be able to squeeze you to death."

He hugs me, reluctantly, and as he does so he finally does shed his tears. He has to turn away; he is having trouble breathing. Naturally his reaction upsets me.

"It's gone," he says to the far wall.

"What's gone?"

"The magic is gone."

I speak firmly. "It is only Yaksha's blood that has been destroyed. Maybe you don't like that. Maybe your fantasies of being a vampire are ruined. But think of the world—it is safe now from this curse. And only you and I know how close it came to being destroyed by it."

But Seymour shakes his head as he glances at me. "I am not worried about my own personal fantasies. Yeah, sure, I wanted to be a vampire. What eighteen-year-old wouldn't want to be one? But the magic is gone. You were that magic."

My cheek twitches; his words wound me. "I am still here. I am still Alisa."

"But you are no longer Sita. The world needed her in order to be a place of mystery. Even before I met you, I *knew* you. You know I knew you. I wrote my stories late at night and your darkness filled them." He hung his head. "Now the world is empty. It's nothing."

I approach and touch his arm, "My feelings for you have not changed. Are they nothing? Good God, Seymour, you speak to me as if I were dead."

He touches my hand but now it is hard for him to look at me. "Now you will die."

"All who are born die," I say, quoting Krishna. "All who are dead will be reborn. It is the nature of things."

He bites his lower lip and stares at the floor. "That's easy to say but it's not easy to live through. When you met me, I had AIDS. My death was certain—it was all I could see. It was like a slow-motion horror film that never ended. It was only your blood that saved me." He pauses. "How many others could it have saved?"

"Now you sound like Arturo."

"He was a brilliant man."

"He was a dangerous man."

Seymour shrugs. "You always have an answer for everything. I can't talk to you."

"But you can. I'm a good listener. But you have to listen as well. You have to give me a chance to explain how I feel. I'm happy the experiment has succeeded. It means more to me than you can imagine. And I'm happy there's no going back."

He catches my eye. "Is that true?"

"You know it is true. There is no more vampire blood, anywhere. It's over." I squeeze his arm and pull him closer. "Let it be over. I need you now, you know, more than I needed you before." I bury my face in his shoulder. "You have to teach me how to be a nerd."

My small joke makes him chuckle. "Can we have sex now?" he asks.

I raise my head and plant a wet kiss on his cheek. "Sure. When we're both a little older." I shake him, but not so hard as I used to. "How dare you ask me a question like that? We haven't been on a date yet."

He tries hard to accept the loss of his world, the death of his magic. He forces a smile. "There's a vampire movie in town. We could see it, and eat popcorn, and jeer, and then have sex afterward." He waits for an answer. "It's what most nerd couples do every Saturday evening."

I suddenly remember. It has taken me this long. There

must be something wrong with my mind. I turn away and swear under my breath. "Damn."

"What is it?" he asks. "You don't like popcorn?"

"We have to get out of town. We have to leave now."

"Why?"

"There was someone here a few minutes ago. A young man—he was knocking at the door."

"Who was it?"

"I don't know. I didn't open the door. But this guy—he called me by name. He called me Sita. He kept insisting I open the door."

"Why didn't you?"

"Because I didn't know who he was! Because I'm human now!" I pause and frown. "His voice sounded familiar. I swear, I knew it, but I just can't place it."

"What makes you think he's dangerous?"

"Do you have to ask that question? No one alive, except you, knows me by the name Sita." I stop again. "He said he would come back. He laughed as he said it. He sounded so sure of himself."

"What else did he say?"

"He called himself my darling."

Seymour was thoughtful. "Could Arturo have survived the blast?"

"No."

"But he was a hybrid. Half human, half vampire. It's possible. Don't dismiss the possibility."

I shake my head. "Even Yaksha could not have survived that blast."

"But you did."

"I floated away at the last minute. You know, I told you." I turn toward the kitchen, my car keys. "The sooner we leave the better."

Seymour grabs my arm. "I disagree. You have said there are no more vampires. What do we have to fear from this person? Better we stay and find out who he is."

I consider. "The government must have known Arturo was using this house. Such records were probably kept somewhere else besides the army base I destroyed. The government might be watching this house now."

"But you said you knew this person."

"I'm not sure about that. There was something in his voice, though . . ."

"What?" Seymour demands when I don't finish.

I strain to remember through my newfound human fog. "His tone—it gave me a chill."

Seymour acts like a wise guy. "In the real world not everybody who comes to the front door wants to kill you. Some guys just want to sell you a vacuum cleaner."

I remain stubborn. "We're getting out of here now." Grabbing the keys off the kitchen table, I peer out the back window and see nothing significant. In the distance, the lights of the Strip come alive and shimmer, colored beacons in a desert wasteland. A nuclear bomb just exploded but human vice will not be postponed. Of course the wind was blowing the other way, but I do not judge. I have always been a gambler. I understand better than most why the atomic dice did not betray the city of sin. Why the fallout fell the other way. Still, I swear again. "Damn. I wish I had my old vision right now. Just for a minute."

"And I bet your old hearing." Seymour comes up at my side and pats me on the back. "You're going to make that same wish a lot of times in the next few days."

ABOUT THE AUTHOR

CHRISTOPHER PIKE is the author of more than forty teen thrillers, including the series Remember Me, Final Friends, and Chain Letter.

The Old Powers are rising.
The apocalypse is drawing near.

The new Night People are determined to
destroy the human world.

But four children have been born, four
Wild Powers who can stop the darkness. . . .

THE NIGHT WORLD...
Love has never been so dangerous.

FROM SIMON PULSE | PUBLISHED BY SIMON & SCHUSTER

Witches
Secrets
Alliances
Destiny

A series by
Nancy Holder and
Debbie Viguié

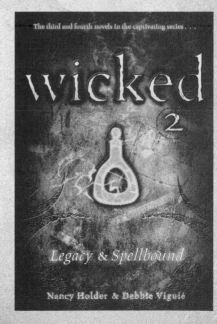

From Simon Pulse
Published by Simon & Schuster